SHE WAS TAKEN

THE BLACK FOREST

P. S. WHYTOCK

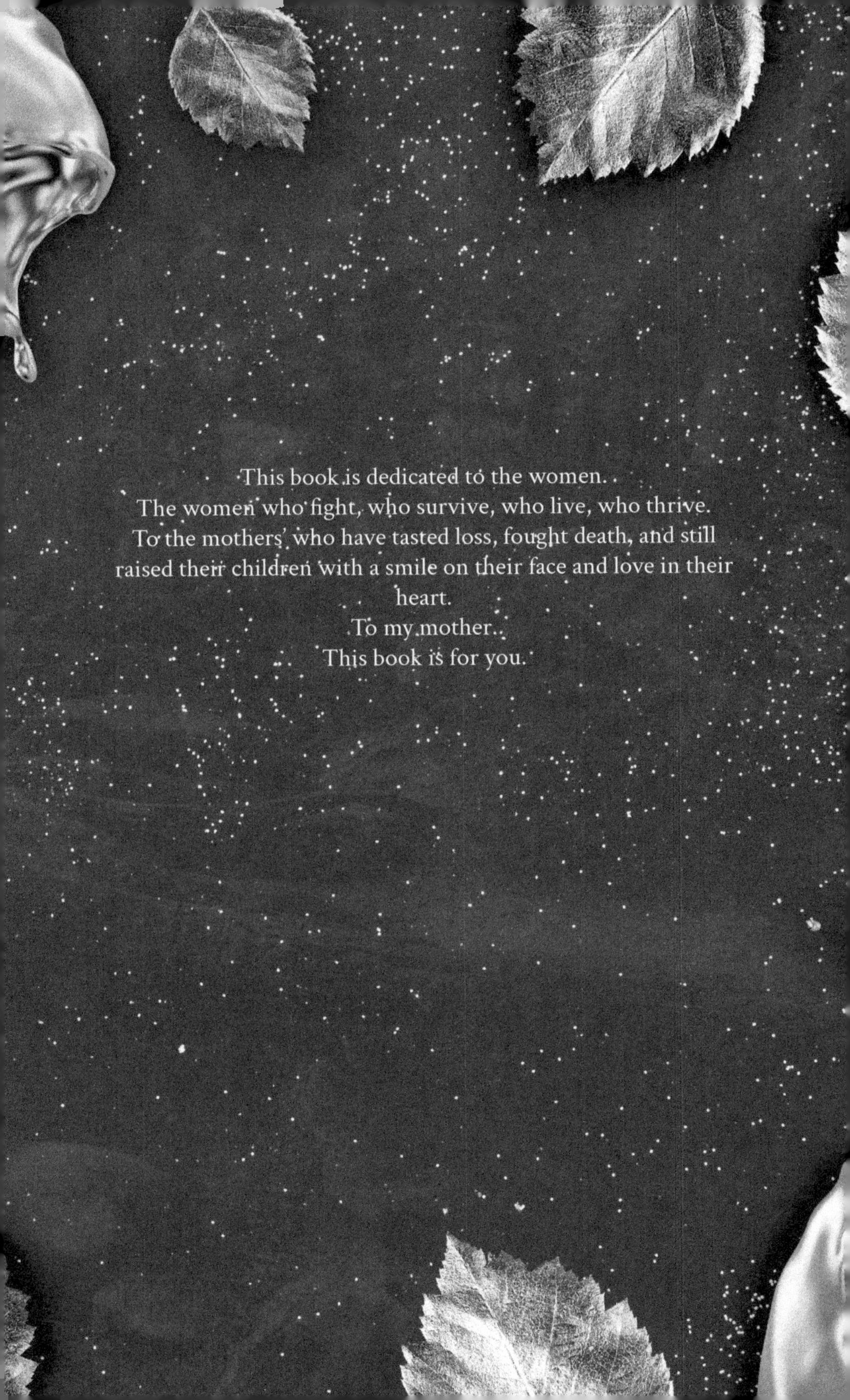

This book is dedicated to the women.
The women who fight, who survive, who live, who thrive.
To the mothers' who have tasted loss, fought death, and still raised their children with a smile on their face and love in their heart.
To my mother.
This book is for you.

ALFABORG
BEL'ONG SEA
N MO
THE FOREST OF LOST SOU
DAUÐINN MOUNTAINS
KI VA
THE BLACK FOREST
ZARREN CITY

ÁLFHEIMR
EVENGILE
THE BLACK FOREST
ELDUR MOUNTAIN
THÓRSMÖRK
HAMMER

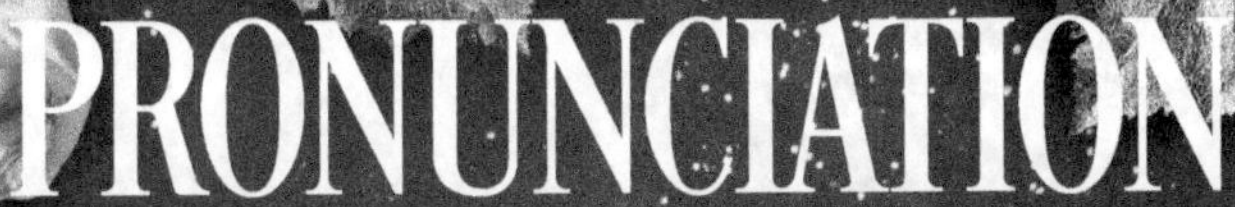

PRONUNCIATION

Places:

Dauðinn: *Doi-th-inn*
Meaning: Death
Origin: Old Norse
Dyagin: *Die-a-gin*
Álfheimr: *Alf-eh-mer*
Meaning: Land of the Elves
Origin: Old Norse
Bel'onc: *Bell-on-k*
Thórsmörk: *Ther-sh-mork*
Meaning: Thor's mountain
Origin: Icelandic
Eldur: *Elled-dish*
Meaning: Fire
Origin: Icelandic
Nal'lian: *Nall-ian*

Names:

Hazen: *Haze-en*
Savven: *Sav-ven*
Brean: *Bri-een*
Lithônion: *Lith-on-nee-in*
Néefar: *Ne-Far*
Tatius: *Ta-tee-us*
Udiya: *You-dee-ya*
Naleen: *Nall-lean*
Ezra: *Ez-ra*
Nazar: *Naz-âre*
Levina: *Leh-veen-nah*
Laudin: *Lah-din*
Valdren: *Vald-ren*
Forndýr: *Forn-dry-er*

PROLOGUE

234 YEARS AFTER BALWIN

Black clouds billowed through the treeline of Álfheimr, city of the light elves. Ash rained down like dark snow as bodies burned, and the flames overtook the fields that lay beyond the forest.

Savven, High Fae Prince of the Elves, stared past the trees, watching, waiting. Moments trapped in numb silence, his breath even, his heartbeat calm. A thin blade lay in his tight grip, ready.

Then they came. The second attack of the *Dökkálfar*, the Dark Ones, the fallen of his kin, rolled through the black ash. With a loud cry, he lunged forward, meeting them halfway, and sparks danced as metal met metal in a deafening ring.

The Dark Ones swarmed around him, slamming his body back and knocking the breath from his lips. His blade came up, slicing through flesh and bones. Blood splayed across his face, his black hair whipping through the air as he spun around the falling body.

A snarl ripped from his throat as he bared his teeth at the arrow aimed for the space between his eyes, and he leapt forward, his blade cutting through the archer with ease. Death came swiftly with every swipe of his sword. Blood drenching the earth in a downpour, he and his kinsmen cut through the mass of defiled elves, reaching the forest's edge as the last one fell.

Beyond the moor sat hundreds of Dökkálfar, bloodlust clear in their hungry eyes. They stood, waiting, watching them as the rows of the fallen shifted with the desire to attack.

Savven's blue eyes scanned the rows until he found *him*. Nostrils flaring in rage, he watched the face of one he used to call friend.

Ezra stood amongst the chaos and death, the look of a thousand demons behind cold eyes. A sinister smile graced his angled features, his black eyes staring at Savven from across the sea of burning bodies.

Savven felt something deep within him stir, a sadness creeping up from behind his rage. Baring his teeth angrily, he pushed it down, drowning the unwanted emotion.

"They will all fall, Savven."

The words were barely registered over the noise of the Dökkálfar, but Savven heard them, nonetheless.

Savven's grip tightened around his blade. "We shall see."

Ezra's eyes turned black as he raised his hands slowly, and from the ground, dark shadows whispered out from the grave beneath them.

"Savven, the King is the only one strong enough to fight Ezra's power."

Savven glanced at Lithônion, his closest friend. Blood trailed down the side of his face and arms, worn scars marking the cords of muscle along his bare flesh. His armour gleamed under the burden of battle. Lithônion's green eyes were serious as he watched Ezra with familiarity, an unknown emotion passing over his gaze fleetingly.

"Ezra wants the throne," Savven stated. "If he takes it, that will be the end of us all."

Lithônion pursed his lips at those words. "I never took you as a coward, Savven. Your father surely isn't one."

Savven gave him a hard stare. "Watch your tongue, Lithônion."

"Adanessa!" Lithônion's voice barked out the command with ease, his eyes on Savven as a lithe female ran out from the ranks behind them.

Her white-blonde hair shone against the flicker of fire in the fields, pale green eyes staring at Lithônion and Savven, waiting for their command.

Savven took a deep breath, calming the growing anger as he glanced at the royal messenger. "Adanessa, bring word to the King; he is needed on the battlefield."

Adanessa glanced at the chaos around them quickly, her head jerking in a quick nod. "Yes, Your Royal Highness." She left on fleeting feet. Disappearing into the clouds of soot that rolled through the forest behind them.

The darkness around Ezra grew into a large wall. The wind pulsed like a heartbeat and roared in their ears in a deafening crescendo.

Lithônion and Savven faced off against the wall of demons, their faces hardened, eyes burning.

With an angry shriek, the darkness dispersed and shot towards them in the form of a thousand black arrows.

Savven shielded his face as the demons enveloped him. When he opened his eyes, he was alone. The world around them was darkness; he couldn't hear or see any of his kinsmen. Lithônion had disappeared, and Savven was left in the shadows.

His breathing was shallow in his ears, a thundering beneath his feet his only warning, and he brought his blade up. The Dökkálfar came at him from all sides, all at once. He pushed them back with the quick jerk of his sword, deflecting the hazardous blows bearing down upon him.

Then they were gone. Those who came fell to the ground, their blood soaking the earth. Then, all was silent again. The darkness parted for only a moment, but at that moment, Savven saw him.

Ezra. Standing alone in the field, the barest hint of a smile on his pale face before he vanished. Misting into the air around them.

Savven felt it, the knowledge that he had fallen for the trap. He stumbled back, tripping over a body, catching himself. Ezra had drawn them from the confines of the city walls, taken their resources, and covered them in an impenetrable barrier that separated them. With no one watching the city walls, they lay bare, ready for the taking.

"Savven!"

He heard his name faintly through the thick black fog. A hand reached out from its depths and pulled him from the darkness.

"Savven!"

Savven cleared his head, his eyes focusing on Lithônion. "How did you escape?!"

"We need the King, now!"

Savven glanced back at the field, knowing he wouldn't find Ezra. "It's too late," he muttered. "Ezra knows the city is defenceless! I need to warn them!" He didn't wait for Lithônion's reply. Sprinting through the treeline towards the city walls.

Adanessa felt the forest walls concave around her as darkness rolled through the tree line, licking at her heels. Her hair whipped through the air, glancing over her shoulder and letting out a cry as the black clouds began to envelop her.

The world went dark, and a chill ran through her body as she stumbled in the sudden abyss. Her knees crashed to the ground, tormented cries echoing through the shadows around her.

Her breathing became shallow, feeling her way around the darkness, small whimpers of terror slipping past trembling lips. Her fingers touched something wet, and the metallic scent of death reached her nostrils. Adanessa's eyes strained against the shadows, and she saw the outline of one of her own. Dead. His eyes were open and void of light, he was staring blankly at her.

Adanessa let out a startled scream, seeing her hand lying across his open torso. She threw herself back, stumbling against another body. Jerking away, she searched the shadows, looking for help. She didn't dare call out for fear of the Dökkálfar hearing her.

The screeches of the fallen surrounded her as the darkness grew. Sudden movement passed her in a blur, and her breath caught in her throat.

She tried to walk forward quietly, her hands in front of her. The forest became deathly quiet, and a cold chill ran up her spine. Ceasing her movements, she turned slowly, her breath heavy in her throat.

The face of a bloodied banshee stared back at her, inches from her face. Its black eyes and sinister smile watched Adanessa with hunger.

She felt her heart stop as she stared at the dark creature.

The banshee let out a sudden piercing scream, grabbed Adanessa by her throat, and threw her back.

Ice filled her veins as she was tossed aside with ease, her body slamming into the base of a tree. Black dots appeared in her vision, but she forced herself to stand. Bracing against the tree, she pushed herself up, the banshee letting out a cry. Terror filled her, and Adanessa sprinted through the forest, the bodies of her kin beneath her feet.

She finally screamed, *"Help!"*

The sound of steel meeting flesh echoed through the white marble halls from the battlefield. Those who stayed behind to guard the palace borders ran towards the burning chaos. Walls threatened to crumble at their feet as they shook, tremors running through the earth.

The dwarves of Zarren brought axes and shields to the battlefield as allied reinforcement. Those left behind stood ready within the palace walls, waiting for the dark armies to invade the territory they protected—the only land yet to feel the grasp of death and know the weight of dead bodies covering its ground.

Savven pushed past scattered dwarves, leaping over a fallen pillar. He spotted a familiar head and called out, "Mirima!"

Spinning around, one of his own turned at his name, bow in hand with arrows sheathed at this side.

"Savven, what is it?" Mirima questioned hurriedly, securing a new string to his bow quickly before lowering it to his side.

"The King and Queen, where are they?!"

Mirima pointed behind Savven. "They're coming."

Savven whirled around and saw them, his parents, walking towards Mirima and him. Their battle armour gleamed under the light of torches set in sconces on the walls; their pace was quick but controlled, and their expressions masked. Savven nodded his thanks to Mirima and ran to their side.

"You're needed at the front." His words were hurried as he glanced over his shoulder in caution, half of him expecting Ezra to appear. "Adanessa was sent to give—"

His mother frowned. "We have not seen Adanessa."

Savven tried to suppress the warring emotions that raged inside him, but his attempts were feeble. They had been naive enough to fall for Ezra's trap. Death was imminent now, and Savven knew his parents needed to leave if they were going to survive. "Then it is too late. You must leave! I cannot allow Ezra to take the throne and you as well."

"Enough, Savven!" his father ordered in an imperious tone that Savven knew too well, his emerald eyes flashing in warning. "We will not leave. I will go to the front if I'm needed there. That is my duty as their king!"

A violent tremor shook the palace, and all movement ceased. Voices went silent. The ground lurched again with a loud crack, and a billow of thick dust rolled through the hall.

Savven felt his heart jump, his breathing coming in quick bursts. "The walls have been breached!"

The momentary stillness exploded into shouts and hurried footsteps as those left took their positions and readied their weapons. Savven turned to his parents and gently took his mother's hand. Familiar icy blue eyes boring into his deep blue. "I beg you— take the west tunnels to the shores of Ligorin. I cannot allow Ezra to take you. I could not bear it. Our people need you alive."

They were alone in the vast hall. Casvara turned to her mate and laid a gentle hand on his shoulder. "Nydeth, perhaps we should. Our people will understand."

"Perhaps they will, but I will live with the shame of it. I will not cower."

"There is no shame in following commands. Savven will guide our armies. You have trained him well. He has guided our people before. Have faith that he will be victorious."

The elder closed his eyes, a hardened look falling over his features. "No, I will not leave our people for slaughter. Until my last breath as king, I will stand with them."

Savven felt his jaw clench with unwanted sentiments, ignoring them as he gave a barely perceivable nod. "Very well, follow me."

He led them down the twisting halls, away from the main corridor that had been attacked, to the hidden east passages that would take them to the forest's edge.

Nydeth stepped around Savven as they approached a marble wall. Waving a hand over the bare wall, he whispered a single word in their ancient language: "*Geyja.*" A crack formed in the marble as a doorway appeared. It opened to worn stone stairs consumed by shadows, leading down into the tunnels below the palace.

"Your Majesties!"

The three turned to see a dwarf running toward them, his barrel chest heaving, his stocky frame covered in dripping sweat and dried blood. "They're coming!"

"Who?!" Savven demanded as his parents started for the entrance.

Gasping for breath, red in the face, the dwarf crouched low, with white knuckles gripping his axe. "*The Dark Ones!* They're coming from the east; they're coming by the tunnels! One of their spells countered ours and struck the ground, collapsing it. They found it! Found them!"

"Savven!"

Savven turned to see the enemy step out from the shadows. No. Not an enemy, but someone he knew. Someone who had crafted the sword on his hip. Laudin, the Blacksmith of the High Fae, grinned through the shadows, eyes black as night. Held in his grip was a taut bow and an arrow flew out from the darkness before he disappeared into shadows.

"Run!" Savven cried out, turning to the dwarf quickly. "Tell the others what has happened! We need reserves at every tunnel entrance! May the Gods help us!"

The dwarf saluted, striking his fist to his heart, and ran back where he had come, his lumbering footsteps echoing in the hall.

Casvara took Nydeth's arm as he reached for his sword. "Come, we must go now!"

The Dökkálfar fell from the shadows, and Nydeth brought his sword around quickly, cutting through the mob of fallen elves. When there were no more, Nydeth turned, grabbing his mate by the hand, and they ran from the infected tunnels.

A single arrow hissed through the air quietly, and just as they reached Savven's side, it pierced Casvara through the heart in one deadly blow.

Time seemed to stop. Mute silence settled in as they stared in horror as blood bloomed like an unwanted flower across her chest.

"No!" Savven cried as his mother gasped once and crumpled at his feet.

The scream that ripped from the King chilled the very air around them, and Nydeth caught her body as she fell, kneeling to the ground.

Savven turned back toward the tunnels and saw the archer. A primal snarl flew from his lips as he unsheathed his sword and charged. He lunged, slicing the once kin in two. More swarmed from the tunnel like ants, swords in hand.

Savven deflected, bringing his sword around lightly, parrying blows and striking when he saw an opening. Soon, the enemies' numbers decreased, but Savven's sensitive ears picked up rapidly approaching footfalls. He ran to his father's side.

"What have you done!" his father screamed, his emotions feral.

Savven flinched as if he had been struck.

Nydeth knelt on the floor over his dead mate, silent tears streaming down his ashen face as he rocked her body in his arms, his copper hair a shield of fire around them.

"We will mourn later," Savven said, his voice shaking despite himself. "She would not want you to die in her wake. By my breath, today will not be the last day you are king."

Nydeth squeezed his eyes shut before he gave a short nod. With a snarl, he snapped the arrow from his mate's back and cradled her in his arms, her blood soaking through his armour, ink-black hair spilling over. Standing, he turned to Savven. "I will take her to the seas of Ligorin. Can you hold them off long enough?"

"Yes, reinforcements are coming. Pass her onto the sea. I will send word for your return when all of this ends." He bent down and kissed his mother's brow. "Fair passage, Father."

Nydeth paused, a coldness in his eyes Savven had never seen before. "Bring death to them all. Show them no kindness." With those final words, he turned and ran. Away from the battle, apart from his son, his dead mate in his arms.

Savven turned toward the approaching enemy, his thin sword dripping with blood, his face grim. The oncoming footsteps shook the ground as he waited. A moment later revealed a mass of black eyes and snarling faces that had once been of his own race, falling through the tunnel's arch like a black wave. They had been lured in by Ezra, drawn by the power he held. They were relentless and merciless.

Laudin stepped through the passage, surveying the hall calmly before his eyes landed on Savven.

Savven's grip tightened on his blade, and he snarled. Thoughts of his mother and what they had done to her filled him with icy rage. He gave a great cry and lunged forward, slicing through the horde, all but a blur.

They would all die for what they had done. Of that, he was sure.

FIFTY YEARS LATER

The wind howled against the mountain, creating an eerie chill in the midnight hours of the summer night. A new moon was overhead, but the stars glowed against the blackness in a vibrant overcast of light.

The Black Forest lay in waiting behind a female figure as she stared up from the base of the mountain. A cloak of dark velvet green was clasped around her shoulders, and a hood thrown over her head concealed her in shadows.

The sound of wings met her ears. She turned to see the body of neither man nor beast land just feet away. His wings were leathery and the colour of the moonless night. His form was scarcely clad, revealing the body of a warrior marked with age-old scars that marred his chest and arms from battles previously fought and won. Black leather tightly encased his lower half. Golden eyes glowed out from the shadows as he stepped nearer to her.

Her voice was firm when she spoke, "Take me to Valdren."

The male stepped forward and bowed his head, a deep gravelled tone filling the silence, "As you command, my lady." He did not wait for her permission but raised her in his arms and expanded his wings. He pushed himself from the earth with one mighty shove, and in moments they were sky-borne.

The earth rushed away from them, and she looked down to see it becoming smaller with each thrust of his wings. The mountain's peak loomed closer as the heavens came within her reach, and the earth was all but a pinprick.

Landing softly, the beat of his wings came to a halt. Setting her down, he stepped aside, bowing his head once and diving off the mountain's ledge. Soaring high into the air seconds later.

Fire was encased in ornate golden globes suspended in the air, lining the smooth stone walls. The air shimmered with heat the further she transcended into the mountain. The walk curved, forking, and she followed it right. Each step allowed her to ease the building emotions that rallied through her chest, she took a calming breath and came to a halt in front of massive wooden doors.

Two dragons were carved into the wood, faced away from each other with wings held high and inlaid with gold—the seal of the dragon council. The doors opened of their own accord with a soft creek, and she stepped inside.

A towering circular room greeted her. Black obsidian floors and sky-high pillars decorated the space, with orbs of fire hanging between each post, flooding the room with a light that bounced off the glassy walls, casting shadows. A golden council table stood curved against the backdrop of the sky, where the black and gold tapestry with the official seal of the dragon council lay as a marker behind it, its gold-fringed hem fluttering in a soft breeze.

At the head of the council sat Valdren, the dragon's keeper, in gold robes cinched at the waist. His grey hair was combed neatly back at the nape of his neck, his bright gold eyes tracking her entrance. The chief of the Drago clan sat beside him; on his other side sat the general of his army and, beside him, the chief's selected heir.

The great golden dragon, Forndýr, lay proudly around the back corner of the council, close to Valdren's side. His massive tail swept idly along the stone floor, the black barbed end barely held high enough to avoid scraping against the stone. Golden scales the size of her head shimmered in the firelight, and long, twisting black horns curved out the top of Forndýr's head. The council room barely held his massive size, and the female, still unused to the dragon's sheer monstrous size, felt her heart stutter when the dragon turned large reptilian gold eyes to stare down at her.

The female took her place in front of them and lifted a hand to her face, slowly removing the hood of her cloak.

"Welcome, Anabelle, Keeper of the Forest."

Anabelle bowed her head in acknowledgement to Forndýr when his voice filled her head, placing a soft hand over her heart in a salute, speaking down their silent connection, *"My greetings, Forndýr."*

Valdren stood at the head, speaking clearly, "Welcome, Keeper."

Anabelle turned her attention to the Dragon Keeper. "I came as you requested of me, Valdren." Her black hair and violet-blue eyes glowed in the orange and yellow light of the fire. The ancient dragon script tattooed upon her skin shimmered like water in the sun every time she moved.

Valdren retook his seat, a look of deep thought etched onto his unmarked face. "We have gathered here to discuss the plight that has eaten at our world, destroyed our villages, and caused so much death."

Anabelle said nothing.

"With this war raging, I must ask something of you that has never been done before. This will not be easy to ask this of you, Keeper."

"What is it?" Her voice was quiet in contrast to Valdren's.

"If there came a time where it was necessary for you to take Ezra's life... would you be able to?"

His question was a simple one, and if it had been anyone else... but it was Ezra, how could she kill him, even after all he had done to this world. Anabelle heard the cries of the earth. They were sobbing. Pain littered everything she encountered, and it drained her significantly of her energy. But Ezra! How could she kill someone she called a friend and kin. He had given her life; she could not take his in return.

Anabelle's heart clenched, and her head bowed, ashamed. "No, Valdren, I would not."

"As I assumed," Valdren said, his voice gentle.

Anabelle looked up at him and saw nothing but kindness, mingled with a sadness created by war, in his gaze.

"We fear the darkness is spreading again, and only the keeper will be strong enough to withstand. To fight at its core. Will you step down and allow this person to be your successor?"

Her brows furrowed. "Was that not my duty, no matter what?"

The chief of the Drago clan spoke up, his voice deep, his dark eyes warm though unwavering. "This will require you to step down within the coming years, perhaps sooner."

Anabelle looked between the chief and Valdren before she shot wide eyes to Forndýr. "This is because of what you showed me, isn't it?"

She remembered the day she received the dragon's blessing almost three hundred years ago and the visions she received with them. Fire, ash, and golden eyes still burned into her memory, and every day since, when life is spilt, and Ezra's name is called in the remnants of ruined villages, she is reminded.

"*Yes, Keeper,*" Forndýr said gently.

"You have served this world and its people well, a feat that is not easily accomplished. With Ezra's dark powers shadowing this world, I fear there may come a time when death must call again by the keeper's hands."

A light laugh filled the chamber. "My, my, you are surely the most dramatic old male I have ever heard."

All eyes whipped to the shadows, where an adolescent girl emerged. Her pin-straight black hair came just below her chin, her eyes nearly black, and her skin pale. Her thin mouth pulled into a smirk as she eyed Valdren.

"Tatius," the Dragon Keeper greeted warily, eyeing her up and down. "You've grown."

"Valdren, war does that to a God of Death," she purred, a glint in her eyes as she stalked forward. A black floor-length gown sheathed her slight frame like shadows as she hopped onto the council table.

The clan leader stood, mouth twisting, his fists anchored to the table. "Why do you come?" he demanded.

Tatius raised a brow, sliding a look to the male. "Tut, tut, Kladine, where are your manners? This involves me too, wouldn't you think?"

His face turned red at her scolding despite her enquiring tone. "I will not listen to the likes of a child!" he blustered, cutting his eyes to Valdren, who sat patiently, watching the girl.

Tatius's face turned deadly, walking slowly on bare feet to Kladine.

The fire flickered in the chamber, dimming as the shadows grew, and Kladine was pushed back into his seat with a thud. Bands of air restrained him as Tatius bent forward, her lips curling back into a sneer. "Child I may look, but I am also the God of Immortality. And while you may be immortal, oh precious clan leader, I am the one who gifted it to you... do *not* make me change my mind."

Her words were barely above a whisper, but Anabelle shivered as ice crawled down her spine.

The flames grew brighter, and the shadows retreated. Tatius skipped down the table and jumped off. Kladine's face had paled, but something simmered behind his dark eyes. Anabelle couldn't place it before her attention went to the small God.

Anabelle knelt before Tatius, going to eye level with her.

A whisper of a smile lifted her lips as Tatius said, "You were never meant to be keeper for its entirety, Anabelle. The world is at play, and change is swift approaching."

Her words struck her, and Anabelle's eyes glittered in the light with unshed tears. "This isn't about Ezra, is it?"

Tatius was silent, and Anabelle found her answer in that silence as the small God tilted her head like a cat eyeing a canary.

Forndýr spoke so all would hear his thoughts, *"Your strength and love for this world is why you were chosen as keeper—Anabelle, you are at no fault."*

His voice ran through the chamber in a warm gravelled wave, and Tatius's eyes rolled in exasperation as the dragon tried to ease the ache evident on Anabelle's face.

"You served this world proudly. We ask now that you allow a successor to come before the time in which the laws of the Fae have been decreed. This one, chosen by the dragons."

Anabelle stared at Forndýr, his words ringing in the hall. She balled her hands into fists, hidden within the folds of her cloak, as her heart raced behind its cage.

Taking a slow, deep breath, she raised her chin and sealed away her emotions, stating, "I have given everything to this world, and while it has given me everything in return, it has also taken much of what I hold dear. I want only to protect those residing in her and the light that this world craves to survive. If I am not the one to do that, I will accept this new successor against all laws if they deem to take on the role." She looked directly at Valdren. "I will fight for you, both as keeper and as nothing more than a soldier. Please do not disappoint me with the one you choose."

Kladine's heir stood abruptly, a winged male with ink-black hair and a cruel face. "You dare make demands?! You dare assume there is fallibility within the dragons?!" His voice was harsh with anger, and his near-black eyes flashed dangerously.

Forndýr lifted his head and looked at the male standing. A deep, rumbling growl filled the chamber until the fire flickered, vibrating the mountain beneath her feet. Menacing and filled with warning, his lips curled back, revealing fangs as long as Anabelle's forearm, and a plume of hot steam billowed from his nostrils. Those gold eyes fixated on the male whose teeth were bared at Anabelle, anger and pride flashing in his dark gaze.

Unlike the heir, the Drago army's general stayed seated, utterly unbothered by the angry dragon at his back. Though his green eyes flashed with annoyance at the heir. It was there and gone before Anabelle could discern it.

Anabelle's mouth pursed at his biting tone, her eyes narrowing slightly, and she rolled her shoulders back as she looked at the male. "Yes, I do," she replied smoothly. "Because *I am the keeper*, I will step down only if I feel they will be selfless in their duties and protect every living thing in this world. We are willing to die to protect what we love. That is the role of the keeper. So yes, I dare to make demands and presumptions against your infallibility. Until such times come, I am the keeper. I must protect this world. So, bring this chosen one. Let us see their strength."

Another rumbling growl filled with approval, and Forndýr laid his head back down, his gold eyes blinking at her and his tail curling behind the table. If Anabelle could guess, those black barbs at the end were waiting directly behind the heir's chair.

The council was silent in her challenge besides Tatius's amused scoff.

"Well, well, Keeper, how far you have come since the day you gave your life to me," mused Tatius, a wicked glint in her eye.

They would bring this chosen one, and Anabelle would soon see if they were worthy of upholding the challenges of this world.

CHAPTER 1

"Now boarding flight 9104 departing to Hornberg, Germany."

Hazel eyes stared up at the ceiling for a moment, as if trying to find a face to match the voice that spoke out of the intercom. With a low groan, Hazen grabbed her laptop bag and stood, pushing her blonde hair out of the way as it got caught in the strap. Following her parents to the terminal gate, where a smiling woman was checking their tickets.

"Have a nice flight," she said pleasantly as Hazen handed her the ticket.

"Thank you," she said softly, following the line into the terminal.

"Hazen, wait," called her mother, and she slowed her steps.

Claris Solvaya lengthened her strides to catch up to her daughter, her ash blonde bun wobbling atop her head. "Hazen, are you okay, love?" Her mouth was pulled into a slight frown, her brows furrowed in worry.

Hazen gave her mother a small smile, squeezing her bicep softly. "Mum, I'm fine, I promise. I'm just tired."

"You just seem so… withdrawn. Are you sure you're okay?"

She hummed, nodding her head and readjusting the strap of her bag. "I'm okay, I promise."

"Is everything okay with Robbie?"

Hazen rubbed her eyes, taking in a deep breath. "We broke up, Mum."

"No!" Claris exclaimed, taking several steps forward as the queue moved, but her gaze was solely on her daughter. "What happened?"

Life had happened. Robbie and she started dating in year eleven of secondary school, and they wanted to take a gap year after they finished their A-levels. For a whole year, Hazen did nothing but work a part-time job at her local pub in Eastbourne and travel a bit locally.

At the end of last year, she had started to look into going to university, but Robbie had other plans; those plans were located in Bali. While Bali seemed like a fantastic idea, Hazen couldn't see herself there with Robbie. So she ended things, and he hopped on a flight to Indonesia the next day.

Hazen shrugged. "I saw us going in different directions, so I ended things."

Claris sighed, looping her arm around her daughter's shoulders. "Well, what if I promise you this is a boy-free vacation, minus the old men. And you can laze around all you want if you promise *me* that you'll try and have a good time. It's been years since your father has gone home, and I know the grandparents will probably want to spoil you rotten." She stopped and turned Hazen, a fierce look in her eyes. "Good riddance to him. He was never good enough for you."

Hazen raised a brow, noting her mother's hazel eyes pleading with her own; her mother's were more green, whereas hers were more gold. Laughing under her breath, she kissed her mother's cheek quickly. "No boys, you promised."

She laughed, giving her hand an affectionate squeeze. "I'll even pinkie promise if that's what you want!" She looked over her shoulder. "We're holding up the queue. Come on."

Hazen glanced behind them, seeing the line starting to form and the impatient stares that followed. Sighing, she followed her mother into the small jet plane.

Her father, Jorg, followed behind shortly after they found their seats and shoved his carry-on in the top compartment before joining his wife and daughter. Starting up a conversation with Claris just as he sat down.

"Are you excited?" Hazen heard her mother ask.

"I've missed home—I mean, you are my home, my love, but I miss..." his words trailed off, and Hazen's heart squeezed, hearing the longing in his voice.

"I understand. It'll be fine, love," Claris reassured.

"I know, I know."

Her father kissed her mother quietly, love softening his weather-worn face and robust features. His salt and pepper brown hair tousled from combing his fingers through it.

Hazen sat her bag on the floor in front of her. Pulling out her phone, she quickly scrolled through Instagram, eyeing the photos her old schoolmates were posting. After a minute, she stuffed her phone in her bag and sat back, willing sleep upon herself as she closed her eyes.

"Please keep your seatbelts on until after take-off. This will be a short two-hour flight. We hope you have a pleasant trip."

"Hazen... darling, wake up," Claris said, shaking her daughter lightly.

Hazen groaned and opened her eyes. "What?" she muttered, sitting up. Her neck hurt, and her back was stiffer than a board. She had managed to sleep in the small space with the reward of body aches and a crimp in her neck.

"We're here."

Hazen looked out the window, grey skies and green hills surrounding them. "I thought Stuttgart was like some huge tourist attraction?"

"It is, but we're staying within Kinzig and Gutach Valley. We'll be beside the Black Forest," Jorg replied, wiggling his eyebrows as he tried to sound spooky and mysterious. His muted blue eyes twinkling.

Hazen laughed, giving him a slight eye roll. "Where's the airport?" she asked, eyeing the rolling hills.

"This is just a stop. There's no large terminal. They offload the passengers flying here and their luggage. You can walk to the station to make calls, or there's a road separate from the runway for pick up," Jorg explained, patting his daughter's back before following the select passengers for their stop out of the plane.

Stairs led into the fresh open air, and a cool breeze blew her hair into her face. Sputtering, Hazen pulled the hair from her mouth and tucked it behind her ears as she took the stairs carefully.

Seeing her parents across the tarmac, she extended a hand and waved slightly. An older couple that looked no more than seventy stood beside her parents, she could only assume they were her grandparents.

She had never met them, once when she was an infant, but she had no memory of that. Of course, she wanted to, but life was always stepping in. On certain holidays growing up, her father would go home, but it had been years since the last time he had flown back. And after the world shut down for a moment a couple years back due to a pandemic, her father was itching to see his parents.

Her grandfather and father stood shoulder to shoulder, towering over her mother's petite frame; her grandfather had a slight rounding stomach, mostly greying brown hair, and a cheery disposition. Though he was older by a stretch, she could see the resemblance between them. Her grandmother was taller than her mum but only slightly, with a slender waif frame and white hair that shone in the grey light, pulled back into a braid down her back. A smile graced her grandmother's features as she conversed with her parents.

"Hazen, come over here!" Claris called out.

She adjusted the strap of her bag as it slid down her shoulder, noting the thunder that rolled overhead.

"Hello," she said quietly with a soft smile.

Her grandfather smiled at her and pulled her into a tight hug. Taken by surprise, Hazen squeaked and hugged him back, though awkwardly.

"It's good to finally meet 'cha Hazen." He let go, allowing her to step away, his German accent thick as the words rolled off his tongue. Her smile widened slightly when she noticed that he had the same eyes as her father. "I'm Charles, but you can call me Charlie, and this is my wife, your grandmother, André."

André smiled at her, pale green eyes shining.

"It's nice to meet you again, though this time, I'm assuming I'll remember it since I was in nappies the last time," Hazen said with a laugh. "My dad has told me all about you and him when he was a child. I'm glad we could all finally be here together."

Claris gave Hazen's hand a slight squeeze.

Jorg looked up to the sky with puzzlement. "Dad, what is with this weather? I thought it would be summer!"

Charlie shook his head, looking up at the clouds in all seriousness. Their usual hot, muggy summer had never come. It only brought chilly rain, grey clouds, and thunderous storms as the clouds rolled overhead. "Odd weather it is. I haven't seen the skies this angry since I had met my André for the first time." He glanced at his wife.

"Well, should we get going?" André asked, clapping her hands together. "It looks like rain. I don't suppose any of you enjoy getting wet?"

Charlie gestured for them to follow. "If we don't hurry, wet is what we will be! Come on, we have your luggage."

A burst of thunder rolled above them that caused all of them to glare up at the sky.

"Best to go now," Charlie muttered.

The five of them hurriedly made their way down the road from the tarmac just as it started drizzling.

CHAPTER 2

Hazen felt rain hit her eye as she glared at the sky, the grey clouds rolling overhead. Goosebumps covered her arms, the cool breeze penetrating her clothes.

They walked to an old black town car, her grandfather and father stuffing the trunk and open backseat with luggage. They all piled in just as the tiny drizzle turned into a small downpour, the sound of rain pitter-patting on the windows in a steady rhythm.

The car ride to the house was filled with Jorg and Charlie's chatter, Charlie's boisterous laughter filling the cramped space. After what seemed like a very long drive through hills, green pasteurised farmland, and untouched brooding forest, Hazen spotted an old stone manor with ivy climbing up the walls, moving its way between the many windows and the dark oak door. Her grandfather steered up the gravel driveway and stopped in front of the garage door.

"Well, we're here," he said, taking the keys out of the ignition and turning around to face them. "Everyone ready to get out?"

Claris and Jorg hurriedly got out of the backseat. Hazen followed suit, chuckling lowly as she watched her parents stretch out their cramped limbs. Closing the door behind her, she walked around the back and waited for Charlie to unlock the trunk.

"Missy, don't you trouble yourself with that. Go on inside with André and look around. Your da' and I got this handled," Charlie said, scolding her lightly.

Hazen started to protest.

"None of that, now go, go." He waved her to the door, shooing her off, before turning to the luggage.

Hazen ambled up to the house, taking in her surroundings with curious eyes. The house itself stood proudly against the grey and green world around them, the backdrop of forest just beyond the house and the road on the other end, though no neighbours were in sight.

She took her time before she walked inside. The crisp breeze grazed her skin, numbing her cheeks, as she inhaled the deep scent of rain that coated the air before stepping through the threshold.

"Just make yourself comfortable, dear," André said as she approached from behind. Unwrapping the scarf around her neck, she hung it on the post next to the entry, along with her coat.

Nodding her head, Hazen took a step further. Pictures lined the walls on both sides, a few old and a few new. Some looked as if they were centuries old—faded and worn. One caught Hazen's eye. It held a girl in it, but you couldn't call her a girl, could you? You could tell she had just reached the peak of womanhood with her eyes bright and shining. There was a glow about her as if she felt all the lightness in the world. She had fair blond hair so light that it looked white and pale skin. She was beautiful.

"Who is she?" Hazen asked curiously, shifting her laptop bag on her shoulders.

Charlie and Jorg took that moment to barge into the house, their arms laden with suitcases stacked on top of one another under their shoulders.

Charlie craned his neck, looking at the picture as he set the bags down with a thud. "Why, that's André," he said, smiling.

Hazen's brows pulled together, and she turned to her grandfather. "That's—but that picture only looks a couple of years old?" Realising what she had said was rude, Hazen blushed and quickly apologised.

"It's alright, girl. You're right, that photo is new, but that picture is quite old. We had it retouched and printed when the original began to fall apart." A faraway look briefly graced the older man's face before smiling back at Hazen.

Claris walked over to the men and her daughter, wiping her hands on a dishtowel. "André and I have dinner started."

Charlie nodded. "Right, well, let me show you to your rooms then."

Gathering their things, Charlie, Hazen, and Jorg walked down the entryway before coming to the door next to the stairs.

"Son, you obviously know your room." Charlie manoeuvred his hand to the doorknob and turned it, pushing the door open silently.

Jorg shoved his and his wife's bag into the room, dusting his hands off. "Right-o, thanks, Dad." Nudging the door wider with his foot, he ruffled Hazen's hair before walking in.

Smiling faintly, Hazen smoothed her hair while she and Charlie ascended the stairway.

"So, what do you think so far?" Charlie asked casually, proceeding not to look at her. He adjusted the bags under his arms as he felt them slip.

"I'm just happy to be here," she stated.

Charlie peered around his shoulder, looking at the girl as they reached the top of the stairs. "I assume you had a whole summer planned out with your friends?"

Hazen gave a small, dry laugh. "Honestly, I was kind of over doing nothing. I took a gap year after school, and I got bored. It's time for a change, and coming here seemed like a good opportunity for that."

"No friends?" Charlie asked curiously.

"I had what you would consider *friends*, but they weren't really friends. Just schoolmates. And we've all gone in different directions since we left. I can't fault them. It's life."

Charlie made a sound of understanding. "Well, there's magic in these lands here, so opportunity is always forthcoming if you have the will for it."

As they stopped in front of Hazen's room, Charlie turned and stared at her, peering at her with an understanding look.

Hazen raised her eyebrows at her grandfather, shifting her feet somewhat uncomfortably. It was as if he could see all of her secrets, not that she had many to begin with.

"I'm glad you're finally here, Hazen. Your grandmother and I both are. It's been a long time coming, and we're tickled we get this time with you, even if we did miss out on a couple of years."

Her chest pinged with sadness, and she leaned forward, hugging her grandfather. "Me too, Grandpa," she said quietly, rubbing her hand over his back before pulling away.

Charlie patted her cheek fondly, set her bags down, and walked down the stairs.

Shaking her head, she opened the door and looked inside. It was a simple room. There was one full bed, a desk, and a dresser. An oval mirror hung over the desk, reflecting the window, and a bedside table. All of which had been—by the looks of it—hand-carved from redwood. The bed had a high headboard with carvings that Hazen couldn't decipher.

All the walls except one were completely bare of anything except a picture of a black birch tree painted onto the surface. Hazen was impressed with their creativity and appreciated the artwork momentarily, taking in the detail of the bare black branches.

Lugging her suitcase over to the bed, she heaved it onto the mattress as she unzipped her largest bag and started to unpack.

It was almost like moving. She hated it. The worst part of moving was the packing and unpacking.

Thirty minutes was her guess before everything would be unpacked—a little game to pass the time, no matter how boring. A race against the clock. But thirty minutes had already come and gone by the time Hazen got to the bottom of her last suitcase.

Just as she was about to toss the last bag in the corner with the others, a folded piece of paper caught her eye. Picking it up, she unfolded it and saw a picture of her with her parents a couple of years ago for her seventeenth birthday.

"Sweetie, let us take a picture of you!" her mother said excitedly.

Hazen winced at the thought of pictures but decided to humour her mother. "Okay, but only a couple."

Claris beamed and shuffled her husband to their daughter's side. "Jorg, stand by Hazen!"

Jorg rolled his eyes humorously at his daughter once his back was turned to his wife, Hazen's shoulders shook slightly with laughter. Jorg threw his arm around her shoulder and squished her to his side. He gave her a goofy smile and exaggerated 'cheeeeese.' Her birthday cake lit up with seventeen brightly lit candles in front of them.

Hazen laughed and looked up at her father as the camera's shutter clicked.

"Perfect! Now me! Jorg, come take a picture of Hazen and me!" Claris hurried over to her daughter's side and shoved the camera at her husband. "The last year our baby is a baby!" she said with a watery smile, looking at her daughter.

A camera snap made both women turn to Jorg.

"Jorg!" her mother exclaimed.

"I thought it was perfect," he said in his defence.

Claris marched over to him and snatched the camera out of his hands. "Can I take one more, Hazen? Please, just one more."

Hazen relented and smiled at her parents, letting it slowly fall when she heard the camera click. "Okay, enough," she laughed, grabbing the knife to cut the cake.

"Happy birthday, baby girl," said her dad gently, ruffling her hair.

"Thanks, Dad."

Fingertips brushed the smiling faces of both her parents. Later, she had gotten a shot with both of them, the camera set on a timer. Hazen set the photo aside with care and stood. Stretching with a groan, she glanced out the window, noticing the black sky.

How long had she been unpacking?

Her stomach growled loudly, and she looked down at it. "Food," she muttered, turning on her heels as she strode out of the room.

The smell of food was mouthwatering, wafting across her nose, and her stomach growled again in protest.

Licking her dry lips, she followed the scent down the hall to the stairs. Taking them two at a time, she met the house's first level and wandered through it casually.

The walls were red with oil paintings scattered throughout. The wall the cream coloured couch was pushed up against had a tree painted onto it in white—just like the one in her room. This one wasn't a birch, though. It looked like a large oak tree. Little cages were painted onto the branches, looking as if they were hanging there freely.

"Beautiful, isn't it?" asked André, coming up beside her.

Hazen looked at her grandmother, turning back to the wall art, and she nodded. "Why did you have them painted onto the wall?"

André sighed contently, a wistful look in her eyes. "It reminded me of my home, far from here. I painted them as a silent token of who I am." André smiled at her softly, her wistful stare turning curious as she looked at Hazen. "I'll have to tell you about my home one day."

Hazen was about to reply, but the clang of pots met their ears.

"Why don't we congregate in the kitchen?" André gently touched Hazen's upper back and steered her to the dining area.

"Oh, wonderful. You're here. I was just about to send your father up to get you," her mother said when she looked up and saw them walking in side by side.

"Lucky timing, I suppose," Hazen stated with a small, pleasant smile, looking around for the food. Disappointed when none was to be found.

"Oh, good, she's here! The prodigal granddaughter has risen!" Charlie exclaimed as he walked in behind Hazen and his wife. "Now it's time for food! The girl needs her food, Claris. She's growing!"

He tossed a playful wink at Hazen, and she felt her cheeks grow hot, but her face broke out into a grin regardless.

André scowled at Charlie though amusement clouded her eyes. "Oh, stop teasing the girl, Charlie. She's stopped growing many years ago."

Scratching the back of her neck lightly with an amused chuckle, Hazen looked at her father, trying to change the subject. "So, what are you doing tomorrow?" she asked, following everyone to the table in the adjoined room.

Hazen looked at the white walls. They, too, had paintings drawn onto them—more reminders of André's homeland, she guessed. Mountains this time, detailed in black, though it didn't look like paint; it looked like ink smeared across the wall in delicate details.

Jorg looked at Hazen as they all took a seat. "Your grandfather and I are going into the city; your mum and André are going to the lake."

Hazen nodded, taking a piece of chicken breast and putting it on her plate along with steamed carrots.

"What about you, Hazen? Is there anything you want to do? You could go with your grandfather and me if you don't."

"I don't have anything planned."

"Well, you could come to the lake with us?" Claris asked, countering their offer, and helped herself to some of the food.

Hazen nodded. "I'd like that, actually."

André smiled wide. "I'll pack us a picnic."

The chatter over dinner was rambunctious and full of laughter. Hazen answered questions and shared stories from over the years, her cheeks hurting from the smile she wore. But as dinner passed and Hazen was about to finish the last of her meal, she felt a gentle wave of fog sweep over her mind. It was like someone placed a blanket over her head, and the noise around her ceased. Her eyes glazed over, fixated on the table, her fork hovered over her plate as she stilled.

Seconds seemed like minutes, and just as sudden as the fog had come, the pain swept in like an unleashed storm. Clamped around her head and squeezing her skull. Sweat immediately dotted the back of her neck, and a sharp, quick gasp left her lips.

"Hazen."

Her brows furrowed, saliva collected in her mouth, she lost the ability to swallow, the pressure building in a crescendo. Putting a hand to the side of her temple, she forced her mouth to move, unsticking her lead tongue. Turning towards her mother, seated beside her. "Yes?" she gritted out, her hand shaking around her fork. She had heard her name in a sweet female voice, too soft to fit her mother or grandmother. Though she didn't pay heed to that minor detail.

Claris looked away from her conversation with André and glanced at her daughter. "What is it, Hazen?"

"Didn't you say my name?" she asked in a strangled voice as the pressure increased, the tightness moving down her neck now like lithe fingers, covering every muscle in a suffocating grip. She felt beads of sweat start to form on her temples and above her lip.

Claris shook her head, her brows meeting as she placed a hand on Hazen's forearm. "Love, are you alright?"

Her eyes skipped between her mother and André, her mother's gaze pinched with concern. Though her grandmother simply stared at her, head tilted and eyes lit with something Hazen couldn't be bothered to place at that moment. Heart racing in her chest, blood humming in her ears, she forced herself to nod. "Yeah, no, I'm fine. Never mind." She turned back to her meal, closed her eyes and took a deep breath—aware that her mother was still glancing at her and of the calculating stare from her grandmother. The pressure dulled, and she opened her eyes, hoping that whatever had happened had blessedly passed.

"Hazen."

It was there again, that sweet ringing voice that brought another wave of pain. Hazen's head jerked, and her fork dropped. It clattered to her dish as she wrapped her arms around herself. It was everywhere, coming at her in continuous waves. The pain was like a hundred hot tiny knives along her back, she gripped the edge of the table for support.

"May I be excused? I'm not feeling very well—stomach ache." The words were breathless, strained, and she didn't wait for a response. Shoving her chair away, she exited the dining room.

She faintly heard someone get up from the table and call after her. She ignored it and continued up the stairs, making her legs move despite their screaming protest as they seemed to turn to stone.

Her body was on fire by the time she reached the top. Her breathing was ragged, and she had to lean against the wall for support. Her fingertips clawed at the plaster to keep her upright, her nails leaving their mark and bits of it burying themselves under her nail beds.

It didn't work. Hazen fell to her knees, her back hunched, and her shoulders flamed. She all but screamed in pain, but only a moan escaped as something clawed its way up her spine. Her eyes blurred from the fire etching into her bones, tears streaming down her cheeks. She pushed past the pain and got to her feet. Staggering to her bedroom and slamming the door behind her.

Feet tripping over one another, she fell back onto her bed. Curling into herself, her fingers fisted into the quilt, tossing and turning. She shook uncontrollably in a sweaty mess as the fire rolled under her skin.

Her mouth parted as another scream took her, and she tasted the cotton of the bedspread. Hair plastered to her skin, her body inflamed, teeth clenched together, her jaw about to snap. It wasn't long before her eyes rolled back into her skull, her body exhausting itself, and the sweet relief of darkness claimed her.

CHAPTER 3

The house was silent. In the early hours of the morning, the sun was just beginning to peek through the kitchen window, and natural light filled the room.

André sighed, glancing at her husband, who sat beside her at their round kitchen table as she tried to collect her thoughts. Last night was an anomaly. She could sense a change in the air, slithering through her home with familiarity—nothing completely noticeable, but noteworthy all the same.

"She's different, Charles, I know she is," she said softly, wonder stitching her voice.

Charlie rubbed his ageing temples as he glanced at his wife: He didn't disregard the idea of magic to be nonsense. While he didn't wholly understand it himself, as always with André, he tried to make sense of it. "How can you be sure?"

"I feel it. You know that I would never lie about something like this... especially for what I am... for who I used to be. My instincts would never lie. They chose her, Charles, for whatever reason it might be."

She sighed, rubbing her eyes with defeat. A small part of her longed for a world she had long been apart from.

She hadn't thought hard about her past life, her youth, and the world she left behind in quite some time; but now, after last night, it was all her mind could think about. And a deep yearning etched its way into her chest.

Charlie studied his wife for a moment and got up from the table. "Yes, I know, my sweet, I know," he said as he came around to her side, sliding her hair back slowly as he saw the slight points of her ears—the only thing left of her old life, a subtle marker.

Caressing the soft flesh, he gave her a kiss on the side of her temples. "So, what are we to do about the girl?"

Grasping his hand to her heart, she whispered, "We wait."

Hazen groaned, her throat clenching as the sound scraped against sensitive flesh. Her head pounded, the sun streamed through the windows, and she tried to turn away from it, her body protesting the movement. Her mind was a blanket of confusion, like a tangle of webs woven together; Hazen couldn't distinguish one thought from another. All she could remember was excruciating pain and then nothing at all.

Sitting up, all the blood rushed from her head. She felt the earth sway, and she opened her eyes to find black spots dotting her vision. Hazen clenched her eyes shut, letting the spell pass before opening them. She cast a critical glance at the window as her gaze was met with a ray of sunlight. No drapes or curtains hung on the walls.

Sighing, she walked over to the window, looking out onto the valley and forest that surrounded them for miles. Her grandparents' house was set in a vast landscape in varying shades of green, springing with life and promise. Hazen could not doubt the country's beauty, even with the bleak overhang of the greying sky.

Somewhere from within the house a door shut and voices from downstairs could be heard followed by laughter. Hazen tore her eyes away from the window and walked over to her door, pulling it open. The volume of the noise increased. She glanced towards the voices but didn't heed them, turning to the right instead. She could feel the sticky residue of sweat on her skin, hoping to find a shower behind one of the doors on her level.

She came upon a bathroom behind the second door she tried. A door lay attached to the small room. She opened it and found that it led to her room.

"Didn't notice that," she muttered.

Hazen locked both doors and stripped out of her clothes from yesterday. Groaning when she stepped under the hot spray, she sagged against the cool tile wall, letting the water run down her body, head pounding like a drum.

Sighing, she grabbed the bar of soap, ran it down her arms, and scrubbed the sweat away. A dark line caught her eye, it curled over her left shoulder, and her hands stilled. Craning her neck, she tried to get a better look, but her muscles twinged in complaint. Rinsing, she turned the water off and got out, grabbing the fluffy blue towel off the rack and wrapping it around herself.

The bathroom had become a wet sauna. The mirror fogged over with steam rolling through like clouds. She used her hand to wipe the glass, staring at her pale complexion.

Turning around, Hazen craned her neck to look at her reflection.

Hazen's mouth parted, and her brows furrowed as she stared at the odd markings on her shoulders. "What the...?" The words died on her lips. Her hand reached to touch it, fingers prodding the skin. To her surprise, the skin was smooth and not tender.

The mark was black-blue like a bruise and stretched across her left shoulder blade. It had eight jagged ends that fanned like wings with four points on either side. Blue and purple veins surrounded it as if her skin had suddenly become translucent. They webbed together, weaving in and out of the mark in a tangle of knots that curled over her shoulder and down her bicep.

"What the fuck is it?" she muttered to herself, brows furrowing in a frown.

"Darling, are you awake yet?"

Her mother's voice wafted faintly through the hall, and Hazen's hand jerked away from the mark. "Yeah, Mum, just in the shower!" she called back.

Tightening the grip on her towel, she unlocked the door to the hall, cracking it open before she slipped through the door connecting to her room. Shutting it firmly behind her, her head fell back against the door with a small thud as she released the breath she had been holding. She tried to remember what happened last night, but unrelenting pain was the only thing her mind could conjure.

Her hand went to her shoulder, gripping it tightly. She gave into the notion that she was going mad and that last night was only a fever dream.

A soft knock jilted her door, her mother's voice following. "Darling? Is everything okay?"

Squeezing her eyes shut, the hand on her shoulder tightening, she said, "Yeah, Mum, I'm okay. Just a bit of food poisoning last night. Good as new now."

"I came to check on you, but you were asleep," she said, her voice muffled.

Letting out a breath through her nose, Hazen stood, opened her door a crack, and saw her mother's worried stare.

"I love you, Mum, I'm okay. I promise."

Her mother nibbled on her lip, nodding slowly. "Okay, are you sure you're okay with going to the lake today? You can stay here and rest if you want."

Hazen shook her head. Even though staying in sounded lovely right now, she wanted to spend time with her grandmother. "No, I'm okay. The lake sounds like just what the doctor ordered."

A smile lit her mother's face, and she clapped her hands. "Perfect, I'll let André know. Breakfast is ready, so come down soon?"

"I will."

After her mother left, Hazen quickly dressed in faded old jeans, a warm white long-sleeve shirt, and her old black trainers. The end of her braided hair created a wet patch on her shirt.

Her feet met the stairs' landing, and she followed the voices to the kitchen, the pleasant scent of pancakes hanging in the air guided her. Hazen pushed her way into the kitchen to find her very awake grandmother humming while she worked over a chopping block. Her white hair was tied back into a bun as she sliced strawberries.

"Those look good," remarked Hazen, walking over to André and kissing her cheek, eyeballing a large stack of crêpes.

André smiled up at her. "Good morning! My, it's nice to see you awake. You were looking a little peaky last night. Did you sleep well?"

Hazen shrugged. "As well as could be expected," she lied.

"Ah," André acknowledged, her brow raising just slightly. "Here" —she handed her a plate full of rolled crêpes stuffed with cream cheese filling and strawberries— "Take these to the table. The others are in there."

Hazen's stomach rumbled in excitement. "These look amazing, Grandma. How did you get so good at cooking?"

André grinned at her. "Trial and error. Now take those to the table, a little sweetness in the morning to brighten the day."

Her parents and grandfather were seated around the table with a plate of eggs and another of sausage in the middle. One clean plate sat primly in front of the chair she had used the night before.

"Good morning," she announced, setting the crêpes next to the eggs. Charlie and her parents looked at her as she grabbed her plate and helped herself.

"How did you sleep?" Charlie asked, reaching for seconds.

"As well as could be expected," she replied, giving him the same answer as she gave André. Her mother held out her and her father's plate, and she placed a crêpe on each one.

"Thank you, love," Claris said.

André came in moments later just as Hazen started on her food. "Claris, Hazen, would you be willing to leave for the lake after you finish? There's a storm coming in this evening, so I thought we would go while the weather is still good."

Claris looked at her daughter and nodded as if asking for her approval. Hazen gave a slight nod of her head. "That would be fine, André."

"Wonderful, I'll go pack us lunch."

Claris thanked her with a smile while Hazen stuffed a strawberry into her mouth.

The sun peaked through the grey blanket of clouds briefly before disappearing again. The Black Forest surrounded them in a towering fortress of giant evergreens. The lake was as black as a murky sea, though it shone like dark onyx—the mountains, with the residue of snow on their granite peaks and the wall of trees, reflected off the watery surface.

Hazen walked across the ledge of the rocky shore. Her grandmother and mother were busy setting up another layer of blankets on the pebble beach. A tan wicker basket full of foods for their lunch lay primly on the rocks. The two women bundled in plain wool shawls, a blue one wrapped tightly around Hazen's shoulders. A brisk wind playfully caressed Hazen's face, and she smiled softly.

"Hazen!"

Hazen turned to her mother.

"Don't wander off too far!"

Hazen nodded, but she wasn't sure if her mother could see it. Turning back around, she continued further away from their picnic.

It was different here than in Eastbourne. The air was fresh, like earth, stone, and rain collided to overwhelm the senses in the best way. Eastbourne was salty and clear as the tide ebbed and flowed from the English Channel, but it didn't smell of earth, only sea. Something about the smell of wet soil and evergreens calmed something inside of her. There was no noise of cars and people. Even the sky, though stormy and overcast, was different.

Her feet carried her towards an unknown destination, following the curve of the shore. Her mind was quiet as the wind played through the loose strands of her hair. When she looked back, she could barely make out her mother and grandmother in the distance.

An eerie quiet surrounded her, the kind where you could

hear the silence as it enveloped you. Her heart pounded like a loud drum. Nothing could be heard from her family. It was just her. Her breathing slowed, her lips parted, and she looked at her surroundings. Without the noise of idle human chatter and feet crunching on the lake shore, you could listen as the forest came to life.

Hazen faced off against the towering wall of trees that lined the rocky shore. Eyes scanning the full branches and misty overhang that drifted between limbs in searching tendrils. She stood there, entirely consumed by the forest, the tug of something unfamiliar pulling her closer to its hidden depths. The gravel crunched underfoot as she took a step towards the beckoning woods.

A small red bird drifted down to a branch on one of the evergreens, its breast as bright as blood. It chirped once and flew away.

The noise jolted Hazen, and she shook her head. Tearing her eyes from the forest, she watched the tiny creature disappear over a horde of trees. The wind whistled through the branches behind her, and she briefly turned back to it, pursing her lips.

Gripping her shawl, she turned away from the treeline, noting the jut of earth. The lake water remained as still as glass, and Hazen found herself walking over to it.

The ground was slick, and she traversed carefully on the patches of grass sticking up from the small rocks that covered the lip. She knelt down, sinking to her knees, her hands supporting her weight as she leaned forward. The water was as black as coal, and she could see nothing but her reflection and the mountain scenery surrounding her.

Hazen peered into the water, watching her face shift slightly as the lake stirred. Hazel eyes stared wide-eyed back at her, almost yellow in the grey light. Her skin paled further in comparison against the dark waters.

A sudden gust of wind blew, and something caught her eye. She blinked, rubbing at it momentarily before staring back at the waters. A pair of liquid gold eyes stared back at her instead of her reflection. Hazen yelped in surprise, throwing her body back. She landed on her haunches, the soft skin of her palm scraping against gravel and dirt. Hazen glanced in the direction of her grandmother and mother. They hadn't noticed. She turned to the water and crawled forward on her hands and knees.

Hazen cautiously looked back at the water, seeing her face on the mirrored surface. She sighed and shook her head. Making to stand, the earth under her—at the edge of the embankment—gave away under her hands, and her body fell forward.

The world turned black, frigid water consuming her, filling her ears, nose, and mouth. It dragged her down, the momentum of the fall serving as a weight that carried her into the watery void.

Her body bounced off the bottom, her shirt catching on a rock when she jerked up. A sound of panic strained her burning lungs, having been unable to take a breath before she fell. She couldn't see anything but water black as night around her. Hazen tugged her arm, the fabric still caught. A whimper filled the silence between her frantic heartbeats, and she blindly followed her arm down to the rock where her sleeve was caught.

Gripping the fabric, she screamed, the last of her air leaving her, her sleeve tearing. She pushed off the bottom and kicked frantically towards the dim light above her.

Her body broke through the surface, and she gasped in a stabbing breath.

"Hazen!"

She saw her mother and grandmother frantically running over to her with a blanket.

"I'm fine," she tried to call back, but they couldn't hear her. They were still too far away, and her voice was barely a whisper. Taking deep breaths, she swam to the shore, calming the ache in her lungs.

Rocks and dirt slipped under her nail beds when she tried to stand. Wincing in pain as gravel scraped against the raw skin on her hand, she heaved her heavy, water-sodden body up onto the shore. Shivering from the cold, she had to clamp her jaw together so her teeth wouldn't begin to chatter. The wind was no longer playful but icy and unrelenting.

Counting to ten, she took in slow, steady breaths before standing. Then, carefully, she began walking toward the two women rushing towards her.

"I'm fine," she said quickly, noting their distressed expressions.

André wrapped a wool blanket around her shoulders, and she gripped it tightly, savouring the shield against the wind.

"You may be fine but won't be if we don't get you out of the wind." A heavy breeze blew by to make her point, and André scowled at the forest quickly before turning her attention back to Hazen. Running her hands over her shoulders.

Hazen said nothing but let the two women drag her away from the lake.

CHAPTER 4

Hazen sat perched by a window, her body stuffed into a large cushioned chair, a cup of chamomile tea in her hands.

A massive storm rolled in just as they had gotten home. Charlie and her father arrived not much later. Shaking the rain from their coats, they hurried through the front door.

The rain and wind whipped at the windows in an angry frenzy. A mournful cry could be heard from the trees as they swayed back and forth like forlorn giants.

Hazen took a sip from her tea and watched the storm from the comforts of her chair.

"Girl, are you hungry?" asked Charlie, perching on the armrest.

Hazen looked up at him, his warm blue eyes smiling at her. She gave him a soft smile in return. "Would it be alright if I said I wasn't?"

"By all means. Though, I don't want you to starve."

"I'll eat later. I'll find some food if I get hungry."

Charlie nodded. "Alright, well, I'll let you be."

"Thanks, Grandpa."

The older man nodded and patted her shoulder. Hazen shut her eyes once he left, and enjoyed the silence, save for the war outside.

It was much later when the outside world was pitch black, and the house was silent as everyone had gone to their separate rooms. Hazen quietly made her way to the kitchen. Washing her cup, she set it back in the cupboard, savouring the silence.

A loud bang came from the living room. Startled, Hazen rushed from the kitchen. Everything was fine. Another blow was heard, and she ran to the entryway. The front door had come open and banged against the wall, the wind pouring into the narrow space.

Hazen rushed forward to shut the door and found herself staring out into the darkness, rays of light from the house becoming lost.

A small bark caught her attention, and from the shallow light coming from the doorway, she eyed a little dog standing just beyond the house. Its fur was wet and matted to its body, and its floppy ears perked up when it barked again.

She groaned under her breath, shivering when she took a tentative step outside. "Hey, boy… or girl… hey, doggy," she cooed softly. Her voice was lost in the wind as it pulsed against her.

"Hey! Come back!" Hazen called after it in annoyance when it ran away.

The dog barked, but the night cloaked him from sight.

Hazen let out a huff. "Fine, stay outside for all I care!"

She turned on her heels and marched inside, shutting the door firmly behind her. Shaking her arms, she tried to wipe the water off, feeling shivers run down the length of her body.

Barking sounded from outside again, and Hazen squeezed her eyes shut. Rubbing a hand over her face, her hand hovered over the doorknob. Another bark, and she let out a slight sound of frustration. She just wanted to go to bed now, damn the silence and the storm.

Thunder rumbled violently overhead, and she heard a small

yelp of terror. She gnawed at her bottom lip, guilt rearing its ugly head. She heard another bark, and Hazen gave in.

Throwing open the door, she stared out into the darkness.

"Here, doggy," she called, walking out onto the gravel. She could feel the coarse rock underfoot as it cut into the soft pads of her toes, cursing herself for not grabbing her shoes. The door slammed into her back, and her body was catapulted forward, the sound of a click echoing as it shut firmly behind her.

Hazen turned to open it but heard the dog again. Turning back, she spotted the mutt further away. "Come here," she cooed loudly over the whipping wind and the occasional crack of lightning and thunder. He didn't listen and barked again.

Groaning, Hazen allowed the darkness to swallow her as she gave into her guilty conscience and went after the small animal.

Once again, her entire body was soaked as rain pelted her through her clothes. Water dripped from her eyelashes, nose, the ends of her fingertips, and hair as she ran into the dark night. A faint bark could be heard in the distance, and Hazen sprinted to follow it.

Thunder shook the skies, and lightning struck in the distance. The sound jarred Hazen as she ran blindly. Her feet slapped against the wet ground, numb from the cold, before skidding to a stop. Her breathing was ragged, her heart pounding, and adrenaline pumped through her veins.

"Where is that damn dog?" she muttered.

Lightning struck again, lighting up the sky, and Hazen jumped as it rumbled closer. Yapping was heard, and Hazen veered right, praying she wouldn't run into anything. A small wet dog with mattered white fur cowered near a cover of trees. The wall of the forest was darker than the night, and Hazen wished she hadn't left the comforts of her grandparent's house for a stray dog. But she was dumb, and she couldn't let it just die!

Her heart pounded as she rushed over to the small dog and picked him up in her arms.

"Finally!"

Just as she was about to turn back the way she came, the wet furry mass in her hands, hoping she could find her way again, thunder roared overhead like a giant's cry. The dog leapt from Hazen's arms and into the dense forest.

"Dammit! Get back here!" she shrieked, her limbs trembling.

The wind picked up, and lightning stuck close enough for her hair to stand on end. Hazen's heart caught, and her feet raced into the beckoning woods. The wind lashed out at her, branches whipping at her face, tearing at her clothes, their spindle fingers desperately reaching to grasp her.

Fear pumped through her body, causing her legs to push past their comforts. Her mind went blank, concentrating solely on the forest floor before her.

"Where could she be?" Claris asked worriedly as she paced the floor.

The house had woken when a sharp slam reached their ears. They had all come out of their rooms dressed in robes, confused and still half asleep. The four adults had found nothing that could have caused the noise, searching through every room until they found Hazen missing. Her bed was empty, and any traces of her were gone.

Jorg stood, ready and on edge. "We have to go out and look for her!"

Charlie shook his head. "We can't. It's too dark. We would only get lost ourselves."

"We can't not do anything!" Jorg argued back in a sharp voice. "That's my daughter out there!"

Charlie walked over to his son, grasping and shaking him by his shoulders. "Get some sense into you, boy! If you go out there, you won't be any better off than Hazen. There is nothing we can do right now! I want nothing more than to join you and find my granddaughter, but we can't!"

André hushed Claris's worried steps and put an arm around her. "The storms here can become dangerous, Jorg. We *must* wait until morning."

Hazen jumped back as lightning struck the ground, not more than a hair's breadth away to her left, the electrified air tinging her wet skin like a sharp kiss. With eyes wide, she veered right and ran further into the woods, knocking branches out of her way as she went. Her heartbeat was erratic as she stumbled on uplifted roots. The trees were packed together, making it hard for her to manoeuvre her way through them.

The world suddenly quieted, and her sharp breaths were painfully loud in her ears. Slowing, her numb feet came to a stop, chest heaving in damp breaths of air. Fingers clenching, she flexed them and walked forward. The forest began to open, the trees seeming to shift further apart. The brambles opened to a clearing where trees lined the aisle ahead like earthen pillars. Tall, dark and foreboding. Their bark was as black as coal—an illusion cast by night—and as wide as two trees.

Dead leaves squelched as they imprinted into the damp soil under her feet. The forest was silent, the storm becoming unheard through the dense thicket of woods behind her. Hazen walked on, her eyes adjusted to the darkness, and before her was an altar of stone.

The stone was worn and old, and moss grew along its arch. Hazen reached the shrine and placed her hands upon its coarse surface, her fingers tracing a knotted pattern along the edge.

All was quiet. No wind could be heard as Hazen stood there in the ringing of silence. Her heartbeat even seemed to still as the forest held its breath.

A sudden deafening roar shook Hazen to the core and vibrated through the whole of the forest. The winds picked up, whistling loudly in her ears, and she slapped her hands over them.

The leaves whipped against her, the trees surrounding her swayed and groaned, and the air around them rampaged throughout the forest like a massive wave.

Hazen's lungs strained against the wind, fighting to take a

breath, but the density of the air grew heavy, and her lungs failed her. Clawing at her throat and chest, she turned to run but fell forward onto the forest floor. Her vision became spotty and blurred, her head fogging over as she gave a strangled silent cry in the chaos.

Something was being pulled from her, tearing her apart from the inside, the feeling of being ripped in two split down her middle and her hands dug into the earth, back arching against the pain. Another roar vibrated violently before her eyes rolled back, and she fell into obscurity.

Leaves cushioned her fall. They covered her gently as the winds settled, the dead leaves gliding softly back down to the earth. As quickly as it had come, it was gone. Everything was once again peaceful and still. The storm passed, the rain stopped, and the wind became silent.

CHAPTER 5

Hazen clenched her eyes tight, the sun penetrating through her closed lids. Rolling to her side, expecting her soft pillow, Hazen's eyes shot open when she felt coarse dirt against her skin. The smell of the earth aroused her senses.

Blinking once, she made to sit up, but her limbs could not move. Looking down, her hands and legs were bound together by thick rope. Struggling, she tried to break free. Panic welled up in her throat, and she let out a frustrated whimper, terror settling in her bones immediately. No matter how hard she pulled, the rope only rubbed deep into her skin.

"Dammit!" she cursed, her heart threatening to rip through her chest.

A rustling came from behind Hazen as she heard someone

speak.

"What did she say?"

The voice was thick with a rough gravel curl, and an accent Hazen couldn't place.

"Who knows? It looks like she's awake now," said another voice, this one much younger, though the accent was still evident.

Hazen's head whipped around, twisting her body so her legs would follow. She felt the earth tilt as she lost balance, and her upper body fell back. She landed on her stomach, her hands trapped beneath her.

Lovely, she thought to herself, her hands digging uncomfortably into her pelvis.

She looked up when two pairs of boots came into view, craning her neck to see the faces of the ones she assumed took her hostage. "Who are you, and what the bloody hell did you tie me up for?!" she shrieked, eyes wild as she looked between them both. They weren't tall at all, maybe five feet at most.

The first had a flaming red beard that reached his knees and covered half of his youthful face. He had tan freckled skin, dark brown eyes, thin lips, and a large nose. The other was the same but with coarse black hair and wrinkles mapping the skin around his eyes and forehead.

Both had axes strapped to their waists by large, brown leather belts. White coarse woven smocks opened at their necks—a mass of curled hair peeked through—and dark pants. Soft, worn boots covered their feet.

The one with the red hair spoke up. Hazen recognised it to be the second voice.

"I'm Tolak. This is my older brother, Ivakin," he said, pointing to them in turn.

"Idiot! Why did you tell her our names," Ivakin snapped with a scowl. Slapping his brother upside the head, he turned a stern eye to Hazen.

Tolak rubbed his head, glaring at his brother in turn. "She asked who we were."

"That doesn't mean you answer her."

"Yes, but it would have been rude. Mother always told us not to be rude."

Ivakin rolled his eyes, his bushy brows furrowing. "Not when we have a prisoner and don't know who she is. Let alone *what* she is."

"But mother always says—"

"Tolak, will you still your tongue!"

Tolak snapped his mouth shut mid-sentence. Ivakin closed his eyes and breathed slowly in through his nose.

Hazen's jaw clenched, her teeth aching as she looked between the two. She was slowly trying to break free of her restraints, the soft skin of her wrists throbbing.

Noticing the movement, the two small men rushed forward and flipped Hazen on her back. Before she knew what was happening, Tolak sat on her chest and Ivakin on her legs.

Ivakin looked over his brother's shoulder to peer down at the girl beneath them with a glare. "Now, where do you think you're going?"

"Back to my grandparent's house, I hope!" Hazen retorted. She bucked her hips, trying to throw them, but found them a solid force atop her when they didn't move.

Tolak made a disapproving sound. "We can't let you do that—"

"—Not until you answer a few questions first," Ivakin finished.

Hazen gritted her teeth in annoyance. "Fine, as long as I get to ask a few questions myself! And you get off me!"

"You won't run off?" Tolak asked.

"Where am I going to go? I'm tied together, and I have no idea where I am," she retorted bitterly, her eyes scanning the area quickly. She was surrounded by a forest, with tall willow trees swaying in the wind, their long branches brushing the ground softly.

"Yes, alright, you have a bargain," the two said in unison. They both got off and sat on their haunches on either side of her.

Hazen sat up, bent forward at the waist with her hands resting on her legs.

"I will go first, then Tolak. After, you may have your turn, and so on it shall go."

Hazen only gritted her teeth, narrowing her eyes at the little man.

"Right, well, your clothing," Ivakin said, gesturing to her body. "Why are you naked? Where's the rest of it?"

She glanced down at herself, a white t-shirt and a pair of blue plaid pyjama shorts. Her bare toes wiggled back at her. "Jamies... they're... I'm not naked!" she sputtered finally. Honestly, she felt more and more befuddled as the seconds ticked on.

Tolak pointed to her head. "Is it customary to have dead leaves in your hair?"

Hazen lifted her bound hands to feel her head. "Oh." She pulled a leaf out of her hair, staring at it contemptuously. "You realise I was lying on the ground, right?"

"Not very appealing, don't you think, Ivakin?"

"Not at all. Silly little custom to have."

Hazen looked between the two, shaking her head with exasperation. "It's my turn now. Where am I, and who are you?"

Tolak pinched the thin skin on her neck. "That's two questions," he stated promptly.

She flinched and jerked away from him, gritting out, "One for each of you, then."

Ivakin looked at her. "To answer the first question, you are in Thórsmörk."

Hazen raised a brow in confusion.

"We are the dwarves of Stonehammer."

Hazen nodded slightly. "Well, most prefer the politically correct term: little people."

The two men glanced at one another.

"Little people?" muttered Ivakin to his brother.

"I have never heard such a word."

"Nor I."

Hazen looked between the men, her frustration welling up quickly. Knots were forming in the pit of her stomach, making her queasy. She clenched her fists, trying to stay calm.

Somewhere in the distance, a crow cawed twice. Ivakin and Tolak froze, glaring at their surroundings, their faces darkening with awareness. Ivakin bent, pulling a dagger from his left boot. He cut the bindings at Hazen's ankles. "Stand up. We're not safe out in the open."

Hazen pushed herself to her feet, the dirt warm under her toes from her body heat. Hazen looked down at the men, realising just how little they were. She had to be nearly a foot taller than them.

Tolak nudged her forward from behind. "Don't try anything. My brother is skilled with a knife, and he's in a foul mood today," he warned in a low voice as they followed Ivakin.

Hazen glanced behind her at Tolak, stumbling over her own feet. She turned around, focusing on Ivakin's back, the deadly edge of his axe glinting in the sunlight.

The forest around them was filled with golden sunlight spilling through the canopy of swaying green limbs and ashy trunks. Black soil was soft underfoot, cushioning her raw feet as Hazen followed between the two men. Her thoughts were a whirlwind of confusion and underlying panic about her situation.

They followed Ivakin until they reached a cliff wall. Boulders were cloistered in one spot against the stone. The eldest walked over to the rocks, his black beard dusting the ground as he bent forward, lightly tracing a crack in the rocks. He straightened and took a narrow blade with a marble handle from his shirt sleeve.

"Watch closely," Tolak instructed Hazen.

Hazen's eyes narrowed on the eldest.

The blade flipped in the dwarf's hand before he sunk it deep into the stone's crevice; a loud crack whipped through the air, and a rough arching outline appeared on the cliff's wall of a door.

Hazen stared with mouth agape at the now visible entrance before her.

"Dwarves' magic," explained Tolak, guiding her towards the cliff belly.

Ivakin pushed the stone door open to let them pass.

"Are you guys from the circus?" she questioned, stepping through the passage. Her comment went unheard as she was led into the belly of the mountain, yellow and orange bouncing off the stone walls from the torches that lit their way.

The tunnel was a maze of confusion. The path split into two, three, and four, which soon connected to more. It got colder the further they went, and Hazen could see her breath cloud in front of her. The stone walls fell away into a black abyss the deeper they traversed.

Hazen brought her bound hands close to her chest, jaw clenched against the cold that was seeping into her bones. The darkness was never-ending, the flicker of firelight barely lighting the path at her feet, and time seemed to pass endlessly.

She opened her mouth, but any complaint died on her lips as the world opened up and warm light filled her vision.

"The dwarven people of the city of Stonehammer welcome you as their prisoner," Ivakin rumbled gruffly as they stepped into the heart of the mountain.

Massive stone pillars rose from the floor to the ceiling, hundreds of feet above their heads. Men and women of like nature stood talking with one another while others bustled through stone streets and market tents with wooden carts. Others worked over fires, hammering at red-hot steel, sparks flying in a shower of orange. Women and men hunched over bubbling cauldrons, steam wafting in the cold air. Children ran past them, and Hazen jumped out of the way, their tickling laughter following closely behind.

None paid much attention to the two brothers and the outsider as they dragged her along, weaving in and out of tents, and wood and stone stands. But those who noticed stared wide-eyed at the girl who stumbled after them, shivering and half-dressed.

Ivakin peered a hard eye around the city before shoving open a wooden door along the right corridor, he slipped through and ushered them inside.

A blanket of heat settled on Hazen, and a violent shiver went down her spine before her body relaxed. She took in the small quarters. A kitchen was in the corner, and two stone steps carved from the ground led to a narrow hall that held two chambers. A wooden stump with a cushion on it lay in the far corner by the hearth, and a table in the centre of the room had three more stumps sitting around it.

A stout woman dressed in a dark brown dress with frazzled salt-and-pepper hair bustled into the room at the sound of the door shutting. She paused, her eyes widening briefly when she saw Hazen before her mouth pursed into a tight line.

"Now, what do you have here?" she quipped with a quick tongue, her rough accent rolling off the words. She stood in front of Hazen, a couple inches shorter than the two men beside her, and one of her hands touched the rope at her wrist, her fingers brushing against her skin. "Ivakin! The girl is chilled to the bone, you boar of a son! You should know better than to tie up an innocent child!"

Ivakin's tan cheeks turned a lovely shade of scarlet. "We found her lying on the ground, and she is neither elf nor Romani."

The woman scoffed. "Look at her! She hasn't done anything! Not even shoes on her feet! What evil soul goes out with uncovered feet?" she chastised, clicking her tongue in disapproval.

"Yes, ma'am," Ivakin said under his breath, taking the dagger from his boot and cutting the bindings at her wrists.

The blood rushed back to her hands, and she rubbed the tender skin gently. Pins and needles erupted in her fingertips, and she felt relief as the sensation slowly crept back in.

"Now, that's better. Come, sit by the fire, dear. Tell me what happened before my fools for sons tied you up like a common thief." She gave her a kind smile. "My name is Dshar. You have met my sons Ivakin and Tolak."

Hazen let the older woman steer her to the cushioned stump by the hearth. Her muscles sighed against the heat waves rolling off the flames, sinking against the wall and revelling in the warmth.

"You have thin blood, not as thick as a dwarf's. I'm afraid our temperatures down here are too low for you. Rest here for a moment." Dshar turned from the girl. "Tolak, Ivakin, pour the girl a hot drink and get the bread!" she snapped as she hurried off to the closest chamber. Disappearing behind a leather flap for only a moment before reappearing with a bundle of fur in her hands. "This will keep you warm while you are with us," she said, unwrapping the fur in her arms and moving it around the girl's shoulders.

Hazen stood and shifted the skin so it lay comfortably; the skin fell to her lower back and instantly warmed her. She smiled. "Thank you."

Dshar waved a hand at the girl. "The least I can do for what my boys have put you through... speaking of whom. Ivakin! Tolak!" She gave a content smile to Hazen as the two men hurried back into the room. Ivakin carried a silver plate full of bread and dried meats. Tolak held an iron pot of water, which he set over the fire to boil, before disappearing again into the kitchen area, returning with a cup in hand and a lidded jar in the other.

"Here, eat while your tea is heating," she told Hazen, taking the jar from her son. "Try this on the bread." Dshar removed the lid and produced a small wooden stick from it. The end dripped with a sticky amber substance.

Hazen eyed the unknown contents. "Is that honey?"

The small woman looked at the girl. "You've never had the nectar of a willow root?"

"I haven't chanced upon it, sorry," Hazen murmured, shifting in her seat.

"Oh, nonsense," Dshar tsked, stealing a piece of bread and spreading a thick golden layer across the top.

Hesitantly, Hazen glanced at the toast offered and took it from the woman, sniffing the nectar and taking a bite. She tasted nothing at first, chewing slowly when a warm sensation crossed over her tongue. The flavour of spiced cinnamon filled her mouth, and she took another bite.

"Good, isn't it?" asked Tolak, helping himself to a piece.

She acknowledged him with a slight nod, finishing off her toast.

Dshar took a seat on the stump closest to Hazen. "Why don't you tell us what happened to you before my sons found you?"

Hazen looked at the woman and Ivakin—who stood leaning against the wall, his face set in a scowl. Tolak took the seat next to his mother. "I'm sorry, I don't remember much."

"Well, dear, tell us what you do know," Dshar encouraged.

Hazen thought for a moment, recalling the last thing she remembered. Muddled images flashed across her memory like shattered fragments, and she tried to piece everything together.

"There was a storm... rain and lightning, I remember the thunder..." She paused, collecting her thoughts, rubbing her temples when her head began to throb. Images flashed through her mind, but she couldn't see them clearly.

"There was a forest. It was dark, but I ran for cover. I ran, and I didn't know where I was going. I just took off." Her voice faded quietly as she stared at her hands, her eyes distant. Her fingernails clicked together absentmindedly, filling the silence.

"There was an altar of stone. I remember the feeling of it beneath my fingers. After that, everything is a blur. I remember... I thought I was going to die. Then I blacked out." Her mind filled with images of the dark forest around her, dead leaves under her feet as the wind picked up. She heard the deafening roar in her ears again and squeezed her eyes shut.

The lot of them were silent as Hazen's words drifted into silence. Dshar was the first to speak. "While your tale is broken and your memories sheltered, I do understand." She held still for a breath. "You are not of this side of the veil, are you?"

Hazen gave a helpless shrug. "I'm not quite sure what you're asking."

Dshar stared warily at the girl across from her. She pinched the bridge of her nose with a sigh before saying, "Ivakin, go continue your hunt for today. Tolak, pour the girl her drink." She waited until her eldest son was gone and a warm cup was between Hazen's hands. "Now, I can't know your story unless I know your name."

"Hazen."

"Drink, Hazen, it will warm you."

Hazen sipped at the hot liquid, savouring the sweetness. She commented on it to Dshar.

"Honey flower," she explained. "It grows in small areas alongside the cliff wall." She studied Hazen as she drank from her cup. "I am about to tell you something—although you may not believe it. But please remember this, all things originate from the truth. Though you may not believe it at first, you will come to understand it in the future."

Hazen remained silent, setting the cup in her lap and giving the woman her attention.

"Where to begin? I would say at the beginning, but I believe others will cross your path and can explain in further detail than I might." She stopped to ponder her following words. "The world you have come from is what we call the New World. You are now in the Old World—a difficult thing to explain without giving false information. The New World is something of... lore, as you would call it. An untouchable place. One that has been forgotten by our children but pondered by those of my time and long before. There is none of your kind here. Romani and north people, but simple humans, do not exist in the Old World. We are a race woven by magic, but that does not mean we do not exist in your world. For what are humans but similar images of us."

Hazen shifted. "What do you mean by race? Who are you? What are you?"

"We are the dwarfs of Stonehammer, of the clan Ironbrow. Underground dwellers and crafters of iron and steel."

"Are elves real too?" she asked with a soft short laugh, disbelieving.

"*Ljósálfar*, the fair race, who live in the mountains and forests of Álfheimr. High Fae who are kin to the fairies, brethren to the *Dökkálfar*—a traitorous mass who have fallen from grace."

Hazen's laughter died. "What are they?"

Dshar's face twisted in disdain, her voice bitter. "A twisted, ugly, and destroyed beauty. They were once the fair race but now as low as the crawling creatures beneath the earth. They are the Dark Ones. Weak against the treasures promised to them by Ezra, the Dark Lord of the Fallen. Their speed and strength surpass even the strongest High Fae."

Hazen shook her head, disbelief evident in her voice. "I'm sorry, but are you saying I've travelled through time or space or... *something...* and now I'm in this world of magic?"

She was sure she was hallucinating. She had to be.

"You have crossed the veil, Hazen. Something brought you to us, something let you pass through. Perhaps you are the one we seek."

Nibbling on her lip, Hazen's hands clenched around her cup, her heart rate picking up. "Ar-are there more like you?"

"Oh, yes, dear girl. This land is filled with unimaginable magic, overflowing from the chalice of our world. Creatures and Fae alike live in vast numbers. Though fair warning, there are those who will tempt you and guide you through the unknown. Caution with those you trust, for even the sweetest sprite will kindly kill you."

Tolak stayed quiet during the whole conversation, but Hazen's attention jumped to him when he stood, taking the cup from her clamped hands. He poured her some more tea and, with a gentle smile, slipped it back between her fingers.

She took a sip, her fingertip running against the rim. Her thoughts turned over in her head. "You know," she started, but the words died on her tongue. Her attempts at logic were feeble, and they shattered the moment she tried to make any of it make sense.

"Hazen," Dshar said slowly, "don't say anything. For now, just think about what I said. Tolak will show you around our village. Perhaps it will offer a small token of clarity."

Hazen stood, setting her cup on the table, weakly replying, "Thank you."

Dshar nodded, reaching for the tray of food and bubbling kettle when she paused. "Oh, Hazen," she called out, stopping the girl when she and Tolak made to leave.

"Yes?" Hazen asked.

"I must warn you. Upon entering our world, you will see, hear, and do things much differently now. If you are indeed the one we seek, your soul within our realm has been awakened."

Hazen stared at the older woman, saying nothing. She felt a tug at her sleeve, and she pried her eyes from Dshar, letting Tolak guide her out of his home.

CHAPTER 6

Massive stone pillars rose high above their heads to support the towering ceiling of the cliff's belly. The entire underground dwellings were cast in a yellow shifting light from roaring fires lit by the blacksmiths and those who cooked in the square. Large black iron pots sat over fires, bubbling to life as steam curled in the air.

Tolak looked critically at his brethren when Hazen passed those who cooked, holding knives poised for chopping the braised meat in front of them and pins for rolling the dough that rose in wooden bowls. Her eyes were wide with wonder, her mouth agape.

Torches lit the numerous corridors, lighting up various footpaths that would have been concealed if not for the flickering fire anchored to the walls.

Tolak steered Hazen to two long, sturdy wood tables, the wear of countless uses marring the surface.

A dwarven woman working the open stove raised her hand in greeting to Tolak but gave Hazen a hard stare.

Hazen pursed her mouth, her fingers balling at her side. She noted the woman's slitted glance before Hazen sat on one of the communal benches. She felt wholly out of place, as if the world would cease to exist if she breathed wrong.

"Wait here," commanded Tolak. He left her to stroll over to the woman glaring at her.

Tracing her fingers along a rough chop that cut through the edge of the table, Hazen watched the two from beneath her lashes. He gripped her hand, whispering something in her ear that had the woman tossing her head back laughing.

Sighing, Hazen's eyes strayed away from them.

The underground city was massive. The sound of the blacksmith's hammer resounded through the stone arches like church bells; wooden carts pulled through handcrafted street paths, homes built into the mountain walls, and children played with whittled wooden hoops, chasing after them in a fit of tinkering laughter. The city was alive, and Hazen couldn't help but stare at it all in amazement.

The ringing from the blacksmith's hammer struck her eardrums with precision as she took in every crafted archway, ally, and stone path. Again, the hammering hit her in a dance of strokes, and she turned. Finding him just beyond her table, the dwarf worked over the red-hot steel of a newly shaped axe. Sparks flying through the air in a shower of glittering embers.

She stood. *CLANG!* The music of the hammer echoed through her body, seeming to wrap around her bones. *CLANG!* She was transfixed, her feet carrying her away from the long table. *CLANG!* Everything settled within her, swaying on her feet, her eyes watched the shower of fire unblinking.

CLANG! CLANG! CLANG! It rang thrice more before he sunk it in a trough of ice water. The sound of hot steel cooling crackled in the air, fire against water. She watched, fascinated when he took it out and placed the weapon back on the large anvil.

Nothing save the strike of the hammer rang in her ears. Her eyes shifted from the smithy to the fire that flamed in the large stone pit. Smoke billowed from its chimney, reaching high above them and away from the masses below. Dancing fiery tendrils manoeuvred through each other in a tangled trance.

Hazen stood hypnotised, her hazel eyes mirroring the orange and gold flames. The sounds of the blacksmith ceased but little to Hazen's attention. Fire played with fire in a game of chase. Her muscles ached for her to move, heat coursing under her skin.

The sound of her steps was lost in the outside noise as her feet led her into the pit. Hot air shimmered around them, her flesh warmed and flushed pink. Orange and yellow light dusted across her face.

It was a distant thought, wrapped in fog and drowned in the watery depths of her mind, of how the fire held her captive. Some place within her mind whispered for her to stop, to turn back, while another voice whispered to touch the dancing flames.

Her fingers twitched at her sides, and she reached for the fire—

A firm hand, with a rough callused grip, took hold of Hazen's bicep. Jerking her out of her trance as the blacksmith whipped her around.

"Wot do ya thin' yer doin'?!" yelled the thickly accented voice of the blacksmith.

Hazen blinked and looked down at the stocky man, his barrel chest heaving, eyes ignited in rage. "I'm sorry! I didn't realise what I was doing!" she explained hurriedly, her tongue tumbling over her words.

God, what *had* she been doing?

He shook his head and held her arm in a bruising grip as he dragged her out of the pit. "I don't kna 'oo ya think ya're, but ya stay out of me 'rea! This isn't a place for a half-naked child!"

"I'm sorry!" she exclaimed, stumbling back into the safety of the streets beyond the blacksmith's shop.

His coal-black eyes flashed in the dance of firelight. "Save yer sorry words fer someone 'oo cares."

Hazen's feet fumbled over each other, taking a step backwards as the smithy stepped forward. Her heel caught the lip of a loose stone, and she felt her ass hit the ground. Pain laced her skin when her hands went to catch her, her palms grating against the rough ground.

"Belard!"

The blacksmith's eyes rounded upon Tolak, who stormed up to them. "Tolak, make sure yer human doesn't come near me' rea again!"

Tolak stood against Belard, his mouth set in a firm line. "Belard, she is a child."

Belard's eyes met Hazen's, and he said in a stone voice, spitting on the ground. "Child or not, she is still human." Rounding on his heels, the blacksmith stalked away, his fists balled tightly at his side.

The hammering started again, and Tolak ushered Hazen away from the smithy.

"Pay no heed to Belard," muttered Tolak quietly. "His dislike for humans is great, but only from the path fate took one unfaithful night."

Hazen glanced at Tolak as he led her through one of the forking paths away from the city square. Her heart beat madly in her chest, and her limbs shook with adrenaline. "What happened?" she questioned.

Grabbing a torch from the hall, Tolak held it high to light the path, silent for some time, leading her down a set of stairs. The only light was the fire in Tolak's hand. The air was like ice against Hazen's face, numbing the warmth that had previously settled along her bones. The fur cape Dshar had given her kept her body enclosed in a bubble of warmth. Saving her from a cold grave set hundreds of feet below the surface.

In a gruff voice, Tolak broke the silence. "It has been seventy years since the attack on our village. We have not always dwelled in these caves. Once, like all races, we lived freely and without care." His low voice echoed along the stone, filling the darkness the deeper they went. "That was another time, though. We stayed untouched by Ezra, left alone to mind our ways in the grasslands of Zarren. Our city was tall and grand. Its walls were strong, the gate doors always open to all, and our children ran without a worry in the golden fields surrounding us.

"One night, Ezra heard talk of a rumour spreading about a child that was said to come baring our salvation, hidden away in our city. That same night, a hundred of his soldiers came under the cloak of a moonless sky. Red rain fell and seeped into the earth that night. Most of us escaped, but not all. Those who escaped are those you see around you; those who didn't were lost forever.

"Belard was the only one who survived from his family. Most families were slaughtered as a whole, or they ran into the cover of the night. Belard was forced to watch as they killed his mate and three children. They meant to kill him but conquered by the poison of grief and anger, he managed to escape."

"He has to live with that," murmured Hazen, and despite herself, her chest ached for the blacksmith.

"Aye, girl, that he does."

"How did he know I was human, but you and your brother didn't?"

"Ah," Tolak said, a sheepish smile turning up his mouth. "My brother and I are still very young compared to some here. My brother may be older than me, but by many, we are only just in the grips of being adults. This is a different age, girl. Things are not as they once were."

Hazen gripped the fur tighter around her, shivering in the cold. "Your mother said I might be the one you need. What did she mean?"

Tolak glanced at her from the corner of his eye. "I'm not sure, Hazen. Ezra is a torrent of darkness I fear we may not find our way out of."

Hazen stumbled when Tolak suddenly stopped in a large hall that split into four separate paths, all concealed by shadows. Along the corridor walls were images carved and painted on the stone mortar in vibrant colours.

Raising the torch in the air, the light cast along the images. "These carvings tell the story of the rise and fall of the light. From the beginning of all the races... to the beginning of the darkness that cloaks these lands in a quilt of demons, holding nothing but great terror and loss."

Hazen walked along the curved edges, her fingertips sliding

lightly across the grooved surface. A circle of eight stars illuminating a black sky fell to the world in four solid figures. Their beauty was apparent, but their wisdom was vibrant even in the paintings. From those four figures blossomed four more.

From below rose a mighty dragon, and the daylight was born from its fiery breath. Four figures stood wreathed in a token of the season they held domain over. Vibrant flowers of pink and purple and red blossomed at Spring's feet, the sun and all its light encompassed Summer, a towering oak tree with orange and yellowing leaves for Autumn, and a snowflake framing Winter. From the Spirits, their world now had seasons. Creatures were created, and life was breathed upon all things. All living things' lives were now tied to the golden web that spread below the surface.

Hazen's steps faltered when she came upon the birth and death of a single soul encapsulated in darkness. Moving on, her brows knitted, frowning when she saw people being burned at stakes, war and death following. And then the wall was forged, dividing their worlds.

The mural continued in beautiful strokes of colourful paint and carvings etched into the stone with feather touches until a bargain was struck, and darkness covered the world.

Hazen turned to the dwarf. "This is your history, all of it?"

"This is our past and our present."

The carvings stopped as they faded out into nothing. "Where is the rest of it?" she asked, her hand brushing the faded ending as if the future might write itself into existence.

Tolak came up behind the girl, gazing at the space. "The one thing magic cannot do is write the future before it has happened."

"Why was I brought here, Tolak?"

"I wish I could tell you, girl."

Hazen pointed to a spot on the mural of a naked woman bathed in dragon's fire towards the beginning of the carvings. "Who is she?"

Tolak looked at the woman, rubbing a hand over his beard. "That is Rose. She was the first keeper."

Hazen looked at the dwarf. "A keeper?"

"Aye," he said, nodding slowly. "Keepers were created to protect those of our world. The Gods created this world and everything in it, but with that comes the inability to change or intervene. Their magic, even then, had laws woven into its very fabric. So, keepers were created, blessed by the dragons, and given the power to protect and keep the balance of this world. But Rose fell into greed, and she met her demise from it. From then on, the keeper was chosen as a half-Fae half-mortal child, so they may know the weight of life and death..."

Tolak glanced at her in thought, his hand stroking his beard once again. "Perhaps that is why you are here, Hazen. Perhaps the world has forgotten what the weight of life over death is like. Perhaps you are to tip the scale. But for your questions, you will not find the answers here. For those, you must find the ones that brought you here. They will give you your answers."

Hazen wrapped a hand around her middle, shivering. "I hope you're right."

Noting the fur shaking, Tolak pressed a large hand to the middle of her back. "Come, it's time we got back to the main hall."

Busier than ever, the square brimmed with dwarves. Children of all ages played while the adults worked, keeping the city alive with different scents and sounds that meddled together in an overwhelming blanket that sent her head spinning.

Hazen nearly fell over when they walked into Tolak's home as exhaustion swept over her anxious mind.

Dshar noted their arrival and bustled into the living space as soon as they pushed through the front door. "Did you show her the city?" she questioned. Taking the girl into the nook of her arm, she steered her to the stump near the hearth.

Hazen gave a hesitant smile, her numb body wanting to melt into the cackling flames. Everything was so heavy. She just wanted to curl up by the fire and go to sleep. "I saw your history. It's fascinating." Her words were more mumbled than coherent.

"Aye, it is." Dshar nodded, rubbing her hands up and down Hazen's arms until she stopped shivering. "Do you need anything? You're our guest, not just in our world but our home."

Body relaxing into the wall, the heat enveloped her, and Hazen stifled a yawn.

The stout woman nodded and gave a sympathetic pat on Hazen's shoulder. "Right, come with me." She didn't wait for her to stand but pulled her to her feet and nearly had to drag her to a room of small stature, the ceiling inches from the top of Hazen's head.

A small bed was placed against the left wall, a rectangular copper and leather crate against the opposite wall, and a round mirror anchored above it.

"This is my room, but you may use it for your stay."

Hazen made to object, her eyes snapping open from their half-dazed state at the idea of sleeping in this… in this *world*. "Are you sure? I can't take your room. I can just leave."

Dshar waved away her words. "Nevermore. Now, I will be in the square for a while. I work as a seamstress. If you need me, go to those who cook in the square. A female named Aunika will tell you where to find me."

Chest heaving, Hazen gathered her wits enough to say thank you.

"It's the least I can do." Dshar swooped out of the room and left Hazen standing there alone.

Glancing at the door, she sat on the bed, feeling it sink underneath her. If she went to sleep, maybe when she woke up, it would be a dream. This could be a dream, or a hallucination. Maybe she hit her head during the storm—why the fuck did she run after that dog?

Hazen cursed silently, eyes darting around the room, her mind replaying everything down to the last detail.

It had to be a concussion. She was concussed, and this was her dream. She just had to go to sleep, and when she woke up, it would be over.

Laying back, her feet hung off the end, and she curled into the fur skins, bringing her knees up. Sleep was a quick thief, and as soon as her head hit Dshar's pillow, her eyes slid shut.

CHAPTER 7

"You really should be kinder to the girl."

"And why should I do that, brother?"

Tolak glanced at his brother from the corner of his eye, noting the firm press of Ivakin's mouth and tight pull of his brows as he gazed through the tree line, a large axe held firmly in his grasp.

"She's but a child," Tolak finally said.

"As are you, still. Yet, I do not coddle you."

Tolak scowled. "I am not a child."

Ivakin finally pulled his eyes from the forest. Shifting on his feet, he looked at Tolak. "You are my baby brother; you will always be a child to me."

"Barely four winters separate us."

"But it's still four winters."

Tolak shook his head with a roll of his eyes before turning his attention back to the forest, the rocky ledge behind them. It was two days past since the girl had arrived, and she still lay like the dead in his mother's borrowed bed. So Tolak and Ivakin went to the surface to hunt.

The sun was shining in golden arcs through the tree limbs, which swayed silently in a near-absent wind. Silence enveloped them, and the two brothers crept silently along, keeping close to the rock face.

Edging around a large bolder, Ivakin's hand shot out suddenly, gripping Tolak by his front, the fabric bunching in his palm. Tolak's protest died when he followed his brother's trained gaze.

Blood drained from Tolak's face, his grip tightening on the handle of his double-edged axe. The sun that shone was no longer bright, and a cold crept in around them as they gazed upon the massive black body of a minotaur.

Its meaty hoof stamped into the dirt, gouging out a chunk of earth while it sniffed the rock face. A crude iron ring was pierced through its snout, and black and white horns tangled through a wiry black mane. A large sword, nearly as long as the dwarves were tall, was strapped to its back in a leather bracing.

Slamming a massive hand into the rock, the minotaur snorted, shaking its head.

Tolak's heart stopped, eyes widening when the minotaur punched the stone again and the earth rattled around them.

"Ivakin," Tolak whispered, his voice barely heard over the splintering of rock as the minotaur laid its fist into the stone over and over again until a chunk fell away.

Ivakin didn't move, didn't breathe, his eyes focused on the beast.

"It's a Prowler," Tolak whispered, shifting his axe in his now sweaty grip.

Ivakin released Tolak's shirt and grasped him by the shoulder, sparing a glance at his brother. "*Run*, Tolak," he commanded in a low voice, his dark eyes glaring at the beast when it let out a low growl.

A snarl twisted on Tolak's face, and he lifted his axe, digging his feet into the earth. "Not on your life, brother."

The wind picked up, and the brothers' hearts froze when the minotaur's assault faltered and it sniffed the air.

"Run, Tolak!" Ivakin barked as the beast rounded on them like an animal possessed, and its roar shook the trees.

The forest whipped by them, their footfalls heavy as the brothers flew over tree roots and under hanging limbs. Beards flying over their shoulders when they dared look behind them.

Black eyes filled with death were trained on their broad backs, the earth threatening to crack under the weight of each of its thundering hooves.

"We need to get underground," Ivakin yelled, cursing when a tree branch flew by his head.

"Why! I thought we were enjo—"

"Tolak!"

Ivakin's feet dug into the ground as his brother went tumbling over the ground, a flying branch catching him around the knees. Teeth bared, Ivakin faced the charging minotaur. His grip tightened on his weapon, and with a mighty cry, he charged forward to meet the beast head-on.

His axe barely lifted over his head when two arrows sliced the air and drilled into its eyes, one after the other.

Stumbling, the minotaur slid across the ground on its knees, blood dripping from its snout, jaw slack. With a cry, Ivakin kicked its chest, and the beast fell back. Dead.

The forest was quiet as another death settled into the earth.

Lips pressed into a firm line, Ivakin whipped around, his eyes landing on the icy stare of a High Fae. His black hair and dark eyes framed by the sun shining through the trees, bow still held in his grip. When Ivakin blinked, the elf was gone.

Tolak's ragged cough tore Ivakin's focus from the forest, and he went to his brother's side, helping him stand.

Looking at the dead minotaur, Tolak began to laugh, belly shaking, and eyes filled with amusement. He pointed to the beast, mystified. "Look at that. We almost died."

"Get up!"

Hazen jolted as hands grasped her by the shoulders, shaking her awake.

"Get up! You have to leave!"

Candlelight lit up Ivakin's face, his face set with urgency. He pulled her upright, and she swatted at him, sitting on the edge of the tiny bed.

"Don't touch me!" she snapped.

"You must leave!"

"Ivakin!"

Dshar entered the room, glaring at her son.

Hazen's eyes bounced between the two. Dshar's face set in a disapproving stare while Ivakin's was made from steel.

"Leave her be, Ivakin," Dshar warned.

"I cannot," he argued. "She must go. It is no longer safe."

"Ivakin—"

"There was a Prowler."

His words hung like a dark cloud in the dimly lit space, and Hazen watched the colour drain from Dshar's face.

Taking in a steadying breath, Ivakin pinched the bridge of his nose. "We saw it while hunting. That is why we came back empty. It was beating into the cliff as if trying to break its way through," he said more calmly.

Dshar, still pale and speechless, let her wide eyes fall on Hazen.

Ivakin gently touched his mother, turning to Hazen for a moment. "Gather yourself, I will be waiting to take you above."

Hazen watched them disappear from the room, the animal hide covering the doorway fell back into place. The room was cast in darkness, and Hazen rubbed a hand over her face. Her mind scrambled.

So, it wasn't a dream or a hallucination.

If the ache in her limbs from the tiny bed was any indication that she was very much awake. Stifling a yawn, she combed a hand blindly through her hair and stood. Back and neck popping, Hazen felt her way out of the room, blinking at the sudden light.

Dshar smiled when she saw her, though her eyes were uneasy. "Come, come, Hazen," she said gently, ushering her to sit beside the fire.

"How long have I been asleep?" Hazen asked, pulling the furs tightly around her and crossing her bare legs.

"Two days," Dshar said.

"Two days!" Hazen exclaimed, sitting up straight.

"Magic is a tricky sort. It can drain you of energy, whether you're awake or not. Coming into our world required an amount of magic that could have killed you had it not been for your blood. I'm surprised my son could even wake you."

"My blood—"

Dshar laid a gentle, steady hand on her shoulder. "All in due time, child."

Hazen's shoulders slumped forward, anxiety bubbling under her skin.

"You cannot stay here any longer."

Hazen looked up at Ivakin, whose dark eyes were firm. She knew he would do whatever he had to, to make her leave.

"Ivakin," Tolak said warily.

"Brother, you know as well as I."

Tolak's lips pressed into a straight line, and he gave Hazen a slight nod. She would leave.

"What is a Prowler?" Hazen asked, remembering what Ivakin said and how Dshar's face turned ashen.

The room went quiet, and when Tolak leaned forward, his face was grim. "They're hunters for Ezra. They roam the land, mountains, forests, and valleys. And they take those who rebel or spread the news of uprising or change to Ezra. But most do not make it to him alive.

"Prowlers helped destroy our home and slaughter our loved ones," Tolak paused, letting out a heavy breath. "If Prowlers are here, it means they have picked up your scent. Ezra will know of your coming before nightfall. Having you here is a risk to us all."

The anxiety turned to dread, which seeped into her muscles and bones until her jaw began to clench, and her fingers dug into the fur.

"Hazen?"

Closing her eyes, Hazen forced herself to breathe, unlocking her jaw and fingers; she looked up at Tolak. "Yes?" she whispered.

"You have many enemies here, but you also have many allies. Take to the southeast, therein lies a village of those who can help you. I will show you the way when we go above."

A shiver of fear ran down her body, making her limbs tremble. Dshar saw this and tsked under her breath, standing. The female disappeared only to return a moment later with a swath of fabric draped over an arm and leather sandals held in her other hand.

"Put this on. You are much taller than I, but it'll provide more shelter than your… garments," she said, eyeing Hazen's shorts with question.

When Hazen returned from dressing, Dshar's skirt falling mid-calf in heavy dark blue wool cinched at the waist with a wool tie and sandals secured, she was fed and made to drink her fill until she wished for the tiny bed and the nap she longed to take.

When they both stood, Tolak held up a hand to his brother. "I will take her above."

Ivakin scowled but nodded, taking his seat at the table again.

Hazen went to remove the fur cape when Dshar stopped her quickly.

"I fear you will need that more than I. Keep it with you."

"Thank you for everything," Hazen said softly, giving her a small smile.

Tolak placed a hand on her arm, squeezing it briefly when she approached him before dropping it and leading her out.

The city was silent as they walked, unlike her first arrival, when Tolak had introduced her to their iron dwellings. There was not a single child out, nor were carts being pulled. The blacksmith's anvil did not ring out, and the females who cooked in the city square were not to be found. The streets were void of life.

"Waiting."

Tolak's response to her silent question made her brows furrow in confusion. Hazen asked, "Waiting for what?"

"For you to be gone."

Her heart stopped, and an inkling of guilt slithered among the fear. "Because of the Prowler?" she asked, eyeing the empty streets one last time before they began the ascent.

"Aye, girl."

They went up and up and up, her legs burning with each push, a sheen of sweat coating her skin. But she stayed silent, focusing on Tolak's back. The air surrounding her began to warm against her skin, and for the first time since she arrived, she felt relief as she approached the surface despite what could be waiting.

The ascent felt shorter than the descent, but she wasn't complaining when they finally faced the rock wall. Hazen was reminded of Ivakin and how he had opened the rocky barrier, but no stones could be seen.

Tolak walked up to the wall and placed one beefy hand upon it. The outline of a door appeared, and he pushed against it. Brilliant rays of the sun shone through the opening, and the pair squinted, stepping into the world.

When they had gathered themselves, Tolak pointed to his right. "Look. That is south. Follow this wall until it ends, and keep going straight."

Her relief vanished as quickly as it came, and the reality of what was happening sunk in. She gave him a shaky nod. "Thank you, Tolak."

Tolak gave her an almost non-existent smile in return. "We welcomed you as our prisoner, but now you leave the city of Stonehammer a friend. I pray there is a time when you may return without fear of what will follow."

"I hope you're right," she murmured.

Tolak looked away from the southeastern lands and turned to Hazen. "We will meet again, though I hope it will be in a kinder time. Without bloodshed."

Hazen could think of nothing to say, so she stayed quiet. Her eyes darted between the way Tolak pointed out through the trees and his dark eyes that studied her.

With a gruff nod, he cleared his throat and bid her farewell. When the rock face closed, she sagged against the towering wall.

Fingers fisting at her side, her brain whirled with thoughts and emotions that caused her chest to squeeze. Gasping in a breath, her throat constricted as her chest fought for a minuscule amount of air. Panic started to weigh heavy on her.

The wind cut across her face, startling her. It was enough for her to force in a lung full of air, and her body sighed in relief.

"Get it together," she muttered to herself.

After a minute, her hands finally relaxed, and she pushed off the wall, rolling her shoulders back. If this wasn't a dream, then she had better get her wits together. And if it was a dream… if she were concussed somewhere and this was an illusion, she would make the best of it.

Eyeing the forest, she began her trek southeast.

CHAPTER 8

The bitterness in the wind, despite the sunshine, made Hazen shiver. The muscles in her knees twitched with fatigue at the same time. Her legs wanted to collapse, but she bit past the deep ache in her bones and made her feet walk on even as they began to drag through the dirt.

Somewhere past the canopy of tree limbs, the sun sat high in the sky. She didn't know if time was the same here, and if it was, she could hardly rely on herself to tell the time correctly based on the sun's position.

She could only assume hours had passed, the rocky cliff long behind her. The willow trees slowly turned to towering birch trees with their narrow trunks and long limbs. The wind danced through the emerald leaves as they fluttered above her, swaying like whispering chimes.

Digging the heel of her palms into her eyes, Hazen groaned before the air stole from her lungs, and she lurched forward. Hands flying out to break her fall, she winced when pain skated across her skin, and she rolled onto her back, trying to ignore the throbbing in her big toe.

"Ow," she cried, though it came out more like a sob, and frustration welled up in her chest as she beat a fist into the ground.

She was tired, her toe was throbbing, she would kill for a shower, and she was almost entirely certain she was losing her damn mind.

Laying there until the ache in her toe disappeared, Hazen took a deep breath, calming the tension coiling in her, and sat up. Dshar's skirt fanned across the ground prettily, and Hazen brushed a soft hand over the fabric, pressing her lips into a determined line as she stood, stepping delicately over the rock embedded in the ground.

Stretching her tired limbs, her back popped, she sighed, eyeing the forest around her. She was alone. Even though the sun was still bright, there was a coldness within it that made her want to step back. There were no shadows, but the light seemed to slither toward her across the ground, and her throat clenched in panic.

Eyes wide, heart racing, Hazen forced her feet to step back. Her blood sang to her, telling her to run, to hide, to *flee*. She had become the prey of some unknown predator.

Leaves crunched softly, and that was all it took before she fled into the forest. Her breathing came in panting gasps, hands out in front of her to push away hanging limbs threatening to tangle in her hair and cape. She didn't know where she was going and couldn't see past the blind panic that raced through her veins.

The forest seemed to close around her, and panic turned to terror when something yanked her back. Her footing slipped, and she slammed into the side of a tree, pain bracketing her ribs. Crying out, she swung wildly at the thing holding her, her knuckles stinging when something hard connected with her fist.

Something banded around her, containing her, and she struggled in its hold, screaming until a hand slapped over her mouth and her eyes snapped open. Hazen froze. Her terror turned ice cold before melting into something hot and rage-filled. The arms relaxed around her, and she took that moment to bite down on the hand over her mouth.

Startled, the hand dropped, and her attacker made a sound of surprise, but she didn't turn to face them, she used the distraction to put distance between them. She had barely taken two steps when she was yanked back again by the fur cape.

Something between a choke and a scream left her when the cape's clasped collar pressed into her throat. Strong hands halted her frantic fingers trying to undo it, and her head whipped around to a handsome pale face and a pair of deep blue eyes staring at her inches from her face.

Her heart stuttered in her chest before she stilled, trying to take a breath. Without looking away, the person reached for her neck, and Hazen tried not to flinch before the cape fell from her throat. The sweet relief of air filled her lungs.

The person stepped back quietly, and Hazen took no time in putting distance between them.

Her eyes glanced at her cape and saw a thin branch caught just right between the fur and brass latch. The tree had been her captor. When she realised this, her eyes snapped to the one who had freed her.

It was a man. But he couldn't have been much older than her. Those dark blue eyes were shaded behind a blank stare that pinned her in place, slightly slanted and framed by black brows. Long blue-black hair fell down his back, braids anchoring the hair away from his beautiful face. And he was beautiful. It made Hazen pause when she opened her mouth to speak, shifting uncomfortably when that guarded gaze tilted to watch her.

He was taller than her, agile but strong. A bow across his back, his black shirt fitted across lean muscle, and black pants tucked into black leather boots hugged narrow hips.

"Thank you," she made herself say.

His full mouth twitched from its flat line but then receded.

The wind flicked across her cheek. Using the back of her hand to brush her hair back when it caught in her mouth, she paused, noticing his hair dance behind him. The delicate arch of pointed ears peeked up proudly through his hair.

She struggled to find her voice, clearing her throat. "Are you... are you..." She couldn't say it. Her mouth opened and closed and opened again before she finally made herself say it. "... An elf."

He quirked a brow, the only indication he understood her.

He stepped forward. Hazen stepped back.

"Who are you?" she demanded.

"I should be asking you this," he replied calmly. His voice was low but methodical.

Hazen's heart leapt when he spoke. "Why did you follow me?"

His gaze flickered beyond her before returning to her. "I've been following you for quite some time."

"How comforting," she sneered.

"I'm not the only one tracking you." He said this as if it would bring her some morsel of comfort.

Her body turned rigid again, eyes darting around the forest. The elf watched her while she tried to source whatever or whoever was hidden.

"They're not long behind. A Prowler. Dumb creatures, especially when corrupted by magic, but brutish enough that I hope you understand you will die if you cross its path."

"What," she whispered, wide-eyed.

"Not by its hands if it can help itself."

"Then by who?"

"Ezra."

Hazen's breath staggered silently. She remembered that name.

"If Prowlers are here, it means they have picked up your scent." Tolak had said.

It had followed her—or they had. She didn't know how many. Panic began to coil in her chest.

"Don't."

The elf's words halted her whirl of emotions, and she sucked in a deep breath.

"Stay focused. Breathe."

"But they followed me," she said.

"Aye. Just one."

She shifted, looking at the forest quickly. "What do you mean?"

"There were two," he clarified.

"What happened to the other one?"

"I killed it."

His simple answer made her want to put more space between them. As if killing it had been a household chore rather than the taking of a life.

After a moment, she asked, "What's your name?"

"Savven."

"Why did you follow me?" she asked again.

Savven was quiet for a moment before speaking. "Because I picked up on your scent when the first Prowler did. Something sweet like a flower but akin to death. Human. I have not seen a human in nearly three hundred years. It makes one wonder."

"Wonder what?" she asked breathless.

"What the Gods have planned with you."

The idea that the Gods of this world were playing with her fate made fire run through her limbs until her hands turned warm. She forced her fingers to unfurl from the fist they had formed, and cool air licked at her scraped palms.

His eyes flickered to her hands, watching them curiously before sliding slowly back to her narrowed gaze.

"Interesting," he murmured.

"Your cryptic words are starting to become annoying," she spat.

"Then you'll love the rest of us," he replied dryly.

Her eye twitched. "I can't wait," she said sarcastically. Untangling the branch from her fur cape, she secured it back around her shoulders, welcoming the warmth from the bitter wind. When she was done, she rolled her shoulders back, not giving Savven a second glance as she whirled on her heels, saying as she walked away, "Now, if you'll excuse me, I have a village to find."

His next words made her stop cold.

"They're dead."

She turned slowly, peering at him. "You don't know who I'm talking about."

Savven looked up at the sky, tracking a bird as it flew overhead. "If you don't believe me, you can go see for yourself. But all you'll find is their mangled bodies among rubble and ash."

Stomach-churning, she turned to face him fully. "Did you kill them too?"

His bitter laugh made her startle.

"No. They died shortly after I had left. By the time I heard their screams and made to return, it was too late. It would seem someone knew something Ezra didn't want them to know. Something worth the life of a whole village."

Her heart had turned to lead, and she whispered, "Do you know what it is?"

He cocked his head in thought, watching her intently. "Maybe." He sighed when she didn't speak and said, "There is ancient magic here. Woven between the worlds. The Gods have their secrets, but nothing remains hidden forever."

Hazel eyes bore into deep blue, silence stretching between them. After a minute, Hazen finally spoke.

"You're not going to let me go alone, are you." It wasn't a question. She knew the answer already. He would follow her silently, unseen, or he would accompany her.

"Choice is yours."

She scoffed. "How kind."

"By all means, I won't stop you."

A hint of amusement shone through his eyes, and her cheeks turned a lovely shade of red.

He wouldn't stop her, and he would watch her get lost or worse. And then she would probably die irritated because she could only picture his smug expression at being right.

With a tight smile, she waved a hand out to the forest, gesturing ahead of them. "Lead the way."

The amusement didn't dissipate, and his mouth quirked into a barely-there smile. Stepping closer until only inches separated them, he leaned forward, speaking lowly, "I should warn you, there is a chance you will die. Many will try to kill you."

"Well, hopefully, you'll be a nice little distraction. Long enough for me to escape."

His smile widened, barely, and he straightened, brushing past her. "Come, night is going to fall soon."

She looked up at the sky, unable to tell the sun's position through the brambles. When she turned away, Savven was already a good pace ahead. Catching up to him, she asked, "Where are we going?"

"Álfheimr, city of the High Fae."

CHAPTER 9

Hazen's foot slipped over a loose pebble, and her arms flailed to keep her upright. Her feet were numb, and pins and needles crawled up the backs of her legs.

It had been hours since they began the trek through forest growth, heading in a direction that Hazen didn't know was south, north, or somewhere between.

"Stop."

She paused, her foot resting above an uplifted root. Watching Savven remove the bow from his back.

"Sit," he commanded.

Hazen scowled. "I am not a dog!"

Savven quirked a brow, regarding her silently.

With a huff, she shook her head and sat. "Is it even safe to stop?"

she asked, leaning against the tree trunk, legs blissfully stretched before her. The moan of satisfaction when feeling rushed back into her limbs was a silent one. Biting back the sound while she watched Savven scan the forest before sitting across from her, his bow seated across his lap.

"The Prowler lost your scent a while ago."

While he had answered her, she noted he had never said it was safe.

Silence stretched between them. The two of them stared at each other. Hazen's expression was annoyed, while Savven's was irritatingly passive as he looked away.

"Hazen," she said after a while.

Savven turned his attention back on her.

"My name is Hazen," she clarified. "So, you can stop ordering me around like an animal."

"I don't think knowing your name will hold much regard in that matter."

"Bastard," she muttered.

He inclined his head, having heard her. "Some might agree."

Biting back a retort, she leaned forward, gently kneading her fingers into her calves as pins and needles erupted across her skin.

"I apologise."

Her fingers stilled, glancing at him. "What?"

"I forget that we are not created the same. Humans and Fae," he said.

"No," she muttered, continuing to work a cramp out of her right calf. "I suppose we're not."

Savven plucked a browning leaf from the ground and twirled the stem between long fingers. "My people lay forever immortal, and with that immortality comes certain rewards to our physical being."

"Your humility is astonishing," she commented drolly.

Savven's answering smile was bitter. "Immortal but not unstoppable. We can still be killed."

Hazen's hands slowed, looking up at the elf again. He stared at the leaf between his fingers. Deep-seated rage burned behind those blue eyes, and a chill of caution went down her spine.

Without warning, her stomach rumbled violently, and her cheeks turned scarlet. Savven's brows rose, and he looked at her stomach.

"It's been a long day," she said defensively.

Nodding thoughtfully, Savven stood, securing the bow on his back. "Stay here."

"Where are you going?" she asked, scrambling to her feet.

"Are you not hungry?"

She chewed on the inside of her lip. "I am, but you're just going to leave me here without a weapon?"

Lips tilting into a smile likened to a cat, Savven removed his bow and held it out to her. "You know how to use one?"

Hazen frowned, eyeing the curved wood. "Well, no…"

His smug look made her glower.

"I didn't think so," he said, replacing it.

She took a deep breath, only to halt in her chest as Savven pointed a finger at her.

"Don't move."

"Don't tell me what to do," she snapped.

With a shrug, he walked away.

He was gone before she could call out to him. "What a pompous ass," she huffed, running a hand through her hair.

Sighing, Hazen peered around at her surroundings. She could see anyone coming from a distance. The narrow trees did little to conceal anything except a couple of trees that stood twisted and gnarly just off their path.

The sun was beginning to wan as she stood and slipped through the trees. Flecks of dust flickering in the last dregs of light that filtered through emerald leaves. She could feel the sun's heat on her hair even as the bitterness settled in the growing shadows around her.

Hazen let her feet quietly carry her through the trees, observing the forest maze before her. Looking over her shoulder, she couldn't tell where she came from but knew she wasn't too far.

The two twisted birch trees off the path were full of lumps and oversized knots. A grouping of tree knots wrapped around the middle of the trunk, while the top of the tree seemed to split from overgrowth.

Stepping forward, palm outstretched, her fingers brushed against the bark before something snapped and cinched around her left foot. A scream froze in her lungs, and a second later, she was thrown onto her back as she was dragged down and up, struggling for air.

Heart racing, Hazen whipped her head around, eyes searching. The forest spun and she pinched her eyes shut, forcing in a breath. Panic made her blood race, the pounding in her head loud with every pulse of her heart.

Looking up, Hazen eyed the rope secured around her left ankle. Reaching up to the knot, she gave a tug, but it held fast. Groaning, she let her body fall back down, her head pulsating with blood flow.

"He's going to kill me," she muttered.

A crack split the air, and Hazen froze. The twisted knots on the deformed tree cracked until a pair of amber eyes blinked back at her and it took everything in Hazen not to move. Another crack raked through the air until the trunk split, and the tree became a beast.

CHAPTER 10

The storm had ended two hours later, the rain stopping as if someone had turned off a faucet. Claris and Jorg hadn't left their spot on the couch, waiting for Hazen to—at any second—walk through the front door. André and Charlie had taken to the kitchen.

André sat at the table, her hands folded under her chin. She watched as her husband paced the tile floor, hands clasped behind his back. He was clearly deep in thought, processing everything she had just told him.

"Dear, please stop. You're making me dizzy," she begged softly.

Charlie ceased his pacing and turned to his wife. "Well, I can't help it. What are we going to tell them when Hazen doesn't show up?"

"My love," she said gently. "Time works differently where

Hazen is. What might be months to her will only be days to us."

Charlie rubbed a hand over his face, feeling every bit overwhelmed and frustrated. "Then what do we do?"

André sighed, knowing he wouldn't like her answer. "There's nothing we can do."

CHAPTER 11

A scream lodged in her throat, and Hazen hurled her torso up towards her feet as a bulbous wooden mallet cut the air where her head had been.

The beast's roar filled the air when it missed.

Thick-bodied and skin that blended in with the surrounding forest, Hazen's eyes lost focus every time the beast moved, shifting like a shimmering mirage.

Heart hammering in her chest, she tracked the mallet, watching a camouflaged arm swing it back, angling for her head. Hazen threw herself back, the rope snapping under the strain. The mallet broke through the rope, and her whole body jerked like a rag doll, flying through the air. Her breath stole from her lungs, the ground bit painfully into every muscle, her bones threatened to snap, and the skin on her left cheek burned as she ate the dirt. Rolling to a stop, she kicked her legs free of the trap and scrambled to her feet. The ground thundered beneath her, and she whirled around, her eyes darting through the trees.

She couldn't see it.

Panic seized her, and her breath froze in her lungs. The ground trembled with every step, and her chest squeezed.

The hair on her neck stood, her only warning, before a snarl ripped behind her and she threw herself to the ground. Grabbing the rope and scrambling behind a tree. The mallet came crashing across the trunk, and she shrieked, running through the forest.

Every lumbering step made her stumble, her legs threatening to give out before a hand yanked her by the hair, and her head nearly ripped from her shoulders.

A gaping mouth of rocky square teeth and rancid breath bellowed a roar in her face, and Hazen squeezed her eyes shut against the spit and bits of debris that flew from its mouth.

Amber eyes of the beast blazed with hunger as its grip tightened in her hair. Scalp screaming and head threatening to snap off her neck, Hazen said a silent prayer before gathering all the air in her lungs and screaming:

"SAVVEN!"

A large hand went to her throat, cutting her off, and the rope dropped to the ground as she beat against the grip. Legs kicking out, her screams were silent, the world around her going hazy.

Blood sprayed the air, and the hand holding her hostage dropped, a beastly howl of pain deafened her.

Hazen collapsed to the ground, sucking in a lungful of air. Above her, Savven stood, one short blade in his hand. His face was twisted in anger and, if Hazen had taken a moment to really look, annoyance.

The creature rounded on Savven, Hazen could barely make out its monstrous body except from the blade embedded in its hand. The sickening slither of the knife being pulled made Hazen wince, and blood dripped from the edges before it was tossed aside.

Savven's eyes flickered briefly behind the beast before he lunged forward. His lean body closed the distance between them before he pushed off the ground. His leg spinning behind him, Savven's foot landed the blow to the beast. It stumbled before Savven whipped forward, and the other knife sunk into its chest.

A rough grunt came from the creature, and Hazen watched the air shimmer; the ground gouged out with every stumbling step it took back. A stream of lagging sunlight filtered through the canopy of trees and across the beast, and for the first time, Hazen could see the monster's twisted face and scar-ridden flesh. Everywhere the light touched, she could see, and Hazen stood, taking a step back as Savven stalked towards it, bow and arrow in hand.

Roaring in defiance, the beast tried to move from the sunlight, but its body cracked. It was turning to stone.

"Savv—" she tried to warn him, but it was too late.

The mallet in the beast's hand went sailing through the air. Savven spun quicker than she could see, but the bow in his hand snapped into splinters, the mallet crashing into a tree behind him.

The rage she saw on the elf's face made her take another step back.

Savven tossed the shards of his bow to the ground, staring hard at the creature as he yanked the quiver from his back. It landed beside his bow. The arrows scattered across the dirt, except one, held tightly in his fist.

"That was my favourite bow," he muttered darkly. His fist launched back, arrow tip glinting dangerously, and he hurled the arrow through the air.

Silence surrounded them, and Hazen stepped up beside Savven, eyes wide and hands trembling. The beast's final cry was permanently etched on its stone face. Savven's final arrow lodged in its open mouth, jutting from its skull.

"Savven?"

Her voice was hushed, eyes fixated on the dead *thing* in front of them. Now that she could see it, she still didn't know what it was.

Savven grabbed the discarded short blade from the ground, wiping it clean across his black shirt sleeve.

"Savven?" Hazen asked again, her voice louder, more sure.

Savven glanced at her, his mouth a firm line, and something akin to irritation was held in that glance. Slipping the blade up his shirt sleeve, he tightened something she couldn't see as he walked over to the beast. One hand on the hilt, his back flexed, the fabric of his shirt straining across taut muscle as he carefully slid the blade free of its chest.

"What was that?" she asked, her fingers fiddling with the edge of the fur cape.

"It's dull," he muttered, shaking his head.

"What?" she questioned.

Huffing under his breath, Savven turned his full attention to her, holding up his short blade. "It's dull, thanks to you."

Hazen scowled. "You're the one who left me alone!"

"Is that so?" he asked, cocking his head to the side.

Hazen swallowed her instant regret, eyes on Savven as he stepped closer to her. Her mind whispered for her to step back, to run. He was a predator, and she was the prey. But she didn't. She held fast, glaring up at him.

"Yes, it's so," she retorted.

"Did I not tell you to stay where you were?" he questioned, his voice cutting.

"Well, yes—"

"And did you stay where you were?"

"Well, no—"

"Perfect! So, I stand correct!" he said, shoving the dull blade into a hidden pocket in his boot.

Hazen sighed, running a hand over her hair. "Look, I'm sorry."

Savven's brow twitched at her apology. "You're going to get us both killed."

"I said I'm sorry!" she huffed, exasperated.

Shrugging, Savven eyed the statue. "It's okay. I wouldn't have let you die, anyway. I knew you weren't capable of staying still."

Something cold washed over her at the realisation of his words. Freezing and then hot, all at once. "You knew... you knew... *YOU KNEW!*" she screamed, storming over to him.

Her fist collided with his jaw, and it was like punching a rock wall. "Fuck!" she swore, cradling her fist while she glared at the elf.

Savven didn't even flinch at her blow, making her want to punch him again. In fact, he looked bored, which made her jaw clench in anger.

"I could have died!" she yelled when he didn't say anything.

He shrugged. "But you didn't."

"But I could have!"

Annoyance ticked on his face.

"Oh, I'm sorry! Am I irritating you? You didn't have to take me with you. You could have left me! But you didn't!" Her anger blossomed like a poison flower, and it began seeping through her. Her hand lashed out, shoving his shoulder. He had the decency to move as if she had been strong enough to move him, but she wasn't, though it felt good all the same.

"Are you done?"

She shoved him again, his bored tone irritating her further.

"You can keep taking it out on me, or you can realise that I did save your life, and you jeopardised your own. You may not want to hear it, but if you had listened to me, all of this could have been avoided."

Her irritation dwindled, but her pride huffed in its own annoyance. He was right. She knew he was right. He knew he was right.

Savven rubbed a hand across his brow with a sigh. "If I tell you to do something, it is in your best interest to do it."

"You might be right, but that doesn't make you any less of an ass," she retorted.

His face was irritatingly passive once more, and she shook her head, turning her attention to the beast.

"What is that thing?" she asked, her lip curling in disgust.

"A troll. Dim-witted, slow, but always hungry. And when they're hungry, it's best to stay clear of them, especially when they're hunting."

Hazen's brows furrowed. "Wouldn't that mean you always have to stay clear of them? Why couldn't I see it?"

"Their magic allows them to camouflage into their surroundings, to become their surroundings. The sunlight exposes them. Turns them to stone."

Savven's gaze worked over her, and she flushed with embarrassment.

"They will eat anything that has a pulse," he said, "and you're their favourite type of meal: dumb and unaware."

"Prick," she muttered under her breath.

Savven gave her a flat stare, having heard her.

"Listen to me, and you won't die. Don't listen, and you'll probably be eaten. The choice is yours." He paused, assessing her thoroughly before he muttered, "It's like watching after a child, only more incompetent."

Her curses followed him as he walked away.

"Sit," Savven commanded, pointing to a small grouping of rocks next to a collection of tall, jagged, oval-shaped stones.

Hazen bristled at the command but sat down, watching Savven. He picked up a small cloth and sat on a rotten log beside her.

They had walked for a short time after the incident with the troll. Hazen's stomach remembered it was hungry and began rumbling loudly in their shared silence.

Savven had ignored her body's complaints, loud as they may be, before the cloister of large rocks rose from the ground, and he had directed her around them. They formed a crescent shape as if it had been some sort of structure long before.

He handed a cloth full of red berries to her. "Eat."

Hazen extended her hand and tilted her head in thanks. The scraped skin along her face pulled painfully, and she winced.

"Let me see," Savven said, kneeling in front of her.

Hazen shook her head, trying to push his probing fingers away. "No, it's okay."

He grabbed her hand, turning it over to look at the ruined skin of her palm. "Is your other one like this?"

She nodded.

"I'm sorry," he muttered.

His hand covered her palm, and her skin became warm under his touch. Heat filled her blood, and she could feel something within her come to life—something foreign, something that crawled along her bones like it had been slumbering.

"May I heal you?"

His gaze was intent, and she couldn't bring herself to look away from those deep blue eyes. Fire and heat coursed through her limbs, melting the stinging pain away entirely. That thing within whispering secrets too faint to hear.

"Hazen?"

"Yes?" she whispered.

"May I?"

"Yes," she whispered again.

Closing his eyes, Savven's brows furrowed in concentration. His eyes moved rapidly beneath his lids.

A bright white light illuminated from his palm, casting shadows that danced across his face. And Hazen watched in awe as veins of white wove around her hands and up her arms. Fire met light within her, and her body went rigid under the sway of magic. Her blood became hot under her skin, and she could feel it coursing, molten, through her limbs.

As quickly as it had happened, it was over. Savven released her hand, the skin unmarked. When he opened his eyes, his gaze was dark, questioning, searching her face.

When she finally found her voice, the overwhelming heat dwindling to nothing, she asked, "Savven?"

"Where is it?" His voice was harsh. Urgent.

"Where is what?" she asked, confused.

His blue eyes were nearly black, watching her, demanding, "The mark. Where is it?"

"Mark? Savven what..." she stopped, the words dying slowly when she remembered what lay tattooed on her shoulder. What had been branded into her skin when she was unaware of the course her life had just taken.

"Where is—" he stopped mid-sentence, listening for a second, before catching Hazen's arm and pulling her behind the mass of large rocks.

"Savven what—"

His hand clamped over her mouth, silencing her.

Savven glared, his eyes warning her not to speak. Hazen was pressed against the rocks, Savven's body against her side. He smelled faintly like saltwater and nothing at all.

A snap of a twig rang like a shot through the silence. Hazen's ears pricked, listening, and she turned her head slowly, waiting.

Seconds later, another snap, directly on the other side of the rocks.

Hazen's breath hitched. Her bones seemed to jolt with the noise. Without making a sound, she peered around the stone, straining for just a glance.

Her eyes came upon a black giant. With long twisted horns growing towards the sky, a massive black snout and dark black fur covered its body in a tangled, shaggy mess; black eyes surveyed the area. Hazen looked at its feet, noticing the large hooves that dug into the earth as it stomped, lifting its snout, sniffing the air. Its meaty hands held tight to a broad double-sided axe.

Hazen spun back around, looking at Savven with wide eyes. He shook his head, his pointed glance commanding her to be quiet.

Savven whispered something so faint Hazen couldn't hear him, but the air around them shimmered before stilling again.

The beast's hoof stomped repeatedly, the ground quaking. Hazen dared to look again, watching it sniff the air. Its head swivelled in multiple directions, sniffing again and again.

Hazen's heart was beating against her ribs, and she rounded on Savven, the beast moving towards them. She opened her mouth but snapped it shut when he shook his head, holding a finger to his lips.

The beast rounded the rock formation, sniffing and searching. It was looking for something or someone.

Holding her breath, Hazen didn't dare move as the beast stopped beside them.

Savven slowly reached for the blade hidden in his sleeve, his fingers hovering over the concealed weapon's location. His eyes never left the beast who stood there.

It didn't see them. It *couldn't* see them.

Hazen didn't move, but her eyes flickered between Savven and the beast.

Minutes felt like hours until a final sniff and stomp of its hoof had the beast walking on.

They didn't move for some time, even after the beast had long disappeared.

When her heart finally slowed and she began to relax, Savven touched her arm and nodded, stepping away. The air shimmered again, and she could feel the gentle brush of air on her cheek once more—something she hadn't realised was missing until just then.

"What was that thing?" she demanded, pointing a finger behind her.

Savven walked over to where the berries and cloth had scattered on the ground, shaking his head silently.

Hazen looked around the forest, turning in a complete circle.

"What was that thing?" she demanded again.

Savven turned to her. "A Prowler." He looked back at the berries. "I should have been more careful," he muttered to himself.

"Was that a minotaur?" Her brain was trying to dust off what she knew of mythology, but none of what she knew was comforting.

"Yes." He paused, glancing at her. "You know of our kind? No, I suppose you wouldn't..." his words were meant for himself again, and his face pinched in thought.

"Is that what was stalking me?"

"No," he said, frowning. "This was a different one. Ezra must have felt the magic shift when you came through the veil. They're hunting you or whoever came through the veil."

Her stomach dropped as fear coated her tongue, its taste bitter and numbing. "Savven, what is going on?"

His sigh was filled with a dozen different emotions, his blue eyes weary. "It's been almost three hundred years since the last human entered our world—the last human being half-Fae. When one crosses the veil, it's felt across our world—a ripple of power. Ezra knows you're here. He's searching for you."

The fear turned to ash on her tongue, and she took in a staggering breath, processing.

"Then what do we do?" she asked.

"We run."

Deep in the heart of the Dauðinn Mountains, in the halls of the Dyagin Castle...

Clouded black eyes stared up through the blood seeping around Ezra's feet. Numbness was like an old friend. Unfeeling, void. His face, blank of emotion, stared back at him as the liquid pooled around him like a mirror.

He was Death. He had become the shadows. He had become the darkness.

Pale skin, unmarked, stretched over high cheekbones and framed by a firm mouth, straight nose, and dark slanted brows. His black eyes, usually full of rage, stared at his face, emotionless.

He watched his reflection tighten its grip on the sword he held;

knuckles bleaching. Blood dripped from its tip, the quiet *plop... plop... plop,* as it fell into the pool around him, filled the stone hall, its echo travelling through the towering arches.

"Throw him off the mountain." His voice was raw, rasping against his throat.

"My lord?"

Ezra rounded on the two Dökkálfar who stood beside the ashen corpse of what was a Romani boy. His once green eyes, full of terror as Ezra tortured him, were now pale and void. His brown hair was caked in his own blood from where he was cut jugular to navel.

"Throw him off the mountain!" he screamed.

The Dark Ones flinched; even the flames in iron sconces wavered against the obsidian pillars.

Nodding hurriedly, they each took an arm and dragged the boy behind them, leaving a trail of red as they exited the grand hall.

It had come—the shift. It had woken him from his sleep, stirring to life the dark magic inside of him. The things that shifted and slithered beneath his skin, clawing against his bones, waiting.

They had said, that little *irritating* God had said, darkness will rise, but fire will come from ash.

Ezra screamed into the empty hall, hurling the sword in his hand. It clamoured against the wall and fell to the floor with a ringing clatter.

The shift had caused talk to rise and whispers to travel. Rumours have begun to spread like little seeds of doubt. Seeds of hope. Hope made his black eyes see red, and he screamed again. Storming up the polished stone steps of the glass-like dais, he threw himself into the glimmering silver throne that sat perched in the centre. Ezra ignored the talons that clicked down his ribs, demons whispering in his head to move to *act.*

Cold white hands shot out from under long black sleeves and clutched at the armrest, fingernails digging into the silver. Long legs stretched in front of him, his black clothing dark in contrast to the bright element.

"Enough," he commanded, and the whispering ceased. "Where is Levina?" he yelled into the empty hall.

A wooden door opened to his right, and out stepped a slight

female. Dressed in a white gossamer gown that gathered under her bust with transparent sleeves. Ezra stared at Levina as if she were a dream. Her dark blonde curls cascaded down her back, and her wide sky-blue eyes blinked down at the crimson footprints that followed Ezra up the dais.

"Ezra," she said curtly.

Ezra frowned at her tone. Her lovely mouth pressed into a harsh line.

"Levina, my heart, come here."

Levina's jaw twitched once before her face settled into a passive, far-off stare. Her bare feet were silent against the polished floors, and her gaze was direct as she approached Ezra.

His smirk was cold, and he leaned forward, grasping her chin between his fingers. "I've always loved your spirit," he murmured softly, stroking her jaw.

She yanked her face away with a scowl. "It's the one thing you can't take from me, Ezra."

"I took nothing!" he thundered. Leaning back in his throne, he calmed a hand over his ink-black hair. "I was *given* everything from you."

"Under false pretence!" she snapped, anger twisting her face.

Ezra waved a hand at her words. "How are you fairing, My Love?"

"I am not your love!"

He jolted to his feet. "Answer me!" he roared.

Levina flinched as the cold darkness seeped into his eyes, turning them into bottomless pits.

Sniffing, she jutted out her chin, nodding to the pool of blood. "I fare better than whoever that belongs to."

The large duelling wood doors of the grand hall creaked sharply as they opened suddenly.

His lips tilted in a whisper of a cold smile, and Ezra gestured to his right side.

Levina had become accustomed to his commands, silent or vocal. Rolling her shoulders back, she took her place on his right side, her index finger quietly tapping her thigh between the folds of her gown.

A Dark One strolled through the hall. Dirty blond hair framed a strong face, his dark brown eyes cold and calculating. Ezra watched his second in command and oldest friend, Laudin, stalk across his grand hall. His powerful build, dressed in all black, commanded attention. Though larger than most High Fae, he was agile and swift as he prowled towards the dais.

Ezra noted a massive black wolf following close behind him in an easy trot. "Laudin, you bring me my dinner still alive? You shouldn't have," he said with an amused smile.

Laudin's grin was cutting as he bowed before Ezra.

"Rise."

"My lord," Laudin said, nodding his head in greeting.

"I'm afraid I'm not hungry," Ezra said coolly, waving a hand to the mess on the floor. "As you can see, I ate a little earlier than intended."

Levina made a soft noise of disgust.

Laudin's brows rose a hair, glancing at her.

"Pay her no mind," Ezra said, waving a hand in her direction. His dark eyes flickered with interest, and he leaned forward. "Though tell me, Laudin. Who is this wolf?" Ezra sniffed the air, pausing before a cold smile slipped over his lips. "No, who is this *shifter*."

Chuckling, Laudin stepped aside. "Shift!" he commanded.

A low growl at Laudin's tone came from the wolf before its body morphed from animal to male. Completely naked for all to see. Silver hair travelled the length of a muscular, olive-skinned back, and piercing blue eyes dared to look directly at Ezra.

Not the slightest bit concerned about his nudity, he calmly said, "My, how the mighty have risen."

Ezra's face shifted from amusement to shadows to nothing at all. His eyes gazed at the male before him as if he were a distant memory he couldn't quite grasp. Pieces of a life once lived and lost floated through breaks in the shadows of his mind.

"Ah," the shifter said, smiling bitterly. "I see."

Laudin's hand latched around the shifter's neck, squeezing until it began to concave under his grip. "You do not speak to the High Lord unless spoken to, Shifter!"

The shifter's eyes latched onto Ezra's, no matter that Laudin had yet to release him and no matter that the world was slowly beginning to dim. His eyes stayed on Ezra, who looked at him through a narrowed gaze of curiosity.

"Tell me your name," Ezra asked.

Laudin didn't let go.

"Release him, Laudin," snapped Ezra.

Sweet air rushed through his lungs when the Dark One finally released him, and the shifter breathed deeply, chuckling softly. "You know my name."

Irritation flashed in Ezra's eyes. "I don't have time for your games, Shifter."

"Néefar."

Ezra blinked once, twice, something fighting behind his eyes before they calmed and their dark depths narrowed. "Néefar, my old friend, you have changed," he commented coolly. He tilted his head in thought, leaning into his throne. "How interesting it is to see you here before me. Where is that precious Anabelle of yours?"

A slight smile tilted Néefar's lips as he said, "She is occupied in that forest of hers, though she remains unmine. Silly girl couldn't choose between me and her little woodland creatures."

Humming, Ezra nodded slowly, his fingers steepling in front of him. "Laudin," he said softly.

Laudin took his cue and went to stand beside Ezra's left side. Leaving Néefar standing naked before the dais.

"And why should I trust you, Néefar? You stood on my enemy's side many years ago."

"I stood on the winning side, as did you," clarified Néefar, his face slowly becoming bored.

Ezra smirked. "Indeed, and look how the tables have turned."

"Yes, you've done very well," amended Néefar drolly.

His brow quirked at the shifter's tone, the shadows beneath his skin pressing into his muscles, their whispers filling his skull again. Closing his eyes, his head twitched as they spoke repeatedly to him.

What does he bring us, the demons whispered.

"What do you bring!" he yelled suddenly, a crazed look widening his eyes as the voices continued to fill his head.

Levina glanced at Ezra before looking expectantly at Laudin, who placed a hand on Ezra's shoulder.

"My lord," he whispered.

Ezra jerked in surprise, pulling away from Laudin's grip, his eyes clearing. Lifting his chin, he stared down at Néefar. "Why do you come before me."

Néefar stared up at Ezra for a moment, hesitating, before stating, "I was there when the God's spoke of the prophecy."

"Yes, and?" Ezra asked impatiently.

"It has been almost three hundred years since human blood has crossed the veil, and you know as well as I that another has entered our world."

"I grow impatient, Shifter!"

"The forest whispers of a newcomer. A girl has come through the veil. She travelled towards the southeast but has changed course due north."

Ezra was silent, staring at Néefar. "A human girl?" he finally asked.

"Aye."

"You're certain?"

"Yes."

"*Nazar!*" Ezra screamed.

Levina flinched at the name, and Laudin shifted slightly as the bone-thin body shrouded in a black robe appeared. Tendrils of shadows followed in his wake as Nazar, Shade to the Realm of the Dead, whispered through the walls to Ezra's side. His sallow skin sunken in around his face, blood-red eyes watching Ezra with a calm assertion.

Ezra stumbled upon the creature half a century ago while prowling the Forest of Lost Souls. Seeking restitution with the promise of serving him, Ezra agreed to the shade's terms and stole the demon from the forest. His own demon's screams filled his head and clawed their way through his body at the deal struck.

"Yes, My Lord," Nazar asked softly, his voice as venomous as a snake as the words slithered past his lips.

Turning his head slightly, Ezra didn't bother to look at the shade. "You are to find a girl. She travels north bound from the southeastern territory."

Nazar's lips pulled back into a murderous smile, torch light flicking across his long white hair. "A girl, My Lord?"

"Any girl who looks out of the ordinary, kill her."

The shade's death-white face turned up into a sharp grin, his red eyes narrowing. "With pleasure."

Levina glared at Nazar even as her palms grew sweaty with fear, quickly turning away when he directed his gaze to her.

Nazar's bloody eyes travelled slowly down Levina's body until they stopped. He licked the air with his black tongue, his smile turning hungry. "The babe grows restless. Soon, it will begin to feed on you, Little Elf," he commented darkly.

Levina bit back the need to wrap a protective hand around her hidden but growing stomach.

"Enough," snapped Ezra. "Go, Nazar."

As silent as the night, the shade straightened, and his body misted into nothing, vanishing.

CHAPTER 13

By the time they stopped to rest, night had fallen in the forest, and the stars lay a silent, glimmering blanket over the treetops.

Hazen stared into nothingness, trying to see past the darkness. But she was blind to the world around her. She sighed softly, frowning.

"You should get some sleep."

Hazen turned away and looked toward Savven's voice. "Here?"

"It'll do," Savven said curtly.

Mimicking him under her breath, she poked her tongue out at him quickly.

"I saw that."

She could hear the dry amusement in his tone. "Good," she said, her smile tight as she felt a hand out in front of her. Her fingers brushed against a tree, and she held onto it, sliding down its base until she could rest her back against it.

"We'll stay here until dawn."

Hazen's ears became hypersensitive, and she could hear him sit not far off from her, her eyes straining to pierce the night with no avail.

"What about you?" she asked, wrapping Dshar's furs around her.

"What about me?" he said.

"Are you not going to sleep?"

"Sleep?" he echoed. His laugh was sudden and hollow, fading until there was only silence.

Hazen shifted away from a lumpy knob pressing into her spine, grunting under her breath irritably.

"Were you always this charming?" Hazen asked ruefully into the darkness.

Savven shifted. She could almost picture him looking at her, and some part of her suspected he could see her.

"Were you always this stubborn?" he countered.

"Yes," she said after a minute, smiling despite herself.

"As was I."

"Oh, I'm sure," she laughed.

More silence followed when Savven didn't reply, and Hazen's mind raced with thoughts of the last few days. Running a hand through her tangled hair, she sighed, closing her eyes.

"You think too much," Savven uttered quietly.

Her eyes opened, and she looked towards his voice. "A lot has happened."

"Hmm," Savven hummed. "Yes, it has."

Swallowing the lump in her throat, Hazen wrapped her arms around her waist and asked, "Tell me something, anything."

"Why?" he questioned.

"Because I'm tired," she intoned. "Because if I have to lay here and listen to nothing, my mind will fill in the silence, and I'm afraid I will go mad."

The seconds ticked by, and when Hazen thought Savven was going to ignore her, his rough, deep voice filled the darkness.

"There was a boy, born of noble blood, who loved his family and his home very much. He had few friends, and while blood did not unite them, they became his brothers.

"One of his brothers grew apart from them. Something terrible had happened to him, and soon this brother grew vengeful. The boy and his brothers sought to help him, but this brother became angry. Light turned to darkness with everything this brother touched. The boy, seeking to help him, tried to aid his brother, but the brother only became bitter, and soon he ran away from them. Hiding within the mountains where none could touch him.

"The boy thought his brother would find refuge in his solitude, but soon the brother returned, destroying the boy's city and his family. The boy lost the things that held his love that day, and his brother spread his destruction across the lands. Darkness eating away the light until only shadows remained."

Savven's words lingered when he was finished, and Hazen wished she could see his face. "What happened to the boy?"

"He lost himself."

CHAPTER 14

"Bones and stones, bones and… stones," uttered Nazar as he glided across dank stone floors through a narrow passage. Shadows clinging to his every move like whispering tendrils.

Thick wooden doors lined one side of the hall, their square cutouts caged by iron bars. Strange markings glowed softly on the wood. Binding spells to keep anyone from using magic to leave the chambers.

Low moaning could be heard from behind the doors, and Nazar stopped, looking through one of the cages.

Light from the torches in the hall barely penetrated the darkness within the cells, but multiple pairs of eyes still blinked back at him.

His smile revealed a row of jagged, rotten teeth, and he reached a pale, bony hand through the bars. "Pretty little bodies, let me have a taste."

The eyes disappeared as the Fae within squeezed them closed, and soft, terror-filled whimpers replaced the pained moans.

Nazar licked the air, tasting their fear, and his eyes rolled back into his skull. "Pity," he hissed. "You would have been delicious."

He retreated from the cell door, cackling lowly as he continued on.

The hall split, and a narrow archway led into darkness as he descended slick stone steps. Dim light broke the shadows, and Nazar slipped into a small, dark room. A cave cut haphazardly into the belly of the mountain beneath the castle. Water trickled down the walls, a slow drip echoing in the space. It smelled of rotting earth and soil.

"Bones and stones, stones and bones," he sang under his breath.

Red eyes glowing in the shadows, he snatched a leather pouch from the narrow wooden table pressed against the wall and went to the stone basin carved from the mountain.

"Bones and stones..." he hissed, tearing the pouch's strings. Bones and stones clattered in the basin, gathering in the middle of the bowl. Nazar leaned forward, dragging a sharp nail across a black stone resting across the ridge of a bleached finger bone.

His head cocked sharply, nostrils flaring as his eyes turned black, and he sent his shadows out into the world.

Dark forest skirted by his shadows as they turned over rock and root. Searching, searching, searching.

Nazar's hands grasped the stone, eyes scurrying as he saw through the eyes of his shadows.

Find her. Find her. Find her! he commanded the spirits.

Root, rock, and tree were overturned until Nazar yelled, throwing the stone back into the basin. "Bring me a female!" he screamed.

Hurried footsteps tapped along the floors, and a cell door slammed shut. The scent of fear filled the room, and Nazar smiled, turning slowly as a Dark One brought in a frail female wood nymph. Her body quivered, beads of sweat bathing her dark brow.

"Bones, and stones, and blood," he sang softly, stepping silently up to the cowering female.

The female squeezed her eyes shut, a low cry forcing its way from her.

Nazar stooped over the nymph, his fingers lengthening to bony ridges, nails turning to short black claws as he dragged one up her brown cheek. "Blood, and bones, and stones. My pretty little pet, do not be afraid."

Her skin bleached, and she shrank back against the Dark One, who held her firm.

"Pl-please," she whimpered.

"Now, now, Little Pet," Nazar whispered, placing his mouth against her ear. "You won't go to waste." His tongue dragged along her jaw, tasting her, and his grin widened when she shrieked.

He grabbed her arm and yanked her forward. The female stumbled, nearly dropping to the ground until Nazar yanked her upright.

"Pretty little pet's blood will find what we seek. Blood for blood. Life for life. Come, little pet," he cooed, bloody eyes narrowing on the basin.

"Please!" she screamed, digging her heels in, green eyes flashing with fear.

Snarling with impatience, Nazar's hand latched onto her black hair, yanking her head back until her neck was bared over the basin.

"Scream for me, Little Pet," he seethed. "*Scream!*"

Her screams filled the room and passage above until they melted into the mountain. She screamed until her screams turned to choking as Nazar sliced a claw across her throat. Her blood gushed into the basin, filling the bones and stones with life.

Nazar licked the trail of blood trickling down her throat before throwing her husk to the ground.

"Bones, and stones, and *blood*," he murmured, eyeing the pool of crimson and the bleached bones that slowly began to feed on the blood.

He dipped a claw into the basin, stirring it until his eyes turned black and his shadows began their hunt.

Earth, and stone, and root. His shadows tore through it all. The forest flew by him as he saw the world through his demons. A minotaur lay dead, its body being pecked through by animals. The shadows moved on. Deeper and deeper they went into the forest.

Blood. *It smelled blood. The shadows paused, smelling the earth and air. Blood, blood, blood, his shadows chanted. The smell of life. The forest whirled past them as they flew through the trees until everything stopped.*

Nazar's eyes stilled their rapid moving as the shadows focused on the forest floor.

A single drop of blood lay forgotten on a dead leaf. They sniffed the blood, searching for more.

"Find her," he hissed through clenched teeth, his hands fisting around the bones and stones, blood coating his skin. *"Find her!"*

The shadows moved swiftly. The deeper they went, the more the dark forest welcomed their search. A dead troll, frozen in time, and more blood flecked the ground around it. Moonlight spilt over the macabre statue through the treetops.

Find her, find her, find her, they chanted, their hissed words filling Nazar's head until they stopped suddenly.

Nazar's heinous smile lit up the darkness.

She was asleep, unaware of the dangers lurking within the shadows, watching her. His shadows stayed hidden, eyeing the female. Something moved, hidden in the darkness with them. Light filled the darkness, and his demons scattered.

Nazar screeched at the light and retreated, his eyes turning back to red; the bones and stones splashed back into the basin, and he lifted his bloodied hand to his face. "I found you, pretty little pet," he sang lowly as he licked the blood from his fingers. "I found you."

Levina leaned back against her door, her head thunking on the wood as she let out a shuddering breath. There was so much and nothing at all—too many emotions and so much numbness that crept along the edges. She felt dizzy trying to force down the dark *thing* that crawled through her, testing the barriers she threw up within her mind for weaknesses. It crawled through her body, limb by limb, weaving through her muscles until she ached from fighting it.

It wanted her to give over control, to succumb. But if she did, she knew she would never find her way back again.

The *thing* came from the darkness that controlled Ezra—her Ezra. Sweet and stoic, he was her friend. He had been her friend. She had loved him like one loves a brother. Even when he confessed his feelings for her, Levina had hoped nothing would change. But she had been a child, naive. And she knew she had hurt him, and for that, she was ashamed.

But the darkness wanted her shame, guilt, hate, anger, despair, and every negative part of her. So, she found herself falling into the abyss, where there were no emotions, no pain, no nothing. She had simply been existing for the last fifty years.

"LEVINA!"

She flinched at Ezra's screeching voice, her name echoing through the cold halls into her chamber. It would be a matter of seconds before he burst through the door. She eyed her room quickly. A small single bed, a trunk of clothes pushed against its foot, and a small desk and chair. There was nowhere for her to go. Nothing she could use to defend herself.

Levina looked at the tattoo branded around her right wrist. A vine of miniature roses crawled up her arm, long thorns pressing against her skin, warning her.

Ezra's bargain.

She had given herself to him; with it, he had taken her magic and so much more with just a simple change of words. She was entirely defenceless.

Backing away from the door, she wrapped a protective hand around her middle. Mouth pursing into a flat line, bracing herself.

The door flew open, slamming against the wall. Levina steeled herself away as black eyes glared at her.

She had done too much in the grand hall—said too much. But she hadn't been able to contain her disgust. It was all slowly coming to a boil beneath her skin every time she held her tongue. Every time he killed another and another and another, she wanted to scream. To run a sword through his black heart and end it all. But she couldn't. So, she wrapped her arms tighter around her stomach and bared her teeth in a snarl.

"Do not," he warned lowly, "make this worse."

"Or what, Ezra? You'll do what?" she spat.

His head ticked, and she saw his eyes look down at her stomach.

"If you touch this babe, I promise I will *rip* your heart out."

Ezra chuckled softly, stalking towards her until he leaned forward and stroked the back of his hand down her cheek, smirking when she flinched. "Darling, don't you know to rip out a heart? You need to have one first?"

"Die!" she snarled.

"I'm sure I already have."

"What do you want?" she asked softly, refusing to step away from him.

"For you to stop undermining me!"

His words rang in her ears, his voice crowding the small chambers.

"Undermining you?! I have done no such thing!"

He grabbed her chin between his fingers, his grip bruising. "Your small quips and sullen glares are enough. This pretty face of yours speaks plainly even when your mouth doesn't move. Need I remind you of our deal?"

The thorns dug into her flesh as the magic tightened around her arm. She bit back her cry, pain shooting through her.

She knew it had been a child's mistake. But time had not been on her side, and she did what she had to. However, in the end, it still hadn't been enough. He had found a loophole in the Fae magic.

"How can I forget when you've taken everything from me?" she whispered.

"Everything?" he scoffed. "You *gave* me everything."

"No," she said, shaking her head. This time, she did step back, yanking her face out of his grip. "I gave you myself so *they* may live. But you killed them... you killed them still... *YOU KILLED THEM!*" she screamed. Anger poured out of her, and the darkness inside her howled in delight. Her eyes turned black, and she wanted to destroy everything.

She lunged for Ezra, her body flying through the air.

He shook his head, and she went crashing into the opposite wall. His magic tossed her aside like a discarded object.

Pain splintered through her, and she dropped to the ground in a bruised heap. Her hand slid to her belly as if she might feel a still beating heart. A soft press from within made relief crash through her, and she released her breath.

"Pathetic."

His disappointed tone had Levina seeing red, and she got to her feet, stalking towards him. "You killed my queen. You killed my people. You burned my home." Her words were quiet, but still, they echoed around them. A look of repulse twisting her face. "All for the sake of what? *Power*? I am not the pathetic one."

"Let me remind you, Levina: you broke our bargain."

"I gave you myself!"

"I wanted everything!"

"So, you took my everything!" Her words ended with a sob, and she pressed the back of her tattooed hand to her lips. Hoping that her tears would not soon follow. "I gave you myself, Ezra. In exchange, you let them live... but it wasn't enough."

"Oh, my sweet," he purred, walking towards her until she was trapped against the wall. The stone was cold and hard through her thin gown. Ezra leaned forward, hands on either side of her head, caging her in. He brushed his nose along her cheek, laughing lowly when she moved her head away. "It will never be enough."

His words jolted through her body like ice. Levina fixated her eyes on the opposite wall, the torchlight filling her gaze.

Ezra brushed his nose along her jaw before placing a tiny kiss on the corner of her mouth and stepped back.

His steps followed him out of her chamber. The door slammed shut, but a single word was still uttered darkly as a warning.

"Behave."

Levina's hands trembled, and she slowly slid to the ground, drawing her knees to her chest. She wrapped her arms around her legs and buried her face in her knees as she wept.

CHAPTER 15

The rain beat against her face as Levina turned her eyes to the towering obsidian mountain before her. Angry clouds rolled overhead, lightning flashing through the grey sky.

Savven had told her not to come. Lithônion had begged her to gain some sense. But still, she didn't listen to her friends, sneaking through Álfheimr after nightfall with a black cloak, its hood pulled around her face, and satchel of previsions around her back. She crept through the city's walls, past the sentries, and into the Black Forest.

It took her three nights to reach Dauðinn Mountain, running on foot and taking minimal breaks. Prowlers roamed the forest, and she took to the trees to rest, watching them clamber over the ground with heavy, loud steps. They were many in number, and she had to seek the comfort of the branches high above until they passed, even travelling through the treetops when it was viable.

A storm cast over the forest shortly after her first night until sheets of rain pissed through the towering branches. There was no escaping it, even with the dense foliage. Her dark blue blouse did nothing to protect her. Still, the oiled leather of her pants was blessedly keeping the water at bay despite the rivulets of rain trickling into her boots. Causing each step to squelch softly.

Now, Levina looked up at the mountain. Its glassy black surface, sleek with water, was imposing and warned against those who sought to enter. She knew what would lay within, who she would find. But even knowing, she still shuddered from the wet, the cold, and the fear.

It had been over two hundred and thirty years since the battle between Balwin and the keeper. Since then, their friend slowly slipped within himself until, finally, he was no longer Ezra. He had become something entirely different. Something darker and twisted.

She should leave him alone. She should turn back. But she couldn't. A shift had come three days prior. Magic had cut through the land like a cold black knife, and when the King and Queen sent out sentries to investigate, they didn't return. Savven and Lithônion were sent out, taking ten of Álfheimr's finest soldiers with them to scout out the lost sentries.

They had found them beside the Forest of Lost Souls. Slaughtered. Nothing but piles of bones and torn flesh that the earth was slowly claiming back.

Ezra had taken something from that cursed forest. Something powerful. Something that could tear apart some of the most skilled sentries of Álfheimr. Levina wanted to know what it was. She wanted to know what was coming.

Leaving her satchel at the mountain's base, Levina unlatched her cloak and let it pool on the ground in a sopping heap before she grabbed a razor-sharp ledge, fingers digging into the crevices, and began the ascent up.

The wind whipped at her back, threatening to dislodge her from the flesh of the mountain. Her arms relished at the stress of the climb, sighing with every stretch and pull of her muscles.

Her foot slipped on the wet surface, and she gasped, hugging herself to the slick side. Prying her eyes open when she realised they were closed,

Levina glanced down at the ground. A painful death waited for her if she fell.

She took one deep breath and then another, and she continued the climb until she pulled herself up over the entrance of a cave.

It was dank and dark within. Rough walls and floors carved out from the stone created a solitary space. The lighting cracked, and its light filled the cave briefly. The shadows skirted away, revealing a set of stairs leading into the mountain before the cave fell into darkness.

Pushing a lock of wet hair out of her eyes, mouth set in determination, Levina stalked into the cave and began the descent into the mountain.

She had never been within the Dauðinn Mountain before. Tales that were more of a nightmare than a fable were told by campfire when she was only a babe. Stories of despair, death, and power. The first kings and queens of their world ruled several territories over the millenniums, but the Dauðinn Mountain and the ancient castle built within was ruled by the Night King.

The Night King was said to have made darkness. One of the first High Fae of the world, he made it come to life in ways that differed from night and day. Stories say the Night King killed his friend; it was an accident, but from that death, he tasted the first true essence of blood lust. The power that came from controlling the outcome of life. From that, the darkness grew, and what was once pure and filled with innocence died, and the Night King was born.

After the demise of the Night King, killed by the Gods, the second and last time the Gods had ever intervened, the mountain remained empty. His shadows lived on, but they were guarded by Naleen, the Lady of the Earth, within the Forest of Lost Souls. But now, for the first time in a very long time, the mountain was occupied.

Ezra had stolen away to Dauðinn Mountain over the years preceding the battle between Balwin and the keeper until, finally, he didn't return. It's been one hundred years since he showed his face within Álfheimr's city walls, but still, his presence roams the lands like the Night King. Bringing shadows and death slowly but surely until people slept fitfully in fear for their lives.

Levina shuddered as she passed a row of empty cells. She could only imagine the death these walls have seen. Following the fork in the hall to the right until it brought her to a set of stairs that wound up and straight,

Her hand brushed against the wall, following it slowly. Her eyes blinked past the darkness until she rounded a corner and firelight dimly filled the hall.

Towering arched, double doors of wood stood before her. Silver handles scripted with tormented faces, gaping mouths and hollow eyes stared at her. Fear licked down her spine as Levina looked at the handles, her fingers hesitating for a moment before she grasped them. Determination steeled her palpating heart, and she pushed the doors open. Gritting her teeth, the wood groaned, heavy and scraping against the rocky floor. But finally, a space appeared, and she slipped through.

It was a grand hall. Empty and dark save for a single torch burning brightly behind a silver throne, perched on a dais at the end of the hall. Levina froze as she beheld the throne of the Night King.

"Magnificent, isn't it?"

She turned sharply. Ezra walked through the shadows until he stood before her. His back was turned, and he stared at the silver throne with pale hands clasped behind his back. Her heart beat wildly in her chest, and she didn't say anything, staring at her friend with wide eyes.

"He left such a mighty legacy." Ezra's voice was soft, but a chill had seeped into the grand hall, and Levina had to stop herself from shivering. "It's a shame it's gone to waste." He turned to her, and where the whites of his eyes had been, only darkness was seen. "But no longer."

"Ez..." her voice faltered, barely above a whisper, and she forced in a calming breath. "Ezra," she tried again.

"You know, Levina, this was all sealed from where you entered. I had to break through it. It took some time, but..." he waved a hand, indicating to the castle within the mountain, "I have restored it."

Her blood cooled in her veins. He had known she was coming. "How did you—"

"—Know?" he finished for her, his lips cutting into a crooked smile. "I know everything, Levina. My shadows know everything." Ezra's steps tapped softly on the ground until his boots toed hers, and he brushed a frigid hand down her cheek. "They whisper the secrets you wish to hide."

She refused to flinch even when her stomach churned. "I have no secrets, Ezra."

"Lies!" he screamed, backing away from her.

He stalked to the throne and took his seat, legs sprawled in front of him, arms gripping the armrests as he watched her approach the dais.

"What secrets do I hide, Ezra," she asked. "Tell me."

His head twitched to the side, regarding her with those unnerving black eyes. "I know why you've come. I know that poor little King Nydeth and Queen Casvara's sentries are dead. I know you, Levina." His tone was mocking, and he leaned forward, sneering. "Always the curious one. Always have to see for yourself. Now, do you see?! Are you not satisfied?!"

Levina flinched, hands fisting at her side. His words filled the space around her, and she shifted her feet.

"You're not wrong," she said quietly. "I was curious. I wanted to know why they died. What could kill them like that? I wanted to know what happened to you, Ezra." Her words ended with a plea.

The soft drip, drip, drip of water filled the silence. Ezra's gaze fixed on her face until he said, "They were nothing to me as they were."

"You left them in pieces!" she spat. Levina latched onto the tether of her magic, holding onto it as the shadows grew around her. Crawling across the floor towards them.

"Pieces?" he questioned, chuckling darkly. "Oh, my dear, that was not your sentries. That was only the beasts they fed upon."

Levina froze, her face paling. "What?" she whispered.

Shadows engulfed Ezra, and he disappeared into black mist.

"Silly little, Levina."

His voice echoed around her, and she whirled around, chest heaving and pulse racing beneath her skin. Her eyes tracked the darkness that slithered towards her, baring her teeth. Her hands ignited in fire, magic coursing through her limbs.

"Ah, ah, ah," he tsked.

A hand wrapped around her throat, and she sputtered, choking as it squeezed around her neck in a vice grip.

"That's not very nice, Levina," he cooed before slamming her body into a black obsidian pillar.

Levina saw stars and tried to lift her hand of fire, but every limb was restrained by bands of burning black shadows, and her skin was searing beneath them.

"Nazar! Bring them!" Ezra screeched, solidifying in front of her.

Darkness crept in around her vision as the pressure on her neck worsened. Her arms and legs were straining against their bindings. She *had never felt power like this before.*

Through her fading vision, Levina watched frost crawl across the ground as a shrouded figure emerged from the walls. She pressed her body into the pillar, wishing it would consume her, when blood-red eyes looked at her. A heinous smile showed a row of rotting razor teeth, and she knew this creature had come from the Forest of Lost Souls. This was the creature Ezra had stolen.

"Nazar is a shade," commented Ezra without removing his eyes from her. "Interesting creatures. Made from the Night King himself, they feast on souls and blood. Commanding shadows and demons, they are darkness incarnate. Nazar wanted to eat your precious sentries, but I had other plans for them…"

Orderly and moving as one, five sentries walked into the grand hall through the shadows that bordered beyond the pillars. Dressed in the royal High Fae army blacks, the golden crest of Álfheimr, a crossed sword, and a branch were visible in the firelight on their left shoulders.

"You… didn't… kill…" her voice sputtered until it faded completely.

Ezra leaned forward, smiling. "No, I made them new. Just as I will all of Álfheimr."

Five pairs of black eyes bore into her, and she was beginning to submerge into the shadows around her vision until his words pierced the welcoming void. He was going to kill them. He was going to take her home, her friends, her family.

"No!" she screamed, thrashing against the bonds that held her.

Ezra ticked his head to the side. "No? No… NO!" he thundered before leaning in, and silence fell. "Do you know what I discovered, Levina?" He continued when she didn't answer. "I found that my blood transcends all power. It moulds it into something else. Something new." His fingers squeezed around her neck, bruising the flesh. "You do not know power, but all of Álfheimr will when they become subject to mine."

Tears streamed down her face, and she took in a wheezing breath. "Take… me." The faces of her friends and family, her king and queen, flashed in her mind, and she whispered again, "Take… me."

Ezra released his grip on her neck, and she took a strangled breath, fire shooting through her lungs.

"Take you?" he purred, regarding her. "What do you offer in their stead?"

The shade hissed, and Levina's attention went to the red glowing eyes and twisted smile. Her face blanched at the seething hatred and hunger she saw.

Her gaze flickered back to Ezra. "Everything. Myself." Her voice broke, but she continued, "I offer you myself. That's what you wanted?" she asked, holding her head high and looking him in the eyes. "Now you can have it. I am yours."

His black eyes slowly vanished, and dark brown, nearly black on their own, stared back at her.

Nazar hissed again, and the sound filled the grand hall. Ezra ignored him.

"All mine?" he uttered, staring.

She could see a part of Ezra begin to show through the shadows within, a part she thought was lost forever. "Yes," she agreed hurriedly. "Forever yours." The shadows loosened around her arms, and she reached out a hand. "Make a deal with me, Ezra."

"Ez-ra," rasped Nazar. The shadows crawled towards the arching ceilings high above.

"Quiet!" Ezra snapped. His eyes transfixed on the hand outstretched to him. "A bargain... Give me everything, Levina," he whispered.

She nodded quickly. She knew then that she was never going to see Álfheimr again. She would never see her friends and family again. Perhaps a tiny part of her knew that when she came here. A deep, aching sadness filled her chest, and hot tears stung her eyes, but she blinked them back. "I give you myself in exchange that you do not harm my people. Leave Álfheimr alone."

His smile was razor-edged. "In exchange for not turning your people, I will have your everything."

Before she could retract her hand, the bargain was struck, his grip iron over hers. She screamed as something cut along her skin, twisting and wrapping along her wrist. Wide-eyed, those tears finally falling free, she looked at their joined hands. There, black as night, twisted vines of miniature roses wrapped along her wrist up her forearm. Long, deadly thorns dug into her skin.

He had changed the words before the deal was struck, and she felt her energy drain from her.

He leaned forward as she dropped to the floor, the restraints vanishing.

"Thank you, Levina. Now I have everything I could have wanted."

Her chest heaved, and she searched desperately for her thread of magic, vehemently scouring every part of her. Her limbs and mind were tired, feeling like lead every time she moved. The thread was gone. "No! What have you done?" she screamed, lunging for him. Her movements were sluggish and sloppy, and her blue eyes flashed fearfully.

"What I should have done a long time ago." He gripped her jaw, fingers digging into her skin until her mouth hinged open.

She whimpered against the pain. It was a new pain, a lasting one. Levina watched as Ezra ran a sharp canine along his wrist, black blood flowing freely from the wound. Dread filled her, and she shook her head violently, her objections and begging muffled.

"Now, now, take it like a good girl," he murmured, holding his wrist to her mouth.

Blood spilt down her throat, burning like ice and fire all at once. Things clawed through her body as his blood filled her mouth. She tore weakly at his hand, but it was unyielding.

The darkness was back, crowding her vision, and her hand dropped to her side like a weight.

"Good girl," he muttered, patting her head. He released her jaw, and she crumpled to the ground.

Levina splayed her fingers along the floor, feeling the texture against her skin. Her mind began to slip into the abyss.

"Take her to my quarters."

Ezra's voice was distant above her, and unknown hands wrapped around her waist, hauling her over a hard shoulder. She could see Ezra's body, though it was becoming distorted.

"Levina."

The one holding her halted, and she glanced up through the persistent shadows of her mind.

"I will burn them all."

She wanted to fight, to scream, to kill, but instead, she fell into the abyss.

CHAPTER 16

Savven's eyes shot open, and a chill went down his spine. He hadn't been asleep, closing his eyes as he waited and listened while the hours passed slowly. But even so, he scanned the dark forest. It had been quick. Something fleeting and cold, something that did not belong.

Claws crawled across his skin, and he bared his teeth, light flaring from his palm and filling the void.

A screech echoed faintly in the distance, and the night was once more just night.

His body went rigid, eyes fleeting to the sleeping girl who lay there unaware.

Another screech, and he was standing, jolting her awake.

"Wake up!"

Bleary-eyed, Hazen grunted, cursing him as she sat up.

"Wha-at is it," she yawned.

Savven gritted his teeth, feeling his neck prickle with awareness. He scanned the forest behind him. "For once, just do as you're told, Hazen."

He could see her stand, rubbing a hand over her face when she yawned again. Her glare narrowed on him. She couldn't see him, though, this much he knew.

A crunch of a twig made his head swivel, and he tracked the noise, hearing Hazen's breath catch, too.

"What was that," she whispered, nearly silent.

"I don't know," he muttered. "We need to move. We aren't safe in the open at night."

"We're not safe during the day, either," she retorted.

Savven ignored her, taking her hand. She jerked back at the touch before realising it was him and relaxed.

"Where are we going?" She stumbled when he began to pull her behind him, guiding her through the night.

"Fallúin."

She stumbled again, growling in annoyance. "And why didn't we go there in the first place?"

"I was trying to avoid it."

"How lucky for me."

Her muttered words made him want to leave her behind, prophecy or not. "How lucky for you, indeed," he snapped. "But how unlucky for them. Do you know how many villages have burned to ash because of Ezra? How much blood this world has tasted?"

Her silence was answer enough.

"It's just over the riverbed," he grunted, tugging her along.

The shuffle of leaves and whispering wind filled the space between them. The crackle of dead leaves on the forest floor as animals meandered made them both turn at every sound.

Hazen tripped upon small rocks and uplifted roots, though Savven never let her fall. Much as he wanted to.

The village came into Savven's sight. The wooden huts and thatch roofs were visible under the crescent of a new moon. Pulling the girl with him, they silently entered the village, shadowing past the sleeping occupants and deeper into their dwellings.

The village was dark. Lights were scarce save the few candles that flickered in the stables they passed.

Savven could feel Hazen shift behind him when he paused, assessing a small fork in the path. Veering right, their footsteps muted on the dry dirt, they slipped along the sides of the huts like thieves in the night.

There was a small hut with firelight flickering from the window. Savven stopped, eyeing the forest that lay behind them. Unease webbed in his chest, and he pursed his lips, glancing at the girl who stared blindly up at him.

Fist clenching and unclenching, he knocked soundly on the door of the lit hut.

It opened with a slight creak. The pale grey face of a worn, crooked, old goblin peeked through the crack, covered in a map of wrinkles. He had a large hook nose, silver eyes, and white tufts of hair ruffled into an untameable mess.

"Yes?" A snap to his gravel voice, eyes narrowed with suspicion.

Hazen noticed his row of sharply pointed teeth, and she swallowed.

"We need shelter for the night. Might you spare a room?"

The old man glanced behind Savven, glaring at Hazen, sniffing the air.

Seconds stretched too long, making Hazen shift.

"Come in," he said finally, opening the door wide enough for them to step inside. Closing it swiftly after.

Heat coiled around them, welcoming them. The home was small enough, with a simple wooden table and chairs in the middle, a fire roaring in a stone hearth built into the wall, and a separate room concealed by a wooden door. An extensive selection of furs was piled into the corner by the fire.

"Only for the night," he snapped. "I do not share my home with strangers, but I make an exception for High Fae. So, I shall grant you a few hours. You will leave at dawn."

Savven tilted his head in understanding. "My people, thank you."

Not saying a word, the minuscule male wobbled to the connecting door, slamming it shut as he disappeared within. A moment later, a small orange glow could be seen from under the door.

Hazen looked at Savven, questions rambling through her head.

"Goblin," he said in hushed tones, eyeing the furs. "A trades Goblin by the looks of it."

Hazen looked at the small pile, walked over to the skins, and kneeled. Her fingers brushed across them, the fur tickling her palm. Unhooking Dshar's cape, she set it at the foot of the pile before collapsing into the mound. Instantly, warmth wrapped around her.

Savven sat at the table, his deep blue eyes watching her, mouth pressed into a firm line.

Guilt chilled her, and she took in a soft breath. "I'm sorry."

He only stared at her. His body sprawled in the chair, arm resting on the table, head cocked slightly as he studied her.

"I didn't realise how many have died on account of Ezra. On account of me."

He shook his head, turning his attention to the fire. "It's not because of you, Hazen. It's the thought of you. The ideal you bring."

She rose on her elbows, looking at the flames, feeling the heat fill the room, and her cheeks flushed. "Do you want to see it?"

Savven turned to her.

"I didn't know what you were asking before." She stood, walking towards him. "But then I remembered what had happened before I came here. A fever dream, really." She grabbed the chair in front of him and turned it so she could straddle the back.

Savven leaned forward as she removed part of her shirt, slipping her left arm out of the sleeve. Her skin was pale and flawless, with a white strap going around her back. Above it, where the white skin was smooth and untouched, were fading black lines that curved and flowed across her left shoulder.

His hand reached to trace the tattoo, though it hovered over her skin. Like a fading bruise, the faint black and blue wings wove across her skin and shifted when she moved. Veins of fading blue and black curled over her shoulder, collarbone, and down her bicep.

"May I?" he asked softly. She nodded, and he let his fingers trace over the marked skin. She shivered under his cool touch, fingers prodding gently.

"Can I ask you something?"

Savven hummed, studying her shoulder.

"Are there more men like you? You're the first I've seen, and it makes one wonder."

Savven chuckled lowly. "There are no men in this world. No humans. Only males. And yes, there are."

"Hopefully, they're not all as annoying as you are," she quipped, though humour laced her tone.

He smiled despite himself, leaning back into his chair. Hazen fixed her shirt, turning towards him.

"Why does he want me? Why is he searching? Why is he killing all for the sake of finding me?"

Pursing his lips, Savven's eyes focused on the smooth grain of the table. "Because of the prophecy."

"I can't help anyone if I don't know what's happening, Savven."

He sighed, pinching the bridge of his nose. "I know."

Hazen waited, the fire crackling beside them.

Running a hand over his face and through his hair, Savven settled against his seat, watching the fire.

"It was half a century after the battle between the keeper and Balwin, and while our world felt light for the first time in many moons, there was a coldness to it. The wind was warm, but slowly, it became bitter. The colours were vibrant, but slowly, they turned dull. You could see the shift, subtle as it might be.

"Ezra had fought alongside Anabelle in the battle. We all did. While he was never physically injured, he was also never... the same again. The High Fae council was summoned by the Gods. My companions and myself, Anabelle, the Fae kings and queens of all territories, and the spirits of season gathered with the great dragon.

"From there, talk was high about what was to come. While most spoke of agriculture and the growth of villages and their cities, the Gods were silent."

Hazen's brows furrowed. "Why were they silent?"

"Because they were waiting for Tatius." Savven scowled. "The most infuriating God in such a tiny little body."

"Tatius?"

"The God of Immortality. Of life and death."

A shiver of something cold akin to fear went down her spine.

"When Tatius finally spoke, it was like the last of the warmth in this world was doused and smothered. '*Darkness is coming,*' she said, '*lasting darkness*'. Then came the prophecy: '*From shadows and mist, and fire and ash: walls will fall, and darkness will reign. As one is, the other will be. From darkness and light, the world will rise*'." He would never forget those words and how they echoed in the chamber. A promise to them all.

The words of the prophecy filled the small hut, smothering the enveloping heat.

"What does that mean?" Hazen whispered, leaning forward.

"She was fixated on Ezra as she spoke these words, and while none of us knew at the time, some deep-seated part of me, of all of us, knew that fire was coming. But at the time, we didn't know how or by whom.

"Word spread and rumours grew as the Fae kings and queens told their villages and cities to prepare. Prepare for what? We didn't know. The years slipped away, and those preparations grew lax. And as those years passed, Ezra slowly disappeared until death started to follow him. Fires burned villages, slowly at first, until whole cities began to crumple under his demand."

Hazen's face paled. Remembering the story of the boy, her heart hurt for the male beside her. It had been his story.

"Not all know of the prophecy. Some went into hiding deep within the earth after their villages were destroyed. There they stayed, cut off from the rest of us. But that's why Ezra looks for you. Because after she spoke the prophecy, she told us that a woman would come from across the veil. Not a female. But a human woman, chosen by dragons, the descendant of High Fae long forgotten."

Hazen fisted her hands in her lap, palms clammy. Licking her lips, she took in a shaking breath. "He doesn't know who he's looking for, so he kills everyone, hoping they might be the one?"

Savven nodded slowly. "He did. But now he knows you've come. The shift is powerful magic. When one enters through the veil, the world will know."

After a moment, Hazen looked at Savven. Firelight flickering in her wide hazel eyes. "I'm sorry."

He sighed, his face grim. "So am I."

Nazar trailed the sharp point of his nail across a pale neck, staring at the face of a hunter. Fifteen tall, brutishly large and muscled High Fae warriors stood, uniformed, waiting for his order. They were dressed in all black with swords and axes strapped across their backs and anchored to their hips. Their eyes pitch black, focused ahead and blank. Perfect little puppets.

The near dawn sky was glittering with stars above them, a crescent moon barely lighting the top of the castle where they stood nestled at the centre ledge of the mountain ridge. The dark forest around them wavering like a black sea in the night.

His smile gleamed, and Nazar dragged his tongue across the small nick in the hunter's throat before him. The hunter did not flinch even when Nazar licked up his blood and hummed with delight.

"How easy it would be to drink from you," he whispered darkly. "*All* of you."

The hunters didn't move, and Nazar chuckled lowly.

Shadows gathered beneath his feet, building like whispering mist around them until they gathered like a wall at the ledge of the castle. A deadly drop to the floor below, waiting on the other side.

"Let us make haste," he said, red eyes glowing. "We wouldn't want to keep them waiting any longer."

The hunters said nothing, their answering footfalls orderly as they marched into the mist. Vanishing.

Nazar watched as they walked into the darkness one by one, falling behind the last hunter as he stepped into the portal. The world shifted, and there was nothing but a void sea before the air cleared, and they were standing by a wide river with the forest behind them.

He sniffed the air, inhaling deeply the sweet scent of life.

"Sleeping souls," he said almost gleefully.

The sky was starting to lighten as dawn fast approached. Nazar's red eyes darkened with the thought of fresh blood, and his smile cut across his face. "Leave no one alive. Burn them. Burn it all."

CHAPTER 17

A distant scream split the air, and Hazen jolted awake. Heart hammering, her breathing came in sharp bursts as she scrambled to her feet, adrenaline pulsating through her limbs. Savven stood at the small window, short blade held in a tight grip.

The fire cracked, and Hazen's head whipped to it, exhaling sharply. Another distant scream, pained and broken, followed before it fell silent.

"Savy—"

Savven held up a hand, and she fell silent.

An eerie calm settled in the air, and she moved slowly to his side, looking out the window. Her breathing was too loud in her ears, and she thought her heart might tear from her chest, hands shaking with anticipation.

Dawn had barely tinted the sky in indigo shades, and the village was quiet as if the screams were only figments of their imaginations. A black fog crawled across the grounds, only seen as it slithered over a lit window and slipped inside like a thief.

Hazen glanced at Savven only to see his jaw flex, nostrils flaring, his eyes fixated on the fog.

Movement flickered in the corner of her eyes, and Hazen watched in horror as figures slipped through the shadows and into the dwelling where the fog had entered. A female's scream, muffled and startled from sleep, also went silent.

Savven gripped her arm, face hard and eyes set. "Be quiet, be quick, and do as I say."

She didn't speak, jerking her head.

Savven reached for the door. "Stay close."

And then they were out in the open, the small hut and its few moments of warmth left behind as crisp dawn air swept across their skin. Hazen blinked in the darkness, eyes adjusting to the dim light.

Savven paused, glancing at the creeping shadows and the bodies that slipped through them. Gesturing, they walked quickly across a forking path, slipping around the curved edge of a hut.

The ground squelched under her feet, and Hazen held her breath. It hadn't rained. She looked down slowly, her chest rising rapidly.

Savven touched her shoulder, garnering her attention. He shook his head, face grim. "Don't look."

He waved her forward as a body slinked past them in the opposite direction. Hazen made to move, but before she did, she couldn't help looking down. A strangled sound choked in her throat, and she clasped a hand over her mouth to muffle it.

Wide, unseeing eyes and mouth gaping was a lone female head. Golden hair splayed across the sopping ground.

Fire lit up the night, and a thousand screams suddenly rang like a death knell. Fear clawed across her skin, her stomach dropping, and Hazen's feet stumbled back, eyes watching the huts that burned hot and bright around her.

"We have to go!" Savven's sharp voice broke the screams, his grip tight on her bicep and then she was stumbling behind him as they ran.

Fire and smoke and the smell of burning flesh surrounded them. Her chest slammed into Savven's back when he halted, a body stumbling from a hut, screaming and clawing at the flames that melted their flesh and ate at their bones.

Bile rose in her throat, but Hazen forced it down. Ash rained like snow in the dawning sky, coating her arms, hair, and face. The smoke was thick as thatch roofs ignited and collapsed. The screaming, though, the screaming filled the air until she thought her eardrums would shatter.

Something wrapped around her ankle, burning her skin, and she was jerked back. Falling to her knees, her nails dug into the wet earth. "Savven!" she screamed. Lashing out, her foot kicked at what held her, hair slashing across her cheeks as she whipped her body around. The shadow had latched around her ankle, shackling her. A massive male fell from the shadows, a large bloody sword held high.

She threw herself to the left, the binding around her ankle tightening and threatening to snap her bones. The sword cut deep into the ground beside her, and Hazen's eyes went wide when it hurled back up, cutting the air—

Savven barricaded her body with his, parrying the blow with his blade. Dancing around the male, his dark hair flying, he struck quickly—a stab to the throat.

Blood slipped down the male's chin, gurgling on it with every straining breath. Savven jerked the blade free, and the hunter fell to his knees, toppling sideways.

Light flared from him, and he shot it towards the shadows. The skin of her ankle burned, and the fog seemed to hiss as it released her.

"Get up!" He didn't wait for her, grabbing her by the wrist and pulling them through billowing clouds of smoke.

Where are you? The shadows seemed to whisper as they melded with the smoke and ash. *Where are you?*

Fear went down her spine, but she sealed herself away even when the whispers and shadows grew. Digging her feet into the ground and sprinting her way through the village. Hazen jumped out of the path of a falling hut as it came careening towards her. Savven grabbed her wrist and tugged her sharply behind him.

They were nearing the river, the sound of flowing water barely cutting through the cries that wanted to mark themselves into the forest like a permanent echo.

A sobbing voice made her want to stop.

"Help us!"

She glanced over her shoulder, seeing terrified eyes locked on her. A hand outstretched and seeking. A male holding onto a limp female, clasped close to his chest.

"Help us!" he begged in a hoarse voice. Pleading.

His words broke her, and she made to take a step back to help them, but then she remembered Savven.

"What about the people?" she cried, running to catch up to him. The riverbed was just beyond their reach.

Savven ignored her.

They made their way across the watery divide, Hazen slipping over rocks, her body shivering from the icy dregs pulsating around them. Savven had shielded them from the wet current when they entered, but now the cool temperatures made her limbs lock, and her skirt weigh heavy.

Relief coursed through her when they made it to the other side. Shivering and teeth chattering, Hazen tried to move swiftly, following Savven as he slid to a small hill mound. The screams beyond them were numerous, and Hazen felt as if she were still in the mouth of the terrorised village.

Fingers digging into the grassy dirt, they watched as bodies were cut down—males, females, and children alike fell to the ground in bloody, burning heaps. Shadows and the things that came from it tore through the village like an enraged beast.

"We can't just leave them," Hazen bit out.

Savven turned to her sharply. "We can and we will."

"You're a monster," she spat.

"What do you suggest I do?" He cocked his head, eyes narrowing.

Hazen bit her lip, looking at the burning village. There was nothing he could do. Not by himself. But it felt wrong. Leaving them felt dirty as if she was no better than the shadows that burned the village.

"Many more will have to die before this ends," he said softly as if understanding her thoughts.

Remorse settled in her chest, and she frowned. "That doesn't make it right."

"No," he concurred. "But if you want peace, then it's what must happen."

A flash of brilliant white caught her eye, and she and Savven turned to the village as a thin figure appeared. Blood-red eyes glowed in the fire amid all the chaos, ashen skin stark in the dawn hours, smoke clouding around him, a smile on his face as he watched the village turn to ash and blood.

Savven grabbed Hazen's hand and tugged her down the mound, urgency in his steps. "Run, Hazen," he whispered sharply. "Run!"

Even with dawn overhead, the forest was dark, and Hazen stumbled blindly. Savven's hand latched on hers and hauled her forward.

"Who was that?" she called, breathless.

"Nazar!"

Branches clawed at her skin and clothes and hair, bleary light beginning to penetrate through the treetops.

Hazen's breath was ragged when she asked, "Who is Nazar?!"

Savven's reply was curt. "A shade."

They didn't look back, but a final mangled scream cut through Hazen's ragged breathing and silence fell in the forest.

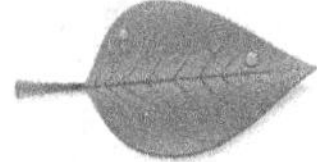

Nazar nudged the half-detached head of one of the hunters with the toe of his shoe. Blood staining his jaw and neck, black eyes unseeing, and his neck gaping open.

Thunder boomed.

He looked up at the rolling grey sky that dampened the dawn, rain sputtering down. The fire hissed around them, whispering a name in their burning tendrils, and Nazar looked back down at the body. The rest of the hunters stood at his back, standing at attention, waiting.

A low hiss slipped through his teeth, and an animalistic screech ripped from his chest. His dark pets within, pulsing against his bones and flesh.

Hair plastered to his sunken face, he turned slitted eyes to the hunters. A village of ash and smouldering piles of what was left lay scattered around them. The blackened flesh of the slain lay like raised mounds in the earth. The ground saturated in their blood.

Nazar smiled softly. *Life* no longer filled the air. It was death that coated his tongue and made his demons sing.

The rain pelted them, and he blinked through the steam that rose. "Blood, and bones, bones and blood," he muttered quietly. Sniffing the air, he could smell *her* through the charred flesh, death, and ash. Smell her life like a rotting flower. Beautiful but decaying. So *human.*

He laughed lowly. Human. He had not feasted on a human in many centuries.

A new type of hunger licked at his bones, and a pointed smile pulled across his mouth.

The wind blew softly, and that sweet, sweet decay made his mouth water. He turned his head to the north as he picked up the faint smell of desperation, the sound of a beating heart echoing from the woods. The sound of a mortal life.

"Find her."

The hunters shifted, and as one, they marched through the billowing steam clouds, rain pelting them from above.

As the hunters disappeared, a raven cawed once and took flight into the storm.

CHAPTER 18

Dark brooding forest surrounded them as the trees grew dense. Tall, thick pillars with black bark and shadowed branches hovered around them. Screeches could be heard in the distance, hidden eyes watching as they tread quietly.

Hazen shivered as her still-damp skirt brushed her legs, wrapping her arms around her waist to preserve the last of her body heat. They had been walking for hours. Or so it felt. Time had mended together, and Hazen could no longer tell the difference between a second, a minute, and an hour. They had run until there was nothing but space between them and the desolate village, and when Hazen couldn't run anymore, she pleaded for rest. But they didn't rest. They couldn't stop, so they continued, slowing to a brisk walk instead.

Savven's shoulders were tense, his eyes constantly roving over every crevice and shadow they passed. Whispers moved through the dense foliage, pricking their ears in every direction, their nerves on high alert.

The sun had disappeared behind angry, turbulent clouds, taking with it its warmth. Rain, at one point in their journey, had come pissing down, and heavy fog made its home in their vision. Savven had to take her by hand to guide her as she tripped over roots, rock, and air.

But the deeper they went, even the fog and rain fled the dreary, damp, isolated woods. Long strands of grey moss hung from the trees and waved like forlorn ghosts, and what little light there was glowed dimly through the tangle of branches.

Savven stopped, and Hazen approached his side, looking at him.

"What is it?" she whispered, eyeing their surroundings.

He shook his head, his gaze narrowing on something ahead of them. Hazen followed his line of sight, but there was nothing there—only trees, moss, and a creeping sensation that left an oily sheen on her senses.

"Something isn't right," he uttered.

She swallowed, shifting her feet as Savven waved a hand through the air. The air shimmered faintly.

"What was that," she breathed.

"A veil." Face grim, recognition flickered in his eyes, and light wreathed his hand as he shot it into the forest. "*Nochdadh.*"

The light cut through the air at his foreign command, and the world wavered until it fell apart like mist.

A large wall of black and grey branches webbed together in a thick, unyielding barricade. Cutting through their path for as far as Hazen could see, it was as tall as the trees around them, its pinnacle unseen.

Something ticked along the fortress from the other side, like nails dragging over dead wood. Hazen shifted uneasily, forcing herself to remain steadfast.

"Welcome to The Forest of Lost Souls."

"How comforting," she muttered. "Remind me why we're here?"

Savven was preternatural still as he eyed the wall before them.

"The forest finds the one it wants to enter. This world has laws it must obey, but this forest commands itself. It follows no natural law and order."

"I feel so lucky," she said dryly.

"We didn't have a choice. Every turn and path we chose was unknowingly guiding us here."

Hazen shivered, bringing her hands to her mouth and blowing hot air into her cupped hands, rubbing them together. Savven stepped forward, and she followed.

"What about the veil?"

"It was only for show. If the forest wanted to keep me out, Naleen could have done so easily."

"Naleen?"

Savven pointed to an old torn tree trunk, twisted and decaying. It had long lost its branches; the jagged ends stretched into the wall behind it, weaving tightly between the branches. "The Queen of the Lost Forest and one of the four Gods of this world."

At his words, the mangled tree trunk crunched and tore, the centre opened to a hollow alcove, and out stepped a beautiful female. Fair green skin glimmered with gold dust along slender limbs, and pale mossy eyes sparkled with curiosity as her cherry blossom hair created a splash of colour in the dreary forest.

She stepped lightly onto the dirt, dark purple flowers gathered in her hair, leaves draped over her hips like a skirt. Her torso was bare, her firm breasts covered by the long waves of her hair that hung to her navel. She was beautiful in a way that disturbed Hazen, like a creature from one of her childhood fairy tales.

"A human in my forest?" Her voice was rich and melodic as she peered slowly between them. Her sights fixed on Hazen, and light filled those green eyes. "Hello, Hazen."

"You know my name?" she questioned quietly.

"I know all things in this world. I hear all things and see all things."

"Except when it comes to the pleadings of your people." Savven's sudden bitterness made Hazen look at him.

Naleen turned hard eyes to meet Savven's. Power radiating from her slight body as she stepped closer to him. "Your hatred for us is garnered by your guilt. Do not blame us for the wrongdoings of the ones we have given free will to."

Savven bared his teeth at the God, and Hazen finally stepped back.

"You let him take one of your *precious* creatures," he spat. "You let him burn our cities and villages and people!"

Thunder boomed, and her green eyes darkened. "We cannot disobey the Fae laws!"

Savven's mouth pursed, and Hazen's eyes bounced between the God, Savven, and the unseen sky overhead.

After a moment, Savven jerked his head. "Apologies."

Naleen tilted her head, her face softening. "Do not let their deaths turn your senses black, Prince. Evil does not only come in the form of the harm we do to others but also the harm we do to ourselves." She turned to Hazen, regarding her. "You have much to learn. You are naive to our world and the one you are about to enter. My forest does not let just anyone enter, especially those who do not belong. This is your path, Hazen. Take heed with where you traverse beyond this wall."

Hazen nodded slowly, her gaze sliding to the tangle of branches.

"But beware, if you find yourself lost and the path unclear, my children might find you to be a delicious meal... and that would be unfortunate."

Her warning sent Hazen's nerves scattering, and she nodded again, rolling her shoulders back.

Amusement flickered faintly in her eyes as Naleen lifted a hand. The wall of branches groaned and snapped, splitting until a gap formed wide enough for them to slip through one at a time.

Savven paused at the entrance, looking at the female. Age-old emotions gathered in his eyes, fleeting through so many Hazen could barely keep count of them.

"The shade is following us." The warning was direct but quiet.

Naleen regarded Savven, humming in thought. "Go quickly now; time does not wait for the living when among the dead."

They slipped inside, Hazen following quickly behind Savven, who stalked into the whispering darkness, his blade now in hand.

The wall began to move, creaking and moaning, and Hazen

whirled to watch it until their way out was sealed, and they had no choice but to move forward.

"That was... dramatic," Hazen commented after a moment of silence.

Savven grunted, keeping his eyes on the path ahead.

"She looks like spring, and this place looks like death."

His chuckle made her brows raise.

"If you met Spring, you would understand their differences."

"There's an actual Spring?"

Savven hummed.

Hazen sniffed, watching his back in front of her. "Interesting."

"Naleen is a God. There are four Gods and four Spirits of seasons. The Spirits were created by the Gods who created this world and the dragons who breathed life into its core. Naleen is known by many as the Lady of the Earth. Taking care of both the living and dead."

"So," Hazen inquired, "she guards this forest because..."

"Because when the dead still roam, the living will die. Naleen keeps them contained for all our sakes."

A howl of despair came from deep within the woods. Hazen stared at her surroundings with wide eyes.

"Time moves differently here, Hazen. Hours can be days, and days can become centuries. Keep close, and *don't* wander."

CHAPTER 19

"Come, pretty bird." Ezra outstretched his arm to the torrent sky, and a sleek, rain-sodden raven glided from above. Latching its talons into his arm, Ezra petted a finger down its back, cooing to the animal.

Néefar crossed his arms over his chest, leaning against the stone altar. Rain drenched the loose black linen of the shirt he now wore, his black leather pants blessedly dry, deterring the water.

"Are we talking to animals now, Ezra? Have we fallen so low?" Néefar asked, bored.

Ezra's eyes turned black as he turned them on Néefar, watching him as he whispered to the raven. "Tell me your secrets, pretty bird. Let me see what you have seen."

The raven cawed, head tilting. Ezra's face went slack, eyes racing side to side. And then the raven screeched, thunder following as if in answer. Ezra's low chuckle made Néefar shift, and Ezra smiled, hand latching around the bird's neck. Then he tore it off.

Néefar contained his grimace when the creature's pained screech was silenced. Blood dripped down Ezra's hand, he lifted the open neck above his mouth, letting it pour down his throat.

When he was done, Ezra discarded the bird, its head rolling across the ground.

"Yummy," Néefar muttered under his breath.

Ezra ignored him, breathing deeply through his nose, his black eyes fixated on the headless body before slowly dragging to Néefar. "He… is… a *fool*," he whispered.

"Who?" Néefar asked, raising a brow.

"Nazar," he hissed. Rage bubbled within those black eyes, teeth bared and blood stained. Ezra's nostrils flared once before he composed himself. "It should take little effort to catch a human, yet she evades even a shade."

Ezra lowered his head in thought. The air shifted, and he looked up at Néefar through lowered brows, thunder booming. "I will send the one who comes and goes like air. Who is dreams and nightmares and death."

Néefar ticked a brow, eyeing the castle top and the sprawling forest around it. "Don't leave me in suspense, Ezra."

"He wouldn't dream of it."

A low, seductive voice brushed Néefar's ear, and the shifter whipped around.

Cold, light blue eyes smiled wickedly up at Néefar. Full lips tilted into a Cheshire smile as Mara stroked a ghostly white hand down his chest, her sable brown hair gleaming in soft waves down her back.

Néefar recoiled from the succubus, baring his teeth in a snarl. "Mara!" he spat.

Mara's grin turned feral. *"Hello, Shifter, it's been a while."*

"Not long enough," he snarled, reigning in the magic in him that wanted to shift and tear out her throat.

Her voice was breathy as she chuckled, pulling down the low scoop of her sheer white gown, exposing her breasts and the silver scar that ran between them. *"Your precious Anabelle thought she could kill me with that cute little trick."* She pressed herself to Néefar, dragging an ice-cold hand along his bottom lip. *"But nothing can kill what's already dead."*

He refused to jerk back, even when she laughed and slipped through him, walking over to Ezra.

"Hello, Mara," he said, eyeing the succubus.

She tilted her head at Ezra. *"You called?"*

"It seems I need a female's touch."

Mara laughed, low and throaty. Dragging a hand down Ezra's body, she grazed the front of his pants. *"Why didn't you say so?"*

Ezra's hands latched around her wrist, shadows seeping from his pores and up her arm, and he twisted until the succubus screeched. "Find. The. Human. And. Kill. Her," he seethed through clenched teeth.

Mara stumbled when Ezra tossed her back and the shadows released her arm. She glared at him, drawing herself up, arm clenched to her chest. *"As you command,"* she whispered, voice turning venomous.

"She travels through your home. Should be easy enough."

Mara's eyes turned to ice shards, and her sly smile returned, her body dispersing into mist.

Néefar looked at the spot where the succubus had been, raising his gaze to Ezra.

Ezra waved a hand to the sky, and a shadow raven took flight towards the Forest of Lost Souls.

Nazar's hand twitched, fingers curling. Red eyes scanned the wet forest and the barricaded wall of branches and brambles before him, the hunters standing at his back waiting for his command. He tilted his head up, sniffing the air. A sly smile cut his mouth, and he wet his lips. "Come out, *Mara.*"

A low, sultry chuckle slipped around him like a phantom.

"I didn't know a little human girl would be so hard for you to catch, Nazar."

Nazar's hiss filled the air. "She will be dead before sundown."

"Yes, because of me." Her body formed in front of him, and her smile was placating. *"Looks like you've been replaced."*

He snarled, hand going for her throat, but she vanished, her voice whispering in his ear. *"Go back to your master, Nazar, and let the big girls play."*

The hunters didn't move, even when Nazar's screech shook the forest.

Darkness seemed to seep from the very ground they walked on, stalking behind them with every step they took. The growth around them became dense, and the road through the crawling forest narrow. Bushes with berries of deep blue hanging from their limbs were accompanied by two-inch, blood-red thorns with needle points that threatened them as they passed by. Moss-covered vines hung from tree limbs. Branches acted like talons, gripping their clothes as they passed, trying to pull them deeper into the growth and away from the path.

"We'll rest here for a moment."

Hazen's eyes snapped to Savven, having been watching a long green tail slither behind a bush.

"Are you sure we should stop?"

Savven raised a brow; his silence was answer enough, and she rolled her eyes.

Rubbing a hand over the back of her neck, she dropped to the ground, stretching her legs out in front of her with a groan. Her emotions played to her disadvantage when she heard every snap of a twig and every howl in the distance. After the first couple hours, she stopped jerking her head around whenever something moved behind her, but it left her neck tight. She rolled her head back, the tension easing.

Savven kept his eyes straight ahead, even when something screeched from the darkness covering the path they had already travelled. Hazen's head swivelled to the noise.

"Relax."

Hazen's eyes fell away from the dancing shadows to stare at Savven. "What?"

"Relax, you need to stay focused."

Hazen sniffed. "Paranoia goes hand in hand with being focused." She was hyper-focused on *everything*.

With a deep, calming breath, Hazen leaned against the smooth, blood-red tree behind her. Dark moss covered the roots and crawled up its base, where she leaned her head.

Hazen picked at a loose thread in her skirt, wishing she hadn't left Dshar's cape back in the village. Shivering at the cool mist that coated her exposed skin. "Can you imagine spending an eternity just wandering this place with no end in sight?"

"A fate worse than death, for only the most damning creatures."

Hazen looked at him as he closed his eyes in concentration. Savven reached out into thin air and produced a purple fruit. It was orange around the bottom, and it darkened to deep purple as it progressed.

He broke it in half; a small flame burst from the centre, leaving a juicy middle weeping over the sides. Savven handed half to Hazen while he took a bite out of the other. "Fire fruit," he explained when she eyed it sceptically, sniffing the centre. "It's usually found only in the deepest regions of the old dragon caves. I'm lucky enough to know they also grow in one other land: this forest."

Hazen took a small tentative bite, tasting it. Rich and exotic flavours erupted on her taste buds, filling her mouth with spices and a sweetness that warmed her entire body.

Something snapped behind them, and Hazen dropped the fruit, her back going rigid. The fruit vanished before it hit the ground.

Savven sighed, finishing his half before he stood. Dusting his hands off, he looked around them before stooping and picking up a long fallen branch. It cracked as he snapped it in half, holding out one of the pieces to her.

"I'm sure that's delicious, Savven, but I'm all full now. Thanks, though." She patted her stomach, despite its annoyed grumbling, eyeing the branch with scepticism.

His impatient sigh was enough to make her stand and purse her lips, taking the half held out to her.

"You need a distraction."

"Kind of you to notice." She twirled the stick in her hand. It was heavy but not too heavy, and she poked Savven with it. Hazen giggled when he glared at her, smacking her stick with his own.

"Look at my feet."

She did, noticing his staggered stance.

"Mirror me."

Her brows shot towards her hairline, and she watched his right foot cross behind his left and his left cross over his right, circling her. She did the same, tripping over her feet as she went.

"Bollocks," she muttered.

"Keep your core tight and the weight on the balls of your feet." He demonstrated.

She did as he said, shifting and turning and crossing her feet over each other. Her calves flexed under the new workout, and her muscles ached happily.

Savven lifted his stick, so she followed. Staring down the end, eyeing the male before her.

"Defend yourself." It was his only warning before he swung, his blow quick, and she yelped when his branch smacked the fleshy side of her waist.

"What the fuck?" she demanded.

He tilted his head. "I told you to defend yourself."

She groaned.

"Again."

And so it went. Savven played the offensive while she attempted the defence. By the time they were done, her limbs shook, and she yawned with exhaustion.

Hazen collapsed onto the soft, mossy ground with a groan. "That sucked." But it had also been fun and helped ease the tension she had been feeling. Though she would rather eat the branch than admit that to him.

"But it was necessary."

She looked at him through tired eyes, a thick white fog rolling across her body, her limbs disappearing. "Because I couldn't relax?" she mocked.

"Because I won't let the same mistake happen twice."

His voice was bitter, and Hazen's brow furrowed, yawning despite herself. "What do you mean?"

"My cousin was ill-prepared due to unfortunate circumstances. Unfair disadvantage led to many being killed in such a short time." His dark blue eyes finally looked at her. "That won't happen again."

She yawned again, her eyes growing heavy.

"Sleep, I'll keep watch."

But even as he said that and her eyes closed, the thick fog rolled up his chest, and Savven yawned. He frowned, making to stand, but his limbs were leaden, and his mind was stumbling into an abyss.

Savven growled, but all that came out was a low breath before his eyes slid shut despite his efforts, and he fell into a void.

Mara hummed a soft, lulling tune, hovering above the unconscious girl. *"So sweet, so unsuspecting. My favourite."* She dragged a finger down her cheek, feeling the warmth of life beneath her cool skin. A soul thrummed behind those human bones, a soul she wanted to taste.

The girl groaned, tossing her head. Mara smiled slightly, dragging her nails across the girl's mouth.

"Let me in, Little Human. Let me feast," she whispered.

Eyes clamped shut, the girl frowned in her sleep. "No," she muttered in a hoarse voice.

"A fighter?" Mara's brow ticked in amusement, leaning forward to brush her lips across the girl's eyes. *"Fight all you want, but your magic cannot outlast me."* Mara's fingers dug into her jaw, nails sinking beneath flesh as she began to pry open the girl's mouth.

The girl's eyes snapped open. "No!" Her voice dragged out of her as if she were fighting her way through the realm of dreams back to reality.

A gentle finger laid on her lips, hushing her protests. A thick fog rolled over the girl's body, her limbs relaxing despite her eyes straining to stay open. *"Don't fight it. I promise you eternal pleasure,"* she cooed softly, her other hand still hinged in the girl's jaw.

"Who are you?" she choked out.

A smile ghosted across Mara's face. *"I am the Lover of Dreams and the Giver of Pleasure."* Mara leaned forward, her mouth hovering over the girl's. *"Now let me in,"* she breathed across her lips.

"No—"

Mara slanted her lips over the girls, silencing her protests. Her vapour form created a dewy veil over the girl's skin, and she watched with wicked intent as the girl's eyes widened, her body jerking in response.

Mara's cheeks hollowed, and she placed her hands on either side of the girl's face and pressed closer and closer until they were one.

The girl's mouth gaped open as Mara slipped inside. Staggered, panting breaths filled the fog-laden air. Her body crumbled in on itself as her bones grew cold, knives stabbing at her insides. Her skin became ashen, and her eyes rolled to the back of her head as Mara feasted on the mortal soul within.

CHAPTER 20

Savven beat against the barrier in his mind, teeth bared in rage. Dark magic lay over him, and he searched the depths of his subconscious state, searching for his own tether of magic. Light flared, and he grasped the bright, searing cord within him.

His eyes flew open as the barrier collapsed, and he jolted up.

Thick, rolling tendrils of white fog whispered over his chest, and he stood, searching for Hazen among the coverage. A sliver of light brown hair peeked through a gap before disappearing.

"Disperse!" he snarled in his native tongue, waving a quick hand over the clouds. At the command of the High Fae language, the fog dissipated.

Savven's eyes narrowed, kneeling beside Hazen. Something was not right about her. His hand grazed her cheek, and he withdrew it quickly. Her skin was ice cold.

He noticed her sunken eyes and ashen skin, blue and purple veins showing through the transparent layer.

Savven swore. "Hazen!" he said firmly, his tone demanding. He grabbed her by the shoulders and shook.

She didn't respond except with a small, barely audible whimper.

Swiftly, he used the sharp edge of his canine and made a small incision in his left arm. Gripping the back of Hazen's head, he pressed the open wound to her mouth. Blood slipped past her gaping mouth as he fed life into her.

Setting her head down. He healed his wound and pressed his mouth to Hazen's frozen lips. A small light illuminated between them as he fed his essence to hers.

A shrill, piercing scream bit the air, and Savven pulled back as Hazen's eyes flew open, and she gasped for air, blood gathering in the corner of her mouth.

Savven's attention was on the female hovering in the shadows, fury and hunger etched on her beautiful face, twisting it into something ugly.

"Mara!" he spat, his eyes flashing dangerously as he stood, facing her.

Mara's sheer dress floated around her, pressing against her naked frame as the fog began to crawl up her body. *"Hello, Elf Prince. Did you like my little trick?"* she asked, giving him a coy smile, reaching out a hand wreathed in thick white fog.

"Go back to the dark hole you crawled out of!" Savven said through clenched teeth.

She pouted, batting her eyes at him. *"But I was just starting to enjoy myself. She is so delicious."*

His blade dropped from its chamber up his sleeve, and he pulled it out, pointing it at the succubus. "Anabelle failed to kill you, but I won't."

Mara huffed, clicking her tongue in annoyance. *"You're no fun, but lucky for you I'm in no mood to be stabbed again."* She rolled her eyes and wafted into the mist surrounding them, leaving nothing but frost and the reaches of death's near hands behind.

Hazen coughed violently, rolling onto her side, her fingers

digging into the dirt. Savven rushed to her side.

Her body trembled violently, and he cursed under his breath. "We need to get you out of here."

"I-I don't kno-know what happened. She just *appeared!*" Hazen stuttered before throwing up clear liquid.

Savven sighed, glancing at the forest briefly. Shadows crawled closer to them, smelling death in the air as it clung to Hazen. She was going to die if he didn't get her out of the dark forest. He stared at their path, seeing a fork in the distance. The forest had many ends, though one could take you back to the beginning. A circle. A never-ending end.

Gripping her bicep, he stood and pulled her with him, slipping an arm around her waist when she began to collapse. "You need to stay awake," he commanded. The arm holding her jerked, and her eyes startled open.

Hazen's body swayed, but she nodded limply, leaning against Savven.

Savven bore most of her weight as they began to walk.

"What... wa-was she?" Hazen gasped out in a short breath.

A clammy layer of sweat coated her skin, and her body got heavier with every step they took. Savven pursed his lips and swept his other arm under her legs, carrying her. She sagged against his chest, her body trembling.

"She is mastered by no one. She is mist and air itself. A demon that steals the dreams of any who let her in willingly or unwillingly. Playing to their desires, leaving nothing but a hollow shell when she's finished. She is a harbinger of death. I'm guessing Ezra sent her because Nazar failed to kill us."

Hazen's head rolled back, nodding limply with each step he took. His heart raced with fear for the first time since he met her, and he quickened his pace.

The poison Mara had seeded was beginning to spread. His essence could only fight off death's kiss for so long before Hazen succumbed. Pressing her close to him, he began to run.

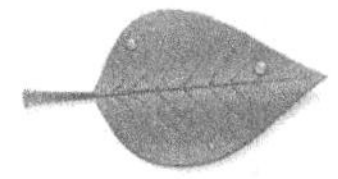

Savven shoved through the forest's tangled walls, branches webbing together in impossible knots. Clawing at their clothes and hair, he gritted his teeth, yanking his snaggled strands free. He had been running for hours and could feel her body become a brick of ice in his arms. Her head lolling, mouth agape, eyes and skin no other shade than that of death.

A ragged struggle came from her parted lips as she took in a shallow breath, striving to put oxygen into her body. Limbs shaking under his hands, her body contracted, and she jerked suddenly, back arching. Savven's grip slipped, and she collapsed on the dirt as he fell to the earth beside her.

He watched her fingers carve into the forest floor. Her body subconsciously curled in on itself as it began to tremble. Savven stooped to pick her up, and she screamed out in protest from the slight touch. He glanced around desperately, his eyes sweeping over the dark spaces.

The shadows crowded around them, and he hissed, throwing light into the darkness.

A girl stepped through the gap in the shadows, and Savven reared his magic forward without thought. The girl tilted her head and deflected the blow easily. Laughing lightly, she stepped closer, Savven's nostrils flared as he stood and blocked Hazen's body with his own.

"Tatius," he whispered.

She tilted her head in regard. Her eyes were as black and bottomless as a pit, narrowing in amusement, accentuating her sharp adolescent features. "Well, look at that, exactly as I want her," she commented softly.

"*Dead?*" Savven hissed.

Her plush yet thin, pale lips tilted into a crooked smile, hooking her jet-black hair behind one ear. Her eyes flickered to Hazen's body hidden behind his. "Death becomes all, Prince. And from it the immortal shall rise, and fire and ash will burn the skies."

Savven's mouth pinched in irritation at the small God's riddles. Stepping to the side and allowing her to see Hazen when she gestured for him to move.

Tatius's bare feet poked from the bottom of her long black

gown. She fell to her knees and swept a hand over Hazen's pale face. Lifting her other hand, palm up, she presented to Savven two small purple berries.

"Spirit berries for the dead. One for the death that lingers around her soul, and the other to restore the blood of her blood."

Savven opened his mouth but clamped it shut when he watched her slip them pass Hazen's lips.

Tatius calmed a hand over Hazen's brow, easing the tension that folded the middle. "When you wake, the world will be waiting for you. Do not disappoint me," she whispered.

She stood and looked at Savven, who pursed his lips, glaring at her.

"Don't give me that look, Prince," she chastised.

"Knowing you can't kill me right now because you need me is my only comfort when I say you are the most irritating God I have ever met."

Tatius picked at her nails, deigning him a sly glance. "The most? My eternal soul thanks you for the compliment," she purred, her smile cat-like in response.

Hazen muttered incoherent sounds under her breath, and the two looked at her. She had stopped trembling, turning as still as the dead. When he knelt beside her, she didn't scream at his touch.

"I've cleared the path for you," Tatius stated, her black eyes fixated on Savven. "*Don't* mess this up."

She vanished in a blink, and Savven shook his head, letting out an irritated grunt. "The most annoying," he muttered under his breath.

Cradling her foetal body close to his, he stood. The shadows that had crowded them were gone, and the path ahead was clear. So, he ran.

Entangled branches scratched at Savven's clothing as he desperately tried to get free of the woods holding them hostage. Their spindly, finger-like limbs clawed their way towards them in a desperate attempt to keep them trapped forever.

Savven picked up his pace, his feet pounding almost silently against the earth as he fled down the narrow path, Hazen held tightly in his arms. He only saw the road before him, and with a burst of speed through the tangles of limbs, a dim light filtering through them, he forced his way out of the woods.

Light bathed their skin, and heat flooded across clammy limbs. Savven let out a ragged breath he had been holding.

The forest behind them contrasted heavily as its dark and brooding gleam ended abruptly, and the gentleness of the mountains before them began.

Savven closed his eyes, taking a deep breath before readjusting Hazen in his arms. Her head rolled into the crook of his shoulder. He peered down at her still face, her ashen skin stark in the sunlight.

The Nal'lian Mountains lay ahead. Two jagged stone pinnacles framed the mouth of the mountains on the other side of the vibrant moor.

Steeling himself, Savven pushed on. Long swaying wheat grass feathered across his hips, a path cutting through the field behind him.

The sound of water trickling filled his ears when he finally stepped through the mouth of the mountain. A lush green gully wound a path through its middle. Rocks, pebbles, ferns, and massive green shrubbery overtook him on either side. Streams of fresh water cascaded from the sides of rocky walls, creating a slick surface despite his sure feet as the water dribbled across the pebbled floor.

The colours were vibrant in the thicket of the mountain, with flowers and trees that bred low-hanging fruit in shades of orange and red. So opposing to the realm of the dammed they had nearly succumbed to.

Spray from the cascading water filled the air with a wet mist that clung to Savven's skin. Warm, humid wind pushed at his back as he climbed the steep ascent ahead.

Hazen stirred in his arms, groaning. Her face contorted in pain.

Savven held her tighter, feeling the heat radiating from her body.

A small white bird with a yellow breast perched on a branch above him, chirping.

"Water!" he cried to it in his native tongue.

It tilted its head once, chirping again, and the bird flew off.

They were surrounded by water, but he needed more than just what fell from the side of rocks and between crevices.

He tightened his hold on her despite her small whimpers and fled after the bird. Away from the known path and into the dense brush.

Néefar's eyes darted around him as he slipped into the shadows along the wall of the grand hall. The space was empty, and his steps filled it with whispered sounds.

He crept along the last obsidian pillar, watching the hall before he went for the towering doors and slipped through them.

The mountain was silent, the narrow passage eating up his footfalls. Wind roared in the distance from the mouth of an entrance at the top of a set of stairs. He took them two at a time, glancing over his shoulder until he was in a cave. The world opened at the cavern mouth, and the wind howled through the pass.

Feet standing at the lip of the cave, a sheer drop below him, he whistled. The noise was eaten up by the wind.

Blue-black wings spread wide, and a raven careened from the sky, sweeping through the air in a wide arc.

Néefar held out his arm, and the raven landed with a wild beat of its wings. He pulled out a small slip of paper and put it in the raven's talons, which curled around it tightly.

"Find him," he whispered.

Clicking its beak, the raven took flight, disappearing into the sky.

CHAPTER 2

Bright fuchsia flowers lit up a crawling bush as it wound in thick tendrils from tree to tree. Savven manoeuvred around them, his feet barely skimming the ground, Hazen tucked tightly into his arms. The small bird flew rapidly over and under tree limbs, getting lost in the overgrowth only to reappear.

Hazen's body was consumed in fire, the heat seeping through his clothes. The bird disappeared through a cascading wall of thick vines, and he cut through them and skidded to a halt.

"Lithônion?"

"Savven?"

The vines brushed the back of his head as Savven took a cautious step back. His oldest friend sat beside a small fire, a steady creek running behind him. The bird landed on a branch, chirping.

"Thank you," he said shortly to the animal, but the bird didn't fly off.

His eyes fixated on Lithônion. His light brown hair pin-straight down his back, face sharp and handsome, though his green eyes flashed with regard.

Lithônion stood, cords of muscle flexing under his fitted dark brown tunic, and threw something into the fire. Savven watched a piece of parchment curl around the embers before it was devoured.

"The last word you sent me, you were out with a scouting party to hunt down Prowlers. That was nearly two months ago." Savven adjusted Hazen in his arms but didn't step closer.

The bird swooped between them, snatching something beside the fire and flew off before Savven could see what it was. Lithônion offered him an easy smile, one he had seen time and time before.

"We got separated," said Lithônion.

He didn't offer any other information, standing there, hand resting on the pommel of his sword strapped to his hip. The fire cracked, and Hazen moaned lowly in response.

Lithônion jerked his chin towards her. "Who's she?"

Savven stared at his old friend, assessing, and his arms tightened of their own accord. "No one."

"You were never good at lying," Lithônion chuckled, turning his body. "Put her by the fire."

Savven didn't move.

Sighing, Lithônion pinned him with a hard stare. "I can feel her fever from here. I promise not to touch her."

He didn't move for some time, seconds ticking by as Lithônion took his seat beside the fire again. Finally, he walked over and gently placed her on the moss-covered bank, brushing a strand of hair away from her sweat-covered forehead.

"You care for her?" Lithônion mused.

Savven stared up at his friend through lowered brows. "I tolerate her."

Lithônion shrugged, but he didn't say anything, amusement rounding the corners of his mouth.

Something uncomfortable stirred in Savven's gut, looking at Lithônion, but he pushed it down. Walking over to the thick growth of weeping ferns and towering floral bushes, he picked up a large leaf from beneath the plant of a Maiden's Blush and knelt beside the stream to fill it.

"What's her name?"

Savven ignored him, hovering over Hazen. Parting her lips, he tilted the water into her mouth, some trickling down her jaw.

"Come now, Savven."

"How did you get separated?" Savven asked quietly, sitting beside Hazen and positioning himself in front of her.

Lithônion busied himself with the fire, stoking the burning twigs. "There were two Prowlers. They cornered us. We scattered when we knew there would be no other option."

"You ran?" His words were muttered, thoughtful.

"There were only five of us, Savven," Lithônion countered.

"Five highly trained warriors." Savven's eyes narrowed at the fire. "Five warriors who have fought in many battles and taken down many enemies... and you all ran?" His gut twisted.

Lithônion was silent. His earlier amusement was gone, mouth pursed, and green eyes cold. "You haven't been home in fifteen years, Savven."

Savven's blue eyes darkened with warning. "But I still know what goes on within my city walls." He leaned forward, a warning in his voice as he switched to the Fae language. "Try. Again."

A muscle in Lithônion's jaw twitched. The Fae tongue demanded truth. Lips curling, he chuckled lowly. "You were always a stubborn one, Savven."

Savven leaned back. "It's a useful trait."

Stoking the fire again, Lithônion put the stick aside and looked at Hazen briefly. "I was sent out by your father. Alone."

"Why?" he demanded.

"No trust, Savven?" Lithônion joked.

"No."

Lithônion's amusement fell. "You've changed."

Savven tilted his head. "And you're deflecting. Why did my father send you out?"

"Because there's a rumour of your death circulating the gossip channels."

"I haven't heard wind of any rumours?" Savven said, frowning.

"I thought you knew everything that goes on behind your city walls, Savven?" Lithônion shook his head with a scoff. "But you don't know everything, do you? Your city is failing, and you don't even know it."

Savven was unnaturally still, feeling the heat radiating up his back from where he guarded Hazen. "Then tell me what I don't know."

Lithônion's eyes flickered back to Hazen. "You first, old friend."

"That isn't how this works, Lithônion."

"No?" Lithônion cocked his head in thought. "I told you something, but you haven't said a single thing."

"For good reason."

"Debatable."

Their eyes locked, unblinking, unmoving.

"We ran into a little trouble with a succubus. I found her in Thórsmörk," he jerked his head behind his shoulder, "and now we're here."

"Who is she?"

"A human."

Lithônion's gaze widened. "A human?"

"From across the veil," Savven said quietly. His friend froze, something passing across his face that Savven couldn't read but made his gut twist again. "Why did my father send you out?"

His gaze was stuck on Hazen, and Lithônion shook his head slowly. "Why does she have a fever?"

"She was kissed by a succubus."

Lithônion's gasp was quick. "She doesn't have much time then."

Savven thought of Tatius, though he didn't say anything.

"Savven?"

"We need to calm her fever."

Lithônion stood. "I'll gather some herbs."

Savven watched his friend walk towards the wall of hanging vines. "Lithônion." He stopped, head turning to hear him. "We're not finished yet."

Lithônion's back tensed fleetingly before relaxing, and he nodded.

"You worry too much, Savven," he called over his shoulder before disappearing.

A fire blazed hot near the stream as Savven stoked it with a long stick before turning back to the flat rock with herbs spread over it. When Lithônion arrived with arms laden with plant roots, golden berries, and other assortments, they filled a round pit they had used magic to crater out with water and lined it with leaves.

Lithônion muttered quietly under his breath and watched as the stones he had placed in the fire rose like glowing ruby gems. They hovered in the air before lowering into the water, a wall of steam rising into the open as the liquid sizzled in protest.

He added small red-hot pebbles as Savven ground the plants before him.

"Here," Savven said, handing him a leaf with the herbs. He watched Lithônion take the large maiden leaf, tip the concoction into the hot water, and stir it slowly as it created a strong aroma.

The two wrinkled their nose as the scent wafted through the air.

"Sit her up," Lithônion instructed when it was ready.

Standing, Savven went to sit behind Hazen and lifted her up, her body resting against his chest as he parted Hazen's mouth gently with long fingers.

Lithônion took a hollowed stick he had found when collecting the maiden leaves, splitting it in half to use as a ladle. Dipping the stick into the warm brew, he carefully brought it to Hazen's lips, slowly emptying the liquid into her mouth.

"That should be enough," he said, setting the ladle down near the pit. "Anymore, and it might react in an ill manner."

Savven heard his words though paid them no heed as he studied Hazen, watching her face. The tea worked quickly enough. Savven could already see the colour flooding back into her once lifeless face, her veins no longer visible beneath her skin. His thoughts went to that annoying little God in the forest, and he silently said his thanks.

CHAPTER 22

Savven stared at the crackling fire as the flames intertwined in an exotic dance. Night had fallen, life thrumming around them, concealed within the dark foliage of the mountain even as it buzzed, chirped, and rustled unceasingly. Glancing at Hazen, he watched her as she slept. Her brow unfurrowed, and her mouth softened; her body visibly relaxed now that the fever had died. Her skin was still pale against the firelight but healthy. Hazen looked as Savven had found her—alive, though her mouth was blessedly silent.

Her head tossed, eyes moving beneath closed lids as she muttered distorted words under her breath.

Savven frowned, fingers reaching for her forehead.

"Humans are interesting creatures. Feeble, but resilient."

Savven's eyes snapped to Lithônion and his wondering tone,

noting his old friend's gaze on Hazen. It was inquiring, and something else, regret?

"She is anything but weak," Savven amended with a sigh.

The girl was a pain in his ass, but she was stubborn and full of fire. She was also slow due to her mortal heritage but hadn't complained... much.

"Where are you heading?"

Lithônion's question was innocent enough as he stroked the cherry embers, but Savven's gut twisted. They hadn't spoken since they had made the tonic for Hazen's fever. Sitting in silence while they waited for her fever to die or take her with it when it did. She had fought, though, body arching and writhing against the heat that Savven could feel coming from her in waves. The life had returned to her face, but they waited hours until her fever finally vanished, and Hazen became still.

Savven wanted to question his friend and demand answers, but he held himself back. Instead, he tilted his head and looked at his friend inquiringly.

"You ask a lot of questions for one who hasn't answered any in return."

Lithônion stilled, his green eyes hardening for a second before that natural ease took over again, and he gave him a crooked smile.

"You were always so stoic, Savven."

"A crown prince of the land has no room for informalities. You're deflecting."

"My apologies, Your Royal Highness."

Savven's tether on his patience tightened to the point of snapping at Lithônion's mocking tone. But instead of growling in response, Savven eased a relaxed smile over his lips and leaned his arm on a bent knee.

"That's better," he said, tilting his chin and haughtily raising a brow.

Lithônion laughed, throwing a pebble in his direction. Savven waved the small stone away with magic, and it plopped into the stream. He gave Lithônion a wry smile.

"Come now, Lithônion, between old friends, what are you doing out here?"

"I told you, Savven," he said with a shake of his head. "Nasty rumours are spreading about you. Your father sent me to find you. Luck has it, you came right to me."

Savven's blue eyes darkened. "How did those rumours start?"

"No idea," Lithônion said with a shake of his head.

His friend's nonchalant shrug of his shoulders and unassuming look were convincing enough to most. Lithônion had always been a good liar. But Savven could taste the lie on his tongue, and it took all his self-control to let it go. Giving another easy smile to his friend, he leaned back on the palm of his hand.

"Will you return to *Álfheimr* now that I'm miraculously alive?"

Lithônion chuckled. "Perhaps, or maybe I'll travel with you? Two of us are better than one during these times."

Savven blinked once, the only sign of his objection before he smiled faintly. "We happen to be travelling in that direction."

Lithônion clapped his hands together. "Ah, well, the Gods have it then. I'll travel with you."

The fire crackled as Lithônion placed another piece of wood on the flames, and Savven watched his friend silently, his face blank.

Hazen stirred behind him, and Savven's attention went to the girl behind him. Her face was soft and peaceful even as she slept, now turned towards him.

"The Saol celebration is coming upon us, the next two full moon spans."

Savven returned his attention to Lithônion, who was staring at the girl. Savven shifted his body in the slightest to shield her and asked, "Who will be in attendance?"

"The nymphs of the northern Kyleast and Taz'ren Seas will make a special appearance, as will the Drago from the high mountains." Lithônion's gaze was still fixated on Hazen, and Savven could feel his patience start to ebb.

"The nymphs have not shown themselves on land for many years," Savven mused. "The Drago have never set foot upon our lands before, either. It will be an honour to feast with them."

"It'll be good to feast with you, Brother. Now that we know you haven't yet left us for the Gods and their golden heavens."

Savven picked up a small round pebble and rolled it between his fingertips, quiet, before he spoke, "We'll have to cross the Bel'onc Sea. It is the safest and quickest way to Álfheimr. She is too naïve of our ways and of the ways of those who want her dead. Crossing the sea is the only way to keep her safe; it will take a day longer than walking, but at least she will arrive alive."

"Aye. Do you think that's wise, though?" Lithônion countered, finally turning his stare to Savven. "I understand what you're saying, Savven, but the seas are open, and there is no place to hide someone, let alone a human girl."

"Who said I was hiding her?" Savven countered.

The quiet stretched between them, the fire crackling in the air, embers lighting up the sky.

"Your father will be pleased you're coming home," Lithônion said, breaking the silence. His lips turned up into a small smile.

The lie was so thick in the air that Savven nearly choked on it. The tension in Savven's shoulders tightened at the mention of his father, his heart rate picking up, and he forced his muscles to relax. Unfurling his fingers that had curled into fists. The pebble turned end over end along his fingers as he played with it absentmindedly. "Home. It has been a while, hasn't it?"

His voice was filled with distant longing. Savven could still see the towering forest that fortified their city, the vibrant colours of flowers and life that had filled their home, and the music that flew through the air from storytellers and musicians.

Life.

His home had been filled with life.

It had been until…

"Aye, fifteen years," Lithônion said, pushing the wood around with a dagger, embers crackling loudly. "It's been fifty years since her death. You never were the same after that. It seems that you died when she did. We all did."

The pebble stilled in Savven's hand.

Lithônion noted Savven's stillness, the cold rage that swept over the prince's face and disappeared just as quickly.

Savven began playing with the pebble again, not saying anything.

"I'm sor—"

"—Don't," Savven said sharply, looking up at Lithônion through lowered brows. Savven cast the stone into the fire. "Don't say you're sorry. Don't apologize for what he's done."

"You can't really blame him, can you?"

Calm, assessing rage filled Savven's deep sapphire eyes, and he said slowly, "I can, and I will. He created them, and they destroyed our city and home and lands and people." He was speaking about the Dark Ones, Ezra's Dark Ones. "Who else am I to blame? Laudin, for firing the arrow? Myself, for not being quick enough?"

"Savven, I didn't mean—"

Savven's eyes narrowed at him. The tether on his patience was at its end, and he bit out, "Do not talk about my mother or who is to blame. Ezra killed my mother, destroyed my city and killed one of my oldest friends."

"She's alive."

That rage fizzled out.

"Who?" he breathed.

"Levina."

Savven's brows furrowed, frowning. "That's impossible."

Lithônion shook his head. "While you were gone, I took to scouting Ezra's territories and picked up her scent by the mountain. It was faint, but it was coming off the wind. She has to be alive. Trapped in that mountain."

Savven's blood rushed through his ears, staring at Lithônion expressionless.

"Levina lives, Savven."

"What proof do you have other than her scent?"

Lithônion scoffed. "Typical, not even a little hope that our friend is alive to rekindle that heart of yours?"

"Show me life, and I will have hope. But blind faith in one's word no longer holds merit. I trust no one, Lithônion, not even you." Maybe he was a fool for admitting that, but Savven didn't care. He didn't trust anyone, let alone Lithônion. Admitting that would only save him face when he didn't openly include his old friend in their doings. He would keep him close, get Hazen to Álfheimr, and sort this out once and for all.

Hazen's head felt like it was going to split in two when she opened her eyes, and just the crack of light through her bleary lids made her head scream. She shifted away from the light, screwing her eyes shut and wincing with a low moan. The sound came out in a strained rasp, and she coughed. Her body was sore as she stretched her limbs slowly like she had trained in the gym for hours or run a marathon.

Something pressed against her cracked lips, and her eyes snapped open. Savven knelt beside her, a ladle in hand and pressed against her mouth. He raised a brow at her, and she bristled at the expectant look. Opening her mouth, she kept her eyes on him as she tipped water down her throat. She choked, sputtering when it went down the wrong pipe.

"You weren't supposed to inhale it," Savven commented dryly.

Hazen shot him a glare.

He rolled his eyes and went to the stream while Hazen flopped an arm over her eyes, shielding them from the light. She would kill for a cup of coffee.

Savven knelt beside her again, ladle in hand with more water. She sipped at it until it was gone, and Savven had to refill it. He did this three more times until Hazen sat up, scrubbing a hand over her face.

"You tolerate me?" she asked lowly in a sweet voice.

Savven discarded the ladle into the stream, glancing at her through lowered brows. "You heard that?"

She laughed, stretching her arms above her head. "I thought it was a fever dream."

"Unfortunately, not," Savven said with a scowl.

"What? You don't want to be besties with me?" Her bottom lip jutted out in a pout.

His brow quirked in question. "Besties?"

Hazen yawned with a nod of her head. Looking back at her grassy bed, she contemplated going back to sleep.

"We don't have time for that," he interjected as if reading her mind.

Her lips pursed in disapproval. "You could use a nap. I think you're cranky."

"Forgive me, I've been awake all night tending to a certain girl who went and got herself nearly killed."

Hazen stood, glowering at the male. "It wasn't my fault."

Savven shrugged, standing with her. "I never said it was."

Amusement danced in his eyes, but his face remained impressively blank until she cracked her neck and back, and then he was looking at her with disgust.

"Did you just snap your bones?" he asked in disbelief.

"Something like that," she chirped, cracking her fingers and laughing at the face he made.

The bushes rustled, and the two turned to see a male emerge with a dead hare in hand.

Hazen lifted a brow, eyes travelling along the obvious Fae male from boot to head. He was broader than Savven, muscles shaped by the black leathers he wore and fitted brown tunic.

Leaf-green eyes fixed on her face before moving down her body, assessing her. Hazen smoothed a self-conscious hand down her dirty clothes, flicking grass off her skirt.

He was handsome, where Savven was beautiful, and broad, where Savven was lean. Hazen finally met those green eyes, and she blinked when a large smile cut across his face.

"You're awake." Was all he said before laying the hare on a flat rock and sitting in front of it.

She watched him pull out a dagger and begin skinning it. "I am," she replied.

Savven was watching the male with a blank expression, one she couldn't place. Hazen raised her brows at him in question.

"This is Lithônion." Savven gestured to the male.

He didn't trust the male, yet they were still with him. Hazen looked at Lithônion, now skewering the animal, and offered him a small smile. "Don't mind him," she said, jerking her head towards Savven. "He's just cranky. It's a pleasure to meet you. My name is Hazen."

Lithônion inclined his head, setting the hare in the flames of the crackling small fire. "Savven was born cranky, and it was even worse as a child."

Hazen giggled as Savven snorted, rolling his eyes.

"That's a damn lie," Savven muttered.

"He's right," Lithônion mused, chuckling. "He was an absolute terror as a child."

She gave the dark-haired male a sidelong look before sitting beside the fire. The flames seemed to dance closer to her, and her blood started to warm beneath her skin. The soreness in her limbs eased as heat seeped into her muscles, and she sidled closer to the fire.

"So, what did I miss while… not dying," she asked, eyes bouncing between the two males.

Savven sat beside the stream, knee bent as he leaned his arm on it. Lithônion turned the hare in the fire.

Hazen nodded her head slowly, biting her lip. "I see, well, a lot has happened. Thanks so much for filling me in."

Laughter played around Lithônion's mouth, looking at her with amused eyes. "I had made camp here when Savven found me by chance," he said after she stared at him expectantly. "After your fever broke, we decided it would be best to travel together."

Hazen looked at Savven, who watched the crackling fire. "Is that it?"

"We make for the docks as soon as you eat," Savven said. "The sea is a day's walk from here."

"Sounds like so much fun," she clipped, taking a piece of the hare as Lithônion pulled it from the fire and cut strips from it. It was gamey, but she didn't care. Taking another piece when she inhaled the first.

Savven and Lithônion didn't eat, watching her devour the animal, and she knew she should offer them some. It was only polite. But something in her growled at the idea of sharing when she felt like she hadn't eaten in weeks.

Pursing her lips, English etiquette overruling her other instincts, she put down the slice of meat in her hand as Lithônion was cutting another for her. "You should eat—both of you," she amended, eyes flicking between the two males.

Savven's blue eyes slid to her, bored.

"That's kind of you," Lithônion said, giving her a soft smile. "But this is for you. You'll need it more than us."

Hazen had to fight not to roll her eyes. "Are you immune to food as well as being immortal?"

Savven let out only what Hazen could call a snort, and she stuck her tongue out at him as he shook his head.

"Not immune," Lithônion chuckled. "Just picky."

"Sounds about right," she quipped, munching on a piece of meat. "Typical men."

"Male." They corrected her in unison.

Lithônion and Savven looked at each other while Hazen ducked her head to hide her smile.

Savven shifted to her left, and she looked at him from the corner of her eye. He was frowning, just in the slightest, enough for her to take note of it and store it away to question him about it later. Her eyes slid to Lithônion while she took another bite of meat. His gaze was fixated on something, and she followed it, landing on a raven that sat perched in the shadows of a leafy branch overflowing with hanging flower vines of vibrant pink and red.

The raven clicked its beak twice, and Lithônion and Hazen watched the bird fly into the forest.

Hazen stared at the once glowing embers, which had now turned to ash. Something inside her stirred at the sight of the dead fire, something akin to sadness. She could still feel the heat emanating from the soft grey cinder pile and shivered when a cool wind grazed the backs of her arms in contrast.

Savven had extinguished the fire shortly after she had finished eating. The two males worked quickly and quietly to erase all traces of their camp.

Standing, Hazen brushed a hand along her skirt and dusted her palms off as Lithônion came to stand by her and looked at the firepit.

"Is everything alright?" he asked lowly.

No, she wanted to say. No, everything was very much not *alright.*

An ember sparked to life, crackling with cherry red light, and Lithônion waved a hand over it, smothering it. The light died, and the fire chilled completely.

Hazen suddenly felt very cold and wished for Dshar's fur cape. She missed the weight on her back and the warmth it provided.

Screams and rolling mist and blood and more screams filled her memory. The scent of copper, smoke, and ash that fell like snow and the head of the female that had lain at her feet, golden hair covered in blood and soot.

Hands balling at her sides, she took a quiet, steadying breath. The cape was long turned to cinders along with the rest of the bodies and homes of Fallúin.

Fire slipped through her limbs like a comforting friend, igniting a path to her fingertips, and she felt her muscles go molten.

"Something troubles you?" Lithônion asked again quietly.

A frown pulled at Hazen's mouth, and she glanced up at the male. Keen green eyes watched her, causing her to shift on her feet and that fire within to smother, but she held his gaze.

"If something were troubling me, you would be the last person I seek for comfort," she said, standing just slightly taller despite the male being a head above her.

Lithônion's lips twitched in a smile. "And why is that?"

"Because I do not know you," she replied firmly.

"You don't know Savven."

"Perhaps, but he's proven himself to be trustworthy."

"So, I have to prove myself to you?"

She shook her head, eyes sliding back to the cold fire. "No. You must earn that right. I've only just learned your name."

"Are you two finished bonding?" Savven snapped from the forest edge. "Or can we get going?"

He didn't wait for them. Weeping vines and large overgrowths of bushes and flowers shielded him as he stalked into the forest.

"He wasn't always this moody," muttered Lithônion.

Hazen snorted. "That, I highly doubt."

CHAPTER 23

Savven led from the front while Lithônion took to the back. Hazen was sandwiched between the two as she kept one eye on Savven's back and another on the floor before her. The trip out of the mountains was slow going, mainly due to her, she assumed. Roots and hidden rocks threating to take her down. Hazen growled in frustration as she stumbled over another creeping tangle of vines hidden beneath a tall fern.

Sunshine streamed through the treetops in thin ropes of hopeful warmth. However, Hazen shivered, its heat scarcely penetrating the cool mist that hovered around them.

Wiping a hand over her face to clear the water that dripped over her eyelashes, Hazen wrapped her arms around herself, gritting her teeth as gooseflesh bristled along her arms, and a shiver went down her spine.

"Are you cold?" Lithônion asked.

Hazen saw Savven's head tilt just a fraction in their direction, and she pursed her lips. "No," she said stubbornly.

She refused to be the reason they slowed even further. So, they continued. Trekking slowly but surely through the forest.

As the sun grew higher in the sky, the three traversed through the forest bed until the Nal'lian Mountains lay behind them, the grassy plains that separated the dark forest and lush mountains at their backs. The Forest of Lost Souls had stood like a gloomy black sea stretching and trying to smother the orange and yellow glow of the woods connecting to it that they now occupied. A world of tall, lean, near barren trees surrounded them. Their dead leaves sprinkled amongst the forest floor, black soil soft beneath their feet.

Looking around her, Hazen sighed. Seeing nothing but trees and trees and more trees. "You know, you never did tell me where we were going," Hazen said nonchalantly, looking at Savven's back with a raised brow. He was further ahead of her now that they had more room, but she knew he had heard her. The waifish trees left little space for creatures to hide, and those that did were no bigger than a squirrel.

Savven's low voice floated back to her, "We're taking a ship across the Bel'onc sea."

"You said it'll take a day to get there?"

Savven didn't deign her an answer.

"Aye," Lithônion replied in Savven's stead, coming up behind her. "A ship ferries people across the mouth of the inlet to several ports along the coastline. It's usually a two-day journey to our port."

"Do you always travel by sea to go home?" Hazen asked, tilting her head up at the male beside her. His hair in the early afternoon light looked like silk, and Hazen allowed herself a moment to be envious of the male's effortless hair. Her own blonde hair in disarray.

Lithônion shook his head. "No, not usually."

Hazen sniffed, her nose wanting to run from the slight chill lingering in the air. "Wouldn't it be faster to cut across the land than going by sea?"

"Faster? With you? No."

Lithônion and Hazen looked at Savven as he spoke, and Hazen scowled, glaring at the male's back. At the same time, Lithônion's eyes just rolled skyward.

"It's usually faster, yes," amended Lithônion. "But he isn't wrong, and the dangers are far greater if we travel all that way on foot."

"Because of me?" she clarified.

Lithônion's grim smile was answer enough, and she looked away.

CHAPTER 24

The sun beat down on the top of Néefar's silver hair, the sky a dull blue above him as he stood on the ledge of the castle wall. A sea of forest spread before him.

A hollow wind pulsed in his ears, and Néefar turned his face into it, breathing in and out and in and out. Trying to calm the churning of his gut.

"You're not like the others."

Néefar turned to the soft feminine voice behind him.

A beautiful female with long golden hair and sky-blue eyes observed him with guarded curiosity. Her frame, draped in a black gossamer gown, was small and delicate despite the growing stomach she carried with a protective hand on it.

"Néefar?"

He nodded silently. He hadn't scented her downwind from him. Néefar frowned, eyes darting behind her. No one followed from the stairwell, and he returned his gaze to her curious one.

"I'm Levina."

"I know."

She tilted her head slightly, surveying him. "Have we met?"

A bird cawed once, unseen overhead.

"No," was all he said, and without breaking her gaze, he stuck his arm out, and a raven soared from the sky. Perching on his arm with quick flaps of its wings.

He didn't look at the bird, watching Levina silently. She watched him back, though turned her interest to the bird.

The raven clipped its beak impatiently at Néefar, and the shifter finally turned his attention to the bird.

Néefar let his magic merge with the raven's, his memories, and the bird's memories, becoming one—forest, river, mountains, and faces. He heard clipped conversations and hushed words until memories faded, and he saw the world from the sky. Néefar pulled out of the raven's mind, and the bird flew off.

Silence fell between them. The only sound was the hollow wind still thrumming with a non-existent hope of life.

Néefar slid a glance at Levina's belly. "How did that happen?" He wasn't asking about the act of it, but rather the why of it.

Her grip tightened slightly over her womb. "Survival."

His gaze flickered to the tattoo as her large flowing sleeve slipped back. Sharp thorns and delicate roses encircled her wrist and forearm, seeming to shift in the sunlight as if it were alive.

It was a Fae bargain.

"What was the cost?" he asked, eyes going from tattoo to sky-blue eyes.

Her face shuttered, and her other hand wrapped protectively around her belly. "Too much," she whispered, her stare going to the ledge behind Néefar.

Glancing over his shoulder, he followed her gaze to the sheer drop over the wall. A forest waiting below. Stepping aside, he waved to the open air.

"I won't stop you," he said coolly, almost bored.

Levina's eyes went distant, and her feet took a single step towards the ledge. A sharp exhale of breath staggered from her chest as if she realised what she was about to do and stepped back. Deep, aching sadness replaced the look of numb submission to her fate. She took another step back, away from the release that would be granted to her over the wall, and another.

Néefar watched her, making sure to keep his face expressionless. "Why not?"

Something akin to pain flashed in her eyes before iron replaced it, and she stood straighter, her hand still cradling her belly. "Because I am a mother. And I have a promise etched in my bones to protect this child. Even if it's from me. My wants are no longer mine. So, I will endure whatever I must, so long as my baby is safe."

Silence pulsed at her words, giving life to the near-lifeless world around them, giving hope. Néefar stared at her for a moment, knowing he should go and that he needed to go before Ezra came looking for him or, more importantly, her. But he didn't move, not knowing whether she would tell Ezra where she had found him or what he had been doing.

"I won't say anything," she whispered, sensing his thoughts. Her eyes lit slightly in earnest.

He stepped from the ledge, making to walk past her, but stopped when their shoulders brushed and whispered a single word, "Good." And he left, leaving her alone to stand beside that ledge and stare at the world he knew she would never see again.

CHAPTER 25

They had been walking for hours, and Hazen had to remind herself that her legs were still attached to her body despite going numb a few miles back.

The good news, though, was that she wasn't cold anymore. A small film of sweat beaded her neck, rolling down her back. She was sure she smelled at this point, and she would give anything for a shower, a hot meal, and a bed that wasn't made of dirt, grass, or a pile of furs. Not that she was complaining about being alive; no, that she was very grateful for.

Lithônion and Savven had ventured further and further away from her, not on purpose but because she was slowing considerably. Her feet dragged through dead leaves and across black soil, barely having the energy to lift themselves enough to take a step.

Her heartbeat was a loud thump in her ears, and she took in a sharp breath when a stitch in her side stabbed suddenly. Hazen's stopped, and her hands grasped her waist while she bent over, heaving in a slow, deep breath. The two males stopped when they heard her inhale.

"Are you okay?" Lithônion called, hearing him take a step in her direction.

"She's fine," Savven commented, unimpressed. "Just human."

Hazen looked up at that and glared at him. He quirked a brow in response.

"Am I wrong?" he drawled.

Nostrils flaring in irritation, she straightened. Taking a deep breath, her heartbeat no longer a relentless drum in her ears, she gave Savven a tight smile. "How observant of you," she quipped dryly. "What gave it away?"

Savven didn't patronise her with a response.

Hazen rolled her eyes when he continued walking and flipped him a vulgar gesture with her hand. Lithônion arched a brow at her raised finger.

"Courtesy of the human realm."

He nodded, smiling slightly.

She waved her hands to usher him to continue when she began walking. "Come on, let's get this over with."

Hazen would have argued hours ago that she loved hiking back in the human world. She enjoyed nature, rain or sun. But not when she hadn't slept in a week and was being chased by a psychotic Fae. She was still convinced she was dreaming but wasn't about to voice that thought to the two males with her. If she was dreaming, her mind had a very, *very* good imagination.

"If it's any consideration, there's only a few miles left," Lithônion said gently, waiting for her until they could walk together.

Hazen looked up at the sky, which could be seen through the thin, spindle tree branches. It was still a bright blue, but the sun had disappeared overhead. It was well into the afternoon already, that much she could say with certainty.

She gave him a tired smile and continued to trudge on.

Another couple of hours passed, slowly and painfully, because her legs had now begun to prick with pins and needles. But the air turned salty. A balmy breeze whispering through the trees brushed a teasing kiss to her cheek and ruffled her tangled hair.

Hazen stopped, breathing in the smell of the sea. It was the first time since she had arrived that anything had reminded her of home. The sea never changed. The scent of salt, seaweed and sand filled her nostrils. Something in her bones called her closer to it, and she picked up her pace. Her legs tightened with the lengthened stride, but soon that walk turned to a jog, the wind picked up, and that jog turned to a run. She ran through the trees, passing Savven and Lithônion, who stopped to watch her.

Trees whizzed by in her peripherals. Orange, yellow, and red were a blur of colour around her until it faded, and grey, blue, green, and white surrounded her.

The world opened to a grassy cliff edge. Tall willowy grass nearly reached her knees, swaying around her in that comforting breeze that came off the sea. Flocks of purple and yellow wildflowers scattered across the ledge. To her left was a crudely made set of stairs down the cliffside. Thick rectangular timber was set into the earth, leading down to an old wooden dock where a massive ship sat moored with impressive billowing sails. Rocks and smooth pebbles filled the space between timber steps, anchoring the wood in place.

Lithônion and Savven came up behind her on either side.

"It's amazing," she breathed.

A sharp whistle pierced the air.

"That's the last call," said Savven. "Unless you want to swim across, we better get moving."

"You can't stop being an ass for even a minute?" Hazen asked, though following him down the wooden steps.

By the time they reached the bottom, her cheeks were stained pink, and the tip of her nose was numb from the wind, which grew stronger the further they descended.

The dock creaked with every step, waves splashing up the wood pilings, and thick lines groaned with every stretch. The ship was massive now that Hazen stood beside it, neck arched back, looking up at it with wide eyes. It swayed with the tide, though the lines held fast, and the wide wooden gangway slid slowly against the dock with the rise and fall of the swells.

"They don't have boats like this in Eastbourne," she muttered, remembering the sailboats that littered the water during summer.

"Ship's 'bout to take off," said the shipping master, who popped up in front of them from behind the gangway. A rotund goblin with a head of crow black hair that sat in a balding mess atop his head. His short, round frame was clothed in sea-worn brown linen pants, a billowing white wool shirt with two patches in the elbows, and brown leather boots that had seen better days.

Hazen's brows went to her hairline when she looked at the well-fed goblin.

Lithônion pulled a small leather sack from his person. "How much for passage to Álfheimr?"

The goblin grunted, scratching his chin. "For the lot of you, six silvers, plus entry into High Fae territory, which is another two silvers, or if you have one gold, I won't say no." His greedy smile was cutting with a row of sharp, pointed teeth; one was gold on the top, and on the bottom, the opposite was silver.

Ignoring his stare on the money pouch, Lithônion withdrew a thick gold coin, a leaf stamped into it, and tossed it to the goblin who snatched it from the air. "One gold."

The goblin turned it over in his long, knobby fingers. He brought it to his mouth and chomped down on the coin, leaving a row of teeth marks behind.

Hazen grimaced.

"Had to make sure it was real," he implored, tucking the gold safely into a pocket hidden inside his shirt.

Hazen watched its weight settle heavily on his garment, and she had a feeling that gold would find a home in the goblin's personal money trove.

"Younglings have been playing with fool's magic, trying to trick ol' Hobsstike," the goblin said gruffly.

Savven's eyes narrowed in the slightest, and a frozen expression passed over his face. "Do we look like the type to play useless tricks?"

Looking from one to the other in ease, Hobsstike replied coolly, "No, my apologies. Though that one may need another look," he said, pointing to Hazen, who raised her chin stiffly and glared at the goblin.

Savven growled lowly in warning, and Hazen felt ice go down her spine at the implied threat. Lithônion took her arm and led her away from Hobsstike's asserting eyes.

Savven waited until Lithônion had pulled Hazen a couple of paces away before saying, "One more thing."

Hobsstike cocked his head in a manner of listening.

"Are there any merchants on board?"

Hobsstike scratched his balding head in thought. "There is a witch named Brean who travels with our ship frequently. She might have what you are looking for. Has a bit of everything she does."

"My thanks." Savven nodded to the goblin before jerking his head to Lithônion and Hazen, who watched him from the middle of the gangway,

Bowing to the elf, Hobsstike muttered, "Fare winds and following seas, Noble One."

As Hazen stepped onto the wooden deck, a rush of energy and awe went through her. Loosening sails, winding ropes, and securing lines; everyone was a blur of movement and organised chaos. Few passengers sat on barrels while some heaved satchels over their shoulders, swaying with the turning of the ship as they walked.

"Go below," Savven whispered to Lithônion and Hazen as he emerged from behind them. "I'll follow shortly."

Lithônion led Hazen away, opening a door that led below and hurrying her down a set of stairs to a dimly lit cargo locker.

"Is this where you kill me?" she muttered, eyeing the stacks of wooden crates and hanging nets full of exotic fruits she had never seen before. Two torches hung on either wall, giving sparse light to the loamy quarters.

"Fire on a wood ship. Great, we're going to burn to death," she remarked dryly.

"It's enchanted not to burn anything but the torch," Lithônion said, ignoring her previous comment.

Hazen tilted her head, watching the fire flicker. "Of course it is."

"Sit here." Lithônion pointed to a crate by the stairs. "I'm going above to watch the deck. Wait here until Savven comes for you."

Lithônion was there and gone before Hazen could reply. She sighed, running a tired hand over her face.

CHAPTER 26

A near-silent echo of a dying wind slipped through the corridors and crevices of Dyagin castle. Nothing stirred, and soon, even the rustle of wind fell still.

Ezra sat on his throne, back straight, eyes closed and unmoving, except for the slight rise and fall of his chest with every sparse breath he took. A black-as-night raven, large and motionless like a painted statue, sat perched on the top left corner of the throne, staring at shadows that ebbed and flowed around the dais like a living thing.

The demons within rattled Ezra's bones. Their claws gouged into his ribs and across each bone in his body until he was sure they had reformed his insides to shreds. The pain spiked through every nerve and along his skin like a friend, grounding him.

Feed us, they whispered. *Find, kill, devour.*

Ezra's head twitched, falling back against the throne.

Kill, kill, kill, KILL—

Ezra's eyes snapped open, black as tar, and fixated on the towering ceiling above him.

They whispered and slithered along his limbs. Pressing against his flesh, seeking a way out. He could feel their talons rake across his throat as they tried to climb out of his mouth, and Ezra let out a low growl. They retreated, though only enough to dig into his chest and bury themselves within his magic.

His head pounded, and their whispers turned distant. An insistent murmur of command.

Find, kill, devour. Kill him, kill him, KILL HIM.

Ezra slowly lowered his head, eyes sliding to the far-right corner of the great hall. A pair of glowing blue eyes came from within the shadows.

"Tell me, Néefar, do you enjoy spying on me?"

Unblinking blue eyes came closer until silver hair and a handsome face emerged from the darkness, and soon, the rest of him, clothed in all black.

Néefar, who leaned casually on an obsidian pillar, cocked his head in observation. "Is it a crime to look upon my most powerful lord?" His tone was dry, questioning as he raised his brows in the slightest, crossing his arms over his chest.

"Do not mock me!" Ezra snapped through clenched teeth. The demons screeched in delight at the anger coursing through him.

"You make it too easy," he replied, unimpressed.

Ezra's head tilted, more animal than Fae. Those black eyes roved over Néefar. "You toe the line between life and death, Shifter."

"A line I've walked my whole life. We're very familiar with one another."

Killlll him.

"I could end you."

"Please do," Néefar replied, bored. "This whole conversation is painfully slow."

Ezra bared his teeth in annoyance, the shadows' voices growing louder in him. Calling, chanting, demanding of him, Ezra squeezed his eyes shut, nails digging into the silver armrests of the throne.

Kill, kill, kill, kill, kill, ki—

"SILENCE!"

Ezra's chest heaved, his voice still ringing in the great hall and filling the corridors. The whites of his eyes returned, and the demons slithered to the darkest parts of him. His chest heaved with every breath, and he slowly slid his stare to Néefar, who looked wholly unimpressed.

The raven, who had sat there unmoving, finally clicked its beak at Ezra as he stood and slowly walked down the dais, eyes fixated on the shifter.

Néefar turned to Ezra when he stopped before him, barely a fist of space separating them.

"I hate to tell you this, but you're not my type," Néefar commented.

Ezra sneered, and his hand lashed out, nails digging into Néefar's neck. The lump in his throat bobbed with his swallow and attempt to inhale the air he was cutting off. "Your jokes will see you dead one day."

The veins in Néefar's temples bulged, olive skin turning red and purple, but still, he gasped out, "Then at... least... I will... die with a per... so... nality."

Ezra snarled at his comment, tossing him away.

Néefar caught himself before he fell to the ground, his shoulder smashing into another pillar as he stumbled forward, coughing.

"Why do you mock me," Ezra bit through clenched teeth.

Rasping chuckles shook Néefar's back as he stood to face Ezra. "You're so dead inside. How could I not? It's almost too easy."

Ezra took a single step in his direction, eyes flashing in warning. "I could kill you."

Néefar stood tall at that threat, squaring his broad shoulders. "Then do it."

Silence followed.

Néefar took a step toward the dark male, then another, until they shared the same breath. Standing at similar heights, Néefar looked him in the eyes, unblinking, and smirked softly. "You can't," he whispered.

Rage flared in those dark eyes. Before Ezra could interject, Néefar continued, "Because I'm the last pawn you have left." He looked around at the empty hall, the silence hanging to his every word. "I see your shade has failed you and Mara as well, and let's be honest, your second in command is useless compared to me. You need me. There's nothing you can do about it." Néefar stepped back, smoothing a hand over his shirt front and eyeing Ezra coolly. "Unless, of course, you want to do it yourself. Then, by all means, oh Dark One, go get your little human."

Ezra's nostrils flared, mouth pinching. "How... do you know this?" he asked slowly, his voice dark and threatening.

Néefar raised a brow as if it were an obvious answer. "Your raven's mind is weak. I can mould my magic to merge with their essence. Their memories then become my own. What they see, what they think—if they think—what they hear, what they eat, where they shit, it all becomes my own until I leave their mind."

The blow happened faster than Néefar could detect, and his head cracked back, body following as he stumbled, hands grasping to catch himself before he fell. The sound of Ezra's backhand connecting with the side of his face cut through the air like a heartbeat.

Néefar's left ear rang, and he shook his head from the power of the blow. After a moment, he straightened, wiping his mouth with the back of his hand. A smear of red streaked across olive brown skin, and pink stained his white teeth when he smiled.

Ezra stared at Néefar with disgust, those demons whispering, reaching, commanding him to kill. To feast on him. They hungered for the shifter's blood.

Néefar watched Ezra with that same indifference, though wariness lingered now behind those eyes. Reaching to draw a nail down his cheek, Néefar slapped his hand away. Growling, Ezra's magic lashed out, pinning Néefar to an obsidian pillar.

He leaned in close, his teeth bared, and gripped Néefar's jaw in one hand, his nails digging into the flesh until bright red pearls of blood beaded down his throat. "You will find the human, and you will bring her back to me, do you understand," he hissed so softly that only Néefar could hear him.

Néefar jerked or tried to, but the bands held him fast, slowly constricting around him tighter and tighter until his bones were screaming to be released, but he bit out through the pain, "And what do I get in return?"

"Nothing," Ezra whispered. His free hand pulled Néefar's head back by his hair, baring his throat. He watched the trails of blood cut a path across his skin, could smell the copper tang of life, and wanted to tear it open and bathe in it. He brought his nose to the blood and inhaled deeply, the demons roaring in his mind, their talons digging into their prison of bones and flesh. "When you return, I will *bathe* in your blood, Shifter," he whispered.

Ezra let go of Néefar, stepping back. His magic dispersed, and Néefar sagged. Relief crossed his face fleetingly before going behind a mask of iron will. Ezra scoffed, striding back to his throne.

"That's a little dramatic, don't you think, even for you, Ezra," Néefar said, not wiping the blood away this time.

Nails dug into the silver throne as Ezra slunk into the chair, his lips twisted into a sneer, eyes dead and black. "Bring me my human, Néefar. Or let me feast on you now. The choice is yours."

Néefar raised a brow, face tightening with anger, but said nothing. Walking backwards until he turned and sauntered from the great hall.

Ezra smirked when the doors closed. "Pity, I was hoping you would say no."

Néefar took in a staggering breath as soon as he was on the castle's roof. The hollow wind cut across his face, and he shuddered, pain wracking his body. His magic slowly healed the pulsing bruises that banded around him and the bones that had cracked beneath them.

He stared southwest towards the forest that lay there, towards the heartbeat he longed to hear again. Sealing himself, he tucked his emotions away, pursing his lips.

The wind thrummed with promise, and he stepped onto the ledge, looking down. A sheer drop and death awaited hopeless souls.

One breath, then another, and he outstretched his hands, and with eyes closed, he stepped from the ledge.

A moment later, a white hawk screeched and shot through the air, disappearing into the cloudless sky.

CHAPTER 27

Savven's eyes slipped from face to face, arms crossed casually on his chest as he leaned against the thick timber railing of the aft deck. Goblins, with their hooked noses and pointed teeth, flocked together, conversing. A pair of young warlocks stood by the bow of the ship, sparks of fire and yellow balls of gleaming light danced around them in cracking streams. And in the nook of the foredeck that led towards the crew quarters, a lone pretty female sat on a large crate shoved into the corner.

She had bright, fiery red hair braided down her back and lightly tanned skin. A dark purple dress fell to her ankles with long fitted sleeves and an open neckline. Her brown booted feet crossed delicately at the ankles as she watched the passengers openly. A brown leather corset cinched her small waist, and a set of daggers belted around her hips in an orderly fashion.

Her red hair was like living embers of copper and sunlight, catching the sunbeams when her head twisted to look at the sea. Savven watched her eyes close, inhaling the scent of briny water. He watched her silently for a moment more, watching stray strands of unruly curly hair fall from her braid and brush her cheek before prowling over to her.

She squinted at the sea when he blocked the sunlight, casting a shadow over her. Her lips pursed, clearly annoyed. Golden eyes turned slowly to him, and her head tilted in thought as she roved a judgmental eye down his body.

"Do you want me to turn you into a big, warty, lumpy toad?" she inquired casually, head still tilted as she decided what spell she would use on him.

Savven's mouth twitched despite himself.

She continued, "Or do you want to be a slug? I hear they're good for the skin. Maybe an old crone can use you as a potion for her delicate wrinkles." She straightened, cocking an expectant brow at him. "Those are your options if you don't keep walking. I'm being generous, so choose wisely." Dry amusement lingered beneath her words, a twinkle in her eye melting away some of the threat's seriousness.

Her face was a map of freckles, and the ones across her nose and cheeks moved every time she wrinkled or twisted her mouth. She looked like a living flame. Exotic and beautiful but fiery, with the bite to match. Savven's brows rose at her choices, and he shook his head.

"I'm sorry, those don't work for me. You'll have to do better than that," Savven said, shifting his stance and looking down at her with a small, amused smile.

The witch scoffed. "I can do better than a toad," she snipped. "I was just being nice. See how far that got me?"

"I'm waiting," he said, crossing his arms.

She huffed, reminding Savven of a firedrake, and half expected steam to billow from her nostrils when she turned those gold eyes to him.

"Are you Brean?" he asked.

"To some," she said, tilting her head again, watching him. "Fire-breathing witch, to others."

He inclined his head in question.

"I wasn't so accommodating to some. A little fire bit a couple of thieves in the ass when I found them rummaging my sacks." She put an offended hand to her chest. "And I'm the bad guy for it?" She rolled her eyes.

A firedrake indeed.

Savven could feel the stares of those on deck as they passed them and his wariness grew, amusement fading. "I was told you were a merchant."

"Goblins," she whispered bitterly, shaking her head and glaring towards the gangway.

Savven cleared his throat.

She straightened, jumping off the crate. She was at least a head shorter than him, and he couldn't help the small chuckle when he saw her slight frame that accompanied such a loud temper.

She scowled up at him, hands on her hips. The movement made her breasts shove against the corset, and he shifted on his feet again, putting some space between them.

Brean noted his movements and the serious look on his face and smiled wickedly. Following him when he moved, just enough so the space between them narrowed.

"Don't worry, I don't bite," she paused, nibbling on her full bottom lip. "Unless you want me to."

Savven clenched his jaw until he saw the teasing light in her eyes. He laughed under his breath, a sly smile tilting his mouth. "I don't entertain dwarfs in my bed."

Her mouth dropped open, head rearing back. "I am *not* that short!"

When he said nothing, she growled and stormed up to the helm, muttering something about the indignance of High Fae and dwarfs. Savven followed her silently, hiding his smile.

Dark green sparks ignited between her fingertips, crackling with energy, and with a quick flick of her wrists, the sparks flew from her fingers. A pile of leather satchels appeared in the middle of the deck, some large while others were so small they could fit in a goblet.

"Usually, all of this is in one carrier, but since my last one broke, I have to transport it all by magic. I was waiting until I arrived at my destination, but you had to mess that up, didn't you?" she quipped.

Savven gave her an impressed expression that made the witch's eyes narrow.

"The High Fae are always so full of themselves," she muttered to herself before pursing her lips and cocking a brow at him. "Well, what do you need?"

"Clothes, warm ones if you have any to spare," he said, eyeing the stacks upon stacks of bags.

"You're scrawny, but not that scrawny," she pointed out. "And while I would be amused to see you flouncing around in one of my gowns, you're a bit flat around the chest compared to myself."

His eyes casually glanced at the swells pressed against the corset with every breath she took. When he met her gaze, amusement sparkled back. "It's not for myself. It's for my female companion."

Brean shrugged a shoulder. "Pity."

He didn't correct her. Let her think what she wanted, but he could feel the stares grow more persistent. The pile of satchels and the pretty witch were not helping.

Brean dug through bag after bag, some big and some small, pulling out a pair of black leather pants, a dark green wool tunic, long black boots, and a pair of short stays that Brean hid between the tunic and pants.

"Don't want the eyes to whisper," she stated.

So, she was aware of them as well. Savven shifted, taking the pile from her outstretched hands. "Thank you," he said quietly, pausing to look at her daggers. "You wouldn't..."

She rolled her eyes, grabbed one of the smaller blades at her waist and plopped it on his pile of clothes. "I hope she knows how to use it."

The blade was small, the size of his hand from hilt to tip, with the bone handle carved with runes. "She will," he promised.

"Mhm," she hummed, disbelieving.

With his free hand, he slipped it into a hidden pocket of his black pants and pulled out his last two silver coins.

She waved it away. "I don't need your money, Prince."

He couldn't keep the surprise from his face. "Prince?"

"I was raised by the High Fae," she explained. A trace of sadness laced her voice, but she cleared her throat, looking towards the horizon. "I left Álfheimr at the marker of my first century."

He grabbed her hand, pressed the coins into her palm, and walked away before she could object.

Hazen was nearly asleep when Savven's silent footfalls creaked on the wooden steps. Her drooping eyelids shot open, and she sat up quickly on the crate she was perched on.

"I brought you some clothes." He set a pile of neatly folded items beside her and a pair of boots on the floor.

She looked at the dagger, picking it up with a questioning look.

"Don't stab yourself with it," he said dryly.

Her questioning look fell into a scowl, and she set it down. "It was so thoughtful, and then you opened your mouth."

Savven gave her a pointed look, already walking out. "Come on deck when you're done. We're casting off soon." And then he was gone.

Sighing, she slipped off the crate and put her hands on her hips, staring at the items. Her fingers reached out and brushed along the blade before setting it aside.

The first item was a dark green shirt, woven and thin but soft against her skin. Sandwiched under it was... a bra. Hazen laughed under her breath, holding the garment up at eye level. A rectangular strip of cream cloth was supported by cloth straps and laces in the back.

A loud *thunk* reverberated overhead, causing her to jolt and set the garment aside.

Shimmying out of all her clothes, she shivered naked in the damp air. The black pants were leather and so deliciously soft against her legs. They were snug but comfortable, worn in, and easy to move in. She tied the laces in the front before pulling the boots over them; they came just below her knees.

Naked from the waist up, she quickly stuffed all her old clothes and the sandals Dshar had given her in a small crevasse between a crate and the wall.

Eyeing the bra with a sceptical glance, she pulled it over her head. Reaching behind her to pull the laces taut, her breasts moulded into the cloth, and Hazen stood impressed.

Another *thunk*, the ship beginning to sway.

Hazen caught the edge of a crate with her hand when she stumbled. Throwing the shirt on, she tucked its edges into the pants quickly, wanting to melt when warmth encased her torso and arms. It was so blessedly warm.

The ship was rocking now, and she snatched the dagger before it slid to the ground, carefully slipping it beneath her waistband. She braced her hand on the wall for support and went up top.

Hazen found Savven on the bow, leaning against the thick wood railing, arms crossed over his chest. He was staring at the sea, a slight frown pulling his face. The breeze coming off the rolling swells brushed his midnight hair. He was beautiful, very annoying, but beautiful nonetheless. And currently, he looked like a dark prince in mourning, dressed head to toe in black, surrounded by the expanse of sea.

"Thank you," she said quietly, knowing he could hear her before she leaned on the opposite railing, hand gripping the wood when the boat dipped into a swell, sea spray misting her face.

"They're warm enough?" he asked, still not looking at her.

"Yes." Hazen followed his gaze. Watching the whitecaps crest and break only to reform and break again.

Grey clouds, dark and full of rage, rolled in the distance, the air cracking with thunder on the horizon. Hazen's stomach dipped when a wave splashed against the bow, and she jumped out of the water's path.

Running a hand over her loose hair, she leaned over the railing, watching the ship cut through the torrent waters.

"There is a story of a female who lives beneath this very sea."

Hazen looked up at Savven, who was now watching her. "What

happened to her?"

He turned his attention back to the sea. "Hundreds of years before my time, there was an elf named Undine. She was created by the sea but cursed to roam these lands, searching and waiting for someone to love her. One day, a human named Huldbrand, a knight, came into our world and met Undine by chance while he was bathing in the sea.

"Captivated by her, Huldbrand stayed by the shore, and as the days passed, Undine began to fall in love with the human and he with her. Though time and happiness were not their end. A witch named Varlaya saw Huldbrand by chance when he had crossed the veil. Enamoured and intrigued, she cast a spell onto Undine, making her ugly and crippled in the eyes of the human.

"Thinking that Undine had deceived him through magic, Huldbrand fled from the sea into the forest, where he met the beautiful witch. Upon taking him, Undine's heart broke. She leapt into the sea, never to be seen again. Though Huldbrand, who stayed in our lands until his death, swore that he could see her in his dreams when he slept. In a crystal palace beneath the waters, as beautiful as he remembered, she sings a haunted melody that fills the depths around her with a longing that breaks his heart with every waking."

Hazen stared at the waves as they crashed into the ship's side, the surf crawling up the wooden barrier and then retreating. "So, what happened? She just stays down there... forever?" she asked, brows scrunching.

"The pain of losing a loved one affects us far more than it would you, Hazen. We can grieve for centuries, and that loss we feel will never truly fade. We do not give our affections so easily." He paused, staring into the water as if he could see all the way to the bottom. And perhaps he could. "No one knows if she still resides beneath the waves. No one has seen her since except one. A southern light, who claimed to have caught a glimpse of her as she was flying across the northern ridge."

"Oh, what a bit of hogwash!" said a flippant female voice behind them.

Hazen turned, noting Savven rolling his eyes to the sky. "What is?"

Fiery copper hair and gold eyes stood behind them. A wry smile twisted a full pink mouth, her freckles mapping her face like stars. The female was petite, shorter than Hazen, and stunning.

"That tale your prince has fed to you is hogwash to me. It's just an old myth," she stated as she slid up next to Hazen, her dark purple skirts swishing with each movement. "I'm Brean, what's your name?"

"Hazen," Hazen said slowly, unsure of her. She quickly glanced at Savven, whose eyes were fixed on the female, lit with amusement, and relaxed slightly. "Why do you think it's a myth?" she asked, shifting her weight and putting space between her and Brean.

Brean snorted delicately, rolling her eyes in annoyance. "Because no female in her right mind would just throw herself into the sea after another female takes her lover. And if she does, then she doesn't deserve him. Real love is worth fighting for." She paused as though noting Hazen's appearance for the first time and cast a critical eye on her body. "I see my clothes fit you well."

Hazen's brows shot to her hairline, her fingers brushing the wool shirt. "They do, thank you." She glanced at Savven, who looked back at her with his typical unimpressed expression. "Thank you," she said again, but this time her words were directed at the Fae male.

He didn't reciprocate, and her mouth pursed into a flat line.

A beam of sunlight broke the rolling black clouds, and Hazen asked, "What are the southern lights?"

Irritation flashed over Brean's features, and she scowled, twisting her freckles over her cheeks. "Fairies. Annoying little creatures."

Savven chuckled. "We call them lights because when they fly, all you see is a gleam of light from them. Southern lights are the summer fairies."

"Who have a bad habit of playing nasty tricks," Brean muttered darkly.

"Only if they find you an easy target," Savven noted dryly.

Brean turned slowly to Savven and raised a brow. Hazen giggled behind her hand, hiding her smile.

Thunder cracked the sky like a hammer above their heads, and Hazen jerked in surprise. Looking up, lightning spider-webbed through the clouds, igniting a fleeting trail of electric blue light.

"If it rains, I swear to all the Gods…" Brean muttered under her breath, glaring at the sky that promised nothing shy of a monsoon.

A fat raindrop plopped down Savven's cheek, and the male huffed a laugh. "I don't think it cares about your idle threats."

Brean covered her hair with a protective hand, wincing when another drop and then another pattered around them.

"I'm going below," she grumbled, making to leave and stopping. She looked at Hazen, mulling over her words before speaking. "They're spelled," she said, jerking her chin towards Hazen's clothes. "I spell all my belongings to conceal. It's one of my magic's specialties. So, no one will know your secret."

Hazen frowned, shifting her stance and sending a fleeting look to those on deck with them. No one was paying attention, mumbling about the rain and heading into the berthing. "How did you know?"

"It wasn't hard to figure out," she paused, "and the wind likes to whisper things to me. Your humanity was one of them." Brean put a steady hand on Hazen's shoulder, squeezing gently. "Don't worry, your secret is safe with me."

The witch sauntered away, her skirt swishing behind her. Hazen's brows folded in the middle, and she looked at Savven.

Savven just rolled his eyes with a shake of his head. "Witches," he muttered.

Rain sprinkled down, and Hazen made to follow Brean, who was the last to go below. Lithônion leaned against the door frame, legs crossed at the ankles, arms folded across his chest. He was staring at Savven, who jerked his head once.

"Go below," Savven said, not raising his voice over the crash of sea and rain.

Hazen raised a brow.

Lithônion looked between the two.

Savven said something in a language she didn't understand.

Lithônion's arms tensed, and his face darkened, but he went below. Hazen looked at Savven with a cocked brow.

"Language of the Fae," he explained. "You cannot lie when speaking in the old tongue. And, in this case, you cannot disobey an order given by High Fae royalty."

"Can I learn it?"

"No."

"Why not?" she asked, tilting her head. Water dribbled down her cheek and across her eyelashes, and she wiped it away.

"Only pure Fae can speak and understand the language. It is our blood right." Savven grabbed a long, thin wooden pole from behind a crate. A sharp metal hook at one end. He snapped it in two, breaking off the hook and tossing it aside.

Hazen gaped at him. "You can't just break that, Savven!"

He looked at the two evenly halved sticks. "I just did."

"They probably use that!' she hissed, eyes darting around the deck to make sure no one saw, but they were alone up top with just the sea and storm as their witness.

Savven chuckled lowly, tossing a half to her. Surprised, Hazen's hand snatched it from the air, and she looked down at it. Something told her what he expected.

"Here?" she asked exasperated.

"Oh good, you're catching on. I was worried for a moment you would be slow."

"You're an ass."

"As you've pointed out before."

He walked over, stood beside her, and shifted his feet. Holding the stick at his side, he nodded for her to do the same. She mirrored him. "Follow me."

And she did.

Every swipe, swing, and stab. She copied him, slowly at first, her movements unsure and jerky, whereas Savven's were smooth and agile. But soon, she picked up speed. The rain poured down, her hair wet and plastered to her head, her clothes mostly waterproof, but her shirt was drenched and clung to her like a second skin. But Hazen didn't feel the cold. Her body flushed, and her muscles warmed with a slowly building ache as Savven took her through drill after drill.

Thunder cracked, and they stilled. Savven faced her, stick at his side, one arm braced behind him. Hazen sucked in a breath, her arms shaking, and swiped hair from her face. He jerked his chin towards her, cocking a brow. Savven looked perfectly at ease, even as the ship swayed sharply and the rain pissed down. She wanted to throttle him for how calm he looked.

Lightning struck the sea, electricity charging the air, and Savven lunged.

Hazen's arm came up, and she grunted under his strength, but her mouth quirked into a smile when her stick and his made contact. Arms threatening to buckle, she pushed back, baring her teeth as she laid into her weapon. The wood groaned under their force, and Savven twisted away, sending Hazen stumbling forward. She barely saw the arc of his stick before it—*SMACK!*

"Arg!" Hazen's back arched, and she whirled as pain laced her spine. Red-hot anger made her skin boil, and she stepped towards Savven, ready to spew fire.

He just stood there, watching her, and looked... impressed.

"*What,*" she snapped, "was that for?!"

The wind howled in her ears, and she had to yell to be heard over it, the rain stinging her skin.

He tilted his head in thought. "You didn't drop your weapon," he said calmly, and she barely heard him. "Good job."

Her anger vanished, and she rolled her shoulders back, giving him a snide smile before heaving her arm back and sending the stick sailing through the air, directly at his head.

It was a perfect shot, but Savven snatched it from the air before it made contact, studying the stick for a moment.

A second later, it disappeared with his, and Hazen saw it reappear, fully intact with the hook, and slip behind the crates. She shook her head, her back throbbing with every heartbeat, and growled under her breath, stalking for the berthing.

She could feel Savven fall in behind her and hear him mutter, "Maybe we should train her on the Javelin." Hazen smirked to herself before slipping below into the welcoming, dry warmth.

CHAPTER 28

Brean waved a beckoning hand to Hazen as she descended into the open berthing. She ducked under a low beam, bracing herself when the ship tilted violently. A floating ball of fire hung in the centre above their heads, its flames flickering and casting shadows over sharp angled faces that turned to study her as she walked past.

It was warm and blissfully dry down below. Her shirt dripped slowly, casting a wet frame around her on the ground when she sat beside the witch.

Brean took one sidelong look at her, pursed her lips in disapproval, and snapped her fingers.

Hazen looked down at her shirt, pinching the now-dry fabric between her fingers. "Thank you," she said, looking at her.

Brean's gold eyes seemed to glow amber in the dim light,

twinkling with amusement. "It's nothing." With a wave of her hand, a crackling fire and a small plate of round, slim white cakes dropped from thin air before them. It thumped on the wood floor, sparking embers snapping around them.

Her mouth opened, closed, and then opened again. "Won't…" she started, staring at the fire. "…won't that catch…" She waved a hand to all the wood surrounding them and then pointed to the orb of fire behind them. "And won't that?"

Brean chuckled, grabbing one of the round cakes and offering it to Hazen. "Spelled fire produces heat, not destruction." She paused, frowning. "Well, it should, anyway. Depends on its wielder."

"What is this?" Hazen asked, turning the thin compressed disk in her hand.

"A wheat cake. It'll fill you up until the storm passes enough to cook proper food."

A wave smashed violently against the port side, and Hazen had to brace her hand behind her to keep from falling back as they rolled viciously across the sea. The wood moaned under the strain but held fast and watertight.

Hammocks along the wall swayed with each toss, and those lying in them slammed into the wood. A collective groan of pain rose, and they crawled from their hammocks, huddling in the corners or around self-serving flames instead.

Hazen devoured her wheat cake. The flavour was bland, but it was something. She ate three more before Brean passed her a cup, and Hazen, in her whole life, had never been happier to have plain water.

When she was done and the cup vanished, she shielded her hands before the fire, letting it warm her fingers. Sparks danced past her, and she reached for them. An ember the size of a grain of sand landed on the tip of her first finger. Hazen frowned slightly when she stared at the sliver of fire that didn't burn her.

Dusting the spark off, she let her gaze wander across the flames to the two Fae males sitting casually against the wall closest to them. They didn't speak, and if Hazen hadn't been paying attention, she would have thought they weren't breathing either. Lithônion was watching her and Brean while Savven's eyes were closed. Hazen didn't believe for a moment that he was asleep.

"Do you miss them?" Brean asked quietly.

Hazen gave the witch a sidelong glance. "Who?"

"The ones you left behind."

Her family. *The ones she left behind.* Hazen swallowed the lump that suddenly lodged in her throat. "I... I do miss them." Her hands flexed restlessly, and she brought her knees up, wrapping her arms around them.

Brean tilted her head, and her eyes turned inquisitive. "Do you have a mother *and* a father?"

The witch looked younger now to Hazen, more innocent and less like a cat about to eat the canary. Hazen gave her a small smile. "I do. They're the best."

Silence stretched comfortably, and Hazen asked, "Do you have parents—a family?"

Brean took a deep breath, chewing on her bottom lip and staring into the fire. "Of course I do, well I did... I didn't know them for very long."

"Oh," Hazen said. "I'm so sorry, I didn't know."

"It's okay," she said, huffing a laugh before sobering. "They were murdered when I was still a wee thing. It's hard to miss what you never had. You can only miss what could have been, and even then, I try not to think long on it. We are what we project into this world."

Her words drove into Hazen, and she gently touched Brean's shoulder and squeezed softly. Seeing the sadness the witch tried to hide behind her strong words. "Whoever raised you did a pretty good job of it."

Brean's eyes lightened, and she gave her a happy smile. "The High Fae took me in when my parents were killed and raised me. They taught me to read and write and to understand combat strategy—"

Lithônion snorted at Brean's words.

The glower she tossed at the male made him quiet instantly.

"I need you to teach me how to do that," Hazen mused.

Brean chuckled darkly.

The space was filled with the cracking of embers.

Hazen sighed. "The last thing I said to them was *goodnight*." Her chest cracked open a little at the homesickness she felt.

Brean nodded in understanding. "You know time moves differently between the two worlds?"

"Yes," Hazen murmured.

"Then don't worry. They'll barely notice you're gone."

"I hope you're right," Hazen said quietly, putting her chin on her knees. "When I get back, I'll tell them how much I love them, and we'll celebrate my birthday and spend time with my grandparents." She missed her family more than she realised now that they were on her mind.

"Your birthday?" Brean asked with an undertone of surprise.

Hazen looked at the witch, raising her brows. "Yes?"

Brean put a hand on Hazen's knee. "When is it?"

She shook her head. "I don't know, um… I've been here a week now?" She used her fingers to count the days and paused. "Oh, today." She laughed shortly. "It's today. Happy birthday to me, I guess."

Lithônion leaned forward. "How old are you?"

Hazen scowled at the male. "Don't you know it's rude to ask a woman her age?"

Brean squeezed her knee, garnering her attention. "How old are you, Hazen?" she asked quietly.

"Twenty?" she said, confused.

Lithônion hummed, and Hazen looked at him, cutting her eyes to Savven, who was now staring at her.

"That explains a lot," muttered Brean, looking at Savven darkly. "Were you going to tell me?"

"Tell you what?" Hazen asked.

Brean ignored her, raising a demanding brow at Savven.

The male sighed, looking unbothered. "I've just met you, Witch. It's not a matter that concerns you."

Gold eyes flashed with warning. "Well, it concerns me now."

"Does it?" he asked coolly.

"Yes," she hissed.

"How so?"

Brean growled, unable to answer because she knew he was

right, but it still boiled her blood.

Hazen waved a frustrated hand between the two, garnering their attention. "Is anyone going to tell me what's happening and why you're talking about me as if I'm not here?"

Brean cocked her head at Savven. "Well, it's not my place, so would you like to explain it to her?"

Savven's eyes narrowed slightly at the witch. "You're very nosy. Has anyone ever told you that?"

Her expression turned charming, and she gave him a tight smile. "Yes, actually."

Hazen made an impatient noise and raised a brow, eyes bouncing between them.

"A keeper comes of age at twenty," Savven said lowly, slowly sliding his gaze to Hazen.

Hazen leaned forward, the heat from the flames warming her skin. "And I just turned twenty."

"Yes."

"Does that mean…?"

He shook his head once. "I don't know."

"Do I have magic?"

Savven paused, regarding her before he said, "I don't know."

Hazen scrubbed a hand over her face, groaning lowly. "So, what are you saying? You think I have magic, but you don't know for sure, and you don't know if I'm the keeper, but I just turned twenty."

Everyone was silent.

"So, what the hell am I?" she demanded.

No one answered her.

Hazen stared at the fire. The ember popped in the air, and the heat blazed against her face when the image of a village on fire filled her mind. Something he had said to her rose through the ashes of her memory. "A woman, chosen by dragons and a descendant of High Fae," she said softly, glancing up at Savven.

Savven's face softened when she repeated his words, and he nodded once.

"My family is very human," she clarified. "I would know if one of them has any magical abilities."

"You wouldn't though, would you?" Brean interjected thoughtfully. "Magic with humans is very tricky. I don't speak from experience, only from reading history books. Still, from what they say, magic chooses only the strongest to be its counterpart."

Hazen shifted to face the witch. "What do you mean?"

"Magic is a living thing within us. It can shape us and use us, or it can destroy us. We do not control the magic; rather, we work hand in hand with it. If we are weak or unskilled, the magic takes over for us. It fills our weaknesses with its own knowledge. And if we are strong, it strengthens us to become a double-edged sword."

"How will I know if I have it?" Hazen asked quietly, glancing at those who were starting to spread out on the floors with blankets.

"That's between you and whoever brought you here," Brean replied.

Hazen stared at the flames, watching it crackle soundlessly. "How does your magic work? Where did it come from? I've seen all of you use it, but where does it come from?"

Brean looked at Savven, who waved a hand for her to continue. She shook her head when he crossed his arms, leaning his head back and closing his eyes.

"Magic is bestowed in many forms to the Fae. High Fae have more capabilities because they were the first created by the Gods. The lesser Fae have more common abilities. Neither magic, though, can be used to harm another. The magic webbed into our world is what funnels into us all. Witches, warlocks, we mould magic into what we need it to be, but the Fae have it innately built into their very beings.

"Only the fallen Fae use their magic to harm others, to go against the natural order of things. High Fae royalty who are crowned High King or High Queen have a direct connection to the magic of their city. Savven and Lithônion have magic by birthright because they are High Fae, but they can only use it to assist them in daily tasks. Only when Savven takes the crown will his magic grow beyond his bounds and tie him to his city."

"So, the magic comes from the Gods? But where do the Gods get it?" So many questions were whirling around in Hazen's head, but she couldn't find the right way to voice them.

"The Gods came from the heavens, but we don't know much about their history. They fell like light from eternal darkness, and from that darkness, they shaped the dragons who breathed life into the core of our world, and from that life, they created the things living within. They created us. The breath of life from the dragons and the Gods was forged with magic, which feeds into us and binds us all."

Hazen stared at Brean. Her mind had gone blank. Could she be tied to that magic?

The fire orbs dimmed, and the berthing darkened as sleep filled the cabin.

"Close your eyes, Hazen," Brean said gently. She waved a hand around Hazen's shoulders, and a blanket draped softly over her. "You'll have plenty of time to have your questions answered."

The ship rocked with every turn of the waves, but Hazen's eyes suddenly grew heavy, and she yawned, stifling it with the back of her hand.

Whatever magic was around the ship had made the journey shift from thrashing waves to being rocked in a cradle. Now that she had paid attention to it, her mind grew heavy with exhaustion.

She glanced at Savven and Lithônion, and she noted their eyes were closed, though she doubted they even knew how to sleep.

Brean gave her an encouraging smile, and Hazen nodded, shifting to lie down. She faced the fire, tucking the blanket around her and curling her arm under her head.

The warmth of the flames kissed her skin, and Brean softly began to hum under her breath. A melody that reminded Hazen of home, but as she tried to distinguish the notes, her eyes drifted shut.

A crack of thunder jolted Hazen from sleep as the ship slammed into a wave. An echo of moans went through the berthing, and she glanced around, rubbing the sleep from her eyes. The fires still flickered with life, the ship creaking with every pulse of the sea around it.

CRACK!

Hazen jolted, heart hammering behind her ribs. Her head whipped to Savven and found him staring at her while Lithônion was staring at the door to the main deck.

Something heavy and foreboding shifted in the air, the ship going nearly silent as if it, too, were holding its breath in anticipation.

Taking in a shaky breath, Hazen stood.

"Don't."

One word from Savven had Hazen halting mid-step.

"I'm just going to look," she whispered.

He regarded her for a moment, and Hazen thought he was going to tell her to sit back down. Instead, he looked at Lithônion and jerked his chin towards her. "Go with her," he said.

Hazen swallowed the knot in her throat when Lithônion appeared at her side, stepping carefully around those still sleeping, though most were waking now and looking around at each other in confusion.

The stairs creaked, and Hazen stumbled when the boat listed sharply. Lithônion's hand went to her arm, steadying her, and she gave him a small smile.

Pushing on the door, Hazen frowned when it barely budged. Her heartbeat was too loud in her ears, her breathing too shallow as she tried to calm her nerves the longer she faced the door.

Something didn't belong, something didn't feel *right.*

"Let me," Lithônion murmured, ushering her aside.

Frowning when the door didn't budge, he leaned his weight into the wood, and it flew open.

Lithônion stumbled forward, catching himself as the world opened up into chaos.

The wind screamed past them, waves rising over the bow in a crescendo every few seconds, washing away everything in its path.

Hazen's hair whipped across her face, stinging her skin. Tears formed in her eyes as the wind cut through her. The storm above was tearing across the sea in sheets of blinding rain and lightning that webbed through thick, rolling black clouds. The thunder shook the air, and her heart nearly stopped in her chest, her breathing faltering in her throat.

Rain-plastered hair clung to Lithônion's face, and Hazen watched him go preternaturally still. She followed his gaze. A flash of something silver caught her eyes before lightning struck the water, and the sea exploded.

Hazen tried to scream a warning as a massive beast shot from the waves, but the sound never made it past the creature's thunderous roar. The creature's large green head and sapphire eyes aimed directly at them, and its long body dived back into the waves.

"Sea dragon!" Lithônion yelled. "*Go!*"

But Hazen was already running below to the others. Savven and Brean were nearly to her when their world shattered, and the sea washed inside.

The sea dragon's body slammed into them, and the port side splintered. Shards flew through the air like spears that sliced across Hazen's cheek and torso before the waves swept her feet from under, and a wave took her down.

Her scream was cut off as water filled her mouth, and she pumped her arms, cutting towards the surface even as the current wanted to pull her back. Hazen took in a lungful of air, breaking the surface, and was overcome by the screams of terror surrounding her.

Bodies littered the sea, splashing as they tried to tread the choppy terrain. Cries for help echoed, and Hazen looked around desperately for Savven or Lithônion or even the bright red hair of Brean. Heart in her throat, eyes wide, desperation clawed through her.

"*Savven!*" she screamed. Her head jerked every which way, choking on seawater as it came over her head.

Sputtering out the water, Hazen blinked the saltwater from her eyes and began to swim. "*Lithônion!*" Her words were lost in the cries of bodies and the clammer of the storm. "*Brean!*" Water filled her mouth, and she choked, coughing it up and swimming away from the ship.

A massive emerald body cut through the waters before dipping below the waves. Hazen's heart hammered when she saw it, threatening to break her ribs, but she kept swimming.

Hair clung to her face, her eyes burned, and the wind roared in her ears before she was dragged under the waves again. Her boots were filled with water, and she tugged at them desperately, her feet getting stuck. Hazen screamed, air escaping overhead, and yanked at her boots. She jerked them off and fought for the surface, breaking through the wall and coughing out a mouthful of saltwater, her eyes blurring.

A loud snap shot through the air, and Hazen watched the ship splinter in half and sink beneath the sea. Floating debris and bodies, so many bodies, lay atop the water.

"Savven! Savv—" her voice cracked, and she choked on the words. A thick, wide slab of the ship's siding floated by her, and she snatched hold of it. Heaving herself partially onto the boards.

A broken sob caught in her throat, her eyes scanning the choppy swells, but all she saw were bodies and no life.

She was alone, in the middle of the sea.

CHAPTER 29

Saltwater lapped at Hazen's sunburned cheek, and the shrill squabble of birds filled her ears as she slowly pried open one heavy eye and then the other. Sunlight penetrated her vision, and she groaned. Her cracked lips tore, and she tasted copper.

Hair caked in salt tangled around her, it stuck to her burnt face when she lifted her head. Her bleary eyes scanned the now calm sea with its flat cerulean waters, noting the emptiness. There was nothing in sight for as far as she could see.

How long had she been drifting?

Groaning, Hazen tried to move her fingers, which were held fast to the board under her, flinching when her damaged skin brushed against the wood. Cracked and raw, she felt her skin break between her fingers and knew if she looked, she would find blood between the folds of her skin.

Her tongue was leaden when she tried to swallow, her throat screamed for water. Arms shaking, Hazen tried to heave herself onto the board further, but the world began to spin, and she collapsed, holding onto the wood with the last remnants of strength. Her vision faltered, and darkness began to enclose around her. Before she knew it, she was falling back into the awaiting oblivion.

Hushed voices tangled together as three females watched the sleeping figure before them. Their once pearlescent skin dull, their concave bodies shaded grey and blue. White hair floated behind them as silver brow-less eyes watched the body with a curious distrust, their sharp faces emotionless.

Silver pearlescent scales appeared as their thin, withered torsos ended, descending into translucent silver tails, shadowed with grey-blue as the fins split. From them grew blue gossamer tendrils.

"What should we do with it?" questioned one of the three.

"Valean should take it to the Queen."

Valean turned to glare at the one who had spoken first, letting out a hiss. "Why must I, Pharien? The Queen shall be angered that we did not present the girl to her at once."

"All the more why you should do it," Pharien said, smiling cruelly.

Valean lunged at Pharien, baring rows of razor teeth in a snarl. Pharien jerked back as sharp nails sliced for her throat.

"Pharien, Valean, quiet, or it will be all of our heads!"

The two gave furious stares at each other as they turned to Narssisca.

"Fighting amongst each other like animals. To call yourselves servants of the Queen, it's a disgrace."

Valean and Pharien bared their teeth at the insult.

"Though this girl may be dead to this world, that will not stop us from joining her if someone hears this argument. Now, enough!"

"Watch your words, Narssisca." Pharien swam around Narssisca slowly, brushing a hair from her sister's face as she leant in close.

"Or it will be your head and not ours."

Narssisca leaned into Pharien, her words slithering between clenched teeth, "Watch your threats, or it will be your tongue."

Valean looked warily at the door connecting to the hall as the two argued. "Let us bring the girl to the Queen. She will do with it as she pleases; we cannot keep it here."

The three glanced at the girl lying on the stone floor. She had strong yet narrow, delicate features, dirty, tangled blonde hair, and tan, cracked skin. She wore travelling clothes that hung in shreds around her slim frame. The gloom of the stone chamber gave her a haughty appearance that said death was near.

"Are you sure she's not dead?" asked Valean, silver eyes flicking between the girl and her sisters.

Narssisca smirked, swimming over to the body and staring down at it. "If she were dead, she would have been food for the creatures, nothing but a carcass left when we found her."

Pharien and Valean swam to Narssisca's side and helped her lift the body. Narssisca took the arms while Pharien grasped her legs. Valean swam to the black coral door and cracked it open, peering outside. A grey corridor stood empty, and she cleared the way, ushering the two out as they hurriedly swam down the bleak, curving hall.

They reached the tall, bleached coral doors of the Queen's throne room. Two guards stood at attention, their silver and blue tails floating behind them. They stared ahead with half-glazed stares as if the three of them weren't there, long poisoned spears held at their sides.

"We have a gift for the Queen," announced Pharien with cold eyes, a cruel smile curling her lips.

The guards eyed the body held between them and moved to open the massive doors. The loud crack of coral echoed through the watery halls, the muscles of their thin arms straining as the door resisted, giving in slowly with every scrape along the floor. With a groan, the doors opened, and the three swam inside.

Tall white coral pillars lined the hall, with cold grey stone floors and black sand walls encompassing them. The court dwellers floated among themselves, though they stopped and stared as they approached the Queen's throne, a hushed murmur rolling through the water.

The Queen was a dark, twisted beauty with silver hair and silver skin, delicate yet sharp features masking the hatred brewing behind her eyes. She sat upon her white coral throne, and her long white tail lay upon the stone floor lazily, gleaming under the orbs of light floating above them in a scattered array.

"Why do you come before me?"

Her cold and monotonous voice caused the three to halt, doubt washing over them.

Masking the fear that began to tremble through her, Narssisca swam forward as they laid the girl at the Queen's feet.

"Queen Nautien," she said, bowing her head, not daring to look the Queen in the eyes. "We found her floating on the surface. We think she is human. We bring her as an offering to you, Majesty."

Queen Nautien stared down at the girl lying unconscious at her feet. Her gaze slowly moved to the three merwomen, who flinched under her assessment. "Leave. And leave this girl here," she commanded coldly. The court stared at her. "Leave before I condemn you all to the gallows!"

Those in the hall scattered until only the Queen and the girl on the floor remained.

She swam from her throne and bent over the body, silver hair floating around her sharp face like silk. The Queen inhaled deeply, her eyes rolling back when she scented the girl. "A *hu*-man," she hissed, sharp teeth gleaming. One long, thin finger trailed a grey nail down the side of the girl's cheek, her cracked skin broke, and a whisp of blood floated before Nautien. Her tongue slipped out and tasted the red drop.

A low groan of approval had her dark eyes turning black, and she wanted to tear into her. To feast. To *devour*.

"Guards!"

Her voice carried through the empty hall, and a guard appeared from a hidden door behind the throne.

"Your Majesty?"

Nautien didn't take her eyes off the girl, digging her hands into the tangled hair and jerking her body closer to her, the human's feet hovering above the floor. She had the appearance of death, this human girl, but her blood spoke of life, of something *more*, and Nautien dragged her nose long the collum of the girl's neck, inhaling the rich scent of her blood.

"Take this girl to the dungeons," she commanded, releasing the girl who sunk to the ground. "We're going to have some fun when she wakes."

He struck his chest with his fist and bent low, taking hold of her in his thin, pale arms. The girl's head rolled back, arm hanging limply at her side. He disappeared behind the hidden door.

Queen Nautien allowed herself the pleasure of a smile as her thoughts whirled together. "Ezra will be pleased."

Brean cracked open one bleary eye and then the other, blinking slowly past the haze of sand, salt, and light that made her head throb. Bringing a heavy hand to her mouth, she wiped away the sand that coated her lips and part of her jaw. The taste of saltwater on her tongue made her mouth drier than the sand beneath her. Sitting up slowly, Brean looked at her surroundings, noticing the beach wrapped around a steep sloping cliff until it disappeared among a bend of rocks.

Scrubbing a hand over her face, she turned a weary gaze to the sea, where the tide lapped gently at her feet. Her clothes were tattered and dirty, there was sand in various crevasses of her body, and her muscles ached with every movement, but that didn't stop her as she stood on unsteady feet. Stumbling, she caught herself, found her balance, and smoothed a hand over the now ruined purple skirt of her dress.

She spotted Savven and Lithônion lying up on either side of the beach. Her head pounded, her ears still ringing, but she ignored the persistent throbbing and stumbled over to Lithônion.

She fell to her knees and leaned over him, shaking his shoulders weakly. "Lithônion." Her voice was nothing but a hoarse whisper.

Lithônion stirred slightly, his brows furrowing. An audible groan left his lips, eyes shooting open, and confusion flashed over his face.

Brean hastily put an arm around his shoulders and helped him sit forward. "Careful, careful, take a moment."

"I'm fine." He brushed her hand away, pressing fingers to his temples and squeezing his eyes shut.

"I'm going to check on Savven." Brean stared at Lithônion momentarily, pushing to her feet when she got no reply.

Savven was opposite Lithônion as she walked to the other side of the beach. He was unconscious and didn't stir as she approached. Crouching down, she grasped Savven's shoulders and slowly sat him up with a low grunt. He was dead weight. "Savven… Savven, come, it's time to wake."

Savven didn't respond. His handsome face remained as vacant and clear as still water. Shifting her weight on the sand, she brought Savven into her arms. She placed a hand on his chest, and her eyes flashed green, magic glowing emerald under her fingers. Warmth flooded from her hand into his body.

Savven's body twitched lightly before his mouth parted, and he threw himself onto his side. Water forced its way out of him, and he sucked in a greedy breath, filling his lungs hungrily.

Brean rubbed soothing circles on his back, trying to calm the tremors raking down his body. "Breathe, Savven."

Savven inhaled deeply, his shaking slowly ebbing. He lay in the sand, his face pressed into the grainy surface, breathing until his body visibly relaxed.

Brean stared down at him patiently as he recovered, waiting for him to sit up. "Maybe I should have turned you into a toad, would have avoided all of this," she commented thoughtfully.

A dry chuckle rasped from him, and he turned to give her a sidelong look. "I am in your debt, Witch."

She snorted delicately. "A prince in debt to a witch? What would the Gods say?"

"Damn the Gods," he said almost bitterly, rising slowly with a groan. "They're nowhere to be found."

"Ye of little faith," she replied, helping him stand. "Don't cast your doubt to them yet."

He gave her a critical stare, which had less of an effect than he probably intended by his weathered appearance. "You favour the Gods?"

"I favour the faith that everything will work as is intended." She looked him up and down with a sceptical eye. "You, on the other hand, I think that sea dragon won this fight." He glared at her, and she laughed, nudging his shoulder.

Shaking his head, he chuckled under his breath and looked down the beach, noting Lithônion, who stood at the tide's edge, watching the waves. "Come on," he murmured.

Lithônion heard their approach but gave them no notice. "What do we do now?"

"Well, since I don't see any half-drowned looking humans, we search for her," Savven said, crouching as a wave lapped at the shore, dipping his hands into the liquid and washing the dust from them. Standing, he looked to his companions.

Lithônion raised a critical brow. "We don't know if she is alive or dead."

"She's out there, Lithônion," Savven countered. "We were making way to Álfheimr, if the girl has any sense in her that's where she'll head."

The two males paused and watched as Brean stepped forward and walked into the water until she was waist-deep.

The wind sang a quiet melody around her, and Brean closed her eyes. She inhaled deeply, stretching a hand over the water. Her body rocked back and forth, swaying with the tide and the life flowing below. And then she stilled. Her body jerked and became rigid. Limbs tensed, muscles contracted, and her eyes scurried beneath closed lids. Brean's hand hovered over the water's surface as she searched below it, among its many seas and under dwellings.

Brean waded out of the water a few minutes later, the bottom half of her gown trudging her down. She bent and rung out the water. "I could not sense her anywhere, but the enchanted clothing might have something to do with that. Though we are alive, which in turn gives us hope that so is she."

Lithônion hummed lowly, closing his eyes as a light wind blew. Then he turned his stare to the sky, muttering, "We're north. If we journey east along the coast, there's a village."

Brean raised a brow, releasing her skirt. "To the east? Isn't that village hunter territory?"

"Yes," Savven confirmed, his mouth set in a disapproving line.

"Are you sure that's a wise idea?" Brean questioned, staring down the shoreline as if she could see the village from where she stood.

"We might be able to catch another ship heading north if it stops in port," Lithônion said. "Evengile is a village of thieves and bounty hunters whose reputation precedes them, so step carefully when we arrive."

Brean looked at Savven from the corner of her eye when the Fae male let out a low, deep breath.

"Do you object, Savven?" Brean asked.

"Yes, because going into Evengile is a marker on any traveller's head."

Lithônion folded his arms casually. "Do you have a better idea?"

The air stirred with tension, and Brean shifted on her feet, eyes bouncing between the two males.

Savven looked north, away from the shore, then east along the coast where the village would be far in the distance.

"No," he said tightly. "A trip on foot will take twice as long if we cannot find a ship willing to take us, but we have to try." The words were begrudging, and Savven's eyes darkened with assessment when they landed on Lithônion.

After a moment, Brean clapped her hands together loudly, garnering their attention. "Well?" she said curiously. "What are we waiting for? If we are to reach this mysterious village of thieves and get to Álfheimr we must go now." She made to start walking but halted in her steps, looking at the two behind her with a smirk. "Unless, of course, you like to stumble about in the dark like fools?"

Savven's brows shot to his hairline. "High Fae, do not stumble around in the dark," he remarked dryly.

Brean put a hand to her heart. "Oh, my apologies, I forgot how *majestic* the High Fae are."

Lithônion snorted.

"I vote we leave her here," Savven muttered to Lithônion.

"I heard that!" Brean was already walking away, but she threw a crude hand gesture over her shoulder at him.

Savven followed the witch, shaking his head.

Lithônion made to follow suit, though dropped behind, turning to watch the waves for a moment. A pit of frustration and rolling knots webbed through his stomach, and he frowned at the sea.

"Lithônion?"

He turned and found Savven watching him calmly. Not saying a word, he walked past him with a tight smile.

CHAPTER 30

Hazen felt like she was floating, but she wasn't. Her cheek was pressed against a hard, roughly cut surface, and when she moved, a cut along her face pulled painfully.

"I think she's awake."

A soft, melodic voice whispered around her, and she squeezed her eyes shut, her heart beginning to pound in her chest. Where was she? Who was that? The memory of the ship, the explosion, the sea dragon, and the *bodies* filled her memory, and Hazen wrenched her eyes open. The images of lifeless faces floating atop the sea stayed with her even when she stared at a blur of colour that slowly came into focus.

The colour moved again, turning to a vibrant, shining gold and silver, and she noted the glimmer of what looked like fish scales...

Hazen slowly moved her gaze up and up, and… a torso, full round breasts covered by those same golden scales, and then emerald, green eyes.

"You're awake!" the one with green eyes quipped.

Hazen jolted upright and skittered back, bumping into something soft. She whipped around and found another gold tail floating idly behind her. Yelping in surprise, but no sound came out, she put a hand to her throat. Hazen scrambled to her feet, and the world spun violently. Bracing her hands on her knees, she waited for the walls to stop moving, her stomach churning with it.

"Are you ill?"

Hazen turned sharply towards the melodic voice, instantly regretting it when she felt her stomach contents want to come up. Those green eyes were gentle and understanding, and Hazen straightened, forcing in slow breaths, eyeing the female. Her raven black hair was braided down her back with vibrant green seagrass woven between its folds, her caramel skin rich even in the dim light that cut across high cheekbones and a firm mouth.

They were all exotic and breathtaking, and neither one was the same. A quick glance told Hazen there were seven of them. Some had dark auburn hair, others silky blonde that looked like gold, and the one before her had hair black as night; no matter how different they appeared, they all held a brand of untouchable beauty. Their torsos were lean, and the naked flesh at their hips slowly started to turn to silver and gold scales as they descended. Where their legs would have been were tails, slim and smooth, the fins curving gracefully as golden tendrils grew from where they split.

"We won't hurt you," said the green-eyed beauty.

Hazen opened her mouth to speak, but no sound came out. Her mouth opened and closed. Nothing. Panicked, air bubbles escaped her mouth, and she grabbed her throat, eyes going wide.

"Mermagic is complicated," said one of the females, whose voice had a soft French accent underlining.

Dark auburn hair floated around a kind face with black almond eyes. She offered Hazen a soft smile as she swam up to her. "If you wish to breathe, the magic will take away your ability to speak; if you wish to speak, then you will lose your ability to breathe. Magic gives, and it takes. It must keep a balance," she explained. "I'm Lilla, and these are my sisters."

Hazen glanced at each face briefly before returning to Lilla, questions in her eyes. *Where am I?* she mouthed, gesturing to the cell. She felt like a lunatic.

"You are in a holding cell beneath the mermaid palace in the sea of Bel'onc. A place unfortunately ruled by Nautien."

Then why...? She gestured to each of them and then to the holding cell, shaking her head in question.

"There is always a balance in magic, just as there is in life. To every good, there is evil. Nautien is of the darkest kinds of magic. She locks us up in holding cells while her followers roam free."

Hazen's brows pulled tight.

Lilla shook her head. "Not every battle is won, especially when the ones you're fighting were the ones you loved as kin."

Hazen looked around the cell. The grey walls were cracked, there were no windows, and the cage bars were made of coarse iron. Sitting on the rocky ledge that jutted from the wall, seven mermaids surrounded her, watching her curiously.

High-pitched voices filled their cell from down the hall, and the females scattered quickly in a flurry of fins. Hazen blinked when they vanished. Her hair floated around her face as she turned and saw a door hidden from view. They hurriedly swam through it. Lilla appeared in front of her and all but dragged her into the other room.

The merwoman put a finger to her lips, shaking her head at Hazen.

Even though she couldn't speak, she pursed her lips tight and held her breath.

Something clanked against the cell bars. *Clank, clank... clank.* Each one was like a hammer to Hazen's heart that thudded behind her ribs.

Pressing against the wall, she peered around the edge of the doorway. Three mermaids hovered near the bars, glaring at the empty cell as they whispered in a low tone to each other. They were not like Lilla and the others who held individual beauty; these three were cold and sunken in—brittle. Where the others were gold and silver, they were silver and grey. They looked breakable, and Hazen knew she could snap them in half if she put her mind to it.

When the half-dead mermaids swam away, Lilla visibly relaxed.

"When darkness devours the light, all that's left is a shell. Nautien feeds on them to gain strength and power. But she wasn't always like this. There was a time when she was like us, but the temptation of power is too great for some."

She wanted to ask: *Like Ezra?* But she couldn't and frowned.

Lilla placed a delicate hand on Hazen's forehead. "Your fever is gone," she murmured.

Hazen stared at her.

"You were feverish when Nautien's guard brought you here. It could have been an ill effect the magic had on you. No worries now; it appears you're very resilient."

Where did they find me? she tried to mouth.

"I'm sorry, I'm not sure what you said."

Hazen waved a hand, dismissing her question.

Lilla was quiet, her thoughts whirling over her face as she concentrated. "What… is it like? Your world."

Hazen gave a helpless wave of her hands, touching her throat. She could only say so much when she couldn't speak.

"I understand." Lilla held up an offering hand. "May I?"

Hazen waved her on.

Dark blue magic sparked from her hand, and she placed her palm against Hazen's brow. Hazen felt nothing and looked at Lilla.

"Say someth—no, think of something to say."

"What did the magic take?"

Lilla laughed, but no sound came out. She paused, tilting her head in thought. *"Can you hear me?"*

Lilla's voice filled Hazen's head, and she stared at the mermaid wide-eyed, a smile blooming.

"It looks like magic created a balance that works in our favour. This prison mutes our magic so we cannot escape, but it's enough, I suppose." Lilla glanced at her sisters briefly. *"I was human once,"* she admitted.

Hazen stared, pointing at her in shock. *"You? I thought no one could enter unless they were of magic descent?"*

"*Everyone has magic within them. It's just a matter of believing in it.*"

"*When did you come to this world?*"

"*Many, many, many years have gone by. It is all a vague memory of my life I once had. When my sister Gene and I came here, it was thirteen forty-eight in the Provence of Béarn in southwest France. We had four other siblings and a mother—our father had died a year before from the Black Death.*"

Hazen put a comforting hand over Lilla's. "*How did you come to this world?*"

Lilla didn't speak for many moments, collecting her thoughts. "*Mother had told my sister and me to pick berries for a tart,*" she started. "*I remember we had been barefooted. Mother had just made new shoes for us, and they pinched terribly.*" A fond smile wove its way onto her lips. "*We had switched our dresses; she had worn my blue one while I wore her red one, and Mother never liked that. The wooded areas were always mysterious, filled with hidden treasures and secrets in which a child could get lost. Gene and I believed fairies lived in the hollows, trying to play tricks on our minds, making us delusional with happiness as our work was forgotten. We would chase each other through those woods, imagining a world not our own to gather us up and take us away.*

"*We never knew how mysterious those woods were until the day when they took us from our world. That day was beautiful. The sun was shining and warm on my skin, and we chattered for so long about the things unseen, or what the church called unholy. The world of fairytales intrigued us to every extent.*

"*Our family was not wealthy; we were a poor family of no stature in society and little money, but we lived a happy life. I suppose it was hard for the others, but for Gene and I, we lived not in their world but another. Our minds were not closed to those things unseen.*

"*Everything changed when Gene and I realised we had to return home. The wind grew wild; I remember being unable to breathe; I screamed for Gene, and she for me. The world grew dark after that. I awoke to a new day and a very new world.*" Lilla quieted, glancing at the lower half of her body, before adding, "*And I had a tail. Which was very shocking.*"

"*Is your sister here?*"

Lilla's eyes filled with sadness. "*No, she is not. My sister was an advisor to our rightful queen—Queen Amatheia—but Nautien slaughtered her when she used her body to shield our queen..."* Lilla turned bright eyes to Hazen, filled with pain, longing, and anger. *"I learned that day we all bleed the same. No matter our titles."*

If Hazen had thought it was possible to cry underwater, she would have been right now, but no tears fell much that she was aware of. Instead, her heart squeezed painfully in her chest. *"Where is Amatheia?"*

"With my sister."

Dead.

"Nautien overthrew her when Ezra gave her the power to do so. She controls us, and he controls the sea through her. She gave herself the title of queen, but she can rot with the rest of her kind. She will never be my queen."

Hazen looked at the doorway, where she knew an iron gate sat, keeping her barred in. *"Then those things I saw earlier..."*

"Were once like me and my sisters. But like I said, darkness devours the light. And Nautien is very hungry."

Hazen stared at the grey clay wall across from her hours later, tracing the cracks with her eyes as she pondered what she would do next. She didn't know how long she had been there; her mind wandered from one thing to another, drifting in and out of consciousness. Hazen noticed that two guards had only passed twice since she had woken, and none stood at the mouth of the cell.

Either they're confident or just stupid, she thought as her mind wandered back to when the merwomen swam hurriedly into the room she had solely occupied.

The time passed slowly, and soon, her eyelids started to fall shut, the soft hum of silence in her ears lulling her into a meditated sleep.

A bang from the hall sounded, and a hand awoke Hazen from her sleep.

"Girl."

Her heart lurched in her throat and met Lilla's worried expression.

Lilla looked over her shoulder quickly. *"They're moving us to another cell."*

Hazen stood mutely, following Lilla as she swam from the

room. Three mermen guards stood at the cell gate, shovelling the females out of the pen in single file. Hazen joined them at the end but was jostled back as she tried to exit.

"Not you," hissed the guard at the cell door. "The Queen wishes for you to stay here."

"*You can't!*" she yelled silently, shoving the hand that stopped her, albeit slower in the water, and sneering at the guard who aimed his long spear between her eyes.

"*No!*" Lilla swam back, reaching for her. "*It's okay, we'll be okay. The spears are poisoned. You will die if they cut you. Do as they say.*"

Only Hazen heard her as her voice filled her head.

The guards hissed out, baring rows of sharp teeth at Lilla. The point of a long spear aimed at her throat. "You will go with the others or face the Queen yourself!"

Lilla extended a hand to Hazen but dropped it, giving her one desperate pleading look before she was shoved down the hall.

"*Fair winds and following seas, Hazen.*" Lilla's voice was faint, but it filled Hazen before the silence took its place.

Her chest heaved in desperation, each breath tightening her lungs as Hazen watched Lilla and the others get taken away. At the same time, she was left there, standing alone in the silence.

She tried to reach out her thoughts to Lilla once they were out of sight but was met only with silence.

Hours passed while she sat on the floor in the corner, her head leaning against the wall, her bones numb and aching from being curled in the same position for so long. She waited. Watching the gate as her fingernails picked at the rough ground, the grain chafing against her skin.

Numbness crept in like an intruder through her limbs. Standing, she tried to walk it off as she paced wall to wall silently, her steps holding a slight buoyancy to them. Her bare feet scraped against the ground, and a muted echo wobbled around her. But it was enough. She did it again and again, her feet moving on their own accord, hair dancing around her face. They crossed over each other, stepped forward, and crossed back as if there was an invisible enemy, and their sword was her end. Her movements were slow but picked up speed until Savven's instructions were burned into her legs, and the wobbling echo of movement was constant.

The cuts on her side and face throbbed as her heart beat erratically, and she stopped, panting, bubbles clouding her vision. Then silence filled the space again. Muted, numbing, silence. She ached to speak, to say something, or even just a constant sound. She remained quiet. Frustration got the better of her, and she slammed her fist into the wall. Pain erupted as it vibrated through her bones, and she gritted her teeth against the throbbing, rubbing her tender knuckles.

The door at the end of the hall opened. Hazen went to the cell gate and lifted her hands to the iron bars. Time seemed to stop as white-hot electricity coursed through her. It crawled over her flesh, branded her bones, and seared every one of her cells as she dropped to her knees, her mouth opening in a muted scream. Her body shook, hands still grasping the iron bars—unable to let go as her body convulsed, silent cries leaving her.

Finally, her fingers dropped from the iron, curling in on themselves, and she dropped to the floor like a stone, blonde hair floating around her. Her body still shook as she lay there, unable to move. Hazen forced her eyes towards the hall. One of the guards stood there watching her, a coldness in his silver gaze. She could only watch him hazily through failing vision, her body trembling from shock, and forced herself to take short, gasping breaths.

It had been hours since she had touched the cell bars, and Hazen sat curled in the corner, having dragged herself across the ground after she regained some control over her body. She didn't know how long she had laid there, twitching, still vibrating from the pain. And even now, her bones felt charred and sore. Angry red streaks glared back at her on the inside of her hands with blistered skin, and she sighed, dropping her palms from her gaze.

She should be dead.

"The Queen commands your presence."

Hazen glared at the guard who opened the iron door without so much as a flinch.

"Get up!"

Hazen stood warily, though squared her shoulders. Seeing the guard pissed her off more than she realised, and she held onto the biting emotion. She let the guard take her. His grip around her arm was icy and hard as he pulled her along, barely flinching when his sharp nails dug into one of the cuts that marred her. The pain disappeared when he let go, shoving her in front of two massive white doors. He hammered on the doors twice with his fist.

A large crack echoed through the hallway, and the two doors were pulled open. The guard yanked on her arm, dragging her into a large throne room. It was empty, except for a female perched stiffly on a white coral throne.

"Your Majesty, the prisoner."

Cold, dark eyes peered down at Hazen. "Leave."

The guard bowed and left. Leaving Hazen and the Queen alone.

"I am Queen Nautien." Her voice was cold and distant as she stood from the throne, swimming towards Hazen. She circled her slowly, her gleaming white tail winding its way around her legs like a deadly caress. "You are human."

It wasn't a question.

Hazen said nothing, her eyes following the queen when she turned her back on her. Everything about the mermaid queen was cold, and Hazen tried to retain the icy emotion that crawled down her back, holding onto the anger she had been feeling.

"You know," the queen commented thoughtfully, "I almost don't want to hand you over to Ezra and keep you as my pet. I want to see what makes you special, to see why Ezra fears you." The queen leaned in close, cold eyes glancing at her body before hissing, "What makes you so important?"

She grazed a finger along Hazen's cheek, digging a nail into one of her cuts. When it bled, she drew her finger across the blood before it curled into the water. It glistened cherry red on the queen's tongue as she licked it off.

Hazen's stomach roiled in disgust.

Nautien's smile turned cutting. "Well, say something." The queen laughed coldly. "Oh, that's right, you can't speak! How sad, you're completely useless. It makes one wonder why the Dark One is so afraid of you. A simple human imposes no threat upon us."

Hazen bared her teeth at the queen, fists trembling at her side. She could be strong. She could withstand this.

She stepped towards her, and Nautien lashed out, her hand gripping Hazen by the throat and squeezing. Hazen sputtered silently, clawing at the hand restraining her.

Nautien clicked her tongue in disapproval, bending her mouth to Hazen's ear. "That wasn't very nice."

Queen Nautien released her with a toss, and Hazen stumbled back, sucking in a lung full of air. The queen glided to her throne, sitting stiffly upon it, her silver hair floating like silk clouds around her, her dark eyes calculating, and she smiled. "The chosen one has spirit, and I am going to enjoy breaking it."

Hazen's body was filled with ice. The anger diminished, smothered beneath the chill raking through her limbs. She steeled herself away, her heart beating wildly, her adrenaline made her limbs thrum with every ounce of fight she retained. She couldn't do anything as the queen swam forward and gently raked her nails across Hazen's cheek and up to her temples. White veins burned in whorls of poison across her skin, and Hazen cried silently at the pain that lanced through her head. Her skin burned like a thousand red-hot needles as the queen's poison branded her before it finally subsided.

"Forgotten by those you have met and those you have yet to meet." Nautien smiled cruelly, tilting her head in thought. "Held in a prison where your thoughts become your darkness. Dreams will turn to nightmares, and the world will never know of your existence after this. To Ezra, you will become a distant memory. He will never know that you lay beneath the sea in a prison within a prison."

Hazen's body jerked, and her bones suddenly burned. Her eyes went wide, and her mouth dropped open in a noiseless scream as her back arched in pain. She was on fire. Tears gathered in her eyes, but she fought them back, her knees threatening to give out. Every muscle in her body felt torn apart, and she took in a gasping breath, trembling when darkness encased her vision.

"You will be forgotten."

Nautien's voice was distant, murmured like a fading echo. Hazen's eyes turned milky, and her body jerked violently before crumbling to the ground, her mouth agape and darkness sweeping in to claim her.

"Take her to the abyss."

CHAPTER 31

Drip, drip... drip.
Lithonion closed his eyes and waited, counting his breaths. In…
out… in… out.
Drip... drip, drip... drip.
He fixated on the sound of the water plopping from overhead to
the stone floor at his feet. His heart wanted to tear out of his ribs,
his pulse thumping in his ears.
In… out… in… out.
Drip... drip... drip, drip.
His hand twitched at his side, and he wiped his sweaty palm on
his black pants, straightening the ends of his black fitted tunic.
In… out… in…
He smoothed a hand over his hair, fixing a hard stare at the

solid wood doors in front of him.

…Out.

The doors crack beneath their weight as he pushed them open and entered the throne room.

It was dark within the hall. Shadows ghosted across the floor like phantom serpents, orbs of light floated above were dim, and Lithônion blinked, his eyes adjusting.

Ezra stood behind the silver throne that sat on the obsidian dais. A dagger was held limp at his side, his unblinking stare on the silver chalice in his other hand. Blood pooled at his feet, dripping from the tip of the dagger, a blood trail vanishing behind a door to the left.

"My old friend."

Lithônion halted.

Ezra's voice caressed the air even though he didn't move. He brought the chalice to his lips, blood trickling down his jaw.

Lithônion's stomach tightened, chest heaving with every shallow breath he took. He opened his mouth, but his throat constricted, and he gagged as his neck concaved, clawing at the invisible hands that held him.

"I don't want to hear your lies!"

The voice was all around him, but Ezra still didn't move. He threw the chalice, and it crashed against a far wall, black eyes fixating on Lithônion.

Lithônion held fast, his vision waning as the bands around his neck tightened.

Ezra's steps slipped across the stone floors, descending the dais. He was leaner than Lithônion remembered, more skeletal than muscle and flesh. His cheekbones looked sharp enough to cut through his skin, and his eyes were sunken. His limbs were too thin and breakable. Even with Lithônion's wavering vision, pulse thumping behind his skin as pressure built, he could see that Ezra was wasting away. He was being consumed, eaten alive, and he didn't even know it.

"My old friend," Ezra whispered when he stood before Lithônion.

A long, bony finger reached for Lithônion as if to touch him, to see if he were real.

Lithônion's hands trembled at his sides, fighting the blackness invading his mind, and held back the flinch when a sharp nail dragged from his temple to his jaw.

Ezra pulled away, red glinting on his nail, and he licked it off. A malicious smile cut his face. "Your blood is sweet, my friend, and my pets are *hungry*."

Lithônion tried to suck in air, his face throbbing, and he bit out a strangled sound, "Né—"

The blood down Ezra's jaw had dried, but his teeth were still stained red when he smiled. "Beg for me to spare you. Beg for your life!"

"—far"

Ezra's smile disappeared. "What did you say?"

"Née—far." The sound barely scraped past his teeth, but he forced it out with the last of his air, and the darkness swooped in.

The bands around his throat vanished, Lithônion crumbled to the ground, and sweet air filled his lungs. He took in a sucking breath and then another. Relishing in the rise and fall of his chest. Black spots floated across his vision as he raised himself off the ground, supporting himself with his hands.

"What did you say?" The words were whispered on a single harsh breath, and Ezra's head ticked to the side like an animal.

Forcing himself to stand, Lithônion faced Ezra with a firm stare. "Néefar. I come with a message from Néefar."

Something thirsty glimmered in those black eyes as they looked Lithônion over with a slight smirk. "Well, why didn't you say so?"

Lithônion didn't move, watching Ezra return to his throne, sitting casually on it.

"My time is limited. I wouldn't waste it if I were you."

The warning was casual but direct, and Lithônion walked up to the dais.

"Where is the shifter?"

Squaring his shoulders, Lithônion willed steel down his spine. "With the girl."

"Then why," hissed Ezra, leaning forward, "IS SHE NOT HERE AND YOU ARE?!" The veins in his neck bulged, turning black against his sallow skin.

The hall grew fridged like all warmth had been sucked from the air, and Lithônion's eyes darted to the shadows growing behind the throne. Fear pierced his body when two blood-red eyes stared at him from the darkness.

Bone-thin fingers curled around the edge of the silver throne, black dagger-like nails digging into the element. Stark white hair gleamed in the shadows as a face only from nightmares emerged.

"I smell *blood.*" The voice was no higher than a whisper, but the words fell like ice.

"Nazar." The name was uttered on a breath as Lithônion looked at the shade.

Ezra's brow ticked up, and he tilted his head in regard. "You know my shade?"

There was an edge to those words, a dangerous one, but he jerked his head once. "Yes. Néefar has informed me of what to expect."

Ezra was up and down the dais steps before Lithônion could inhale a breath, his hand latching around Lithônion's jaw in a grip that threatened to shatter his bones.

"A *spy* in my mountain?!" Ezra screamed in Lithônion's face. His nails sunk into flesh, and five trails of blood fell down his neck.

"No!" rasped Lithônion, nostrils flaring with every sucking breath he took. "Néefar is no spy, and neither am I! We work towards the same goal!"

Ezra leaned in close, his breath bitter with the scent of copper. "And what goal is that?"

"To bring the kingdom down."

The words hung between them, and Lithônion stared at Ezra with cold eyes, willing the years of his training as a warrior to take over.

"Álfheimr's finest wants to crumble the kingdom walls?" Ezra inquired. He let go of Lithônion's jaw and stepped back, eyeing the male thoughtfully. His footsteps echoed in the frozen hall as he strode to his throne, his black eyes fixed on Lithônion when he turned.

"And where does Néefar fall in all of this?"

"He has his own agenda with the kingdom. You can never trust those who change their faces. But I know we both want to see it fall into ash, and you're the only one who can do that."

The remark had Ezra's face shifting from one of distrust to one of satisfaction. Nazar bared his row of sharp teeth, and a hiss that sent nails raking down Lithônion's skin slipped from the shade.

"I smell *lies*!"

"Quiet Nazar!" Ezra snapped.

Nazar's head whipped to Ezra, baring his teeth. His face turned savage, morphing into something Lithônion could only imagine lived in the darkest pits of the underworld.

"He spews *LIES*!"

Ezra shot to his feet, rounding on the shade. "I. Said. QUIET! You have already failed me once! You have no place to speak!"

Something dark flashed in those blood-red eyes, and the snarl on Nazar's face fell, replaced by a sly smile. "As you wish, My Lord."

Lithônion could see the leashed rage in Ezra when he turned his attention back to him.

"Foe or friend." He stepped from the dais slowly. "Friend or foe." Another step, and another. Ezra stepped up to Lithônion, dragging a nail through the drying blood on his neck. "We will see where your allegiance lies, but not yet."

Black eyes regarded bright green ones, and Ezra stepped back.

"Nazar, take him below until I'm ready for him." Ezra stepped back as Nazar swept in. "Nazar."

The shade halted, skeletal fingers hovering over Lithônion's arm, twitching.

"Do not touch him."

Nazar sneered at Lithônion, telling him he was lucky, and retracted his hand into the shroud of darkness and shadows that cloaked his frame.

"Move," he hissed, pointing to a wooden door to the left of the throne.

Lithônion pursed his mouth into a firm line, striding for the door.

"LEVINA!"

Lithônion froze.

The wooden door opened and outstepped his memories—only she was wearier, and a tiredness had replaced the sparkle in her sky-blue eyes. Her blonde hair was still soft and flowing down her back. She stood ramrod straight with that confidence he knew so well, even for her slight frame.

Levina's blue eyes widened when they fell on him. However, it lasted only a second before they became indifferent, and she made to walk past.

His eyes fell on the soft, rounding belly hidden behind black gossamer layers, and her chin notched a little higher when she passed. She had seen him notice.

"Move, Elf, or I'll rip out your soft flesh."

Nazar's words cut him out of the haze, and he blinked. His feet moved only because he forced them to, and his face remained neutral from years of training, but as he walked through the wooden door, he looked back over his shoulder.

Levina caught his eye briefly before striding up the dais to Ezra. "You screamed for me?"

The snark in her voice eased something in Lithônion's chest even when Nazar's shadows shoved him further into the tunnel, and the door slammed shut.

CHAPTER 32

The abyss was a bottomless pit of the darkest waters, where no light could penetrate. The creatures that lingered had protruding jowls and elongated razor teeth, while others had long, slippery bodies encased in electrical currents that promised death to those around them.

Suspended within those dark waters was a slate cube. No iron gate, windows, door or exit of any kind. In other words, it was a coffin at the bottom of the sea.

Two of Nautien's guards swam through the inky waters, their tails sifting through the current with ease despite their skeletal frames. A limp body was held between them. They slowed when approaching the cube and cautiously pressed through the slate wall. The wall gave way under their hands, and they passed through it as if it hadn't existed.

The darkness was cold as ice, and even with their mer eyes, they couldn't penetrate the shadows. They were blind, light did not exist within the cube, and the guards shifted restlessly because of it.

Tossing her into the dark depths of the isolated prison, they couldn't see as Hazen's body floated there, her blonde hair wafting around her pale face. If there was light, they would see the delicate white whorls of poison now branded along the left side of her face, both intricate and deadly. But the guards couldn't see anything, and their eyes darted back and forth while slowly swimming backwards.

It was a prison for the insane, and the guards left before they could succumb to it.

Hazen's body twitched violently, but she was unaware of her movements as the darkness in her mind grew claws that sunk into her like teeth. Pain lanced through her, and she screamed into the void, but none heard her.

Levina's footfalls were silent, the stone cold beneath her bare feet as she plunged deeper into the mountain, spiralling down and down and down. The stairs opened into the mouth of a long hall lit by torches that burned without end. A row of thick wooden doors with iron bars caging the small square observatory cutouts sat to her right as she walked down the hall. Hands reached through the bars, those that could fit through the narrow spaces, while others gripped them with white knuckles, scared and weary eyes penetrating the darkness from within. The cells were cursed, entrapping the prisoners within with dark enchantments that sucked dry their abilities to use magic, making escape impossible.

Her gut twisted sharply at the sharp tang of copper. She shoved down the darkness Ezra had embedded within her, fighting the hunger the demons felt. She knew her eyes had turned black, and she paused, breathing deeply through clenched teeth. The tension in her eased, and the demons, already starved, crawled back into the hole she had shoved them into and locked them tight within her.

With the hunger under control, she drew a shaking hand through her hair and peered into the cell beside her. A body lay mangled and half-eaten on the ground, browned blood pooled around what was left. She cocked her head slightly, and a pair of grey eyes blinked back at her from the shadows.

Exhaling sharply, Levina turned away and continued walking.

Door after door, until a scent made her stop near the end. It was familiar and calming, and she faced the door. Her blood rushed through her ears as she peered within the cell. Bright green eyes, sandy brown hair, a tall, muscular body, and a face that generally had a teasing smile attached to it, but now was a wall of steel emerged from the darkness. Lithônion stepped into the little light let into the cell, and Levina wanted to sob.

But she didn't.

She kept her composure, sealing away her emotions.

Silence stretched thin between them until she finally asked at the same time he spoke.

"Why are you here, Lithônion?"

"You're alive... I knew it."

The awe in his voice couldn't be missed as he searched the planes of her face, and Levina shifted on her feet, placing a hand over her belly.

"You've been here this whole time?" he asked, his hands gripping the iron bars.

Levina sniffed, straightening her back. "Yes."

When she had seen Lithônion, she thought she had been seeing one of Ezra's many tormenting hallucinations he provoked her with. But when he had passed her, she could smell the world beyond the mountain on him. He smelled like life, family, and friend; it had taken everything in her not to fall at his feet in relief. Or to scream at him to run and flee before he was trapped within the mountain like she was.

Instead, she walked past him straight to Ezra, who had kept himself entertained with her for hours both in the throne room and his private chambers. When he finally fell asleep, she slipped from his room to find Lithônion, but now that she saw him, she didn't know what to do.

Her eyes darted down each end of the hall when something creaked loudly from one end. "How did you find me? You shouldn't be here, Lithônion."

He looked offended at her words. "I shouldn't be here? *You* shouldn't be here, Levina!" His voice was harsh but low, the words forced between his teeth.

"My reasoning is my own."

"Damn your reasonings," he retorted.

"How did you find me, Lithônion?" she asked again.

He regarded her silently, eyes dropping to the peak of her rounding belly she still held a hand to. "I could smell you faintly while scouting around the western territory. It came on the wind nearly a season ago, and I knew you were somewhere within. Whether you were alive or dead, that I didn't know, but I had to find out."

The sorrow in his words made Levina's chest squeeze painfully, and she rubbed a hand over her face, breathing deeply.

"You let him take you?"

Her breath stilled in her lungs. She dropped her hand slowly. Lithônion's words cut her like a blade, and it took her a moment before she could look at him. "I didn't have a choice."

"The Hel you didn't!" he snarled.

She hissed as his voice carried down the hall, and those within the other cells stirred. "Keep your voice *down!*"

"You had a choice, Levina!" he bit out in a whisper. "You didn't have to come here. No one asked you to!"

Her heart was hammering wildly in her ears. It was all she could hear. The wild rush of her blood filled her head. Squeezing her eyes shut, she tried to block out the memories of home, her family and friends, and the night it all ended.

"You could have stayed, Levina! That could have been your choice!"

"He was going to destroy us!"

"He was going to try regardless, whether he had you or not!"

The memories vanished, and a cold numbness swept in, and she wrapped both her hands around her belly. "I know that now," she whispered, eyes downcast to her stomach.

Lithônion reached a hand through the bar, not getting far before his muscled forearm couldn't fit. Seeing this, Levina stepped forward, close enough that his fingers could brush her cheek as tears fell silently down them. For the first time in fifty years, she felt genuine comfort.

"I thought I could get through to him," she whispered, laying her cheek into his palm. "I thought I could protect everyone."

"I know," murmured Lithônion, stroking his thumb over her jaw.

Someone stirred from within a cell down the hall, and Levina's spine stiffened, remembering where she was. Lingering for a second longer, she forced herself from the comforting warmth of his hand.

"You can't help me, Lithônion," she said, sealing away her emotions back into the box where she kept them within her. "I am bound to him, through this babe and through magic."

She lifted the loose sleeve of her black gown, showing him the thorns and miniature roses bound around her arm. The tattoo shifted as if showing off its power to Lithônion, and Levina saw him blanch.

"It is my burden to bear, Lithônion. There is nothing you can do." She stepped back from his cell door. "Leave. Find a way and go, and don't come back for me. My fate has been sealed; you still have a chance."

She left before he could say something to try and change her mind, but that didn't stop the tears from falling as she walked away.

"Udiya."

"Tatius."

The small God stepped up beside the spirit of elements who stood at the lip of a sheer cliff ledge, watching the sea churning. Sunlight sparkled from behind rolling clouds and lit across Udiya's black skin and dark red bodice.

Udiya's green eyes glanced at Tatius with a faint regard. "What do I owe this pleasure?"

"She is dying," Tatius stated simply.

"I know." Udiya turned her attention back to the sea, where the girl Tatius spoke of lay below.

"She cannot die. Not yet."

Udiya's black brow arched softly. "You have a soft spot for the human?"

"No. I just simply need her." Tatius folded her hands behind her back, her black gown shrouding her whole body down to her toes even when the wind made it rustle around her.

"And you want me to do what about it?" Strands of her black hair came loose from the interwoven braids down her back as the wind blew and curled around her face.

Tatius's black eyes narrowed on the sea. "I need you to make sure she lives."

Udiya turned to look fully at Tatius, brows furrowing on her beautiful face, her leather encased legs shifting. "You forget who I am."

"I do not forget," stated Tatius simply.

"I am a God!" Udiya demanded, her green eyes flashing in warning. "I helped create this world; do not forget that, Tatius!"

Tatius finally turned to Udiya with cool regard in her eyes. "I do not forget, Udiya. But do not forget, you are elemental, and I am death." Her words were heavy and unforgiving but calm, her expression turning stormy. "We are bound by Fae law, laws *we* wrote, but *I need her alive.*"

"I cannot intervene."

"You must."

Udiya's chin jerked, taking in a harsh breath as she stared at the sea. "If I don't?"

"Then we're all damned."

Udiya took another breath, her black boots digging into the grassy lip beneath her. "Fine. But if I alter fate, then it is on you."

Tatius glanced up at her. "You are saving our fates."

Darkness surrounded her. Tearing at her flesh only for it to knit back together and be torn from her again. It was in her mind, her memories, her emotions, controlling her. Hazen tried to run, but she was frozen. Her body couldn't move, and the claws dug through her.

She could feel every fibre in her tearing apart; she could feel her hot, sticky blood coating her as it gushed from the wounds… and then it would be gone. The blood, her ragged limbs and peeled skin, everything would vanish, only to start again.

Hazen screamed into the void.

Udiya stepped out from the shadows. Her almond eyes, green like new leaves, seemed to glow in the abyss. The silver whorls tattooed up her arms from her fingertips in long graceful lines, curled around her shoulders and collarbone, emanated a faint light that scattered across Hazen's haggard appearance when she stepped close enough to touch her.

She gently stroked the floating hair from Hazen's cheek as she silently whimpered into the darkness, her face contorted in pain.

"It seems, young one, that Tatius has plans for you," Udiya said gently. "I've been instructed to not let you die yet."

Gathering Hazen's limp body in her arms, they vanished from the abyss.

Dawn broke the night sky, and a flood of colour painted the ceiling in an array of orange and pink as Udiya and Hazen stepped from the sea to the world above.

She placed Hazen on the sandy beach as she whimpered in pain. Laying her down, Udiya covered Hazen's eyes with a soft hand.

Her body visibly relaxed as the darkness in her mind disappeared, and the demons that tormented her over and over again vanished.

"I hope Tatius understands the dangerous game she plays." Udiya stood, watching the girl for a breath and vanished as Hazen's eyes opened.

The gentle lap of water and the soft crunch of sand beneath her hands made Hazen stir. She coughed dryly, licking her cracked lips. The world tumbled around her, light blurring in her eyes as she sat up, her head spinning dangerously.

Water licked her toes, and she curled her legs away from it.

The world came into focus, and she looked around, sluggish.

How had she escaped?

Hazen looked around for the person who had helped her. She was alone on a beach. A forest was to her right, and a rocky cliff lay to her left and at her back. Hazen looked back at the sea, the tendrils of water seeming to reach for her as if it wanted to lure her back to its watery depths. She shivered when the memories of pain seared into her bones.

The fog in her brain was diminishing, and she made herself stand, knowing full well that just as it had been under the water, it would be on land. Everyone would want her dead.

Hazen brushed the sand off the ruins of her wet clothes and hands with a low, pained groan, the sound of her voice bliss to her ears. The cracks in her lips bled, and she licked it, coughing at the dryness in her throat. Her hair fell around her face like a sopping bird's nest, and she pushed it off her eyes, wincing when she touched a scabbed cut on her face.

She was a mess, and she felt like she had just gone to war mentally and emotionally for the last ten years. Her body ached, her hands shook, and she wished for home.

But home was a foreign concept, something Hazen could barely compute in her mind.

Her legs wobbled at her first step; she braced herself, and the second step was steadier. Rubbing a hand over her face and hair again, she took a calming breath and made for the forest.

Nautien cut through the black waters of the abyss. The twisting in her gut whirled in a frenzy, and she snarled with impatience, swimming faster, her tail slicing like a whip. There was an imposter in her waters. She had felt them enter and exit through her barriers and knew who they had come for.

With a set face, she reached the slate entrance and pushed herself through the wall. The cell was bare, and the queen could feel her rage boil the blood in her body.

She let out a bloodied, piercing shriek and slammed a fist into one of the walls, the power of it cracked the stone.

CHAPTER 33

It had taken them two days to reach Evengile, the village of thieves. The weather had turned harrowing, and they stayed off the main path, slowing them considerably. Yet they had made it with the last dregs of sunlight left as the sun sunk beyond the horizon.

They camped just outside its grey, crumbling borders, hidden within the sea of white deadwood trees, their blanched limbs barren and making a spindled cover over them. An angry ash sky of another coming storm rumbled to life overhead as its clouds rolled through the branches, the wind beating against the magic barrier Savven had created around them. Firelight flickered in the twilight with the last light of the crescent moon that began to rise, the sea crashing its waves upon the sand just over the dunes behind them.

Savven sat on a felled tree, eyes scanning the darkness. Lithônion shifted beside him, poking the blazing twigs with a thin branch he had snapped in two earlier. The branch ignited, and Lithônion huffed, tossing it onto the burning pile.

Brean looked up at green-eyed Fae warrior with an arched brow, and he gave her a sidelong look.

"Can I help you, Witch?" he drolled.

She shrugged, looking back at the fire. "Unless you know of a good summoning spell that works for lost things, then no, Elf, you cannot."

He cocked his head at her. "And what did you lose?"

"Everything on that blasted ship," she growled, annoyed.

"Can't you just flick your little witchy fingers and summon them back?"

The snark in his tone made Brean turn her growl on him, and he smirked at her.

"Don't make me use my little witchy fingers to snap your neck, Lithônion."

"Promises, promises."

"Both of you are bickering like children," intoned Savven.

Brean rolled her eyes. "He started it."

Savven cut her a look that said: *Point made.*

One hour turned to two, then three. The night turned black, and the moon rose higher into the sky, the stars peeking through like twinkling lights.

Brean's brows furrowed as she muttered under her breath, magic sparking at her fingertips with every spell she recited. The firelight made her hair glow like living embers, and her eyes shone with a fire that seemed to glow brighter than the flames before her.

Savven paced through the trees that stood around them, feeling the magic of the barrier press against his side as he walked.

"At least it's not cold."

Savven looked at Lithônion, who fell into step with him. "Cold?"

"Aye," he said with a nod. "Bitter and cold."

Savven stopped and looked at him. "I'm not sure I know what you speak of, Lithônion?"

Lithônion looked over at Brean, who was focused on the

ground and turned back to Savven. "Anabelle?" he said lowly. "The bitterness that came that winter after Balwin."

Savven was silent momentarily before he nodded slowly and said, "Yes, I suppose you're right." Something in him stilled preternaturally, turning on edge. He began walking again.

Following close, Lithônion asked, "Have you heard from her? Anabelle, I mean."

"No, I haven't. I haven't heard from my cousin in many years."

They walked silently until Lithônion asked again, "Do you suppose we will see her in Álfheimr?"

"I don't know, Lithônion," Savven uttered quietly, watching Lithônion in the corner of his eye. He saw his friend chew on his words, his eyes darting to the forest when the branches knocked together. "Why do you ask about Anabelle?"

Lithônion looked at Savven and shook his head. "I was only inquiring. Being in these woods brings back memories."

Savven opened his mouth to reply—

"What—damn it all!"

The two males turned to the witch, who had shot to her feet and stood glowering at a pile of sopping wet satchels—some large, some tiny, and all very, very *wet*.

Brean glared up at them while wiping water from her cheek. "It was at the bottom of the damn sea."

"We can see that," commented Savven with a wry smile, watching her pinch a piece of seaweed between her fingers and flick it away with a scowl.

Flames lit her golden eyes, the annoyance kindling in them aimed at Savven, who smirked back at her before wrenching the top of one large satchel open. Brean wrinkled her nose in distaste before she plunged her hand into it, the leather and cloth bags squelching.

Lithônion bent and picked up a small stone, rolling it between his fingers and sitting beside Brean.

Brean pulled out a wooden spool with black silk thread wrapped around it from her bag, a sharp needle stuck through the middle. She looked at the male beside her. "You're quiet, Lithônion."

"Am I?" he asked, watching the pebble in his hand.

"Yes," she said, pulling out a long swath of black wool fabric.

He shrugged, humming under his breath. "Apologies."

Brean shook her head in regard, waving her hand over the wet fabric. Steam rose from the wool and vanished into the night, leaving the fabric dry in her lap. Grabbing the needle, she licked the end of the silk thread and began trying to weave it through the tiny eye.

A soft wind blew through their camp, and she went rigid.

Lithônion gave her a side glance when he felt her stiffen. "Are you well?"

Brean looked up from the needle and thread in her frozen hands. The wind grazed past them again, and she inhaled deeply, her eyes widening and narrowing on him.

They stared at one another, a palpable silence between them. Brean's fingers curled around the needle until blood dripped down her hand.

"Brean?"

Savven's voice cut through the building tension, and she gasped softly, the needle dropping to her lap. She looked down, and blood smeared her palm where it had stabbed her.

Savven's blue gaze strayed to Lithônion, who had gone still as stone, his face unreadable. "Lithônion, go and collect more wood for the fire."

Lithônion didn't answer.

"Lithônion," he said again, steel etching through his voice. A command.

Lithônion blinked slowly. He turned his head to Savven, though his gaze stayed on Brean until they eventually followed and fell to Savven. "What?" he asked tersely.

"Go and collect more firewood."

Nostrils flaring with contained emotions that slipped behind his eyes, Lithônion stood, the stone dropping from his hand, and disappeared into the forest.

Brean's unblinking stare followed Lithônion's back into the white woods. When he disappeared, she took in a sharp breath, dropping her gaze to her bloody palm, which she cradled in her other hand.

"Let me see it," Savven murmured.

Before she could say anything, he already had her hand in his own, his skin warm against hers.

"Savven…" Brean studied his face as he covered her palm with his, a soft blue light emanating between them. "Savven the wind… it whispered—"

"—I know." Savven released her healed hand and cast a sideways glance in her direction. "I know."

"What are we going to do?" she asked, her eyes darting between the woods and Savven with trepidation. Her heart was beating in her throat, and her muscles were tense.

"Nothing for now." He stood, looking at the wool the witch had now forgotten in her lap. Savven pointed to the material. "Focus, Brean. That's what I need you to do right now."

"But—" her words died when he cut her a hard stare.

"Focus," he said again and walked away.

The night passed on without visitors. Animals had wandered close to their camp, but Savven had kept them at bay with small bouts of magic that sparked at the edge of their base. The sky lit up, fading from black to blue as it turned from night to day; the fire had long gone cold, and both males stood rigid at the forest edge, watching the village as it slept.

Later that morning, an annoyed huff came quietly from Brean's lips as she finished the cloaks she had made through the night and some hours into the morning. She had spent the night sewing every stitch by hand to keep her mind occupied and her thoughts at bay, even when her fingers had gone cold and stiff. With a wave of her hand, emerald sparks danced over the still semi-damp bags, and they disappeared. Where? She didn't know, nor did she care. They were probably below the sea again, but fate had been altered, and she no longer needed any of it.

She stood, thick black material draped across her arms and walked over to the males who turned at her approach. "I have done my part," she commented darkly, dropping one cloak in each male's hand. "Now, you two may do yours. Get us to Álfheimr."

Amused, though they did not show it, they thanked her, and the three of them quietly shifted the material over their shoulders. The wool fibres warded off the damp chill that bit through the air, mist and clouds curling around trees and creeping over dirt and rock. They pulled the hoods over their heads and slipped from the cover of the white woods into the misty land of thieves.

Thunder rolled overhead like giants warring above them as they entered Evengile. The fog crept throughout the creaking village, damp air clinging to their faces the further they ventured. Old, worn-down huts still stood, fragile and withered. Dew and greying moss clung to the timber. Rain sprinkled down, and the sky darkened with the threat of a downpour.

Savven stilled when they came to a broken cobble road, the skin on his neck prickling with warning. A withered tavern lay just up ahead, the sign of an old inn creaking in the growing wind; scattered shops lay decaying along the way, forgotten by most.

He could feel Brean and Lithônion shift on either side of him.

"What is it?" Lithônion muttered in a low voice.

Savven's eyes peered from under his hood over the buildings, his ears keen. "We're being followed."

Brean looked behind them, ahead of them, and finally to the rooftops. Her eyes found the dirty face of a child crouched low, peering from behind a smokestack. "It seems so," she murmured under her breath. "It's a child, Savven. Let it be."

Savven grunted lowly and glared at the child, who didn't flinch or shrink away but simply stared back.

"We have to keep moving," Lithônion said, his voice hushed, eyes darting from store to store.

The village streets were empty, and the creaking sign of the inn was a constant in the hollow void. They didn't speak a word but followed the broken path to the tavern. The door wailed on its rusty hinges, their arrival not going unnoticed by the occupants inside. Those who sat in the dimly lit tavern stopped what they were doing, their voices hushing, and turned to stare at them when the beaten door slammed closed at their backs.

None stood, but every pair of eyes was trained on them as they took a seat in the corner, their hoods still concealing their faces, until one by one, they fell away, and the wave of chatter resumed.

"Are you sure it was wise coming here?" Brean muttered under her breath, her eyes darting from grubby face to grubby face.

Beggars and thieves of different species huddled over pints of ale. Goblins, warlocks, Romani, and other lesser Fae took shelter in the shadows, searching gazes eyeing those around them.

The people in the tavern were worn and ragged. Their clothes were patched and fraying, and their hair lay in stringy tangles around their faces. They looked swept in from the sea and smelled of it, too.

Lithônion made himself more comfortable, draping an arm on the tabletop as he leaned back into his seat. "We had no other choice." The corners of his mouth tilted slightly. "I never took you as one who would be afraid of a village of thieves."

"There is much you don't know about me," snapped Brean.

A couple eyes turned in their direction, and Lithônion's chuckle rumbled low in his chest.

Savven's fingers drummed the tabletop until the eyes turned away again, and he said, "Lithônion, get a room at the inn. We will need a place for the night."

Lithônion raised a brow at him. "What about the ship?"

"Storm is coming in; they'll delay departure until it passes."

A look of impatience crossed Lithônion's face, but he stayed silent. Glancing at Savven for a moment, his stare frozen. Words were held on the tip of his tongue, but he bit down on them. His chair scraped the rough wood underfoot, and he made himself scarce.

Brean leaned forward as soon as the tavern doors slammed shut. "What are we going to do?"

Savven let his thoughts wander, taking note of the room's details—faces, stances, cracks where the wood was weakest. "We wait."

Brean peered at him from under her hood. "Wait for what?"

"We wait for the truth to come to us."

"Your riddles make my head hurt," she grumbled darkly.

Savven's answering smirk made her glare at him.

"Arrogance does not become you, Elf."

"And yet," he murmured, leaning forward until they shared a breath, "I think you quite like it."

The tavern door slammed, and Savven leaned away.

Brean and Savven glanced over to see Lithônion's dark cloak slip between leaving patrons, shaking the rain from his shoulders.

He tossed a large iron key in the middle of the table. "Our room is on the second level, the first door."

"That didn't take you very long," Brean noted.

"They don't have many guests."

She nodded her head, arching a brow at the weathered tavern. "I don't suppose they would."

Savven stood, his chair scraping softly, and the two quieted, watching him approach the wooden bar.

A rotund faun with his ruined clothes, greasy, pock-marked skin, and beady eyes scanned Savven greedily.

"What do you want?" A row of yellowed and browned teeth flashed as he spat out his words.

Savven leaned on the bar top, noting the long crack in the worn wood. "When is the ship's next cast off?"

The bartender's hooves scraped the floors as he returned to wiping the bar top. "Two days or so, I reckon. Storm is coming. It'll wipe the sails from their masts if they try to make way in it." He narrowed his eyes on Savven, eyeballing him slowly and leaning forward to try and see beneath the hood of his cloak. "What is it to the likes of you?"

A silver coin clattered on the bar top. "For your silence," Savven said shortly and stalked away.

He jerked his chin slightly towards the door when Brean and Lithônion caught his gaze before he slipped out. The quiet scrape of the chairs followed, and a second later, both Lithônion and Brean stood behind him.

When they stepped onto the cobbled road, rain pelted their cloaks, and the wind threatened to rip the wool from their shoulders.

The inn was only two shops ahead, sitting crooked and weatherworn. The stone base was cracked and crumbling, and the wood planks were grey and covered in moss.

Inside, the inn was dank, like the bottom of a murky swamp. Black filth defiled even the candles that burned in the musty air, and a thick layer of dust coated the wood counters.

An oversized woman, as filthy as the inn, sat at the counter in a patched green dress and a black smudged apron that had once been white. She gave no notice to them as they passed her, taking to the stairs. They reached the second level, and Lithônion produced the iron key and opened their door. The three stepped in and were met with the foul smell of mould.

"A toad would have better accommodations," said Brean in a low, sarcastic voice.

A bed was pressed against the far wall, a white wood desk was against the opposite, and a single candle was sitting promptly on it, waiting to be lit.

Brean went to the candle, put her lips close to the wick and gently blew. A small orange flame sparked to life, and she stepped back. The room was cast in a weak glow as the dim light of day faded from the single shuttered window beside the bed.

"Lithônion and I will take the floor," Savven said.

The shutters banged against the window, and Savven grimaced in annoyance every time they slammed against the glass. Letting loose a harsh breath through his nose, he strode to the window, forcing it open as it groaned with protest. When the shutters flew back towards the window, he grabbed them and secured the little black latch between them.

The room was immediately filled with darkness except for the soft glow of candlelight.

Brean took one glance at the musky bed and grimaced. "How lucky." She fingered the quilt, eyeing the holes and questionable stains. "What are we to do now?"

"Now we wait until morning," Savven said, sitting on the floor. His back was pressed to the corner facing the door, the window to his right.

Lithônion leaned against the desk. "Have you ventured here before, Savven?"

Savven stared at a spot on the floor, his face impassive. "You and I got drunk here once before the attacks."

Brean sat on the bed, the hay stuffing rock hard beneath her bottom, but she stilled at Savven's words.

Lithônion nodded thoughtfully, pursing his lips as if trying to remember. "It's a bit foggy, but I think I remember. It must have been some good ale to make me forget."

Savven hummed, turning a steady eye on Lithônion. "Aye, a few hundred years have passed since then."

Brean wasn't breathing, her body frozen, eyes darting between the two.

"With so much happening, it's difficult to remember everything."

"Yes," Savven said, turning his stare to the door. "A hard thing to remember…"

The night grew steadily, the hours dwindling, and the glow of candlelight dimmed as the wax melted. Brean had long since fallen asleep, using her cloak as a blanket after giving them the blanket on the bed to share. Lithônion sat, arms crossed and head back against the wall in a corner near the bed while Savven kept the first watch.

Drunkard's shouts could be heard from the tavern across the road, the sounds floating through the window's crevice. Savven listened to every moan and creak of the inn, hearkening for any subtle changes in the night during the storm. The rain trying to fight its way through the barrier their little room provided.

The night passed into the first hour of the new day, and Lithônion woke to relieve him of the watch.

Savven slipped into the corner Lithônion had occupied. Picking the blanket off the floor, he draped it over himself and closed his eyes, but even as the world of dreams wanted to claim him, he didn't dare sleep.

CHAPTER 34

At first light, Savven awoke to a cold, dark room. He had fallen asleep. He noted Brean sleeping peacefully, her wild red hair strewn across her pillow, a soft snore emanating from full parted lips. But his lip curled when his eyes slid to the corner Lithonion no longer occupied. Rage ignited a hot path to every nerve in his body, and his hands fisted at his sides.

Wood moaned softly as Savven stood, breathing deeply to calm the inferno that spiralled within, inhaling the inn's foul smells, and slipped out of the room.

The inn was empty.

The woman behind the desk was nowhere to be found, and stale air hung like a murky blanket over it as if cloaking a sleeping beast for the night.

A meek wind glided through the alleyways as Savven stepped outside. Shaking the edge from his limbs and flexing his fingers to relieve the pressure building, Savven glanced down the empty roads and quickly crossed over to the tavern, hesitating when he heard voices talking.

His hand whispered over the tarnished handle of the tavern door before he removed it, ears straining as he tried to listen to what was being said.

The voices were mumbled, and whoever spoke didn't want to be heard.

One of the shutters on the window had come undone and creaked loosely on its hinges, leaving a small gap. Savven slipped silently over and peered through the opening, his eyes falling on Lithônion, his back to him.

Savven growled under his breath, that rage simmering hot beneath his skin. He watched Lithônion say something unheard, pass a couple gold coins to one of the locals, and then the same to the bartender. The two bobbed their heads with sly smiles, and the bartender pointed to somewhere beyond the tavern's walls while the other bit into the gold. Lithônion nodded in understanding and turned to the door.

Savven ducked into the alley, eyes narrowing on Lithônion as he turned left out of the tavern and left again when the road veered in multiple directions.

Savven followed him.

Rubble, chunks of driftwood, rocks, and sandy dirt scattered across the road as it turned primitive. Dome huts made from mud and clay with thatched roofs were dispersed in the wild seagrass that stretched along the coastal front to his left.

Lithônion veered and cut through the field, eyes darting over his shoulder briefly. Savven knelt behind a broken-down wagon when he turned his way.

Whacking once on the wooden door of a rounded mud hut that sat along the edge of a small levy leading down to the beach, smoke wafting from the crumbling chimney into the grey wild, Lithônion shifted on his feet.

Savven could smell the unease coming from him downwind.

"*Yes?*" A gruff male voice snapped from within the hut, the door opening a second later on rusted hinges.

An old Romani peeked behind his door, eyeballing Lithônion with bloodshot brown eyes. Withered with age, the burden of his life was etched like a map of wrinkles in his skin. A rotund belly made his once white tunic strain with threats of tearing, and a silver scar glinted across his right cheek in the pale morning.

"Tomhal…."

Lithônion's voice was drowned out by the wind, and Savven shifted closer, straining his ears.

"…Tomhal would sell himself for some coin…"

"…Map…"

Savven growled silently when their words vanished in the wind.

The man looked over Lithônion with sharp eyes and let him in, glaring at the outside world before shutting the door with a slam.

 Savven stood, the crisp wind brushing across his face. Gravel shifted under swift feet as he slipped from behind the wagon quickly. Voices drifted from within, and he followed the curved edges to the window that lay exposed except for a thin flap of animal hide pulled up by twine. Savven crouched low, barely peaking over the sill while he listened.

"Now, what is it that Tomhal has promised I can provide?" the old Romani asked, his voice ragged and harsh. The words tumbled out of a scarred mouth, several teeth missing and rotten.

"A map."

"Of what, precisely? I have many maps." The piggish male went to his stove and opened it, stoking the hot coals.

Lithônion glanced around the hut; shelves upon shelves lined the walls with scrolls piled high, some strewn in piles on the dry clay floor and propped against the wall. Stacks of candles burning low on the ends of the shelves, with their drippings cascading over the edge. "One you stole many, many years ago."

The Romani straightened with a low grunt and turned, his wrinkles pinching with annoyance. "I have stolen many a map in my time, Elf."

"I want the Seers Map."

Savven's blood chilled.

The male stilled, suspicion narrowing his bloodshot eyes. "And what would the likes of you do with such a map?"

Lithônion turned a hard stare at him, reaching within his left boot and producing a small leather pouch. Four gold coins spilt out into hand. "The map, if you will."

Bloodshot eyes turned hungry, fixating on the gold that glimmered in the yellow candlelight. The male whipped around, riffling through the pile of scrolls, some falling from their stacks to the floor and unravelling. "It's here… somewhere…" he muttered under his breath.

A sound of triumph followed, and he scurried to an old chest tucked by his lumpy bed.

Savven straightened further, straining to see within the chest.

Tarnished gold trinkets, sheets of paper, and scrolls bound together with leather were piled within. The male shifted the items out of the way until he pulled out a small scroll, a dark blue satin ribbon tied around it. He stood, holding it protectively to his chest, and stretched out his hand. "My gold first."

Lithônion handed him the four gold pieces, clinking as they fell into the Romani's palm.

He tossed the map, and Lithônion snatched it from the air.

Savven ducked when Lithônion turned towards the window and waited, listening to the shifting of feet. He peeked over the sill again, Lithônion's back to him.

The Romani bit into the gold, focusing solely on his earnings.

Lithônion slid the ribbon off, glancing at the contents before rolling it back up and securing it. "How did you come by this?"

The male gave a sly grin. "I won it in a gamble."

Lithônion lifted the edge of his tunic and placed it securely beneath the waistband of his pants, sliding his shirttails over it. "Winning and cheating are two very different things."

Grinning wickedly, the male asked lowly, "Is it, though? When the end results are the same?"

Savven turned away from the window, fire engulfing his veins, and he quickly returned to the inn.

Savven paced the small room at the inn once, twice, before stilling. His mind was calm, though a torrent of emotions rained through him like a storm, and he bit down on his control.

Brean leaned against the wall near the bed, watching him. She had awoken to an empty room, only to have Savven storm in minutes later with an air that could chill ice. She had seen his eyes and had known that the day would only worsen.

"You will wear a hole in the floor if you keep pacing like a caged animal," she commented dryly.

Creaking floors gave way to the approaching footsteps, and Savven's veins filled with fire and ice. "Keep quiet," he warned darkly, shooting Brean a hard stare.

Lithônion walked in no sooner than the words left his tongue.

Before the door had shut, before Brean could inhale another breath, Savven's fingers grasped the handle of the dagger from his boot, and threw Lithônion against the wall, blade at his throat.

"Who are you?" he snarled.

The calm was gone, and the storm raged chaos within him. He tightened his hold on his blade, years of training the only thing holding him back from gutting the male pinned in front of him.

His voice had a venom to it that made Brean want to disappear from the room, and she pressed herself into the wall, jaw locked and eyes wide.

Lithônion was not of the same standing, his face only a mask of confusion.

"Savven, what are you doing?" he demanded, throat bobbing against the dagger. His eyes darted to Brean quickly before falling back on Savven.

Savven's fist lashed out, punching a sizeable hole into the wood beside Lithônion's head. "Who are you?"

Silence stretched taut in the room.

The shadow of a smirk barely curled Lithônion's mouth, and he regarded Savven. "You know, I'm actually surprised you had the patience to wait this long." Green eyes flickered to Brean. "I thought the witch would have given me away."

Savven's eyes flashed with a warning. He tightened the blade across the impostor's throat, his knuckles turning white, and the grip of the dagger bit into his flesh. "Where. Is. He?"

The impostor inclined a brow, frowning.

Savven exhaled sharply, his limbs rigid, vision going red. "Who are you?" His voice was deathly calm against the silence in the room.

The imposter was silent.

Savven nicked the blade across his skin, drawing blood.

The imposter sighed, exasperated. "Don't be so quick to take my head, Savven. I'll show you. But I would appreciate it if you would remove your knife. I don't want to be the one at fault for decapitating myself."

Savven didn't move.

Lithônion's face gave him an expectant look.

"Savven," Brean whispered, her eyes bouncing between them.

Savven snarled, pressing into him. "If you make to escape, if you even think about it, your life will be forfeit." He removed the knife, the sound of it scraping across flesh, leaving a thin slice across his neck. Savven put his body between the impostor and the door while he moved towards the middle of the room.

"I ask again: who are you?"

The impostor gave a secret smile, and his features began to change—first his height, then his hair, and then the rest of him. Soon, what stood before them was another male entirely.

A male with piercing blue eyes, olive-brown skin, and thick silver hair that travelled the length of his back stood before them.

Savven went preternaturally still. "Néefar?" he breathed.

"Hello, Savven," replied Néefar coolly.

The blood in Savven's veins had turned to solid ice. He stepped back, his back brushing the door. "Where is Lithônion?"

"In Ezra's dungeon now, I suppose."

Savven's heart leapt in his throat. "How?" he demanded.

"With careful planning," Néefar elaborated. "Mostly on his part."

Brean's eyes narrowed, finally moving from her spot on the wall. "Were you Lithônion the entire time?"

Néefar glanced at Savven's dagger, still held in a white-knuckled grip but now at his side. "No." He walked over to the bed, sitting on it casually and nodding in approval while he patted the thin blanket. "That floor was awful. Next time we should get a room with two beds. You and I could cuddle, Savven."

Savven's snarled warning was swift, and Néefar held up his hands, chuckling.

"It was Lithônion who I met in the mountains?" Savven asked.

"Yes."

Brean eased closer to him. "You said he planned this?"

Bright blue eyes gave her a cursory glance. "Yes. We traded places during the shipwreck." He paused and then added, "Sorry about your things. I was more focused on not killing anyone. Not that it did much good."

Brean shrugged, crossing her arms.

"Is he…" Savven couldn't make himself say the words.

Néefar pursed his lips, knowing what Savven wanted to ask, and he shook his head softly in understanding. "No, Savven. He didn't betray you."

Relief was swift, relaxing the rigidness of his limbs, and he let out a breath he had been holding.

"Don't mind me," Brean said casually. "But who are you?"

"Savven and I go way back. Don't we, Savven?" Néefar remarked.

Irritation flashed over Savven's face. "Yes," he replied tersely.

Brean raised her brows, waiting for him to continue. When he didn't, Néefar cleared his throat and spoke up.

"Friends because of battle and brothers because of marriage."

"A shifter, not just a friend of the High Fae, but also a brother?" Brean asked, turning her amusement to Savven, who stood there with a look of agitation, his jaw flexing as he ground his teeth.

Savven slipped his blade back into his boot. "Why do you need the Seers Map."

Néefar's brows arched. "So, you were following me. I thought I saw you in the window. I stand impressed, Savven. Your restraint is well applauded."

"The map, Néefar," he intoned lowly.

"What is the Seers Map?" Brean asked despite rising tension.

Savven ignored her question, frowning. "Map. Now."

Pressing his lips into a flat line, Néefar stood and pulled the map from his waistband.

Two bounding strides had Savven snatching the map from Néefar's hand, who growled low and vicious, more animal than male.

"Give it back, Savven," Néefar warned darkly, his eyes glued on the map.

Savven handed it to Brean, who tucked it close to her chest. "Tell me why you need it."

"Dammit, Savven!"

"Tell me!"

"I bought it to ensure my wife is still alive!" Néefar ran a frustrated hand through his hair, the silver strands catching the watery sunlight.

Savven cocked his head, weighing his words. "For Anabelle?"

Néefar stepped up to Savven, nose to nose as he seethed. "There is no one else in this whole damn world that I would do anything for. I do everything for her. She is my world. Not by mates, not by circumstance, but by *choice*. I choose her, and only her, and because of this damn war, I am apart from the one person who has all of me." He jabbed a finger towards the map. "And that blasted map is the *only* thing that lets me know she is alive."

"Savven, we should give him the map." Brean's voice was soft with understanding. She made to open her caged arms, but Savven held up a hand.

Néefar stepped back, sighing. "She made me help Lithônion. He came to us, begging. She couldn't say no to him, and I couldn't say no to her when she asked me to go with him."

Savven leaned against the desk. "What did Lithônion need help with?"

The room was tense as they waited for him to answer.

"He needed to get into Dauðinn Mountain."

Savven narrowed his eyes, crossing his arms. "Why?"

"Because he thinks Levina is alive."

Savven's nostrils flared with shock. Remembering Lithônion's words.

"She's alive."

"Who?" he breathed.

"Levina."

"Is she?" he whispered.

Néefar took in a deep breath, scrubbing a hand over his face. "Yes."

Savven was staring at the wall, his blood humming in his ears. Levina was alive. Lithônion had tried to tell him.

"Savven?"

Brean stood in front of him, but he didn't look at her.

Levina was alive.

"Savven," Brean said again.

Savven took a deep breath, finally looking at her. She still had the map, and Néefar's gaze was focused on it. "Give me the map." He removed the ribbon and spread it over the desk when she did.

Néefar was at his side before the scroll was completely open, eyes scanning the paper.

It was blank.

"It can't be," whispered Néefar, brows furrowing.

And then ink began to spread over the scroll. Mountains and trees, oceans and valleys. It all came to life in inky drawings that blossomed slowly.

"Show me Anabelle," Néefar demanded. The map shifted its geographical location as if the ink were alive, black coating the scroll until it sunk back into the paper, and they were left with a mountain range and surrounding forest.

Anabelle's name appeared within the inked trees; *The Black Forest* etched across the forest scape. She wasn't alone. Autumn and Winter's names both floated beside her own.

Néefar's sigh of relief filled the room, his fingers grazing across her name softly.

"Show me Levina," Savven demanded of the map.

Néefar sucked in a breath when Anabelle's name disappeared into an inky sea.

The map revealed the jagged cuts of Dauðinn Mountain, and Levina's name floated within its depths.

Savven closed his eyes when he saw her name. Memories of the last time he had seen her reared up from the depths of his mind, and he clenched his jaw.

"Promise me," he begged her.

Levina gave him that charming smile that he knew too well. "You worry too much, Savven."

All this time. She had been there all this time.

"It's enchanted," breathed Brean in awe, hovering by Savven's other side.

Néefar looked at Brean, nodding his head. "Say a name, and it will show you where they are. It's old, very old, and it was by luck many years ago that I heard it had been stolen in a game of chance by a thief in Evengile."

"Can we find Hazen with this map?" Brean asked, her eyes widening with hope.

Savven frowned, rolling the map up again. "No."

"But—"

He spared her a glance. "It only works on the occupants of this world, not those who come into it. The magic doesn't take note of outsiders."

Brean sniffed, stiffening, and her brow arched, but she said nothing.

Néefar stretched out an expectant hand, his brown tunic stretching across the muscled plains of his chest and bicep. "You've had your go, Savven. Now give it back."

Savven's stoic nature grew irritated, and he thrust the map at Brean. "Burn it."

"No!" Néefar lunged for the map, but a magic wall slammed into his chest and pressed him to the desk that rattled violently against the wall.

"This is too dangerous to have with us. It could leave us defenceless if it falls into the wrong hands!" Savven rounded on Brean as Néefar thrashed against the magic's hold. "Burn it. Now," he ordered.

Brean looked torn and opened her mouth to say something but snapped it shut when Savven shot her a warning glare. He was right, and she nodded her head in defeat.

A heartbeat later, the map burst into flames and turned to ash within moments. The remnants scattered like snow on the old wood floors.

Savven's magic released Néefar, and the shifter stumbled forward, looking at the pile of ash.

His lip curled, and he rounded on Savven, shoving him hard in the chest. Savven stumbled back at the force, the desk now rattling behind him.

Néefar grabbed him by his black tunic and slammed him into the desk once, then twice. "Damn you!" he snarled. With one last shove, he released him and stalked away, groaning low while he scrubbed a hand over his face.

"I'm sorr—"

Savven stopped abruptly, eyeing the door.

Néefar released a heavy breath and turned around at the silence, following Savven's stare. He straightened, muscles tightening, eyes and ears on alert, and shifted his stance, waiting.

Brean cocked her head, listening to the deafening silence. Raising a hand, she looked at Savven, waiting, her magic thrumming beneath her skin.

Slipping his blade from his boot, Savven jerked his chin at Brean. The witch's magic wrapped around the door, and it flew open.

CHAPTER 35

A boy fell through the doorway.

He gaped at them, his wide black eyes bouncing between the three, and he scurried on hands and knees backwards to the hall behind him.

The door slammed shut at his back, and he flinched, freezing in place.

Savven, blade still in hand, knelt before the child. "Why were you spying?"

The boy's pale complexion worsened at his commanding tone, and he hurriedly tried the door handle.

"You really have a way with your words, Savven," commented Néefar dryly. "Even the children run."

Savven shot a glowering look Néefar's way.

Brean shook her head, stepping around the males. "Send a male to do a female's job and watch them dash it all to pieces," muttered Brean darkly.

She lowered herself to the ground, kneeling and placing her hands in her lap. A small smile lifted her mouth, and her amber eyes softened as she greeted the child. "Hello there."

The boy wiped a surprisingly clean hand over his matted black hair that hung across his forehead, sniffling. "Hello," he said in a small wobbly voice. He couldn't have been more than ten.

"Don't mind that big mean elf. He's just hungry and gets cranky when we don't feed him." Brean offered a hand to the child, who looked at it, his hand dropping from the door handle. "It's okay, I promise we won't hurt you."

He hesitated before reaching out a bone-thin arm and taking her hand.

Brean pulled him gently towards her, and she straightened his twisted shirt made of rags and patches. His pants were made of scraps of patchwork and frayed at the bottom, but otherwise, they were also intact. Sweeping a hand over his hair to brush it from his eyes, she smiled at him brightly and stood, his hand still in hers.

When she looked at Savven, the freckles on her face twisted with a scowl. "Apologise."

"What?" Savven asked, bewildered.

She raised a brow at him. "Did I stutter?"

His jaw tightened, teeth grinding at her tone, but amusement sparked behind that annoyance, and he loosened a breath with a roll of his eyes. "I'm sorry if I frightened you," he said, turning his attention to the child who stared bug-eyed at him.

Brean smiled down at the child. "That's better." She guided him to the bed and had him sit. When he was comfortable, Brean sat on her heels before him and tilted her head in question. "I saw you on the roof?"

The child nodded softly.

"Why were you following us?" Brean prodded.

The child looked to Néefar, then to Savven, who he quickly looked away from, and then back to Brean. "My master said you would come to us. She told me you would be here. She wants to see you. All of you."

Savven shifted, and the boy's eyes snapped to the blade in his hand. He glanced down at it and slipped it back into his boot. "What is your name?" he asked.

The boy shifted, looking at Brean. "I have no name."

The look of recognition settled in Brean's eyes. "A nameless face." The words were uttered in the softest whisper that barely left her lips. "Your master is the old witch of the sea?"

Savven pulled his gaze to Brean.

The nameless child nodded his head. "Yes."

Brean stood and turned to see the confusion on Néefar's and Savven's faces. "She is spoken of between witches. They say she foresees visions of the future and is the last of her kind among witches. But her power takes a toll on her body, and with every vision she sees, she loses a year of her life. So, every hundred years, she takes a child in, orphaned, nameless, and..." Brean glanced down at the child with horror. "...She sucks the youth from them. They don't live past a hundred years."

The child tugged on Brean's hand, garnering her attention. "May I take you to my master?"

"I..." Words failed her, and she dropped to her knees, pulling the child to her chest.

Pulling back, the boy frowned at her.

Brean searched his face before standing and stepping back. "I'm sorry," she said softly.

"May I take you to my master?" the child asked again.

When Brean didn't speak, Savven took the two cloaks from the table and handed one to Néefar as he secured his own. "Show us the way."

Néefar followed closely behind the boy when he opened the door for him.

Brean grabbed her cloak from the bed and stopped Savven with a hand to his bicep when he passed her.

Savven glanced at her hand wrapped around his arm, then slowly at her. Her amber eyes were full of sorrow. "It's not our place to interfere in his fate, Brean."

Brean chewed on her lip, looking up at him through thick lashes and nodded once. "I know."

Making to move past her, Brean stopped him again with a tug on his cloak. He let out a sigh. "What?"

She shifted the cloak over her shoulders, and when she looked at him again, the sorrow was gone, replaced by kindling flames in her stare, and her mouth pressed into a firm line. "In case you've forgotten already, you're an ass for burning the map."

He opened his mouth, but she flounced past him in a red and black flurry, leaving him to follow, shaking his head.

The wind shrieked past their ears, slicing their faces. Their cloaks whipped behind them, doing little to shield them from its torment.

The boy had led them away from the village to the outskirts. Down alleyways and crumbling roads, ruins lay where homes once stood many years ago, only a shadow of what the village had once been.

Rubble turned to sand and small rocks, softened by the salt and years of rain, while beach heather lay in patches of greying greenery amongst the sand dunes.

The boy veered from the scattered road and hastened over one of the dunes, scuttling on hands and feet when it gave way under him. They followed him closely, though they remained upright. Stopping at the top, watching the waves crash on the sand below, the boy ran down the slope, black hair flying behind him.

At the bottom of the hill was an old yet sturdy hut on the beach. Wind chimes of shells and hollowed dead wood hung from its support, playing an eerie melody in the wind. A fisherman's net, browned from the years, was knotted up on the railing, hanging helplessly over the edge as the wind blew through its crevasses.

A grey wood door creaked open as the boy pulled on it, gesturing for them to follow him. Candlelight was seen from the entrance, and one by one, they entered.

Sage incense drifted in the air, tickling their senses, along with the smell of the fire that crackled in the stone hearth, which was seated in the middle of the surprisingly sizeable room. Its chimney curved and narrowed until it disappeared through the rafters hung with dry fishermen's nets and old shells. An overstuffed, high-back patchwork red chair that had seen better days sat warming in front of the fire, set at an angle to face the door. The door in question shut behind them, and the boy hurried through another doorway covered with a flap of black animal hide.

Fish skeletons were laid out on shelves that lined the walls, dried starfish and sea urchins, shells by the dozens in every colour and size overflowed jars, and small vials full of liquids ranging from transparent to black as night lined the top shelf.

"Cozy," remarked Néefar.

Brean rolled her eyes but made no comment, straightening her haphazard cloak and ran a hand through the tangles of her wild red hair.

Savven was silent but eyed the home, if you could call it that, with ill regard when he noted a bleached skull tucked within a bookshelf to their right. It was small, the size of a child, and he made a face of displeasure.

An old woman hunched over a knotted black wooden cane entered the room. Her hair was grey and long, with wisps falling around her face and framing the map of wrinkles carved into her skin. Her mouth had shrunk and curled in on itself as she silently pursed what was left of her lips. A grey cloak hung from her shoulders, concealing little of her grey dress. Her eyes were closed as she entered, though she found her seat by the fire with no problem.

"You three have travelled a great distance. Separately, though, that may be," said the old witch. Her voice was weak and crackled like fire.

"The boy," Savven started, eyeing the child who seemed to press himself into the black hide over the door as if it would conceal him.

"He is a creature of the seas, washed ashore at infancy. Nameless and forgotten he is, I took him in." Her eyes finally opened, and the milky whites were revealed. "I sent him to you. To bring you to me."

Néefar raised a dark brow. "You're blind? A blind witch, that's perfect."

The witch stood slowly, her hand wobbling on her cane. Sliding one foot in front of the other, her cane scraping along the wood floor, she stood before Néefar, who towered over her hunched form. A withered, bony hand reached up to stroke his cheek, and in that crackling voice, she said, "You yearn to go south to where your heart resides. She is the light you crave. Your loyalties lie only with her." She dropped her hand and shuffled back to her seat, sitting with a heavy sigh. "Though I may not see the world, it does not mean I cannot see."

Néefar looked the witch up and down with suspicion and shifted his stance, brushing his hand across his cheek as if she had left a mark on it.

"What do you want? We have a ship to catch," Savven inquired, the hard edge in his voice hinting at his growing impatience.

The witch turned her head toward Savven, her bones cracking, and the whites of her eyes stared him down. "Oh, Prince, I wish many things of you and your companions. How I would love to see within your minds, see the world you see, and *taste* your eternity. I wager it would taste divine." Her tone became wistful and hungry, and the three shifted just a little closer to the door. "But for now, I only have one thing for the witch that travels with you."

Brean straightened, brows furrowing when white eyes locked on amber ones. "Me?"

"Aye, you, Witch."

The older witch stomped her cane on the ground with surprising strength, causing the boards underfoot to rattle. The boy ran to her side. She held out a hand, and he deposited a small leather pouch into her waiting palm.

Brean watched the boy scurry back into his hiding place by the door, and her jaw clenched, stomach churning with unease.

Chuckling softly, the witch tilted her head. "You think I am a monster?" She inhaled deeply, her mouth parting as if smelling a divine meal and revealing decaying teeth. "I scent your animosity for me, Witch. Come here and let me *taste it*."

Brean sniffed in disgust, her jaw clenching, and fire flamed in her eyes. "You can be damned," she spat.

The witch cackled, long and loud, her head thrown back, brittle hands gripping the armrests of her seat.

"We'll be leaving then," Brean bristled, rounding on her heels.

Cackles turned to low, rumbling laughter that seemed to fill the sea-worn home. Darkness edged around them, the firelight flickering with a warning. The three of them shifted restlessly. Savven went for the blade hidden within his tunic sleeve, claws grew from Néefar's fingers as the beasts within him surfaced, and magic sparked Brean's fingertips.

Silence filled the home, and the blind witch ticked her head at Brean. "Come here, Witch." It wasn't a suggestion but a command. A command laced with age-old magic.

Brean swallowed, feeling the push of magic around her. She begrudgingly walked towards the grey witch, shoulders back and every nerve on alert as she neared the elder, her body buzzing with energy.

"Kneel," she ordered in that crackling voice, and Brean had no other option than to obey as magic pressed in and around her. "Your hand, Witch."

Taking in a deep breath, Brean held out her hand.

The witch turned it palm up and dropped the small pouch into her waiting hand. Brean instinctively curled her fingers around it and retracted her arm, looking down at the small bag.

Brean frowned, glancing at the witch through lowered brows. "What is this?"

The grey witch's rotting teeth smiled at her in answer. "Only the dead can kill the dead. Only the dead can command the dead."

"Say that three times," muttered Néefar.

The elder hissed at his words. "You jest, Shifter. But the dead will rise, and power, once given, will return to its master. Let's see you jest then."

A shiver went down Brean's spine, and she stood, taking a small step back. "What's in it?"

"The blood of the Nexus tree."

A cold wind cut through the chimney, and the fire flickered violently, threatening to go out.

Silence bit through the house like a knife before Savven said quietly, "The Tree of Souls."

"Ah, yes, you know your history, Prince," rasped the witch. "You know it as the Tree of Souls, but once long ago, when the Gods created this world, and the dragons blew fire into its belly to give it life, there was a High Fae called Nexus.

"Nexus was one of the first Fae created and wanted to show thanks to the Gods, so he went deep into the forest at the heart of winter. When the ground was frozen and everything slumbered, he buried four small seeds into the dirt and said his prayers to the Gods before he *sliced* a dagger across his throat."

Brean's sharp intake of breath was matched with Néefar's low groan of exasperation. The grey witch ignored them both, stomping her cane sharply on the ground.

The boy scurried over with a glass of amber liquid. Drinking deeply, the witch ran her mottled tongue across her thin lips and continued, "There his blood watered the seeds, and come spring, the earth had eaten him piece by piece, and four small saplings had sprouted. Though the Gods heard his prayers and saw his sacrifice, they webbed their magic into its roots to connect all creatures within these trees. Both dead and alive. His body lays forever beneath The Nexus Tree, cradled between its roots and home to the dead things that crawl beneath."

When they didn't speak, the grey witch sunk low into her chair, her eyelids drooping. "See them out," she muttered.

Brean's fingers gripped the pouch tightly before she slipped it into a hidden pocket within her skirt. When she turned to leave, the grey witch spoke quietly.

"One more thing, Witch."

Brean did her best not to let her bubbling emotions show as she turned back and met the white stare aimed at her.

"Mix it with liquid fire."

She waited for a breath, and when the grey witch slumped back into her chair, she followed the others outside.

Once outside, she heaved in a sharp breath as if she had been holding it all this time.

"Well, that was unsettling," commented Néefar over the heavy wind, brushing at his leathers as if he were brushing the feeling of the house away and righted his cloak.

"Did you see the skull?" Savven asked, his lips curling.

Néefar nodded, and the two glanced at the boy when he sniffled. He stood with the house to his back but shifted from foot to foot in the sand anxiously.

Brean nodded for the others to go on, and she knelt before him, grasping his hands. "You can come with us," she said gently.

He shook his head, his black hair falling across his eyes, and Brean stroked it back from his face. "I'm an orphan, nameless. I will be forgotten."

His small voice made Brean's chest squeeze painfully, and she gripped his hands harder.

"No," she said fervently. "Not all orphans are lost."

"The witch brands her nameless, so she can always find us, so we can never escape," he explained, his eyes filling with unshed tears before he quickly blinked them away and pursed his lips in defiance.

"Oh, my sweet darling," she cooed softly, lifting a hand to stroke one of his cold cheeks. "I am an orphan too, but I was not nameless, and neither will you be." Her eyes darted to the house quickly before returning to the boy. "If you could be called any name, what would you want it to be?"

She was desperate for him to give her an answer, desperate for him to know—to truly *understand*—that he was not nameless, he was not orphaned, and he would not be forgotten.

His bottom lip trembled, and he bit it to make it stop, sniffling. "I have a memory," he started quietly, and Brean strained to hear him. "A soft voice calling me Alaric. When the witch is asleep at night, I hear it whisper to me in my dreams. It calms my nightmares and makes me feel strong when I want to cry."

Tears, hot and painful, gathered in Brean's eyes, and she swallowed the hard lump that grew in her throat.

"Perhaps it's your mother, letting you know that you will never be alone." Her words were strained, and she took in a ragged breath, making the tears fade as she fixed him with a firm stare. "You are *not* nameless. You are Alaric, child of the sea, and you will *never* be forgotten."

She gathered him close, wrapping her arms tight around his too-thin frame. "I will never forget you, Alaric," she whispered.

As the sun sank below the horizon, the darkness within the old sea house grew, the shadows coming to life from within them and outstepped Tatius.

Her feet whispered over the floorboards, her long black gown dragging softly behind her. Unending firelight from the hearth flickered over her onyx hair, brightening her pale features.

Tatius stepped up beside the sleeping witch, who snored softly and regarded her with black eyes before slowly turning them to the child curled in the corner on a torn blanket.

"It is done."

The crone's crackling voice filled the silence, and Tatius raised a brow at her.

"You did well, Witch."

The grey witch harrumphed, waving a hand at the fire that blazed hotter. "And what do I get in return?"

"Your life," Tatius stated darkly.

She cackled lowly in Tatius's face. "You are not very good at bargains, Little God."

"Watch your tongue, or I'll take away the boy." She narrowed her eyes at the witch in warning.

With a click of her tongue, the crone leaned back into her chair, basking in the warmth of the fire. "And what does the God of Death want from those three? I could have had them for my dinner."

"I just need the witch," Tatius said shortly. "You could have eaten the other two."

Humming lowly, the witch used her cane to stroke the fire, the embers filling the chimney. "And what about the fates? A God tampering with the fates is forbidden within the laws of Fae."

Tatius slid the witch a long look, her face giving way to boredom. "That's why I had you do it."

The crone's cackles followed Tatius as she vanished into the growing night.

CHAPTER 36

Levina sat at the foot of her bed and drew a shaking hand over her hair. Closing her eyes, she breathed in slowly, though try as she might, nothing eased the tremors.

Despair gripped her heart, and she let out a broken sob.

A single candle burned lowly on the desk in front of her, the shadows seeming to come alive even as the dim light fought it back. She wished those shadows would devour her.

It was one of the rare moments Levina allowed herself to feel something, anything other than numb. Knowing her friend was held captive below made her feel *so much*. She felt things she hadn't in a very long time, and her heart felt like it was breaking all over again.

Her hand went to her belly when the child within kicked at

her ribs. "Yes, Little One," she said with a strangled sigh. "I haven't forgotten about you."

A tiny hand, this time, stretched the confines of her belly as if to say *you're not alone*, and she put her hand over it, pressing back. "I'm right here," she murmured softly.

When the babe calmed, she pinched the bridge of her nose, squeezing her eyes closed.

She had to find a way to get Lithônion out of the mountain. His cell would soon become his tomb the longer he remained, and she couldn't live with herself if she watched him die like all the others who entered the dark castle.

But she didn't know how.

She had no magic.

She had no immortal strength.

She was simply, just a body trapped within a nightmare.

The shadows grew and grew until the candlelight flickered, and the flame went out. Levina was left in the darkness, and the things within her that clawed at her insides and tested her for weaknesses howled in delight.

The air grew cold, and Levina could feel herself slipping into the abyss that had beckoned for her every waking moment since she had entered the mountain.

Her chest squeezed painfully, and her mind grew hopeless, tears stinging her eyes as they cut a path of fire down her cheeks.

Her sobs cut the silence.

Broken.

Raw.

They consumed the darkness.

Suddenly, the babe pressed against her left side and her right. Stretching its small limbs within her belly.

Levina blinked through her tears, the pressure moving from side to side as her child shifted every which way.

That darkness vanished in a single moment.

She was a mother.

She did not need magic, immortal strength, or even the blessings of the Gods. She carried so much more within her, and with both her hands, she cradled her belly, sighing as the tension in her chest eased. The dark things within snarled in outrage, retreating.

"Thank you, my Little One," she whispered.

A loud knock rasped at her door, and her head whipped in the dark room towards it.

Another knock, more impatient.

Jaw clenching, she stood, rolling her shoulders back when a fist banged at the door.

Walking to the desk, she found the flint by the candle and struck it. A flame lit the darkness, and the shadows retreated.

Another loud bang.

"I'm coming!" she snapped.

She swung the door open and glared at Laudin, who smiled back at her.

"*Levina*," he purred, leaning against her door frame. His fitted black tunic and leather pants stretched over thick muscles as he crossed his arms over his chest.

She crossed her own arms and frowned up at him. "What do you want, Laudin?"

Brown eyes travelled the length of her body, hovering over her full breasts that expanded with every breath before going back to her eyes, which were now narrowed to slits. "I want a great deal of things, Levina," he drolled, eyeing her chambers over her head.

Levina gaped when he pushed past her and entered her room.

"I did not invite you in! Get out!" she demanded, seething.

Laudin ignored her, going to her bed, running a hand over the thick quilt, and then dragging a finger over the small side table. He looked at his finger as if inspecting it for dirt, and Levina fumed.

Gripping his arm, she used every ounce of her measly strength to turn him around, fury fuelling her blood. "Get. Out. Now."

He leaned down to her eye level and smiled. "No."

His fingers drifted to her neck, and Levina made to step back, but his grip tightened, restraining her.

Fear flashed through her, and her eyes went wide, her hand gripping his as he *squeezed*, and spots floated in her vision.

"Lau-din s-to-p," she managed to get out. Blood rushed through her ears, and all she could hear was her heart beating wildly.

His low chuckle echoed in the shadowed room, his hand

slackening.

Levina took in a sucking breath, the babe in her womb pressing against her ribs in protest.

Laudin leaned into her, his thumb brushing against the bruised flesh, and she knew her skin would soon be purple. His mouth replaced his thumb, and he kissed the skin of her neck, laughing darkly when she jerked back.

"I told you I want many things, my dear," he whispered, allowing her to escape him. His eyes had turned black as coal, and they glowed with hunger. "Let me taste you. Let me feel you around me, Levina."

She couldn't help what she did next. She laughed. Loudly. She laughed until tears formed in her eyes and held her belly as her whole body shook.

"I'm sorry," she said between dying laughter. "Could you say that again?"

Laudin's face turned murderous, and he growled in warning. "You laugh at me! I granted you the ability to say yes, but you *laugh at me*." He stalked towards her until she was trapped between the desk and his towering body. He gripped her wrists painfully, twisting them to her sides in an iron grip when she fought him. "I can just take what is mine," he warned darkly.

Levina spat in his face. "I will *never* be yours!"

A sly smile cut his mouth, and he tilted his head in thought, his blond hair catching the candlelight. Levina wished on everything that she had her magic and could set that blond hair on fire. "And what if I promised to free your precious Lithônion?"

Blood drained from her face. "What?"

Laudin's eyes simmered, and he bent his head, dragging his teeth across her neck and biting the skin painfully.

"You heard me," he murmured against her skin.

The pain doused her shock, and she struggled against his hold, her knee slipping between his legs. She reared her leg back, as much as the desk would allow, and brought her knee to his groin.

Laudin's face immediately paled, and he doubled over, his hands going to his groin.

"Don't you *dare* touch me again!" she spat venomously.

He straightened, despite the look of lingering pain, and grabbed her as she tried to run, throwing her on her bed and using his weight to pin her.

She was trapped.

"Do not make me hurt you," he snarled.

"You already have!" she threw back.

His body shifted, all of him covering all of her, and she could barely breathe at the weight pressed on top of her.

Laudin reared her body up and slammed her back into the bed.

The bed muted the blow, but it still jarred her bones.

"Make a deal with me," he hissed between clenched teeth. "I will free your Lithônion if you give yourself to me."

She smiled bitterly up at him. "To be freed from one nightmare, only to be a slave to another? No, thank you."

Rage, pure, unaltered rage, morphed his face, and he snarled viciously, swearing as he got off of her. "You're a fool! I can free you!"

Levina laughed, rolling herself to her side to push off the bed. Her dark blonde hair tumbled wildly around her face, and she brushed it back, sitting on the edge of the bed. "I will never be free, Laudin, and *you* will never be good enough to best Ezra and destroy his bargain."

His face turned red under that rage, his lip curling at her words.

"You will never be strong enough."

She knew her words struck home when his face turned bright red, and his eyes became impossibly black. But she didn't stop. She stood, squaring her shoulders. "You can't touch what doesn't belong to you, Ezra's precious little *pet*."

Laudin's hand whipped out, connecting with her face, and her head snapped back, body following. The bed broke her fall, but she could feel blood trickle across her cheek where the skin had broken, and she breathed through her nose, hand gripping the quilt.

"Then you and your babe will rot here forever!"

His voice resounded in her chambers even after he left, but still, Levina didn't move. Her one hand cradled her belly, the other gripping the quilt as if it would keep her from floating away into the abyss that crowded her vision.

CHAPTER 37

Hazen's toe caught the lip of a tree root, and the ground tilted under her. Groaning, she sat back on her heels, fatigue numbing her legs, feet, head, *everything*. She was sure her bones had long since vanished.

Brushing the dirt off her thighs and scraped palms, her shoulders slumped, and she scrubbed a ruined hand over her face. She had been wandering through the forest for days and hadn't seen a soul. The thought that she could be going in circles was constantly in the back of her mind, and she refused to acknowledge it.

It was dark in the forest most of the time, dim beams of sunlight slipping through the dark evergreen needles high above her. This was unlike Thórsmörk, where willowy trees grew tall and lean, their long branches draped in vibrant green leaves. These trees were as wide as they were tall and dark as night. Vibrant moss covered the protruding roots and dusted the base of the trunks, tiny purple flowers sprouting in between the folds.

She was starting to slip into a state of delusion. However, if she had been more conscious, she would have thought the forest beautiful in a dark and quiet way, but she wasn't. Hazen blinked as the world tilted on its axis.

Taking a slow breath, her lungs almost too tired to work, she tried to blink away the shifting earth.

The world stopped moving, and she slumped against the tree she had tripped on, the large roots cradling her heavy body. Hunger had long since vanished, but her mouth was like sandpaper, and she would give anything for water.

She had survived a troll, a minotaur, a psychotic mermaid queen, and she would survive this too—even if Savven wasn't here to save her this time and then lecture her for almost getting herself killed.

If she were honest, she missed the bastard, though she would never admit it to him.

Her thoughts went to the watery prison far below the sea, Lilla and her sisters, the queen who stole the throne, the black cell... and the darkness she saw within it every time she closed her eyes. Hazen owed her thanks to whoever helped her escape the abyss that still haunted her dreams. She could still feel her flesh being torn away, the darkness ripping her apart from the inside out, and she swallowed hard, shaking the memory away.

She would survive this; she had to; she refused to come this far and die.

Her limbs shook violently from dehydration and fatigue, and she leaned her head back against the trunk. A quick nap was all she needed, not that she had much choice. Her brain was shutting down her body even as she tried to stay awake.

No sooner had her eyes closed they snapped open as a bird cawed from overhead.

Hazen's heart shot to her throat, and her head swiftly looked up, her eyes searching and focusing on a raven with blue-black feathers perched on the lowest branch of the tree before her.

Wide-eyed with her heart thumping in her ears, she swallowed and unstuck her tongue from the roof of her mouth, but no words came out when she tried to speak.

What would she say? Hello?

Beak clicking at her, its head tilted sharply before looking to her left. It cawed again and flew off.

Nostrils flaring, Hazen was fully awake now, her limbs thrumming with adrenaline.

A twig snapped to her left.

Hazen jerked her head towards it. Standing slowly, careful of the roots, her eyes scanned the forest, but the trees were too thick. They stood like small, impenetrable walls to her vision.

Sunlight penetrated the forest ahead of her, and her breath caught in her throat. A centaur walked around a tree, the beams of light falling across its pale blonde hide and igniting the honey-brown hair that curled around its feminine face.

Her hoofs padded across the black dirt, pausing.

Hazen darted around her tree when the centaur's eyes came her way. After a moment, she leaned on the trunk, peaking around it to watch the creature she had only seen in mythology textbooks.

She was breathtaking. Olive skin glimmered almost gold in the light, and her long hair hung curly and untamed around her face. Her chest was bare, her breasts small and nearly concealed by the hair that curled around them, and her narrow waist disappeared into the body of a horse.

Hazen stared, mesmerised.

"CAW!"

The raven cut across Hazen, the tip of its wing nearly slicing across her face. She gasped and stumbled back.

Startled, the centaur reared up, her front hooves kicking sharply.

Hazen caught herself before she fell, eyes locking with the female centaur, and then the sickening spray of blood and the crunch of bones was all she could see and hear.

Flecks of bright red blood sprayed her face even from several feet away, and she blinked in shock, watching the centaur's head slip from her narrow shoulders. That long curtain of curly hair falling away in two sections.

A scream lodged in her throat, and Hazen took in a sucking breath, stumbling over her feet backwards.

The centaur's body stood for a few more seconds before crumpling beside the dislodged head.

Slowly, so slowly as to not make a sound, Hazen put space between her and the body, chest heaving with short breaths. Her head jerked quickly from the axe embedded into the tree and followed its trajectory. All the blood drained from her face as a towering, bullish creature stepped into sight.

A Prowler.

She ran.

Hazen's feet barely touched the ground as she flew as fast as humanly possible. The forest screamed by her in a black, brown, and green blur. Adrenaline fuelled the blood in her veins like a drug that narrowed her vision to just the path in front of her and limited her hearing to the erratic heartbeat pulsing in her ears.

"You're going to get yourself killed."

Savven's voice seemed to chase her, and she gritted her teeth.

I. Will. Not. Die. It was like a mantra in her mind as she ran.

The earth rumbled like thunder as the minotaur crashed through the forest. Hazen said a silent prayer of thanks to whatever Gods ruled this world for the trees that she easily dodged around but sat like pillars in the minotaur's way.

She didn't dare look behind her and sucked in a sharp breath when she stumbled over another root. Jerking forward, she tumbled a couple steps and pushed off again, a roar so close it jarred her bones.

Survive, her mind seemed to whisper. *Survive, Hazen.*

Run.

Faster.

RUN.

Her feet pounded the earth, and a strangled sound escaped as she bit down on the sharp pain that lanced her neck when a low-hanging branch whipped her skin, baring her teeth in defiance. She would not fall. She would not fail. Not then, not now.

Survive.

Above her, the raven cawed.

Something whizzed by her head, nearly tangling in her hair.

Then another, and another.

A voice cried out from ahead, but she couldn't focus on it or make out what it said; the blood rushing through her ears was deafening.

Survive.

The voice called out again, but it was distant, buried under the beat of her heart. Then, hands grabbed her.

Hazen's body jerked back, her head whipping forward. She screamed, lunging at the ones that grabbed her, lashing out with fists, nails, and feet. She would bite them if they came close enough.

"Stop!" the voice barked in a deep baritone.

Whoever held her shook her roughly, and Hazen sucked in a long deep breath, blinking rapidly. The world around her came back into focus, and she blinked again, realising she was staring at a barrel chest.

Looking up, rich brown eyes met her hazel ones in a firm assessing stare. They belonged to a man—male—who couldn't have been older than forty if he were human, of course.

He had a close-cropped black beard, grey hair sprinkled throughout, and black hair starting to turn a little more salt-and-pepper. Deep olive skin gleamed in the sudden sunlight Hazen hadn't realised had appeared.

He stepped back with a frown, his black brows furrowing in question as he looked her up and down. He wore a white workman's shirt that lay open at the collar, tucked into brown leather pants that were tucked into brown boots.

He looked... human, like her.

Hazen *knew* she looked like shit. She felt like shit, and she smelled like shit.

He crossed his arms over his barrel chest, tilting his head in thought, his eyes sliding beyond her.

Swallowing the sudden lump in her throat, her heart still beating like a drum that would crack her ribs, she turned.

Three arrows, one to the head, one to the chest, and the other to the neck. All in a perfectly straight line down the minotaur's upper body, protruding from its back.

The minotaur was sprawled, face down on the ground, its head bent at an unnatural angle from where it had skidded across the ground and smashed into a tree.

Hazen whipped around, the world tilting dangerously. "You killed it?" It came out in a croak rather than coherent, each sound grating on her throat. She needed water.

"Aye, we did." Frowning, the male reached for her as her world tipped on its axis again, and she swayed with it. "Eh, watch it, girl."

"Who…" But she couldn't finish her question. Her tongue was lead in her mouth.

His large grip was a steady, warm band on either of her arms, and Hazen's head swam. Her heartbeat slowed, that adrenaline ebbing out of her muscles and bones, and whatever fibre she had in her to keep upright vanished.

Darkness swooped in, and Hazen went willing into it.

Something wet and spongy pressed against Hazen's mouth, water trickling past her lips, and she turned her head away from it, groaning softly.

Someone tsked beside her, a splash, and then a comb was run through her hair.

Hazen forced an eye open as fingers replaced the comb and began to tug at her hair softly.

"You've slept for two days."

Both eyes opened now, fully awake, and they darted up to the female who sat beside her, braiding her hair. Almond eyes met her own, and her heart rate spiked. Eyes going wide, she jerked away and rolled to her feet.

Chest heaving from the sudden burst of movement after apparently being asleep for two days, Hazen tried to calm the erratic way her heart skittered across her sternum. "Who are you?" she demanded.

The female sighed as if exasperated with her, leaning back onto a vibrant orange pillow stitched with intricate florals. Her long black hair kept loose, falling over an exposed brown shoulder. She raised one arched brow, a thin silver scar that ran from her right brow to her jaw pulling tight.

She looked at Hazen expectedly as if asking her if she was going to run or not.

Hazen's eyes darted around the room—the tent—she was in.

Incense hung in thick clouds as it wafted lazily through the air. More pillows of vibrant burnt oranges, plums, and yellows were strewn in a corner and around a table that stood only a foot off the ground, with hinges down the middle that suggested it folded in two.

The ground was covered with colourful woven rugs. A trunk sat in the corner near the entrance, and a long table against the side of the tent served fruits and meat on silver platters.

Hazen's stomach rumbled loudly at the sight of food. The hunger had returned tenfold.

"Who are you?" she asked again.

Loosening a breath, the female pursed her lips and stood, dark red skirts skimming the tops of her black boots and swaying around her.

"I will go get Luca." The light Russian accent that rolled off the words made Hazen's brows shoot to her hairline. "Eat." And she was gone, the tent flaps fluttering in her wake.

Hazen looked around the tent, then down at herself. Her clothes had been changed. Bringing her nose to her underarm, she sniffed. Someone had bathed her.

The tattered scraps of what had been Brean's clothes were gone. In their stead, she wore well-worn brown leather pants, a dark blood-red shirt with loose sleeves that fit around her wrist, and a black bodice with golden clasps going down the middle and gold flowers embroidered. With every breath she took, the bodice pushed her breasts up into the long V of her neckline.

Running a quick hand over her hair told her it had been washed, brushed, and French braided down her back. The silky strands were soft under her small callouses and still healing scraps of her palms.

Her body was sore and stiff but whole. She was in one piece, and Hazen's shoulders sagged slightly in relief.

Stomach rumbling in a reminder that she hadn't eaten in four days, Hazen reached for the first food item she could grab. A purple melon-type fruit, sweet and tart all at once. A yellow berry that looked almost like a strawberry and tasted like one, too. She ate a handful of those. Meat. Her mouth salivated. Dried meats littered a tray to itself, and she wolfed down bite after bite.

The tent flaps ruffled, and Hazen swallowed the piece of meat in her mouth quickly, a blush rising at being caught.

"I thought you dead when you collapsed," said the male who entered the tent.

The male stood beside the black-haired female whom Hazen suspected was the one who bathed and clothed her. His baritone voice was familiar.

What did she call him? Luca?

Luca gave her a small smile, his brown eyes lit with warmth.

"You killed the… Prowler." It was more of a statement, and she shifted when the female shot her a look of contempt.

Luca waved dismissively at the female as if he could sense that look. "Don't mind, Vika. She's like a cat, a little skittish around new people."

Vika's mouth dropped open.

Hazen smothered her laughter, but not before a small smile slipped.

The smile dropped from Luca's face, and he faced her with a look that reminded her of her father. The kind of look that once made Hazen tell her parents she was hiding a baby squirrel in her closet when she was five. It was the worst day, having to give the squirrel to the animal hospital. It was that same look. The kind that got Hazen to spill her secrets.

"Ezra's dogs don't usually wander this deep into the outskirts of the Black Forest," he said lowly. "Which means they're hunting something… someone." His head tilted in thought, and those brown eyes bore into her as if they could dig out the truth. "Why are they hunting you?"

Could she tell him about the prophecy? Did they know? Savven said not everyone knew what was foreshadowed. Chewing on her tongue, Hazen looked between Luca and Vika.

Did she want them to know who she was? Did she even know who she was?

"You're wasting our time," snapped Vika.

Luca frowned at her, clicking his tongue. "Ignore her." His gaze softened on Hazen, who frowned at them both. "It's okay. We won't press."

Vika scoffed. "If you bring in a stray, Luca, more will follow. It's too dangerous for her to be here."

He shot her a sidelong glance, brow raised and the previous amusement returning. "If you remember, Vika, you were once a stray yourself." He clapped his hands together loudly and gave Hazen a beaming smile. "Well, welcome to my tribe. You will stay with Vika in the meantime. She will show you around."

Hazen caught the annoyed shake of Vika's head, the female raising a brow at her. "Are you sure that's a good idea?"

Luca chuckled. "Her bark is worse than her bite."

Laughter and the soft tune of a fiddle slipped through the tent entrance when Luca paused halfway, looking pointedly at Vika. "Her name is Hazen, not Stray; remember that, Vika."

Vika scowled at the tent entrance.

"How does he know my name?" Hazen demanded, stepping back. Her stomach shifted with unease.

Pinching the bridge of her nose, Vika turned slowly and looked at her through lowered brows. "The same way he knows who you are." She said it like she was talking to someone who didn't speak the same language. "The same way I know who you are."

Hazen's jaw clenched in annoyance. "And how is that? Or would you prefer I solve a riddle to get the answer?"

Vika chuckled darkly. "Don't tempt me." She flipped her long black hair over a brown shoulder and motioned for Hazen to follow. "Come, you can't stay hidden all day."

"I didn't realise I was hidden," mumbled Hazen.

Warm air, laughter, children's shrieks of happiness, and the quick strums of a fiddle all greeted her. Hazen tilted her face to the sunshine above, a soft smile curling her mouth. This place, oddly enough, reminded her of home. The normality of shrieking children, laughter, music... For a moment Hazen could see the

Sunday farmers markets she and her family would go to, then she blinked, and it was gone. Reality making her smile drop a fraction as she glanced at her surroundings.

They were in the forest, but the trees were more dispersed. Wagons circled one after another, weaving in and out of the trees. Red and cream tents were pitched beside them or within the large circle they created. The wagons acted like a wall against the forest, and in the centre was a blazing bonfire with a black cauldron hanging over its flames.

Something chimed in the breeze, and Hazen looked over her shoulder. Pieces of blue glass strung together on a long white branch sang softly as the wind danced through them, catching the light. The glass hung from an enclosed wagon beside the tent they had just exited.

Three boys went screaming by with wooden swords in hand, and Vika grabbed one by the back of his collar.

"*Maa-ma!*"

Vika clicked her tongue. "Enough, don't complain." She knelt, licking her thumb and scrubbing a bit of dirt off the boy's caramel cheek.

His golden curls caught the sunlight, and his freckled nose wrinkled as Vika fussed over him. His hand pushed away her picking, and he glanced up at Hazen when she laughed.

Hazen's laughter died when she noticed he had one eye exactly like Vika's, the same light almond brown, but the other was a bright indigo blue.

"This is my son, Makari." She stood, pressing Makari to the front of her skirts, his face tilting back to look at her when his mother wrapped a protective hand around his shoulder. "Makari, this is a stray Luca brought in."

Hazen shot Vika a deadpan stare. "Really?" Shaking her head, Hazen knelt to eye level with Makari. "My name is Hazen."

Makari shifted the wooden sword in his hands, looking more than ready to run off and continue his chase.

"Hello," he replied.

Vika brushed his curls back, kissed the top of his head, and gave him a gentle push. "Off with you, Little Hellion."

Makari's smile challenged the sun, and he waved at Hazen before dashing off.

"He's beautiful," Hazen said softly, giving Vika a small smile.

Vika's eyes were set on Makari, watching him raise his sword and charge one of the other little boys. "He's my blessing."

"How old is he?"

"Seven."

The fiddle playing changed to a dark humming melody that sang of magic and fate, and Hazen's eyes fixed on the fiddler swaying beside the bonfire.

Vika followed her gaze, eyes darting between Hazen and the music.

"You're gipsies," Hazen breathed when the realisation struck her.

"Romani, but yes," Vika corrected.

Hazen spun to Vika. "Does that make you human?"

Vika's silence followed as she walked away, and Hazen pursed her lips, striding after the female.

"Wait." Hazen reached for Vika's arm and tugged. "Wait, Vika. Are you saying you're human?"

Vika took in a long breath, studying Hazen's face momentarily. "Yes… and no."

Hazen looked at Vika, stunned, and hurried to catch up when she resumed walking. "What do you mean yes *and* no?"

"Once the veil claims you, you become something *more*." She paused, turning to Hazen. Her mouth was pressed tight, and she combed a hand through her long hair with an audible sigh. "I'm not Fae if that's what you're asking. The Fae are all those who were born within the world of magic, born of magic. We are not born of magic; we are *blessed* by magic. Chosen by the magic of this world to be something beyond ordinary."

"I thought I stepped through the veil?" Hazen clarified.

Vika's head ticked, and Hazen could tell the woman was thinking.

"In a sense, yes, you stepped through the veil, but only because the veil chose to let you pass. It claimed you as part of this world, so you came through the divide. It's why we never remember crossing through the veil. It transforms us into something more as it brings us through."

"What do you mean it *chose.* You talk about the veil as if it's a living thing?"

Vika looked like she was entertaining a child's questions, but Hazen couldn't care less. She wanted answers.

"Vika," she said, a demand in her tone when the woman didn't answer.

Vika's eyes darted beyond to the children playing, Hazen following her stare. Makari ran freely, his gold hair wild in the breeze, and his smile cut ear to ear.

"The Gods made this world, but the world has a mind of its own. The Gods made the veil, dividing the world into two, but the veil chooses who it lets pass through. Magic is a very real, very living thing, Hazen." Vika looked at her with regard. "They made the veil with ancient magic, magic so old it does not exist within us anymore. So yes, the veil is alive and has the ability to shape us."

Makari saw them and waved wildly before dashing off with the other boys.

"So, what happened when you crossed the veil?"

Vika crossed her arms over her chest, jaw ticking, and Hazen could see the darkness creep into her eyes before it was blinked away.

"My family, my tribe, migrated from a tiny village in northern India by sea for nearly a year before we reached Russia. My mother died of infection during the voyage halfway through." She loosened a shaky breath. "My father, malaria, two months after Luca welcomed us into his tribe. It was the middle of summer when Luca took me in as a child, and a year later… we were in the village next to Lukh when they began… the hangings and… the burnings.

"Luca took us all into the forest, and we travelled for days, weeks, and months. We didn't stop because we knew it would be our end if we did. Luca protected us all until one day, the air grew heavy, and it was stolen from my chest, and then I was waking in a different world.

"We soon realised this wasn't like the one we came from. This was new, different, and *safe.* I stopped aging on my twentieth year.

Those beyond twenty stopped ageing, and children grew until they did too."

Vika picked at a spot on her sleeve, frowning. "We're immortal for however long this world deems it acceptable."

Hazen wanted to reach for Vika's hand; she could see the pain the past had caused her, but something told her the woman wouldn't appreciate it.

"So that's why Luca called you a stray?" she asked instead, an amused smile lifting her lips.

Vika snorted, shooting her a sidelong look, the darkness in her gaze easing. "Death is a fickle thing, even after so many years."

Bodies upon bodies filled her memory. Those in Fallúin shifted to those floating upon the sea, but it was all the same. They all died because of her.

Swallowing the lump in her throat, Hazen smiled tightly. "So, did the veil grant you the ability to guess my name, too?" she teased wryly, changing the subject.

The tension in Vika's shoulders eased, and she rolled her eyes, but there wasn't any annoyance there this time. "Yes, but not in the way you think. Cards, and little magic tricks, tea leaves. The veil grew those skills into something *more*. We can't predict the future, but we can see what is close to us, close to those around us."

"So, you saw a human girl was coming your way?" Mirth lingered behind her words.

"No," Vika said, frowning. "We saw a dragon."

Hazen's blood chilled, her prior amusement fading.

"Mama!" Makari ran up to them, breathless. "Come play!" He tugged on her hand with his free one, the other still holding the wooden sword.

"Oh, you little hellion, I wish I could, but I have to start the roast." Vika smiled gently down at Makari, ruffling his hair. "They caught us a boar for the feast."

Makari's eyes lit up, and Hazen chuckled.

"Can you play with me?" Makari asked, turning to Hazen.

Vika folded her arms over her chest. "What happened to the other boys?"

"Toblin and Ragar got called to help collect firewood for

tonight," Makari said with a frown.

"Shouldn't you be helping them?" chastised Vika.

Makari shrugged with a mischievous smirk. "I hid before they could see me."

Vika just shook her head. "Whatever am I going to do with you?"

"Can she play with me?" he asked his mother this time, insistent.

Vika raised a brow at Hazen.

Hazen looked between the two and huffed out a laugh, nodding. How could she say no to a child? "Sure, what are we playing?"

"Bandits! I'll go get Toblin's sword! He's the biggest!" Makari sprinted off before Hazen or his mother could object.

Standing, she crossed her arms. "There's a feast tonight?"

Vika nodded, humming.

"What are you celebrating?"

"You." Vika rolled her eyes in exasperation at Hazen's bewildered look. "Don't ask me, Luca said we are to celebrate the coming dragon. So that means *you.*"

Makari was already sprinting back, a longer sword in his other hand.

"Don't let it get to your head," Vika muttered as her son approached.

Hazen frowned. "What?"

"When you get bested by a seven-year-old." Vika knelt and opened her arms to her son, scooping him up and covering his face in quick kisses. Makari's laughter filled the air. "Don't go easy on this one," she whispered just loud enough for Hazen to hear.

Stumbling back when she set him down, Makari nodded, smiling.

"Vika!" Hazen quickly called after the woman.

Vika paused, glancing back.

"Thank you for… you know." Waving a hand down her body at her clean clothes and washed skin.

Vika shrugged nonchalantly. "You were starting to smell like *asafoetida.* I had to for the sake of the tribe."

Hazen narrowed her eyes.

Makari giggled, tugging on her hand.

She looked down at him with raised brows.
"You were starting to smell like rotten eggs."

CHAPTER 38

She was sore *everywhere*. Hazen rubbed a diligent hand over her hip, walking into Vika's tent.

Vika sat in front of a small mirror perched on the folding table, brushing a wooden comb through her dark hair. One look at Hazen's haphazard face and disarray braid had her laughing.

"What did I tell you?"

Hazen blew a strand of hair out of her face. "I didn't doubt you for a second."

She did. She one hundred per cent doubted Vika's warning, but Makari didn't let his mother down. He was seven, and they were *playing* bandits. They were *play duelling*, but he would still whack her on her hip and tell her she was dropping her arm and then complain when he beat her too quickly.

Savven would be proud of the kid.

Something white sailed to Hazen, and she snatches it up. "What is this?" Opening the soft white material, she notices it's a shirt with flowers and vines embroidered into the sleeves and wide neckline.

Vika jerked her chin towards a copper bowl with a linen towel draped over the lip where the food had been, now cleared off. "I don't need you smelling during the feast."

"You're hilarious," Hazen muttered as the woman went back to combing her hair.

Undoing the vest and pulling the dark red top off gingerly, her still healing skin sensitive, she set them on the table. She made quick work of washing her upper body. Noting the new purple bruise forming on her left hip courtesy of Makari, it mingled with the yellow and green bruises that made a kaleidoscope of colours on her torso and arms.

Pursing her lips, she gingerly slipped the new shirt on. It fit off her shoulders, the sleeves fanning out at her wrists. Tucking it into her leather pants, she donned the black vest.

"Come. Sit."

Vika set her comb aside, brushing her hair out of the way, and Hazen sat on a bright purple cushion she had patted in front of her.

A small bowl of yellow oil was placed on Hazen's right, and Vika dipped her fingers into it. She could hear Vika rub her hands together, and then she was combing her fingers through Hazen's hair. Hazen moaned lowly when the woman began massaging her scalp, her fingers making quick work of the braid and loosening the leather strap tying off the end.

Her blonde hair fell around her shoulders, and Hazen tilted her head back, eyes closed, as Vika continued to massage her head.

The tension of the last few days or weeks she had been here melted under the woman's skilled fingers.

Vika grabbed the comb and worked it from root to end before she began braiding her hair, tilting her head down as she went.

Hazen caught her reflection in the warped glass. Gold hazel eyes went wide, blinking back at her. Her lips were still healing, and there were abrasions and minor cuts along her cheek, forehead, nose and jaw that had scabbed over and were on the mend. A fading yellow bruise on her neck caught her eye, but not before she noticed the white whirling tattoos branded along the left side of her temple and up to her hairline.

She lifted a hand to the mark, tracing it slowly.

"You will be forgotten."

Nautien's voice whispered cruelly from her subconscious, and Hazen sucked in a breath when she felt those dark claws rake across her bones, the ones that tore into her in that darkness. She visibly shivered and quickly shook the memory away.

Vika stilled, catching her reflection. "Are you okay?"

Hazen nodded softly. "Yes, just bad memories." She drew her knees up, wrapping her arms around herself.

Humming, Vika continued braiding, gathering tiny sections of hair at a time. "It took me a while to stop thinking about my scar."

Hazen glanced up through her lashes; brown eyes met hazel ones, but Vika's face was expressionless.

"We were on a trade route when we took shelter for a night in the village of Baith along the western ocean. Luca was bartering a deal with a warlock, so he proposed we stay a night... but that night, Ezra's hunters slipped into the village and slaughtered nearly everyone." Vika's lips pursed into a hard line, tugging a little harder on Hazen's hair, her eyes darkening. "Our carriages were overturned, and we had loosened the horses and were fleeing into the forest until I heard a scream that would live in my bones for the rest of my days.

"It was a child. A girl. She was trapped beneath the dead and was trying to claw her way free. So, I did the only thing I could. I turned around."

Vika began wrapping the leather strap around the end of Hazen's hair. "I got the girl free and screamed for her to run. The hunters saw me and heard my scream, and I *fought* them within an inch of my life, but it was worth it because the girl got away. Now I have this scar and my son." She finished wrapping her hair and leaned forward, looking at their faces side by side in the mirror.

Hazen stared at Vika's scar, the thin silver line pulling from her right brow to her jaw, and then looked at her own, the delicate silver whorls marking her left temple, her hands balled into fists.

Jaw clenching, threatening to snap her teeth as anger boiled in her veins at what they did to her—what they *took* from her. She wanted to scream in outrage and horror for the woman at her back.

She knew what it felt like to have unwanted hands on her. To feel that terror, to think there would be no escape no matter how hard she fought. At fifteen, she had only been a child, and the man had been her teacher. If not for her classmate forgetting her mobile in her gym bag, her story might have ended like Vika's.

"Scars are a sign of power, Hazen. They're a sign of survival. That we fought for something, that we fought for ourselves, that we *lived*." She grasped her shoulders, squeezing them firmly. "Wear it with pride. It is now a part of you. Own them so they cannot own you."

Vika stood, holding out a hand to Hazen.

Hazen took one more look at her reflection and grabbed the offered hand.

The day abandoned them to the night, and the moon slipped slowly over the trees. Embers from the bonfire crackled and popped, igniting the sky above it like burning stars.

Laughter, music, and the smell of food floated through the tents. Hazen's mouth watered when she spied the roast, slowly turning over the fire, golden and delicious.

Small wooden chairs, thin woven rugs, and vibrant plush pillows were strewn around the bonfire like an outer ring. Between the fire and seating, fiddlers danced with their instruments, another with a tambourine, and one with a small drum attached to a leather strap hung around their neck.

Hazen smiled, clapping along with the female musician who caught her eye and shot her a wink before whirling away in a storm of colour and dark hair.

Twirling in and out of those who danced around the fire, their arms up, skirts held high, and cheering with every pound of the tambourine and strum of the fiddle.

Breathless and wide-eyed, Hazen found a spot on the outer ring. A smile cut from ear to ear, she clapped in time with the music, waving off a man who offered his hand with a laugh, a crooked smile coaxing her to join the festivities.

Feet tapping in time, she let her body sway, seemingly forgetting all her worries in that moment. She felt… normal. Hazen's smile slipped slowly, her eyes straying to the fire, watching it crackle and burn bright. She felt normal here. She felt *free.*

Luca's bear of a body sidled up next to her, two silver cups nearly swallowed by his hands. He handed her one, and she looked at it, eyeing its contents and sniffing.

Wine.

"To the dragon," he said, lifting his cup to hers.

She hesitated before toasting with him. "To the dragon."

The wine was good, a little dry but sweet, and she downed it.

Wrapping her hands around the empty cup, she watched a fiddler play feverishly, their body getting lost in every strum of their instrument.

"Luca?" she asked. "What dragon do you think is coming?"

Luca's bushy brows rose, and he gave her a slow, knowing smile. "There is old magic, and then there is the old ways. The Fae follow the old magic, the magic that structures this world. But we follow the old ways. We take only what is given to us by the earth."

"I'm sorry I don't follow?"

Luca grabbed a clay pitcher from a passing woman, shaking it in small circles. He set his cup on a wooden chair behind him, reaching for hers. "Give me your cup."

Hazen watched him pour an amber liquid into her cup and hand it back to her.

"Drink."

She looked up at him through lowered brows.

His laughter was deep and rich when he saw her untrusting stare. Grabbing his cup, he downed the wine, filled it with the amber liquid, and tossed it back.

She chuckled and shook her head, taking a sip and trying to refrain from immediately wincing. It was tea—a very woody, very earthy tea.

Luca saw and threw his head back, laughing. "It's an acquired taste, but it does the trick. Drink it all."

So, she did, trying not to breathe, hoping it would dull her tastebuds. It didn't. She wished she had more wine.

"Look at the bottom."

Tea leaves stared back at her.

He was reading her tea leaves.

Realisation dawned on her, and she looked up, showing him her cup.

"Now move it in a circle three times, quickly, and tip it on its side to drain."

She did and looked from the cup to him, raising her brows.

Luca's face turned serious, and he looked at her cup. "What do you see?"

Soggy tea leaves, she wanted to say.

Pursing her lips, she squinted at the leaves in the dim firelight, turning her cup towards the bonfire to see better. They lay clumped on one side from top to bottom; a tiny bit towards the middle was shaped like a small, misshapen heart, but the rest... Hazen shook her head. "I don't know."

Luca peered at the leaves and nodded, humming under his breath. "The rim of your cup resembles your present, the middle your coming future, and the bottom the distant future. This heart" —He pointed to the small heart— "symbolises a coming lover. And this" —His finger moved to the large mass— "is your complete future."

"What is it?" she asked, leaning closer to look.

"A dragon."

He pointed to the head, which split open like a mouth, and then the long, thin neck that travelled down the middle. The body laid near the bottom but never quite touched it.

She stared at it for a long moment, until it took shape and she saw what he saw.

To the coming dragon.

"What does it mean?"

"Change, girl. Great, transforming, *change*."

Cheers and whistles filled the air as the tune crescendo, the fiddlers' bows flew across their strings, the tambourine chiming wildly, and the drums pounded like a heartbeat. Everyone was a whirl of bodies and colours. Skirts raised, men grabbed the women and spun and spun and spun them around the fire.

"This world is full of mysteries we will never understand. Magic so old it transcends time itself. But I know this: change is coming. Great, unfathomable change."

Hazen chewed on her lip, her eyes studying the faces that whirled by and the forest surrounding them.

Luca gave her a crooked smile when he saw the millions of thoughts cross her face as she looked up at him. His hand was warm on her shoulder, comforting. "We don't celebrate you, Hazen. We celebrate what comes with you—the change you symbolise."

A woman with dark, curly brunette hair sidled up to Luca, wrapping her hands around his large bicep and tugging it playfully. Large green doe eyes staring up at him. Her petite body arched into the side of his. "My darling, come dance!" she said, breathless from the festivities.

"My wife, Nola," he introduced.

Nola smiled prettily at Hazen. "I saw your name in the bones."

Hazen's mouth parted in surprise, eyes darting to Luca. That's how he knew her name.

His crooked smile became vibrant, and he winked at her, drawing his wife into his side. "One of magic's great mysteries! Change is coming, Hazen! So tonight: feast, celebrate, and dance, for tomorrow, we face it head-on!"

Luca's words boomed across the tribe, and everyone cheered as Luca and Nola spun in time with the music and got lost in the dance.

"Hazen!"

Makari ran around the outside of the bonfire, his face flushed and blond curls bouncing across his forehead.

"Hazen, come dance!" He tugged on her hand, pulling her towards the throng.

Laughing, a smile cut across her face, and she followed.

The music seemed to amplify within the inner ring. Filling the spaces and the people, weaving a spell that had Hazen closing her eyes, her feet following in time with the music.

Her heartbeat sang in her chest, thrumming with every strum of the fiddle, her veins pumping through her body in time with the drum.

Around and around, she danced, her hair falling from her braid around her face. Men twirling her this way and that, women taking hold of her and spinning in time with her.

She was free. So long as the music didn't stop, and her feet kept moving, nothing could touch her. There was safety within this ring of dancing music and fire.

Hazen's eyes locked on the amber light, turning quickly, her head snapping around and fixating on the fire again.

Again.

Again.

Again.

At every turn, the fire met her gaze and pulled her closer with the beat of the music.

Tendrils of flames kissed the night sky, embers cracking off and igniting the air around her. She turned and turned, and… the music became a distant echo, fire filling her body and heating along her bones and muscles in a song of magic.

The air pulsated with power, and Hazen's mouth parted, drawn in by the flames that seemed to reach for her. Her feet stilled, and she stood transfixed in front of the roaring bonfire as men, women, and children danced around her.

The fire called to her. Her name whispered within every crackle of the embers and snap of the wood.

It called for her.

Hazen outstretched a hand and slid a foot, one after the other, closer.

Closer, it whispered.

She could feel the heat radiating off it, her skin flushing, her body singing from its power.

Closer.

One more step… her fingertips brushed the edge of the flames, and the night held its breath as a kernel of fire ignited within her.

Life rushed through her limbs like a tidal wave, and she submerged her hand in the flames.

Power. Pure, undiluted power filled her body and soul. It knitted through her muscles, flowed through the blood in her veins, down to the marrow of her bones.

And then it was gone.

Someone yanked her by the arm and jerked her away from the flames.

A strangled breath left Hazen when the fire was sucked from her, and that power dwindled into icy coldness.

The music had ceased, and every eye in the tribe was trained on her.

Hazen swallowed the lump in her throat but couldn't contain the chill down her spine.

Vika's stern eyes darted between Hazen's, her mouth pursed, but underneath that stern gaze was a worry that had Hazen shaking her head and muttering an apology.

"I think it's time for you to rest."

The bodies parted around them, and Vika guided her out of the ring of fire and dancing.

Luca stood in the outer ring, Nola by his side, and a small, knowing look in his gaze as Hazen glanced his way.

When they neared the tent, Hazen looked down at her hands.

The skin was unmarked.

CHAPTER 39

Nazar dragged a sharp nail across the flesh of a Dark One; a thin line of blood, black as tar, slipped down its neck. His black tongue slipped across the collum of skin, eyes rolling back in near pleasure.

"Nazar."

The shade's lip twitched with a snarl at the warning in his name, and he flicked dark red eyes to Ezra, watching him, waiting.

Ezra walked through the rows and rows of stagnant, Dark Ones, the tap of his feet echoing against the towering cave ceilings deep below the mountain.

Nazar's hand gripped the Dark One's neck, nails piercing the soft, cold flesh. The Dark One didn't move. Black blood slipped over his nails, and long, bony fingers and his nostrils flared with hunger.

"*Nazar!*" Ezra's eyes flashed with warning, turning black.

He released the Dark One with a look of pure malice, dropping his hand to his side, letting the blood settle on his skin.

The Dark One didn't so much as flinch despite five gaping punctures to his neck that flowed freely with blood that slowly began to recede, the skin stitching back together.

Ezra faced off with one of his Dark Ones, a female faun. Her dark copper skin and auburn hair lacked vibrancy in the cold chambers and hibernated state they all stood in.

Nazar slipped between shadows and rows of bodies until he stood over Ezra's shoulder, watching him reach out and touch the female faun softly along her cheek.

"How interesting," Ezra murmured in thought. "How different my pets affect each of them."

A soft snarl left Nazar, and his eyes darkened with rage. He watched Ezra as Ezra watched the female.

"Some become puppets, like this female," he continued, paying no attention to Nazar. The female's stare was blank, and her hazel eyes were cast with a white haze. Those eyes had no flicker of life, emotion, or physical feeling. She just stood there, still as death but breathing. "While others become weapons, like Laudin… and eventually, Levina," he murmured the female elf's name gently, and Nazar's eyes narrowed.

"What about the male?" hissed Nazar, walking around Ezra and the female faun. His black robes hung over his thin, skeletal body like a shroud of darkness that misted around him into the shadows.

Ezra's black eyes blazed, watching Nazar circle them.

"What about the male?" he hissed again. "The one that comes with *lies* on his scent." His bloody eyes darkened, and he stood behind the female faun, staring at Ezra over her head. "He wastes away in the cells. Let him feel the control of your dark power. Let your pets shape him into a weapon."

"Lithônion would make a useless weapon," Ezra remarked coldly.

Nazar hissed at his words. "Your underlying affections rot your mind."

Ezra's black eyes flashed with warning. He stepped around the faun, and his hand latched around Nazar's thin throat, his fingers nearly overlapping. "You forget who you speak to, *Shade*."

The grip on his neck did nothing to him. *You cannot kill what is already dead. Stupid Fae.*

A dark, humourless laugh echoed in the cave. "*I forget… forgive me, My Lord. I forgot whose presence I stood in.*" His row of teeth glimmered in a saccharine smile, bowing his head like an obedient pet, and looked up at Ezra darkly.

Releasing him, Ezra folded his hands behind his back and walked through the bodies, eyeing them like they were trophies he had collected.

He stopped in front of a Fae male, regarding him thoughtfully. The male looked similar to the elf who sat waiting in the cell.

"Lithônion, you say?" Ezra asked.

Nazar's head ticked sharply to one side, and he moved through the shadows, dancing around Ezra and the male. "Only the weak become puppets to the darkness," he whispered from the growing darkness. "But the strong… the strong become weapons forged from the pits of Hel. The strong survive."

His teeth could tear Ezra's ear from his head if he moved just a breath closer as he whispered into the dark lord's ear. Saliva dripped between his teeth, and he slipped between shadows, closer… his mouth opened… closer…

"Do it."

Nazar's growl of menace was silent, his lips curling into a snarl.

"But not now," continued Ezra. "Tomorrow marks the blood moon. Tomorrow, he will bleed. Tomorrow, he will feel the mark of a thousand deaths. Tomorrow, he will be reborn."

Nazar's eyes lit with cold calculation, and he let the shadows meld around him, consuming him. A sinister smile cut sharply over his hollow face. "Very well, *My Lord.*"

CHAPTER 40

Scorching heat blazed across Hazen's face, and her eyes shot open.

A strangled, horrified sound left her lips; scrambling to her feet, Hazen stared in shock. Eyes wide and glassy, fingers pressed to her lips as it all *burned* and *bled* around her.

In front of her was a large white ash tree, its skin consumed by flames, and at her feet, *surrounding* her, bodies—children, mothers, fathers, animals, and warriors of all races lay bleeding out. It saturated the ground until red pooled in divots and outlined bodies, half mud, half blood, and all death.

The earth, for as far as she could see, was covered with a layer of death, limbs, and lost souls. Flames roared in a continuing crescendo that filled her ears until it was all she could hear. She couldn't hear her ragged, strangled breaths that squeezed from her tight chest, or the rush of her blood, or the pounding of her heart. Fire *filled* every inch of her as it blazed brightly and consumed the ash tree.

The tree stood alone in the night, like a burning torch for Death, so that he may find his victims.

"This is our history."

Hazen's heart lurched, whipping around.

A male stood amongst the sea of bodies, firelight glinting off his long braided grey hair, bright gold eyes fixated on the loathsome site.

"Who are you," she demanded.

His pristine dark golden silk robe, black pants and boots stood in stark opposition to their surroundings.

"It is not a matter of *who* I am but *what* I am." His voice was calm and almost thoughtful as he turned his gold stare to her.

Smoke wafted around them in thick tendrils, curling around her hands, heat going through her limbs.

"*What* are you," she bit out through clenched teeth.

His head tilted softly, and he clasped his hands together in front of him. "I am your beginning."

The words made her jolt, and she clenched her hands at her sides. Gaze darting from body to body, blank stares followed her; no matter where Hazen looked, the dead kept their eyes on her.

Nostrils flaring, ice went down her spine when she stopped on a child's head: that's all it was, just the head of a small boy. The body had been completely severed and was somewhere within the fray.

"This is our past. It was in your name that they died. The *chosen one* that Ezra fears. This is our present and will soon become our future."

"This isn't my fault!" she yelled, the ice in her bones melting under the inferno that began to rage.

Savven had said it wasn't her fault. It wasn't. It couldn't be. She didn't *know*.

"These people are dead, they are dying, and they will perish!" his voice rising above the roaring inferno.

Stalking towards her, his golden eyes consumed the fire, holding its power within his gaze, and the world pulsated with it.

Power. Unyielding power pulsed around Hazen. It crushed every bone in her body at his presence until she dropped to her knees, her bones jarring from impact, but she barely noticed it. Bloody earth saturated the leathers of her pants, the scent of copper and fire infiltrating her senses.

Tears burned her eyes as her rage conflicted with the power pressing around her and left their stinging path down her cheeks. "They will not die!"

She threw her hands out wide and looked up at the male looming above her. A helpless feeling in her gut gnawed at her like a rat eating flesh. "This is not what I want!" she screamed.

Desperation, anger, agony, her voice broke with it all. *This is not what I want! They cannot die because of me*, even her thoughts raged in opposition.

"They will all burn to ash because of you!" His bellowed words were suffocated by the roar of fire consuming the ash tree.

"They will not die! *I will not let them die!*" she screamed wildly, the words scraping against raw vocal cords.

A thunderous explosion shattered at her back, and she arched against the blow, falling to her hands. Nails digging into the sopping grounds, she turned to see the ash tree crack, and numbing silence followed the deafening roar before it splintered apart. The flames flew into the sky, moulding, expanding, and shaping themselves until the fire was no longer just fire but a dragon made from flames and embers.

Flying through the sky, the dragon arced and fell back, wings tucked tight to its body. It neared closer, its size terrifying, and Hazen's scream broke the night.

The great dragon's wings flared open at the last second, righted its body, and consumed her in a blaze of fire.

The male stood, unmoving, and watched as the great dragon took its rightful place.

Shattered screams split the air, and gold eyes shot open, fire igniting every fibre within her body as Hazen jerked upright, her unbound hair falling around her face in disarray. Her chest heaved with sudden adrenaline, and she stilled, numbing silence wavering as the seconds ticked by.

Vika's tent was dark and empty, save Hazen. The flicker of firelight shining through the crevasses of the opening flap gave some leeway to the blackness.

Had she imagined it?

Another cry broke through the canvas walls, and she tossed back her blanket, rolling to her feet.

Hazen pulled on her boots, sprinted out of the tent, and barely dodged the sharp edge of a blade cutting through the air, close to her face, too close as her breath snagged in her chest.

The outside world had erupted into chaos.

Bodies of beasts and Fae stampeded through the Romani camp. This was no army, but they slipped into the camp like a tidal wave of destruction.

Hazen's breath quickened, and she dashed around a... a *harpy,* whose claws dug into the face of a Romani man, blood spraying the air and the right side of Hazen's face when she twisted around them.

Startling, Hazen blinked the blood from her eyelashes and ducked under the wings slicing the air.

The harpy screeched, her half-female body withering furiously as her wings flapped into the night, taking half the man's face in her talons. Flying off to find another when the man dropped, lifeless.

Steel slicing through flesh was a sicking ring beneath the roar of fire and beasts. Tents burned brightly, women and men stumbling out of them, half ravaged by the blaze.

Bile rose in Hazen's throat like acid. She sprinted through the onslaught, looking for Vika.

Leaping onto an overturned wagon, its wheel spinning endlessly in the air, Hazen's eyes darted from face to face, not lingering for longer than a second. She searched for the telling scar that ran down the woman's face.

Adrenaline turned to fury as she watched with growing horror the demise of the Romani tribe. The fire around her was nothing compared to the flames that ignited a red-hot trail through every crevice of her body.

Molten power lit an inferno within, and she let it pull her under.

"MAMA!"

She heard Makari's terrified screams through the roaring in her ears, and she turned. She felt like the world had slowed, like time had stopped, and her eyes widened with outrage.

Beyond the carnage, a Fae male hauled Makari, kicking and screaming, deeper into the forest. Makari bit down on the male's neck viciously and tore his teeth through the skin, ripping flesh away, blood dripping down his small jaw.

Hazen could see the fear in his eyes, even from where she stood, and then she was running, sprinting as fast as her feet could carry her. She *flew* across the bodies, smouldering tents, slain horses, and protruding tree roots.

The male roared and threw Makari like he was nothing.

Makari crashed into a tree and collapsed in a small unconscious heap.

Hazen's mouth pursed tightly, and she saw red, willing herself faster, eyes narrowing into murderous slits as the inferno consumed her.

She was fire. She was flame. She was death.

The male pulled his sword from its sheath on his hip, arced it overhead, and she drove her body into his.

They went tumbling to the ground in a tangle of limbs. Even consumed by the cresting fire, stars erupted in Hazen's vision when her head smashed soundly against the ground.

"They will die because of you!"

They. Would. Not.

Hazen snarled in defiance, rolled to her feet, and immediately charged the male who had stumbled to his.

He yelled when he saw her and lunged for the blade that had flown a couple feet off when she had charged him. Hazen saw this and threw herself towards the sword.

They grappled for the weapon, Hazen's fingers wrapping around part of the cross-guard; simultaneously, the male grabbed for the handle. She snatched it back and jabbed her elbow into his nose, hearing it crack.

The male roared in pain, a hand going to his face.

Hazen rounded to her feet, sword now firmly in her grasp. It was heavy, but not heavy enough that she couldn't slice the male in front of her into two.

Sneering, the male dropped his bloody hands, his eyes black as coal narrowed on her as he lunged.

Nothing but pure power was rushing through Hazen's body. Something unfamiliar, something *new,* shifted and tightened around her. It moved her like a chess piece with strength and sureness that steadied the shake in her limbs. That power wove through her in a blaze of heat that would burn anyone around her. Taking one look at the blade and the charging Fae, Hazen flipped her hand to the underside of the handle and drew her arm back.

The sword sailed sure and fast through the air like a bullet.

Bones and flesh and a sharp gasp and then silence.

Her empty hands fisted at her sides, nails biting into her flesh before she relaxed her fingers and breathed sharply through her nose.

The male was pinned to a tree, his sword penetrating him like a tack in a board, his feet dangling in the air, head lolling forward. Finally, his body followed, slumping over the hilt.

Thunder rolled violently overhead, shaking the forest and jarring Hazen. She blinked, rounding, and ran to Makari.

She brushed golden curls away from his forehead, cradling him in her arms protectively. He was still unconscious, and her thumb brushed his small chin, frowning. The blood was gone.

"Makari!"

Vika sprinted through the trees, a hand holding up her long black chemise. An embroidered shawl hooked into the crooks of her elbows as it tried not to fall off. Her black hair whipped behind her, and panic set in those dark eyes.

"Makari!" she gasped, dropping to her knees in front of her child. Vika gathered him close, and Hazen dropped her hands to her lap.

"What happened?" she demanded, turning furious eyes on Hazen, whose attention was on the boy. "What happened to my child?!"

"He was thrown…" her voice travelled off, and she looked around.

Hazen blinked slowly. The body was gone—the sword, the body… she jerked around, looking at the now quiet camp. Except for the small blaze of the dwindling bonfire that still glowed, the fire was gone. There were no bodies, no blood, no beasts and screams. It was all gone.

Her heart sank like a stone into her stomach, and she swallowed hard.

Had she imagined it all?

Vika grabbed her by her chin and turned her sharply to face her. *"What happened?"*

"It was all burning," she whispered, her eyes still fixated on the slumbering camp despite Vika's punishing grip. "There was so much blood and… *fire.*" She took in a shuddering breath. The power that had consumed her slowly dwindled until she felt a coldness chill her to the bone.

She wanted it back. She wanted the fire back.

And then it was there, a tiny kindling ember flickering inside her, warming her like it had heard her, reminding her that she had control and was not powerless in this world filled with magic.

Hazen finally turned her gaze on Vika, and the woman sucked in a sharp breath through her teeth.

"Your eyes," she whispered. "They're gold."

Hazen barely registered her words, turning back to the tree where the male had been pinned and hanging limp. Getting up, Hazen traced a hand over the rough bark where the sword should have been. Not even a scratch marred the tree.

"He was dead," she whispered to herself.

"They will die because of you!"

She dropped her hands to her side, fisted her fingers, and her eyes darkened. That ember flared briefly with power within her before settling back into the small flicker of life.

She could hear Vika shift and stand beside her a moment later. Vika looked at the tree and then at Hazen, studying her silently with pursed lips; Makari cradled protectively in her arms.

"Come," she finally said, nudging Hazen's shoulder with her own. "There is ancient magic at play. Let us go back."

Hazen studied the tree for a moment more, furrowing her brows as a thousand thoughts spiralled deeper and deeper into her mind before turning and walking silently back to Vika's tent.

"Was that necessary?"

Tatius flicked disinterested black eyes up to the Keeper of Dragons as Valdren walked up to her side, sliding his hands into the long open sleeves of his dark red robes.

"Completely," she drolled.

Valdren arched a grey brow at her, softly slanted ancient gold eyes following her stare. They were narrowed curiously on the head of blonde hair that disappeared into the circle of wagons and tents.

"She was taking too long," she added as if discussing the weather. When Hazen vanished from sight, she looked up at Valdren, cocking her head. "Thank you."

Valdren tilted his head in response. "And what is the little God up to?" His mouth quirked in a ghost of a smile, and Tatius refrained from rolling her eyes.

"I'm sorting out my priorities, if you must know." She frowned, glaring up at the Keeper of Dragons. "You are the only one I don't flay alive for calling me little."

A soft chuckle huffed from Valdren, and he shook his head. "The laws were written for a reason, Tatius. Do not tamper with the old magic."

His warning was noted, and she shrugged a small shoulder nonchalantly. "You forget I helped write those laws, small as I may be. I helped create the first weaves of magic within this world, and *I,* as Death, helped create the cycle they all live and die by."

He raised a hand before folding it back into his robe sleeves. "Apologies, Tatius."

Tatius sniffed delicately, turning dark eyes back to the Romani camp where Hazen was settling into her bedroll, her mind was turning over and over within itself, and where that ember of power now burned hot and bright, waiting within her.

A small, calculating smile whispered over her thin lips as Tatius said, "I think it's time for some of the laws to be rewritten."

CHAPTER 41

André awoke with a strangled gasp, beads of sweat dotting her forehead. Hand to her chest, she tried to steady the fibrillation of her heart. Eyes darting around the dark bedroom, they landed on her sleeping husband, and she laid a soft, shaking hand on his shoulder as if his touch would help ease the pounding in her chest.

Letting out a breath, André slid silently out of bed, her long white satin nightgown falling down her legs. She tucked the quilt around her husband before slipping out of their bedroom.

The house was silent and dark, except for the soft patter of her feet and the scrape of wood as she opened one of the drawers in the desk in the living room, her eyes adjusting to see in the darkness.

"Hazen," she whispered to the silence. "What has happened to you?"

The silence didn't answer back but wrapped tightly around her. Magic hanging heavy in the air, sweet and tempting and dangerous.

Her fingers grasped a small wooden box with a large oak tree carved on its lid and pulled it out, brushing across its top with a yearning that still nudged her mind from time to time.

Fire filled her vision from her dreams. Hazen... she had seen Hazen consumed by the dragon, and then magic had awoken her. Her magic, her power that slumbered in an eternal sleep in this mortal land, had woken her and was now wrapping around her, urging her to move.

André's hands trembled as she lifted the lid.

It was the only thing she had taken with her when she crossed the veil, the only thing she had left of her heritage, her history, and her people. An amber teardrop held on the thinnest gold chain glimmered in the darkness. It had been her mother's, and before that, her mother's mother and so on, and then soon became André's when she was in her first century.

She grasped it tightly, closed the box, and sealed her past.

The night air was crisp and wet as the storm slowed to a sprinkle. Her son and daughter-in-law finally went to bed after André and Charlie had forced them to regroup in the morning. It's only been hours since Hazen disappeared, but time is fickle and slips away at its own pace. She knew in her bones that her granddaughter was living a lifetime within their seconds.

Her bare feet dug into the sopping ground, the towering black trees yielding around her as she walked into the forest. The wind caressed her skin, her nightgown like a beacon of white in the night, her white hair falling around her shoulders.

The earth seemed to sigh at her presence, and she laid a familiar hand on a passing tree.

"Hello, my old friends," she said softly into the night.

For a moment, she was home, and the forest breathed a sigh at her return.

Silence had long since enveloped the forest. The further she treaded within, the creatures did not stir, the wind ceased its restlessness, and the woods waited on bated breath as she stepped into the long aisle of trees. The stone altar sat catatonic at the end of the aisle. André stood there for a long moment, staring at it with familiar eyes. This was the marker of her mortal existence. This was where she had crossed the veil.

Swallowing the lump in her throat, André pursed her lips softly and stepped forward.

Sunrise slowly paled the darkness, turning it indigo and purple, and soft beams of light streaked dimly through the branches high above.

She traced the knots carved into the stone with the tip of her finger, burning the feel of it into her memory. Her eyes read the ancient script she had long thought she would have forgotten. However, her people's tongue still rang true within her and fell more easily than the mortal languages she knew.

"All ends have a beginning."

Sighing, she opened her palm, and shining brilliantly in the dawn glow the amber tear lay against her slowly ageing skin. André looked up to the forest, and her heart was held in her throat as she called out, "I have not forgotten! I have not forgotten!" Her hand trembled, and she brought the necklace to her lips. "I have not forgotten..." she whispered. "With the remainder of my people's blood that lies within me, I beg that you give her the last of who I am!"

Her words got lost in the dewy morning, the quiet remnants of rain dripping from the branches like a symphony, before an invisible force wrenched a hand into her soul, taking what little magic was left.

Her bones felt heavy as if the age she bore was now the age she felt. André's body shook in an effort not to slump beside the altar. She was tired; she needed to rest.

Dropping her hand away, she glanced down at the necklace. It was shining like an ember of fire, and she laid it down on a patch of moss covering the altar.

André gave one last glance at the altar, committing it to memory, for it would be her last time seeing it, and turned her back on it.

CHAPTER 42

"If the rain does not cease, I'm going to send up a strongly worded prayer to Udiya." Néefar rung out the end of his cloak, laying it over the rotting log he sat on to dry by the fire.

"Well, at least we're not shipwrecked out at sea this time," snipped Brean, wringing her hair out and tossing it over her shoulder.

Savven snorted softly, eyeing Néefar through lowered brows. "I didn't see any sea dragons, but I'm not sure who I have to thank for that."

Néefar rolled his eyes, scrubbing a hand over his tired face. "I'll be sure to make it up to both of you next time if there is a next time. Sea dragons are a thing of the past, I'm thinking… firedrake?"

"Oh good, so we can burn to death instead of drowning." Brean removed one of the three spits they had roasting over the fire with fish and handed it to Savven, giving another to Néefar. "I always wondered what it would be like to have my flesh melted off my bones."

The two males looked at Brean with raised brows.

"Sometimes, what comes out of your mouth concerns me," Savven stated dryly.

During their blessedly calm voyage across, Brean had let slip that she had always wondered what being a fish in the sea would be like. Then she added: *"But then I also wonder what it would feel like to be eaten by a bigger fish. Do you think I would feel my bones break, or would it all go black? Or... does a fish not comprehend that amount of pain?"*

Neither male could comment on that statement, and she was left staring into the water with her strangely specific thoughts.

Brean huffed. "Well, that makes one of us." She snapped her fingers, and their cloaks hissed with steam before drying out; she did the same to her hair.

The wind howled like a banshee, trying to pierce the small barrier Savven had cast around them, shielding them from prying eyes, but it did little to shelter the elements, fighting the storm around them tooth and nail.

The storm had come out of nowhere. Every day was a battle between being dry and staying wet, as it rained most days now, and the three huddled around the fire.

Thunder cracked, and lightning split the sky in a flash of blue.

Brean's shoulders flinched.

"Are you afraid of a little thunder, Witch?"

Amber eyes flicked to amused blue ones. "No, I'm not."

Thunder rumbled, her hands twitched, and she balled them into her skirts.

"Convincing," Néefar remarked.

"Leave her alone," rumbled Savven.

Brean began to hum under her breath when thunder rolled again violently, and the lightning that cracked shook the trees to their roots. Picking at the fish from the stick she held with idle hands, Brean looked up at the sky with distant eyes. "When I was a child after my parents were killed and I was taken in at Álfheimr, I was placed in the care of a guardian. She was beautiful. Hair the colour of chestnuts, eyes like this storm, and a smile that taught me there is beauty in the pain. She took care of me—raised me." Fire reflected in her bright eyes, but the tilt of her lips turned sad and reminiscing. "Her name was Brilyn."

Brean threw the fish skeleton into the fire and wiped her hands along her skirt. "I was a wee child when a massive storm, much like this one, rolled in. I remember dashing from the warmth of my bed and down the hall to her chambers, fleeing like my feet were on fire..."

An audible gasp wrenched from Brean as she sat up in the darkness of her room, her blanket tangled around her tiny legs. Another crash clamoured beyond her window, just like the one that had awakened her, and she sucked in a sharp breath.

Dashing from her bed with a squeak of terror, her hair a wild mess of copper curls around her tiny body, she rushed to the two wooden doors that led to the balcony. Throwing them open, she stood wide-eyed as a wild storm battled above.

The wind dashed her bright red hair in tangles, and her long blue nightgown glued to her as the rain pelted down. Lightning crackled in the distance, and thunder roared, splitting the sky.

Brean screamed, fleeing her room, her heart lodging in her ribs.

She didn't stop in the dim hall, lit by two mounted Fae lights; she didn't stop running until she stumbled through the wooden door at the end of the corridor. Righting herself, she ran to the bedside and climbed on top, sitting on her haunches, small mouth pursed, amber eyes wide as she poked the sleeping female.

"Brilyn," she whispered, her breath catching as her eyes skittered to the window.

Another bought of thunder rumbled through, and she gave a frightful scream.

Brilyn jolted, reaching for the blade on her nightstand, and Brean scuttled back, curling in on herself, head tucked down and her hands covering her ears.

A gentle hand untucked Brean's head and tilted her chin up. Her mouth wobbled, and her eyes were glassy with tears.

Brilyn gave her a small smile, stroking her hair. "Are you afraid, Little One?"

Brean pursed her lips defiantly, shaking her head just as the sky roared, and she gave a little shriek.

Pulling her close, Brilyn tucked her into the safety of her arms and pulled the blankets up around them. "It's okay to be afraid," she whispered softly. "It gives us the courage to be strong."

She stroked her hair idly, and Brean looked up at her, her heart still thrumming like a hummingbird.

"It reminds me of my parents," she whispered in a watery voice.

Brilyn hummed under her breath, pressing her cheek to the top of Brean's head. "I understand, Little One."

Brean looked up at Brilyn again, wide amber eyes watching the grey ones that stared back. Brilyn had said once that they were the same. She didn't have a mother or father either. Her mother was a beautiful Romani woman, and her father was a High Fae. They had fallen in love and soon bore her, but like she, her parents were killed. "You cannot choose who you love." She had told her. "But when you find love, you must love with all that is in you because you never know when the time will run out." Brilyn was her friend and guardian, and she loved her. They had each other.

"Were you scared when your mamma and papa went up to the heavens?" she asked in a small voice, curling into Brilyn. Lightning ripped the sky, and she forced herself not to scream, biting it back and balling her little hands into fists under the blankets.

Brilyn stared off with a pained look, and she gave Brean a small, sad smile. "I was terribly afraid. But then I remembered every time I was afraid, my mother would sing to me until all my fears and worries disappeared." She brushed a wild curl away from Brean's forehead. "So now, when you're afraid, I will sing to you."

Pulling her tightly to her side, Brilyn wrapped protective arms around Brean, cradling her close as her voice filled the tormenting darkness around them.

She blinked the memory away, her eyes drilled into Néefar's. "I'm not afraid of a storm, Néefar. I'm afraid of the memories it brings."

Néefar watched Brean, thinking of his own past. They weren't very different, she and him, so he tilted his head in answer; glancing at the fire with distaste as if the flames held memories in them, a distant expression drawing his brows together.

"What happened to her?" Savven asked, stoking the fire, embers dancing into the watery sky.

"She died." Brean turned her head to the heavens, watching the rain beat against the barrier. "Murdered, not by Ezra, but by a drunk Goblin who wanted her coins. He followed her into the forest on the outskirts of a village and left her body for the beasts."

She let out a bitter huff, wrapping her arms around her middle. "I was informed of her demise by the village head a month later by letter. I came and buried what was left of her under the black ash tree she had died beneath, and every year in the spring, blood red flowers bloom where she is laid… like the earth refuses to forget."

CHAPTER 43

Children's laughter pealed the air, and Hazen's mouth twitched into a smile, watching three girls run after a much-smaller boy, a look of regret on his face.

A horse nickered impatiently, and she looked over her shoulder at the end of the caravan to see a man loosening a stone from the horse's front hoof. Wagons and carts trailed one after another in a long procession that travelled through the thick forests.

It had only been a day, but she felt a lifetime had already passed in those twenty-four hours.

Glancing down at the flower she held between her fingertips, she twirled it softly, watching the colours melt together in a palette of blue and purple. When she brought it to her nose, it didn't have a scent, and she gently rubbed a soft petal between her fingers.

Hazen tapped one of the children ahead of her on the shoulder, a small girl with chocolate skin, dark blonde hair and brown eyes. "A flower for you," she said, offering the flower to the girl.

Shyly, the little girl took the flower and looked at it before turning a small smile to Hazen and dashing off in a whirl of blue skirts and giggles.

Hazen huffed out a laugh, shaking her head in amusement, but it was short-lived. Impatience rolled through her limbs, and she flexed her hands to disperse the energy. That impatience turned to confinement, and she closed her eyes and sighed heavily.

"What did you see?"

She had awoken to a restless Vika rattling her awake and nearly pulling her along until she stood in the middle of Luca's candlelit wagon, with scrolls and books stacked around his surprisingly large wooden desk. He sat, elbows braced on the desk, fingers steepled in front of him, his usually bright eyes, now dark and serious, as they stared at her.

Hazen didn't bother avoiding Luca's gaze. Her voice fell flat as she recalled the massacre. "Death."

Luca, if he had any reaction, didn't show it. "What else did you see?"

"A dragon made of fire, it... it consumed me."

He nodded slowly, his brows furrowed in thought, shuffling through scrolls until he pulled one out and spread it across his desk.

Hazen stepped closer, leaning forward to glance at the scroll. It depicted roughly sketched forest terrain with mountain peaks, rivers that cut through, and a sea marked with little swirls like waves beyond the borders.

"This is Eldur Mountain," he said, pointing to one of the large sharp points that represented a mountain range. "And within is the dragon."

"How cryptic," she drolled. "More dragons."

"No," he said, a shadow of a smile revealing itself. "My tribe calls them Cer Diavol, or Sky Devil. That is who you will find within the mountain."

Hazen looked up at Luca through lowered brows. "Sky Devil?"

"Men with wings, who come like death and wield the strength of dragons." He pointed to a spot within the forest. "We are here, for now, but we move today along here."

How he knew their location based on a section of roughly sketched trees, she didn't know. However, her eyes still trailed along with his fingers, watching it cut close to Eldur Mountain.

"Your time with us is slowly coming to an end, Hazen."

Memories of this morning fade, with a low groan, Hazen scrubbed a tired hand over her face and fell away from the caravan when her chest began to tighten, and she couldn't take in a breath.

She casually braced one hand on a tree, trying to look relaxed, and held the other to her chest, willing a breath into her lungs. Gritting her teeth when voices rose in conversation behind her, she stumbled further until those voices became a distant murmur.

In. Out. In… Out.

A breath hissed from between clenched teeth when the tightness in her chest eased, and she leaned against a tree, letting her head drop back and squeezing her eyes tight.

When the pressure in her chest vanished, she opened her eyes, and her mouth dropped open.

The world had gone molten around her.

Trees, the ground, and the thick leafy ceiling above became translucent, almost iridescent, and gold.

Hazen pressed away from the tree cautiously, and a steady harmonic hum filled the air as thin gold veins pulsed with life beneath her feet; then, they shot towards the trees and up to their branches until every leaf shone and dripped with golden energy.

The world was a spider web of lifelines all around her, connecting everything to each other. Even where she stood, gold illuminated under her feet.

She was a part of this world now. Connected, bound, and *unified* with every creature, person, and thing within it—good or bad.

Hazen outstretched her hand, watching the leaves drip with the golden energy like honey as it fell into her open palm. The energy shimmered and slipped between her fingers, weightless, she held her hand up to watch it trail down her wrist and sink into her skin.

Gasping, heat flared within her chest, and Hazen stumbled back until she leaned against the tree. Power surged through her limbs and crawled up her neck, the scar along her face and back grew warm. She was burning in the purest sense, where she did not cave under the heat, but something within her, something *wild*, grew and became restless.

"I see Valdren did not disappoint."

The world went opaque, and her heart lurched as she whipped around.

A female, not much older than herself, stood patiently, her hands folded in front of her, head tilted softly as she watched Hazen with a slight, curious smile.

Violet-blue eyes clashed with hazel ones when Hazen met her stare. The female's ink-black hair shined almost blue under the midday sunlight that penetrated overhead. She was tall and willowy, her pale face kissed by the sun. When she shifted slightly, the skirts of her long, sage green dress moved with her. The long sleeves and scoop neckline covered most of her in a modest cut.

Despite the faint fatigue Hazen noticed smudging under her eyes, she was beautiful.

Her stare swept over the female, and something familiar about her made her pause. Something… male… *Savven.*

"My cousin was ill-prepared due to unfortunate circumstances," Savven had said.

The female's eyebrows rose a fraction, and her mouth twisted in amusement as if she could read Hazen's thoughts.

"He is my cousin, and I'll have to thank him eventually for taking care of you despite his reluctance," she said, answering Hazen's silence. "He wasn't always like that, you know, crass and angry, but death does that to you…"

"You're his cousin," Hazen said finally.

"Anabelle."

"And you…"

"Are the Keeper of the Forest and guardian to the veil." Anabelle nodded her head slightly in greeting. "And you are Hazen Solvaya from across the veil."

She wasn't wrong, and Hazen pursed her lips, eyeing the female. "How do you know my name?" Everyone knew her name, apparently.

"I know everything concerning the veil, Hazen." She paused, amending, "Well, almost everything. There are secrets the Gods don't reveal."

Sunbeams fell across Anabelle, and she inclined her head towards the warmth, a fleeting sadness crossing her face before she turned to Hazen. "Walk with me."

Anabelle offered her hand, and Hazen, hesitating, took it. The keeper slipped it into the crook of her elbow.

There was quiet within the forest. A softness that Hazen hadn't felt before, and it seemed to come from the female by her side. Like the forest knew who was among it.

"We are alike, you and I," Anabelle commented softly. "Halves of what we appear to be."

The ember within Hazen flickered in acknowledgement.

"An age has passed since the dragons have chosen a keeper, bestowing that right to the Spirits of Season." Anabelle slid her attention to Hazen. "But that changed with you."

"Why?" It was all she could ask. Why her, why now, why the dragons, why, why… why.

"Because I cannot fulfil what is asked of me. I owe a life debt to someone, and because of it, it hinders what I would be tasked to do."

"So, now I have to do it?"

Anabelle's steps paused, and Hazen stopped with her, watching the keeper.

"No," she said slowly, chewing on the word. "There is something… there is something at play, Hazen." Anabelle dropped her hand and turned to face Hazen, uncertainty in her eyes. "Something out of my control, and yours, and the dragons. The Gods are playing a game that I do not know of, and we are their pawns."

"Well, it definitely feels like that," muttered Hazen in agreement.

Anabelle put a warm hand over hers, her eyes searching Hazen's. "They call you the new keeper, but I don't believe you will be."

Hazen frowned. "I'm sorry, I don't follow."

"We are puppets," explained Anabelle. "In a game of charades played by the Gods. The strings that bind us, they control. They brought you here, you were chosen by the dragons, and you were bestowed with that magic, but I don't think they ever wanted to make you keeper."

Hazen let out a disbelieving laugh, licking her lips with a shake of her head. "Then why am I here?" she demanded.

"To be forged into a weapon."

The words hit Hazen, and she jerked her hand from Anabelle's.

"You're saying I was brought here to fight, and kill, and then possibly die and… then what?" Hazen's smile was cutting, and she scoffed. "A puppet… I am no one's puppet."

"No, you're not, but some will try and make you into one." Anabelle glanced towards the caravan when laughter slipped through the forest. "You will have a choice to live or die. It's not an easy choice, and I had little time to think it through for myself. But you, Hazen, have some time, but not much."

Hazen's heart stuttered in her chest. "When you say live or die…"

Pain flickered beneath suddenly tired violet-blue eyes, and the weight of the world seemed to fall onto the keeper's shoulders. "Remaining mortal or becoming immortal. A keeper, a weapon, whoever you choose to be in this lifetime, Hazen, falls to whether you decide to live a life as a mortal and die like one or to live for eternity."

"Forever is a very long time," whispered Hazen.

"It is," agreed Anabelle solemnly.

Hazen sucked on her teeth, looking away from Anabelle.

The world around them, even within the forest, was so vast that the trees stood like mountains. Tall, unyielding, and strong. They withstood the rise and fall of kings and queens, keepers, wars, and the changes of history. She would be like the trees. She would withstand whatever this world threw at her. Whatever they demanded, she would withstand.

When she turned back to Anabelle, she found satisfaction gleaming in those violet-blue eyes, like she knew where Hazen's mind had gone and the promise she had silently made to herself.

Taking in a long, slow breath, Hazen rolled her shoulders back. "Have any decided to remain mortal?"

"No."

"When do I have to make this choice?"

Anabelle shook her head. "I don't know. That is between you

and Tatius."

More laughter drifted from the caravan, and Hazen glanced in its direction.

"You know," Anabelle said slowly, "you are in the Black Forest, and if you continue northeast, you will find Álfheimr, the city of elves. They would offer you protection and safety—if you wish."

Hazen frowned. "Wouldn't I just be hiding then?"

Anabelle didn't respond.

"They want a weapon, then I'll show them how deadly I can become, on my terms, and not by hiding behind gilded city walls."

She would withstand. Even if it killed her.

Anabelle's smile was small and relieved, she tilted her head in regard. "Well said." Her hand slipped into a hidden pocket within the folds of her green dress and pulled out a tiny amber gem the size of a seed on a gold chain. The amber glinted like fire in the sunlight. Spots of yellow, orange, and red melted together, and a soft glow emanated from its core. "This belongs to you. A gift from beyond the veil."

Hazen took the offered necklace, brushing careful fingers over the delicate gold chain. When she touched the gem, her brows rose. It was warm.

"It's Fae made."

Hazen looked up at Anabelle.

"Someone knows you're here, someone who loves you."

"My parents aren't…" It couldn't be; she would know, wouldn't she?

"I never said it was your parents, Hazen," Anabelle said gently. "It's imbued with magic. Whoever wants you to have it has given you a very special gift."

Hazen slipped the necklace over her head, and the amber gem pressed between her breasts, warm against her skin.

"We always have a choice, Hazen. The foundation is laid, but you choose the way ahead. It is why the Gods do not interfere, and the spirits have all but vanished from this world. You have the power of choice. No one can take that from you, not even the Fae."

Hazen glanced between the necklace and Anabelle, her mouth pursed tight.

You will withstand, the power within her seemed to whisper. *You will withstand.*

"Another village has fallen."

Anabelle closed her eyes for a long moment, took a steadying breath, and turned to Autumn.

Sunlight reflected off his deep olive skin and high cheekbones. His chestnut hair was tied loosely at the nape of his neck, and his all-black ensemble was stark in the light.

Anabelle looked into his hazel eyes. "Couldn't you have lied to me for just a moment?"

A hand lay gently on her forearm, drawing her attention. Winter's pale green eyes stared down at her warmly. Silver-blonde hair fell down her back in soft folds, contrasting against the deep blue of her gown and silver-fitted gossamer sleeves. "Unfortunately, moments are all we have left."

Shaking her head, Anabelle turned back to where Hazen and the caravan travelled. "I can feel it," she murmured. "It's happening again—the decay in the world, but this time I can't stop it. I don't think I was ever supposed to stop it." The last words were barely audible and meant only for her. She was so tired, and she felt the burden of death weighing on her bones.

With a sigh, she turned around, facing the spirits. "I had to know. I had to know who they chose."

"Do you approve?" asked Autumn gently.

Anabelle gave a slight nod. "Yes."

The silver of Winter's sleeves caught the light as the spirit stepped aside, and Anabelle walked past her. "Do you think it was wise to tell her everything?"

Anabelle paused. "Secrets are harmful. Secrets destroy even the most innocent reasoning. So, yes, she had every right to know what others will be expecting of her." She fiddled with the small gold band around her finger, twisting it in thought. "How is Néefar?"

Her heart contracted painfully in her chest when she said his name. She missed him dearly and hated the distance between them.

She hated not knowing if he lived or died and the sacrifices he made for his friends—their friends.

"He travels with Savven and a witch," Winter replied.

An unsteady breath loosened past her lips, and she nodded. "And Lithônion? This was his plan. What becomes of him?" She refused to let the bitterness slip into her tone even though she could feel it on her tongue. She had told Néefar to help him because Lithônion is their friend—their family. Still, she had hoped her husband would talk the male out of his ridiculous plan to storm the mountain. He hadn't been successful.

"He is within the Dauðinn mountain. Beyond that, the dark magic bars us from seeing within."

"So long as they're both okay." Anabelle's fingers dropped from the ring, and she continued walking, the spirits falling into step behind her.

"Anabelle?"

Anabelle looked over her shoulder to Autumn. "Hmm?"

"That necklace. Who sent it across the veil?"

There was a pause, and then she said, "Adanessa, the royal messenger to King Nydeth and Queen Casvara."

CHAPTER 44

"How much for the horses?" Savven inquired, approaching the Romani man sitting outside a lean-to stable.

A greasy, pock-marked face and bloodshot hazel eyes stared up at Savven. He oozed with the scent of stale piss, his clothes hanging off his oversized body in tatters.

They had come upon a hap-haggard Romani caravan just east of Evengile, at the edge of the Black Forest sea boundary. The camp was small and secluded, filled with future seekers, drunkards, and thieves.

Swaying on his seat drunkenly, the man burped once, loudly, and then spoke, "Twenty" —he burped again, grabbed a brown tankard from beside his chair, and took a long swig— "silvers… each."

Savven's eyes narrowed in disgust, his lip curling in a slight grimace. "Are you cheating me, Romani?"

Néefar, who leaned against a wooden cart, arms folded over his chest, chuckled in amusement when the Romani's glassy eyes blinked slowly at the prince. With a shake of his head, he pushed off the cart, letting Savven negotiate their means of travel.

Travelling with the witch on foot was slower than he cared to admit to the female, who he could see currently eyeing the Romani man with revulsion.

"Where are you going, Shifter?"

Néefar glanced at Brean, her amber eyes now narrowed in suspicion at him. "I was going to find a secluded area to transform into a big scary giant to terrorise everyone with," he said casually, looking at his nails before sliding her a sly smile.

She rolled her eyes with a huff. "Well, make it quick. This place makes my skin crawl." Brean said this with a shudder as a thin man stumbled out of a muddy tent, fixing his pants as a woman followed behind him. He leered at her, blowing a kiss in her direction, and the witch visibly shivered.

The glare Néefar shot the man made him go pale and scurry off. With that, he ambled into the scattered tents.

The ground was thick with mud, and rain lingered in the air. Dirty, mud-covered tents sat around him in tatters, their frayed edges hanging in the hollow air that promised thunder and lightning. The trees were thick around them with grey-green moss that hung on tall branches like eerie tendrils.

An old, stooped-over hag with a nest of wiry grey hair around her creased face looked at him as she limped around a tent to his right. A rotten smile of cracked black teeth grinned at him, one of her eyes milky white, the other dark as night.

Néefar didn't smile back and watched her disappear into a tent covered in patches.

Maybe he *should* turn into a giant.

He made to turn around when a woman stepped out from around the side of a tent, blocking his path. Her hair was a murky brown and dreaded down her back, beads interwoven through a couple, her black eyes sharp as she peered at Néefar. The clothes she wore left little to the imagination, clinging to her and falling off her shoulders until only her large breasts kept the dirty white fabric from slipping off. The dark blue skirt flowing from her hips was torn up her legs, one end tucked into a thick brown belt, so it draped across the apex of her thighs. A bone handle dagger at her hip.

"Hello, Traveller," she purred, stepping up to him until her breasts pressed against his chest. "Do you fancy a tumble? No charge for handsome travellers." Her fingers skimmed beneath the hem of his tunic, her other hand sliding down the length of his torso.

Steel fell over his expression, and he grabbed her wrists, squeezing the one that slowly searched his waist.

She let out a soft gasp of pain, eyes widening when he tilted his head, looking at her with repugnance. "You will find nothing, whore, for I have nothing worth stealing." He brought her in closer, dropping his voice as he let the predator show in his eyes. "And the only woman allowed to touch me is my wife." Néefar released her, and she stumbled over her feet, falling into the mud with a soggy squelch.

When his back was turned, the woman let out an outraged snarl, and he heard the slip of a dagger. Néefar twisted back as the dagger sailed at his head, and he snatched it from the air.

He nodded, looking at her impressed. With a crooked smile, he lifted the dagger in salute. "I'll just take this, so you don't try that again."

The woman spat profanities at him in a language he didn't know as he walked away, and he just shook his head, slipping the small blade into his boot.

Savven and Brean stood by three strong, chestnut horses, readying their bridles.

"Where were you?" Savven asked, not taking his eyes off his mare, who nudged his hand with her nose.

"I was looking for people to torment," Néefar mused.

His horse nickered at his arrival, and he pat the animal's hindquarters gently. He grabbed a fistful of the horse's mane and hauled himself into the saddle. The animal shifted its feet, accommodating the new weight.

"Did he take you for all your coin?" Néefar inquired. The horses were pretty—too pretty to be in such a desolate tribe. And he would bet all his money—which wasn't much, that they were stolen or winnings from a gamble.

Brean and Savven mounted their horses, and Savven scowled darkly.

"No." Savven adjusted the reins in his grip, shaking his head. "He decided to take a more hospitable approach."

Brean laughed mischievously. "More like Savven forcibly persuaded him."

Blood-curdling screams tore the air from beyond the walls of Dyagin castle as souls succumbed to eternal darkness. Obscurity wrapped around the Dauðinn Mountains. The ash sky met them in an eerie embrace as fog and clouds crawled over the peaks like whispering tendrils. Rain blanketed the skies and coated the grounds—as if trying, with what little power it held, to wash away the sins and death that now grew in the very soil of that land.

Ezra looked down at the blood staining his fingers, wrists, and up his arms, as he stood quietly on the ledge of the castle. He turned black eyes to the forest spread before him. His ink hair was slick with rain as water slid down his sharp features.

The world was as silent as the male's dying breath, who was strapped to the altar made of swirling shadows behind him.

He closed his eyes. Claws ran down his ribs and along his other bones, demons whispering to him, but it all fell on deaf ears. He heard only his heartbeat once… twice… Ezra opened his eyes on the third beat, and the rush of rain and terror-filled screams penetrated his ears as the sound came rushing back.

Ezra turned, his black boots keeping sure footing on the slick stones, and watched Nazar press a hand to one of the three males they had brought up from the dungeon. This one that Nazar held down was a faun. The hair of his lower body was so coated in blood that you couldn't see the once vibrant copper colour, and his black skin was shiny with his fluids.

Two males were strung up along a rocky wall, constrained by bands of shadow manacles that tore their arms from their sockets, their toes barely brushing the ground. They screamed as they watched the other male lay banded to the altar of darkness. Nazar's white skeletal hand splayed across the faun's lolling lifeless head as he bent over his torso, using a bone knife to carve binding runes into the skin.

Nazar's low cackles of joy whispered manically through the torrent of rain. He dragged his black tongue over the male's carvings, blood dripping from his lips before his jaw cracked and lengthened, and thick black tar fell from his mouth and coated the desecrated torso.

The dead body twitched. The runes glowed with a dark light, searing into the flesh, and the faun's eyes opened wholly black.

The two chained males had gone silent and paled when the faun sat up, the shadow bands vanishing.

Nazar's laugh was almost giddy, and he slid bright red eyes to Ezra, who raised a brow at the shade.

Ezra stepped down from the ledge and walked around the altar slowly, eyeing the undead faun. "An army of the dead?"

"Imagine what I, what *you*, could do with an army of undead *puppets* at your command." Nazar's nostrils flared, eyeing the blood trail that went down the male's torso when he stood.

He watched the shade, emotionless, despite the hot, black thrill coursing his limbs at the thought of so much control. Of the power he would possess. It would be endless. The demons within him sang with approval.

Ezra dragged a finger under the male's chin, turning his face to look at him. The faun stood, waiting, like a good soldier awaits orders, and his mouth twitched. "Kill them," he hissed.

Nazar's eyes widened in delight, a smile cutting across his face.

And they watched as the faun turned slowly to the males chained along the wall.

The males thrashed in their bindings, seeing their counterpart walk towards them.

Perfect little puppet. Perfect little soldier.

Limbs separated, soul-wrenching screams filled the air, and blood fell heavy until both rain and blood were one, and you couldn't tell where one began and the other ended.

Pieces were all that was left of the males on the wall. The shadow manacles vanished when there was nothing left to hold, and piles of what were once two males now covered the stone floor.

Nazar licked the beads of blood off his lip that sprayed his face, and his stained red teeth gleamed at Ezra. "Shall I get the liar?"

Ezra's face was a splattered canvas of blood and ghostly pale skin as he looked back at the shreds of flesh and bones. A hint of a smile tilted his mouth. "Yes."

"Come, Liar! It is your turn!"

Lithônion stood slowly when the door to his cell opened, the shifting air made the smell of piss and shit fill his nostrils, and he kept the bile down as it burned his throat.

Nazar's thin, shrouded figure filled the doorway, something akin to joy filling his cruel eyes.

Heart pounding behind his chest, Lithônion's hands fisted at his sides, and raised his chin defiantly, walking towards the shade.

"Faster!" Nazar snapped, and the shadows at Lithônion's back shoved into him.

Lithônion stumbled close enough for the shade to grip him by the hair and drag him from his cell.

Nazar's cackles raked down Lithônion's spine, his teeth clenched painfully, his head jerked back, hair still in the shade's vice grip. Feet stumbling over each other, Nazar shoved him towards the stairs with excitement.

"I have a surprise for you, Liar," he whispered.

Dread filled Lithônion's gut. It twisted and roiled within him like a serpent, and his limbs went numb with realisation. He was going to die. Not in the literal sense, maybe, but in some regard, who he was would perish tonight.

He could fight, but he wouldn't get far within the mountain, where dark magic rules.

He never thought he would see the day when he would cease to exist. As a warrior, he knew there was always a chance, but as an immortal, there was always a hope that he was wrong. An arrogance and ease that came with living forever and thinking one could avoid Death.

His steps became automatic, the mountain around him a haze of reality as his mind took him to a place of comfort, of refuge, of home.

When the rain pelted his face, Lithônion closed his eyes and absorbed the feeling on his skin. He felt the wind caress his cheeks and cool the stinging of his eyes.

The world was with him now.

He would not die alone.

Levina cradled her stomach as she ran down the corridor. Cell doors whirled by her, her breathing was unsteady in her ears, and her heart raced uncontrollably.

The screams rattled the very foundation of the mountain, the shadows active and slithering through the castle. When the screams stopped, Levina nearly ceased breathing when she realised whose screams would next fill the mountain.

She ran past cell after cell until she stopped in front of one whose door was still open. It was empty except for the fluids in the furthest corner, and she pressed the back of her hand to her nose when the smell made her nausea churn violently.

Lithônion was gone.

"No," she whispered and sprinted back down the way she had come. *No, no, no, no,* her mind whispered feverishly.

The hem of her black gown caught on a rocky step, the fabric tearing up the side, the stone cutting into her palms when she made to catch herself.

A foot pressed against her ribs, and she brushed a calming hand over her stomach as the child within her womb shifted restlessly.

Righting herself, she cradled her belly in one hand, grabbed the ruined remnants of her gown in the other, and bolted up the stairs.

Rain, thunder, lightning, and wind all assaulted her as she stumbled onto the castle's roof, eyes wild as they landed on Nazar and Lithônion.

"What are you doing with him?" she demanded. Her heart was a wild thing in her chest.

Levina's blonde hair clung to her face, rain coating her skin, eyelashes, and the thin fabric of her dress that moulded her body. She blinked the water from her eyes, her gaze landing on Ezra, who stood beside an altar made of creeping shadows, his eyes impossibly dark.

"Ezra, what are you doing?" she asked quietly, this time as if she were addressing a skittish animal.

She noted a male faun along one wall, his shiny black skin, wholly black eyes, and runes carved into his torso. The faun didn't move or even gaze in their direction.

Nazar hissed, turning red eyes on her. "We have no need for a *whore*. Leave!"

She didn't flinch at the shade's words and narrowed her eyes on the undead creature. "I wasn't speaking to you, Shade."

Lithônion, forgotten, Nazar took a menacing step towards her, and she pursed her lips, refusing to cower.

"You have no business meddling in affairs that do not concern you," Ezra said lowly, his cold and uncaring gaze sending ice through Levina.

Levina's bare feet were silent against the wet stone when she stepped towards him and hesitated when something squished under her toes. Chest heaving with every quick breath, she made herself look down. A scream lodged in her throat, and shock, disgust, and bile all rose within her, and she clenched her hands to keep from jerking back. Gingerly stepping off half the face that looked up at her, Levina forced herself to look at Ezra.

"Lithônion is our friend," she said softly. "He is your friend and mine; he does not deserve this."

At the mention of his name, Lithônion turned just enough to show the sadness and regret within those beautiful, mossy eyes.

Her heart tore out of her chest, and her eyes stung painfully when she met his gaze, but she forced every emotion back down into that deep box within her. Determination blasted through Levina, and she walked towards Ezra, who stared at her without a flicker of recognition. The demons had a firm grasp on the dark lord. Body parts and shards of bones pressed under her with every step, and she could smell the copper that coated her feet.

"This is not you, Ezra. Lithônion is our *friend*." She was on the other side of the altar now, and she could feel the murderous rage to her right from Nazar and the despair from Lithônion, who watched her silently. "Let him go," she whispered, her steps halting feet from him. "Let our *friend* go."

Ezra's gaze flickered, the darkness in his eyes wavering.

Nazar screeched and was behind her before she could react, shoving her into the sludge of remains.

Her head hit the ground, cushioned by a severed leg, but spots of light still flashed in her eyes, her body screaming when bone fragments cut tiny lacerations into her skin through her dress and one lodged into her thigh.

"Stupid bitch," seethed Nazar. "You are getting in the way!"

Levina's eyes widened through her spotty vision when Lithônion's whole body went careening into the shade's.

"Do not touch her!" he snarled venomously. The regret in his eyes had been replaced by the pure Fae warrior he was—and always would be.

He grabbed a discarded arm, a long shard of bone jutting out like a dagger, and he threw it at the shade's head.

Nazar vanished into shadows with a wicked gleam in his eyes, the arm sailing right through the darkness to Ezra, who caught it before it pierced his chest.

Ezra's head tilted, and his face turned murderous.

The darkness grew behind Ezra, and Nazar's eyes glowed from beyond him. His mouth was inches from the dark lord's ear. "*Kill him.*"

Blood mixed with rain on her skin, smearing across her chest and splaying along her neck and cheeks, her wrists and hands staining bright red as she pressed herself up. Arms trembling with the pain, Levina gritted her jaw and made her body stand.

She did not need magic to be strong.

Levina grabbed the bone from her thigh and *pulled*. She bit back the scream as her flesh tore open and blood-soaked down her thigh.

She would be strong.

She would be strong.

She *would* be strong.

Blue eyes filled with rage, she lunged, not for the shade, but for Ezra. Bone held in her grasp, she lifted it with a cry, ready to stab it through his heart.

Nazar's smile gleamed in the shadows, and he vanished as hands yanked Levina back. She was pressed against a solid body, arms banding around her with bruising strength, and she shrieked with rage.

The bone was snatched from her hand, and she gasped, "No!"

"Don't move, or the next place this bone will cut will be the child," Laudin whispered harshly against her ear, moving the sharp end to press into her belly.

Levina froze, eyes widening at the feel of the bone against her womb. He would cut her baby out of her if she didn't stop.

Her eyes bound for Lithônion as shadows gathered in front of him. The warrior's eyes trained on Laudin with killing intent, and he was already sprinting towards her.

He was going to die.

Heart thundering with the sky, Levina shook her head quickly. *No, no, no,* her mind sobbed uncontrollably.

"*LITHÔNION!*" she screamed as lightning splintered the sky, and Nazar apparated in front of him, dagger poised.

Lithônion ran right into it.

His body jerked, shock marking his face.

Nazar's manic cackle filled the mountains, and the world around Levina went mute.

Everything seemed to slow.

The shade slipped around Lithônion, dagger still in his grasp, and he yanked Lithônion's head back, blood spurting around the blade.

Levina froze and could feel the rumble of Laudin's chuckle reverberate through her back. She shook her head, blue eyes wide and unblinking.

Lithônion's steely green gaze met her, and it didn't stray.

They looked at each other, as if willing strength into one another, from one prisoner to the other.

There was nothing but them.

Levina held his gaze unfailingly, willing her tears back, and she nodded once with a short jerk of her chin. *Go,* she said silently, *go with honour.*

Nazar sliced the dagger across Lithônion's throat, and his blood sprayed across Levina's face, but she didn't flinch. She held his gaze.

She held his gaze until the light left his eyes. Nazar slid the dagger from his nearly severed neck, and Lithônion's body crumpled.

Levina didn't scream. She didn't cry. She did not falter.

Ezra toed Lithônion's head. "You weren't supposed to kill him."

"Apologies, My Lord. I couldn't help myself," Nazar intoned, though his voice was anything but apologetic. "We have others we can use."

Levina's body began to shake, whether from shock or rage, she couldn't tell. But her hands balled at her sides, and she gritted her jaw against the tremors.

I will live, I will survive, she chanted to herself silently. If not for herself or her babe, then for Lithônion. So his death wasn't in vain.

"Toss her into a cell, Laudin," Ezra said tonelessly. "I find the time has come. I've grown tired of her. And Nazar, get me another body."

She would live. She would survive.

Laudin's grip branded her arms as he dragged her away, her eyes only leaving Lithônion's when the castle walls obscured his body from view.

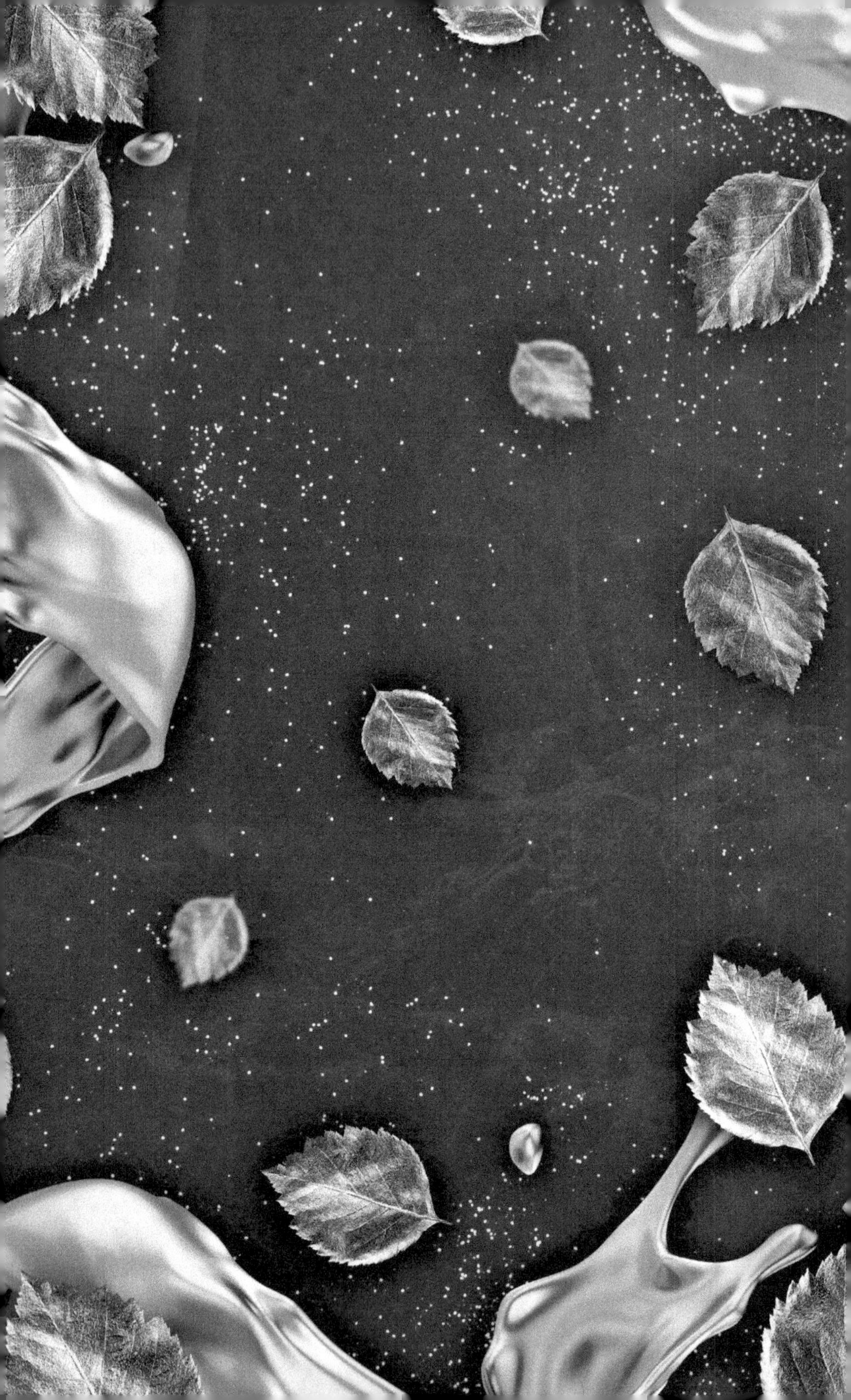

Next up in the Keeper trilogy:

The Veil

Coming 2024

ACKNOWLEDGEMENTS

Where to start?

Most say at the beginning, but this isn't the beginning, is it? This is book two… never thought I would live to see that happen—let alone see it turn into two books. (Book two is one of those anomalies that magically split itself in two, and now *poof*, the trilogy is a four-part series. I'm not even kidding—I wish I were.)

I want to thank the women in my life. This book is dedicated to women, so it's only fitting that I first thank them.

To my mother, who, in the face of adversity, has triumphed and flourished into the most amazing woman she is today. Who has taught me to be strong, have grace, and take absolutely no shit from anyone. I love you and thank you for being the woman you are today and the mother God has blessed me with.

To my alpha readers: Hannah Curtin and Jazmyn Michélle Akita Brandon-Lowe (YES, I used your full government name!) THANK YOU so much for reading this novel before it hit the editors and pointing out the things that needed to be fixed, changed, or added. I couldn't have done it without you.

My PA Baddie, or @batwingbaddie, thank you for being a gem through and through. You are a superwoman, and I don't know how you juggle so much, but you're amazing. I hope you know that every day.

To Brandy Gibson, my amazing line editor, THANK YOU. Without you things would have gone unchecked, and the book would have been mayhem. So, thank you for taking my novel into your hands and honing it to be the best it could be. You are an amazing woman, mother, wife, friend, and editor, and I don't know how you manage it all but you are extraordinary. I am so proud of you and cannot wait to see you flourish even more!

To Stacey, my lovely proof editor. Thank you to the woman you are... Not only did you edit my novel(s), but you also helped get the word out about them and took time out of your personal life to tell people about my work. Your belief in me is top-tier, and I'm so grateful to you. You are a one-of-a-kind person.

To Charly, my cover designer, I will sing your praises everywhere, woman. EVERYWHERE. You are a stunning, creative, and just an overall lovely human being with whom I've had the honour of working with once again. Thank you for making my stories come to life with your covers and formatting. I couldn't have done it without you.

Maddie, by the time this comes out, you'll be all graduated from university! I'm so proud of you! During your time at school, between classes, and during your breaks, you have made artwork for my books, and I'm so blessed to have found you. Thank you for being my friend on the other side of the world. You're incredibly talented, and the world is at your feet, Darling.

Ashlyn M. Pugh—Audiobook narrator, CEO in the making, and instant best friend. (Don't you know, Slytherins and Ravenclaws make the best friends—anyone who says otherwise is wrong.) What an unlikely friend I found in you. I slid into your DMs, and the rest is history. Thank you for taking a chance on book one, The Keeper, and being supportive and graceful throughout the process. You're an extraordinary woman, and God took His time when He created you. Never, ever forget that.

To Gina-Marie, Jacky, Jeff, Sirine, Yasmin, and all my lovely friends in our Barnes and Noble book club, thank you for supporting me. I get very shy when discussing my books because art is subjective, and I know it's not for everyone. I also know the flaws of my novels like I know the flaws of my body. And if you stare at them too long, that's usually all you see. But, you guys cheer me on and support me despite them, and it fills my heart with so much joy to know that I'm surrounded by beautiful individuals such as yourselves.

To my father: I love you.

To me: I love you more.

About The Author

P. S. Whytock is a thirty, flirty, and semi-thriving adult who is just trying to figure out life. She currently lives in Florida and is a Merchant Marine when she's not pretending to be an author.

www.ingramcontent.com/pod-product-compliance
Lightning Source LLC
Chambersburg PA
CBHW060612300726
48975CB00005B/1539